Praise for the novels of Sa...

'Unbridled passions run riot' *Daily Mail*

'A rich, vivid, three-dimensional, gutsy narrative
which has you turning the pages into the early
hours' *Eastern Daily Press*

'Sizzles with passion' *Guardian*

'An excellent book combining humour and
passion' *Telegraph and Argus*

'A ripping yarn' *Bury Free Press*

'Here is a vivid evocation of a way of life'
East Anglian Daily Times

Also by Sally Worboyes

Wild Hops
Docker's Daughter
The Dinner Lady
Red Sequins
Keep on Dancing
Down Stepney Way
Over Bethnal Green
At the Mile End Gate
Whitechapel Mary
Girl from Brick Lane
Banished from Bow
Down by Tobacco Dock
Time Will Tell
Jamaica Street
Room for a Lodger
East End Girl

About Sally Worboyes

Sally Worboyes was born and grew up in Stepney with four brothers and a sister, and she brings some of the raw history of her own family background to her East End sagas. She now lives in Norfolk with her husband, with whom she has three grown-up children. She has written several plays for BBC Radio 4 and Anglia Television. She also adapted her own play and novel, *Wild Hops*, as a musical for production at the Mermaid theatre.

SALLY WORBOYES

Where Sparrows Nest

HODDER

First published in Great Britain in 2003 by Hodder & Stoughton
An Hachette UK company

This edition published in 2016

1

A CIP catalogue record for this title is available from the British Library

Paperback ISBN 978 1 473 65384 9

Typeset in Plantin Light by Palimpsest Book Production Limited,
Falkirk, Stirlingshire
Printed and bound by CPI Group (UK) Ltd, Croydon, CR0 4YY

Hodder & Stoughton policy is to use papers that are natural, renewable
and recyclable products and made from wood grown in sustainable
forests. The logging and manufacturing processes are expected to
conform to the environmental regulations of the country of origin.

Hodder & Stoughton Ltd
Carmelite House
50 Victoria Embankment
London EC4Y 0DZ

www.hodder.co.uk

For my brother John Lipka who with his handsome Tony Curtis looks drew many hopeful Fifties girls to our front door and several small bars of chocolate to my pocket. The sound of those fabulous songs coming from his first record player stay with me for ever as do the artists – Nat King Cole, Fats Domino, Louis Armstrong, Ella Fitzgerald . . .

I

---◆◆◆---

1952

On this clear early August morning, as she watched her belongings being lifted and stacked on to a rickety old truck that looked as if it might not make the short distance to her new home, Edie Birch felt a sense of dread and anxiety wash over her, wakening feelings that she had so far managed to keep at bay. Combing her fingers through her sun-streaked brown hair, she told herself to be strong and that she was on the brink of a new beginning. A new life.

Having burned the candles at both ends with all of the sorting and packing that goes with moving from one home to another, she was tired and low on energy and felt as though it hadn't just been boxes she'd been packing but parts of her life that she had somehow been storing away. Now, with most of the work at this end of the move over, she had to use every bit of will-power to maintain her usual feisty spirit and hold back the now threatening tears. The floodgates must not open yet. Until now she had managed to shut her emotions away, deep inside, keeping them under lock and key until she was ready, or able, to open the door and let them out. Perhaps later, alone in her bed, with the long night stretching ahead of her, she would allow herself the luxury of crying into her pillow.

In this determined mood she was reminded of two of her mother's sayings: *Never wear your heart on your sleeve* and *Shed not one tear in public else a flood will follow.*

Turning her back on the house that had been her home and safe haven since birth, Edie leaned against the crumbling brick wall and closed her eyes, berating herself for not having the will-power to suppress her fear of the unknown. This row of terraced slums in which she had been living was infested with mice and damp, she reminded herself, and without any of the modern comforts she would enjoy in her brand new flat. Common sense told her that the move was the best thing she could have hoped for, but her heart was wishing for something else: wishing that the clock could be turned back to when she was a child and living here with her younger brother and her parents, that things had gone differently.

Glancing along the war-damaged street, scenes from the past floated across Edie's mind: the hopscotch, the skipping, the ball games and, best of all, the world of make-believe. Focusing on what used to be her favourite play area, a forbidding derelict building with a morbid history, which, of all places, should have been blown to smithereens, she smiled at the irony. But then again, she mused, the sinister Victorian workhouse had also been to her a weird and wonderful, haunting place where fantasies were created. A place she had often crept into alone to explore with a mix of terror and thrill urging her on.

Edie lifted her pale face to the sun, which was emerging from behind a cloud, and thoughts of the future returned. What if she didn't like the people she would from now on be living so close to? Or what if they didn't like her? Worse still, what if they didn't take to the no-nonsense side of her nature? Having lived in this turning all of her life, she was not only leaving familiar ground but neighbours who had, over the years, become close, more like an extended family, rallying round in times of trouble, comforting her mother through the dark times when her father had seemingly disappeared into thin air.

As the memory floated across her mind yet again she wondered if it would ever stop haunting her. It had been an ordinary Sunday morning and an ordinary errand. Her doting father had gone out as usual to buy his Sunday newspaper, a sixpenny bar of chocolate for her mother and a bag of pink and white sugared coconut chips for her brother and herself. She could see the expression on his face now, the strange smile as he stood in the doorway – a smile that said everything but had meant little to her at the time. How could she possibly have imagined, all those years ago, that she would never see him again?

On that Sunday, and for days and weeks afterwards, Edie the child had not been able to fathom why the neighbours were consoling her mother and speaking in hushed voices. There hadn't been an accident. No sudden heart-attack. No murder. Her father had simply not come home from the errand. Thankfully, her mother had, in her wisdom, chosen to tell the truth without frills or fuss. The man Edie had thought she knew so well had in fact been leading a double life. Her father had been seeing another woman for as long as he had been married to her mother, and the woman had had his child, a son. He had ended up choosing one life to lead, and it wasn't with them.

Now, in the wake of leaving the only home she had known, Edie wished that her brother, Jimmy, was by her side. He had offered to take a day off work to help her move but her determination to cope alone had put paid to that. Her firm insistence that he mustn't lose a day's pay and that she could manage had put his mind at ease and a smile on his face when he had said, as he had many times before, 'Too bloomin' independent, that's your trouble, Sis.'

In a way he was right and she knew it, although her independence had not come from choice but necessity. Once the reality had sunk in that her father was not going to return all those years ago her mother's depressions had worsened and her happy-go-lucky nature had vanished. In consequence Edie had been thrown into adulthood before she had reached her sixteenth birthday, when she had not only to care for Jimmy and her traumatised mother but hold down her job as machinist in a local dress factory, working all the hours God sent.

Two years after her husband had gone from her life, Edie's mother had still not got over the pain of losing the man she'd loved and trusted to another woman.

Over and over she had asked the same question: how could he abandon us? It was obvious to all those who knew her that she was losing her grip on life and reality, and that she had all but given up until she finally lost the will to live. It came as no great shock to her neighbours when she took her own life.

To Edie and Jimmy, however, her suicide had come as a devastating shock and neither of them had been able to get over it. The only saving grace had been that the tragedy of losing their mother had brought brother and sister closer than they had ever imagined they could be.

Now in her early thirties, with most of her possessions on the back of a truck and her old life shut away behind a paint-peeling brown door, Edie forced herself to look on the bright side. A new life was stretching out before her, full of possibility. Peering along the turning, she saw a smart removal van pulling away and smiled inwardly. It was followed by a truck filled with the Cooper family. Showing a hand as they passed, she smiled gamely back at the mother of four, whose expression somehow pushed Edie's blues away. Even though they all knew, as they bravely waved cheerio, that they would most likely never set eyes on each other again, there was a look of optimism on Mrs Cooper's tired and lined face, and determination on her husband's. They had chosen to take up the offer to move out of London to Harlow and a brand new terraced council house, and they had not been the only ones to opt for different surroundings.

More East Londoners wanted a new way of life

closer to the countryside. Some families were heading for Norfolk, or Basildon and Dagenham in Essex. It was a time of change, but although there was a sense in the air of better things to come away from the 'Smoke', Edie felt safer in London – her familiar home ground. Safe and at home. Even if her new neighbours would all be strangers in the beginning, at least she would still be in the city of her birth.

Not only had she lost both parents, she was a war widow – at least that was how she saw herself. She had certainly come through enough grief to realise that it was futile to hang on to a shred of hope that her husband Harry would be found alive now. She had spent too many nights when younger hoping that her father would return to keep a torch burning for her husband.

The main priority of Edie's life now was to be amid people she knew and trusted, shopkeepers, stall-holders and neighbours. Finding someone to take Harry's place was not an option. He had been her first love and would be the last. She had her daughter Maggie, her brother Jimmy and her great-aunt Naomi, the flamboyant seventy-year-old who had spent all of her working life, since the age of twelve, around actors in the worst and best of British theatres. A widow herself, having lost her husband in the First World War, Naomi had been the one to show Edie the way forward when the devastating telegram arrived in 1942 telling her that Harry was missing, presumed dead.

According to the War Office, the rescue boat on which he was stationed had been detailed to search for survivors who had been aboard an allied war plane, which, while crossing the mountainous region of Turkey, had crashed close to Kemer. The rescue boat, on arrival into the region, had gone into a sea severe and rough with waves reaching monstrous heights. The last radio SOS message from a crew member had been on the rocky coastal shore near Oludeniz. The boat had capsized in the area and the crew were listed as missing, presumed dead. No survivors had been found and there had been no trace of the wrecked boat on the shore.

'Better to be loved by one good man than by a dozen wasters,' had been Great-aunt Naomi's few words of comfort to Edie, which were followed by unbending advice: 'First, have as many lovers as you want, my darling, and second, never, *never* marry twice.'

Edie had taken the second piece of advice, but as for having many lovers – here she differed greatly from Naomi. Edie had loved Harry deeply and had married young. Her modest wedding day had been wonderful and she was content with her memories. After her marriage, and before the Second World War had broken out, the couple had lived in Edie's family home with Jimmy, who had regarded Harry more as a real brother than an in-law. The two had spent hours fishing in the Cut, a narrow river that flowed from Essex through Hackney and down into the Thames at Wapping.

Feeling a little easier now as snapshot scenes of better times flew across her mind, Edie brushed away rust coloured dust from her skirt, which had come off the crumbling brickwork of a house ready for demolition. As she turned her front and back door keys in her hand, worn-out and familiar thoughts were crossing her mind. That maybe Harry was alive. That maybe he had been captured by the enemy while trying to make his way home. That maybe he had been taken to some God-forsaken prisoner-of-war camp and would one day return. That she would wake up in bed to find him lying next to her, softly snoring.

'Penny for them, Edie,' came the slow voice of the coalman who today was clean and spruced up to the nines. 'I hope you're not having second thoughts.'

'Of course I'm not, Ben, but . . .' she slowly shook her head, pinching her lips together. '. . . I can't help thinking that some of us won't see each other agen. After all these years.'

'Don't be mad. We're not all trotting off to live wiv the carrot crunchers, thank God. Don't worry, we'll all be rattling against each other like bad pennies, in the eel shop, the markets, down Brick Lane, in Balmy Park . . .'

'Maybe so, but I think I might miss this old house,' she shrugged, 'once it's been flattened with the rest and it's too late to do anything about it.'

'Well, I shan't miss mine,' he chuckled, continuing on his way. 'You women, you make me laugh. It'll take a cleverer man than me to fathom you! A clever man and a lifetime twenty furlongs too long!'

Laughing at his strange rhetoric, Edie shook off her nostalgia and went back into the house where her removal man, Mr Crow, was struggling with her old settee. 'You're sweating like a pig, Mr Crow,' she smiled. 'Leave that for a minute and I'll make us a cup of tea. I expect you're ready for one.'

'Ooooh,' he said, lowering the end of the piece of furniture he had been heaving and dragging along. 'That lad of mine's bin gone for half an hour,' he puffed, wiping sweat from his brow with the back of his hand. 'You wait till he gets back. I'll give 'im what for. Popped off to get me some Golden Virginia. You can bet yer bottom dollar he's slipped into the Carpenter's Arms for a pint. Left an old man to it. Lazy little bugger.'

'You're not so old, Mr Crow. What about a nice cup of tea, then?'

'Can a duck swim?' he laughed. 'Four sugars, if you don't mind, dear. I'm sweet but not sweet enough.'

Edie looked from his rosy face to the tatty old sofa. 'You know, Mr Crow, I'm sick of the sight of that fing. I don't think I'll take it to my lovely new flat. Don't bother with it. We'll leave it behind for the mice.'

The old boy pushed back his cap and scratched his head. 'Sure about that are you, ducks? They don't make 'em like that nowadays you know. Well sprung, that is.'

'Maybe so, but it's old, it smells of damp, and them springs you're talking about don't half dig in your bum.'

'Well, then, you put a coupla cushions on top. You don't wanna go getting in debt. Bloomin' tallymen wait on street corners for you women and your fancy ideas of buying this, that and the other.'

'Even so. We'll leave it behind.'

'Well, if you can afford new, buy from a factory and sod the middle men. Go into Johnny Carpenter's shop floor and tell 'im I sent yer. You can't miss 'is place – it's slap bang on the end of the other furniture makers' just off Columbia Road.'

'Ah, but will he give it me on tick?'

'Probably. But you'll end up paying more'n the cost in the long run.'

'Well, I don't 'ave much choice, do I? Us lot hardly have bank accounts to draw from.'

'That's true,' he sniffed. 'Very true. Tell you what. Come and 'ave a look round my yard in Tobacco Dock. I don't only moonlight with moving families from one place to another. I clear the odd 'ouse and office now and then. You'll find summink that takes your fancy. A couple of quid for a settee. Can't be bad, can it?'

'Depends on the state of it.'

'Oh, I don't waste floor space on rubbish. No point. This old one of yours wouldn't find its way into my yard. I could find an 'ome for it, mind. Some poor old bugger'll be pleased to 'ave it for four or five bob. I'll dock that from the price of a decent one. How'd that suit yer?'

'I'd need one straight away. Don't want to sit on orange boxes for weeks on end.'

'Well, you wouldn't do, would yer? Tell you what . . . once I've moved you in I'll come back and fetch this and the rest of the rubbish you're leaving behind and drop by your flat tomorrer with a settee you'd be proud to let your neighbours see. That suit you, will it? I'll only charge a dollar for all the manoeuvring and let's say two quid for the bit of furniture.'

'It's a deal. But if I don't like it—'

'You'll like it,' he said. 'It'll give you a few years' wear and it'll be a darned sight better'n this old fing.' He looked into her face and grinned. 'Four sugars for me, then. I'll load that tea-chest up while yer brewing.'

Back in the scullery, Edie filled the kettle and smiled. The people in this part of London would be the same no matter where she moved to. Wheeling and dealing was a way of life.

She was so deep in thought she didn't hear her daughter arrive. 'You ain't taking that bleedin' old settee, are yer?' groaned Maggie, her hands firmly on her bony hips and her green eyes glaring. 'Flea-bitten old junk needs—'

'I'm not taking it! And where'd you skive off to? There's your clothes to be packed into a tea-chest yet.'

'Went and 'ad a look at the flat. Peeked froo the winda. Kitchen looks like a palace. Don't know what all the fuss's bin abaht. It'll be like living in one of them American films. Fresh paint everywhere, sparkling white sink and silver taps. Cupboards on the walls all brand new and painted cream. And you could eat off that stone floor it's so clean. Mice won't be able to chew froo that, will they? And they definitely couldn't get up them stairs.'

'Maybe they'll use the lift,' said Edie, tongue in cheek.

'That's a point.' Maggie raised her thick ginger eyebrows. 'They could sneak in every time the door's pulled open. I went up and dahn six times to check it works properly. I don't want you gettin' stuck in there.'

'Oh . . . and I didn't think you cared, Maggie Birch.'

'I don't.' The wily fourteen-year-old shrugged. 'But you might 'ave the shopping bag wiv yer and I'd starve to death while you suffocated.'

With her back turned to her daughter, Edie smiled inwardly. 'So you like the flat, after all. That's good.'

'They've put up an enamel sign on the stairs. "No spitting." As if we'd spit!'

'I'm pleased you like it, Mags. Makes a big difference to me. You did say before you thought it was more like a prison or a lunatic asylum than somewhere to live.' Edie was relieved that her cantankerous daughter had had a change of heart.

'I never said that. Aunt Naomi did. Anyway, it wasn't finished when we went to 'ave a look, was it? And there was mud and builders everywhere. Got grassy areas round the block of flats now. You could sit out there wiv yer new neighbours and gossip – jus like when we went hop-picking that once.'

'I don't think so.'

'Uncle Jimmy's right. You *are* a snob. Never liked it, did yer?'

'No, I never. Tin sheds with a hole in the ground for lavatories. Straw to sleep on and cooking on a camp-fire. It was like the poor living in the Dark Ages.'

'I might go wiv Uncle Jimmy and Aunt—'

'You will not! No more time off school – and that's final!'

'You're *allowed* by the School Board to go!' growled Maggie, turning away and peering into the back of the removal truck. 'The country *needs* us to pick 'ops.'

'I'm sure it does but you need *education* and in my books *that*'s more important.'

Ignoring all of that, Maggie sniffed and looked her mother in the face. 'There's a Tarmac playground, you know. One for each block of flats and a big cement one for them who're gonna live in the cottages and maisonettes. Some boys was already playing football on it.'

'Sounds all right, then.'

'Course it does. Should 'ave moved out of this dump years ago.' With that, Maggie eased the brace off her teeth, tossed it over her shoulder then pushed a hand through her thick red hair. 'Don't need that any more. They're straight enough now.' The wolf-whistle from one of the boys playing football had left its mark.

'Don't be too hasty now,' said Edie, as she cupped her daughter's face. 'The dentist thought another month.'

'I know, but look at 'em. They don't stick out any more and the gap where he took that one out has nearly gone. You can 'ardly see it.'

'That's true.' Edie didn't really think so but she had to admit that Maggie was smiling properly for the first time in ages and the improvement from when she first went for treatment on her teeth was as good as she had hoped for. Giving her daughter's flushed cheeks a little squeeze she winked at her. 'I said you'd turn into a swan and I bet you do.'

'No, I won't, Mum. Stop pretending. So I don't 'ave to wear the brace any more, then?'

'No. And do you know what else?' said Edie, slowly removing Maggie's National Health glasses. 'I think it's time you got yourself a Saturday job so you can save to buy a nicer pair of these.'

'But I only need 'em for reading. So it'd be a waste of money. No one sees me when I'm in me bed, do they? And I couldn't care less about being called Four Eyes in class.'

Moved by this sudden change in her daughter, Edie went quiet, carefully choosing her words. Maggie had been hiding behind her glasses since she was six years old, pretending she couldn't see properly without them. The school nurse knew differently, and so did the optician, but Edie had long since given up trying to persuade her that she had lovely eyes and should show them off – lovely sloping green eyes and thick, nicely shaped eyebrows to match her healthy head of lustrous copper hair, just like her father's.

'Too lazy to get yerself out of that bed of a Saturday morning, eh?' she managed to say, inspired by the new look of confidence on her daughter's face.

'I never meant I wouldn't try for a Saturday job. I meant I'm sick of wearing these fings all the time. I ain't gonna waste me money on another pair, am I, when I need some new clothes? And you've got other fings to buy off the tallyman. New curtains and that.'

'That's true,' said Edie. 'That is *very* true.' She nodded thoughtfully. 'I saw a notice in Woolworth's window and in the fabric shop down Bethnal Green Road. They're looking for Saturday girls.'

'I'm not working in bleeding Woolworth's!' declared Maggie, and then, in a quiet voice, 'I'll try the curtain shop though.'

'Whatever. Go and pack the rest of your things into the tea-chest I've left in your room.'

Maggie turned away from her mother, sullen. She had been excited when she inspected the new flat that was to be her home, and relieved when she had seen that others in her age group were arriving in lorries and trucks. The expressions on some faces seemed apprehensive and that, in a strange way, had boosted her confidence. The mix of people she had seen moving on to the estate had surprised her. In the street where she lived the neighbours had been white and mostly Church of England. Jewish and Catholic families tended to live in separate areas, or at least that was how it seemed to Maggie. They certainly moved in their own circles, the Catholics using certain pubs and churches, while the Jews had their own markets, shops and synagogues, the Anglicans here, there and everywhere. Apart from the Turkish barber shop and the Maltese café at the end of the turning, foreigners seemed few and far between in Stepney. But today she had seen a West Indian family moving on to the estate, had spoken to a fair-haired woman with a strange accent who turned out to be Polish, and had laughed furtively at an Irish Catholic, who had sat on the wall of her tiny front garden continuously crossing herself and asking Mary, Mother of Jesus, to help shift a mountainous pile of furniture off the pavement and into her house. Her husband, like other husbands moving on to the council estate, was offering his custom to his new local and believed it the duty of the removal men to carry everything into the house. Removal men who had been paid between five and ten shillings for the deal of carting their belongings from one place to the other and no more than that. The discovery that hardly any men were waiting at the houses at the other end to help unload had not gone down too well, and the women had had to take the flak. Maggie had witnessed more dramas in the couple of hours she had spent wandering around the Barcroft council estate than she had seen in her whole life in this back-street.

The last thing she had done before she pulled herself away from the bustling place was help an Italian woman carry a pram filled with kitchen pots and pans up three flights of stairs. The woman didn't believe or trust that the lift would take her safely to where she wanted to go. Her sixteen-year-old son, carrying a blanket box on his broad shoulder, had been one reason why Maggie had offered to give a hand. He was the handsomest boy she had ever set eyes on – and he had flashed a smile and winked at her.

'I s'pose I've gotta let Mad Woman keep my rabbit?' said Maggie, her thoughts nipping from one thing to another, as she watched a mouse scouting for crumbs in the doorway leading into the scullery.

'Just try taking it back from 'er now,' chuckled Edie. 'And don't you think it's time you stopped calling your aunt Naomi Mad Woman? It was all right when you was little but you're fourteen and—'

'She likes me calling 'er that and, anyway, she *is* mad. The theatre work never made her bonkers – the film studios did. She said so.'

'Oh, whatever . . .' sighed Edie, pushing a hand through her hair. 'I can't see her settling on the estate, though. Too clean and clinical. I s'pose you popped in to see 'er?'

'Course I did. She's all right. Finks 'er neighbours are old and boring but she likes it all right – now that she's draped her Chinese shawls everywhere and put her pictures and photos up. She was really beautiful before she turned into a prune.'

'And a very good actress, according to the reviews in her scrapbook. So Naomi's settled in. That's good.'

'She's planted seed potatoes in 'er bit of garden already and she's nicked some plants from the old-boy-next-door's garden.'

'I don't wanna know,' said Edie. 'Come on. Time's marching forward. It'll be afternoon before we know it and the nights are drawing in. I planned for us to be all settled in by nightfall. I'll be ready for my bed by then, that's for sure.'

'I won't. I'll be in the flat next door watching their television. They've got a brand new nine-inch. Oh, and I think you might 'ave to go round to Mad

Woman tomorra. She's goin' up the rent office to cause pandemonium. She reckons they're charging 'er ninepence over the top. You've gotta argue it for 'er.'

Edie slowly shook her head. 'I knew it was a mistake to persuade 'er to live on this estate. Why didn't I listen to myself instead of you?'

'Because she's family!' Distracted by more mice scampering around the fireplace, Maggie gazed around the empty room as a wave of panic rushed through her. The moment had finally come, and once she was out of this house she would never see this room or her bedroom again. The bedroom that knew all of her secrets and had listened to her crying softly into her pillow. She spoke in a broken voice: 'Do you fink they'll pull this house down straight away, Mum?'

'Course not,' said Edie, sensing that her daughter was feeling the same as herself – a bit on the low side and with past memories swimming through the mind. 'They won't demolish till everyone's gone from the turning and some will stay put for as long as they can. Five or six don't want to move from their roots.'

'So they'll just board ours up, then?' said Maggie, avoiding eye-contact.

'No. They don't do that any more. Tramps and down-and-outs must have somewhere to sleep. And there were enough of the poor sods from the first war never mind the second. Better they camp out in these old places than in doorways and parks. Let's 'ope they'll be in here over winter – and the next come to that.'

'Mad Woman said that life's like a roller-coaster.'

'It is. Ups and downs. An even life, if you can get it, is the best you can hope for.' Edie gave a gentle tug to her daughter's long pony-tail, which was scurfed back and tied with a strip of rag. 'Welcome to the real world, Mags.'

'What's that s'posed to mean?'

'Time'll tell. This month next year you'll be looking at things differently. My little girl will 'ave turned into a young lady.'

'And we'll be settled in our new 'ome.' Her eyes shut tight, Maggie slipped her arms around her mother's soft, warm body. 'We'll be all right, won't we? You'll meet some new friends and you won't miss Dad so much.'

'I'll never stop missing him, sweetheart,' whispered Edie, with a tremor in her voice, 'but at least I won't be lonely with all them people around me. Let's hope our close neighbours'll be as good as the ones in this turning. I think we're both gonna take time to settle down but we'll like it. I know we will. We'll love it,' she said positively. 'And now we need to get a move on. It's time to go, Mags. Time to put the last of our things on that truck. Mr Crow's a good man and knows that this is a bit emotional for us but . . . he's got a living to earn and time is money.'

'I know,' murmured Maggie, and then, 'Promise me you won't cry?'

'I won't if you don't. We'll be brave soldiers for each other, eh?'

Maggie nodded and managed a weak smile. 'I can't

wait to sleep in my new bedroom or soak in that gleaming white bath.'

'Nor can I,' said Edie. 'Nor can I.'

Two hours later, Edie was standing in her sparkling new kitchen with the afternoon sun streaming through the window and on to her face, while the smell of fresh paint and new pine timber lingered in the air. The décor throughout the flat had a spring-cum-summer feel to it. Doors and picture rails had been painted fresh apple green and walls emulsioned cream. It was airy and bright, with no hint of the smells and atmosphere she had lived with for so long and had got used to – damp, mustiness and the gloomy dark. To close the door for the last time on Cotton Street had seemed an impossible task. Now she was glad, really glad, to have done it.

Catching Maggie's expression as she came into the kitchen, Edie knew that she had made the right decision in choosing this second-floor flat. It was almost as if their name had been on it before the paint was dry. The face of her only child, who was on the brink of adolescence, was glowing. The adventure of new beginnings during the past few months had now turned into solid reality. All thoughts of things going wrong in so far as Edie was concerned were diminishing by the second. Gone was the nagging worry that if they hated living here there would be no turning back. Edie no longer wanted the option of a second chance to change her mind. New housing was in demand and people like Edie, whose homes had suffered major or minor bomb damage, were desperate for the new flats or cottages on offer. And even those whose homes had not been damaged wanted to move out of the slum dwellings. The working classes had had enough. They had had it with showing the stiff upper lip, of making do on bread and cheese, of being freezing cold in the winter and of being looked upon as if they were third-rate citizens who smelt and didn't care if they had hot water to bathe in or not.

Most, if not all, wanted new, decent places to live where they could hold up their heads and be shown some respect. Some were even determined to climb the sanctimonious class ladder and grin into the faces of those horrified to have the working classes at close to touching distance. There was a distinct air of determination and an atmosphere so thick you could feel it. Determination, indignation and pride. Poverty would no longer be tolerated. Men and women were beginning to march forward, not to save King and country, but themselves, their children and their children's children.

Waiting in her new kitchen for Mr Crow to arrive with her belongings, Edie gripped the rim of the sparkling white sink with its pine draining-board and looked through the window at the light blue sky with its sprinkling of cotton-wool clouds. The echo of talk and laughter on the staircase outside was music to her ears. Especially since the laughter was interspersed with swearing coming from two dockers struggling with an oversized, overflowing trunk filled with bedding. 'Home from home,' she murmured delightedly, then went out of the flat to look at the two men as they struggled with a bulky piece of furniture. Her neighbours might have found the manoeuvring easier had they been of similar build, but the elder was short and round while the other, a man in his mid-twenties, was tall and broad. Leaning on her elbows on the balcony Edie viewed the comings and goings below while being entertained by these two men and their banter . . .

'Gawd, Jack . . . This can't all be pillows and sheets! I reckon Laura's got the Crown Jewels hidden in there!'

'All my half-crowns that I can't find more like! Nicked all me notes, didn't she? Save for a rainy day and it gets blown on daft machines. What do she want with a vacuum cleaner in a brand new place? Broom'd do!'

'It's 'er house-warming present to 'erself, Jack. She's not stopped talking about it for weeks so don't start moaning when 'er and Liz get back from the shop with it. Anyway, me and Lizzie put 'alf towards it so you're only fifty per cent out of pocket. Stop yer moaning.' Taking a rest when they'd reached the top of the flight of stairs, he wiped his brow. 'I'm not as young as you, don't forget. Must be a lot of half-crowns in there to make it weigh this much.'

'Stop *your* moaning Bert,' mocked Jack, as he grinned his handsome smile. 'Let's get this out of the way and slide off for a pint. Laura, Liz and our Kay can fetch all the bits and pieces up once they get 'ere.'

'Hold on a minute, if you don't mind!' came the magisterial shriek of a woman on her way to the third floor. 'We've all gotta use this staircase, you know!'

Glancing sideways at Bert, Jack covered a smile. 'Sorry, love,' he said, trying to sound sincere and gallant as he moved aside to give her space. 'You don't 'ave to walk up, you know. That's a smart old lift we've got.'

'If I want to take the lift I'll take it. If I choose to walk up I will.' She stared into Jack's face, weighing him up. 'I've seen you before?'

'Might 'ave done, luv. Dunno.' Jack scratched the tip of his ear and glanced sideways, catching Edie's eye. Giving her a flirtatious wink, he turned back to the other woman and showed a concerned face. 'Need 'elp with your bags, love? Cos Bert 'ere—'

'Oh, yes! Your face looks familiar! I've seen it. I get the East London paper every week, you know.' Her eyes narrowed, as she looked accusingly at him.

Knowing full well what she was alluding to, Jack thanked his lucky stars that his name had never been in the court columns. 'Mine's the *News of the World*.' He sniffed, turning his face to give Edie another little wink, as she turned the bright new keys to number forty-one, Scott House, in her hand. Relieved to find that although this block of flats was a far cry from what she had always been used to, the people were no different.

'I might 'ave guessed you'd read *that* paper,' said the woman from the third floor, 'all filth and gossip. Any beer parties and I'll report yer! Mark my words!' That said, she climbed the next flight of stairs. 'The name's Sarah James, *Mrs* James to you, and my 'usband is George. He works for the railway in the offices, so watch yer step!'

With a hand cupping his mouth, Bert just managed to hide his laughter; his eyes, however, were glistening. Making sure the woman was out of earshot he released a muffled burst of laughter. 'She's a bundle of joy, ain't she?'

Jack let out a low moan as he half turned to include Edie in the conversation. 'There's one everywhere you go!'

'Looks like it,' she chuckled.

'I reckon we can handle 'er, though. The name's Jack, by the way, and this is Bert.'

'Pleased to meet you both. Mine's Edie.'

'And don't think I never heard that because I did!' came the high-pitched voice of their neighbour from above. 'I'm not deaf!'

Pulling faces, the men went quietly about their business. 'I thought Carlton Square was bad enough,' murmured Jack, 'Gawd 'elp us if we've made a mistake . . .'

'I told you not to take a place on an estate, but you wouldn't listen,' said Bert, lifting his side of the trunk. 'Still, that bleached blonde we saw earlier should perk up yer Percy.'

Struggling along the balcony towards their flat, Jack bore a grin but a nervous worry was starting to nag at him. Women. Women next door to him. Women above and below. And far too many for his liking. The rooms he and Laura had moved out of overlooking a small tree-lined square were far more romantic, to Jack's way of thinking. He had flirted with more than one pretty lady while hidden by the shrubs and wrough-iron fence. When Laura had been at work and he hadn't, he had also slipped into one or two other rented rooms for a little bit of loving on the side. Their rooms, the top half of a Victorian house, had been cramped but at least it had felt more secluded than this estate. The fact that they had been only a five-minute walk from Stepney Green Underground station, which he often used, was another advantage.

'Fat chance of a bit of the other with all these windows,' grinned Bert, reading his mind. 'But, then, it's not the windows you need to worry about, Jack, mate, it's the balconies. I've seen flats similar to this and rows of 'ousewives leaning on their elbows on every floor enjoying the view. Nuffing'll be missed, I'm telling yer. Wink at one of the women and another'll spread the word that you're cocking 'er. You'll 'ave to live like a saint now, mate. No more sneaking in and out of back doors. You're gonna miss Albert Square—'

'Carlton Square. I've told you enough times it was never called that.'

'And I'm telling you it was! Way back. My great grandmuvver knew what she was talking about. Ask any of the neighbours when you pop back for a cup of tea. It was changed when young Queen Victoria met 'er Albert and fell in love. They changed a lot of squares from Albert to summink else. Political, my old granny reckons.'

'Load of rubbish,' said Jack. 'Anyway, I might not need to pop back. I fancy the one in number forty-one. Little cracker she is.'

'Oh, leave off. Poor cow's a war widow, according to Liz. She bumped into 'er when they first come to view. Any'ow, she's out of your class, mate, she is. Out of your class.'

'Don't let Laura 'ear you say that. Did Lizzie catch 'er name? I never did.'

'Cos you was looking and not listening. It's Edie. And the kid's called Maggie.'

'Edie, eh? Sounds all right. Nice and soft. Which is 'ow I like 'em.'

'Well, you would do, wouldn't yer?' said Bert. He arrived at the flat door and lowered his end.

Taking a breather, Jack leaned against the balcony wall and pulled his tobacco tin from his pocket. 'Edie . . . yeah, that name suits 'er.' He ignored Bert's disparaging response. To Jack, life was too short to miss opportunities – especially when they came wrapped in a lovely feminine parcel.

'I ain't listening and I'm taking no notice of yer. Should be ashamed of yerself,' sniffed Bert, wiping his brow with his handkerchief. 'Talking like that after all your Laura's bin through.'

'I'm not talking about now, Bert. Give it a few years.' He winked, saying, 'Anyway no 'arm in dreaming, is there?'

'More'n you think, mate. More than you think.' He dug deep into his trouser pocket and pulled out his Zippo lighter before Jack could ask for it.

Lighting his roll-up, Jack drew on it and raised an eyebrow. 'And Laura's not the only one cut up over what 'appened. I'm not made of stone, you know. I loved baby John as much as she did.'

'I know that. Just don't act like nuffing's 'appened. It's not clever and it don't do none of you any good. Not you, not Laura and not Kay. Never mind my Lizzie. She still cries in her sleep over it.'

'That's it, Bert. Rub it in. Rub the salt right in! I was just trying to look on the bright side, that's all. Strike me dead for it if you must, though. Take me dreams away and gimme a razor blade.' He said, berating his brother-in-law. 'Life's too hard to get too soft.'

Bert answered with a short nod. He and Jack were close and he knew him well enough to realise that it would take him a long time to get over the loss of his baby son. This pair were best friends and worked as a team. Even so, Jack didn't seem to have control of his dick, as far as Bert could tell. It seemed to have a mind of its own. His very own water-diviner.

The sight of another lorry pulling into the grounds but no sign of Mr Crow and her belongings was causing Edie to feel nervous. Maybe there had been an accident. Or perhaps his old truck had finally given up the ghost. Telling herself to be patient, she watched as three families alighted from the lorry and ran all the good things through her mind to calm herself: lights at the flick of a switch, hot water at the turn of a tap, a fireplace fitted with a gas poker to get the coals burning quickly. The brand new grey and white flecked gas stove in the kitchen.

A natural blonde who looked about the same age as Edie was stepping down from the back of the latest lorry. It was Jessie Smith, mother of two: the lively thirteen-year-old Billy and shy ten-year-old Emma-Rose. This family was about to move into their flat on the top floor, the fourth. Jessie's assumed husband Max, unable to take time off from work, was not there to help her. But, then, Max Cohen hadn't been as eager to move in here as Jessie and the children.

Max Cohen's hopes and dreams of owning his own house in Golders Green had been dashed but his aspirations were not yet dead. An accountant by profession, he had realised, when the Second World War had finished, that his business would take a nose-dive. Most of his clients had moved upwards and onwards, to other territories, the West End in particular where there was more money to be earned, where more and more nightclubs were opening with wealthy owners at the helm who would require protection against rival and jealous club owners. Not all of Max's clients were of this ilk by any means, but most of those who were honest businessmen found that after the war the buildings in which they had run their business were no more than a pile of bricks and rubble.

Now, employed as an accountant for a small wine and beer merchant, Max's one ambition was to work for himself again, to rise from the ashes. He had spoken openly of his discontent at being employed instead of running his own business, but the hurt he felt because his beloved Jessie had not filed for divorce from her husband Tom, from whom she had been separated since the end of 1945, he had always kept close to his chest. Why she hadn't set the wheels in motion to end her broken marriage was something only she could explain. The fact was that she had never stopped loving Tom, even though he had been an unreliable and reckless husband.

Now, standing in the Tarmacked grounds, Jessie looked around her, feeling light inside. The sun streaming down on to her face, she closed her eyes and thought of her comfortable bed up there on the fourth floor, up in the sky and away from the world, with all of the hustle and bustle and worry of what had been so far a difficult life.

Before the war Jessie had had to cope with the discovery of a twin sister, whose existence had been a tightly kept family secret. Also her engagement to Max Cohen had been broken, thanks to his interfering sister who did not want a Christian marrying into their Jewish family and her new romance with Tom Smith just weeks afterwards had introduced her to a world of petty crime, which eventually led to the police turning up at her door and a search of her house for stolen goods – stolen goods which Tom had hidden in *her* wardrobe.

Now, with all of the worst behind her, Jessie felt she could look forward to a peaceful, untroubled life and concentrate on bringing up her two children within the confines of this safe council estate. The place had a village feel to it. On such a glorious day it was easy for her to be confident that she could settle down with Max and continue to bring up Billy and Emma-Rose without the never-ending strain of having to worry or look constantly over her shoulder for trouble brewing. She glanced across to the grassy area and low wall surrounding the flats and cottages, which had new young trees planted. She imagined a rug spread out and a picnic basket. She could see her children playing there with others from the estate. She pictured herself sitting on her rug with other young mothers, out of their homes and taking a break, chatting about their children, schools and their hobbies.

Her ten-year-old Emma-Rose tugging on her sleeve brought her back into the present, the real world and the task in hand. Tired from all the packing and carrying, Jessie gazed into her daughter's innocent face. Emma-Rose's pale blue eyes squinted against the sunshine as she shifted her weight from one thin white leg to the other while screwing up the material of her summer frock with both hands. 'Can – can – can – can I—' rushed Emma, excited and anxious to get out her words in lightning time '—can I go in the lift?'

'Calm down, sweet'eart. We've got a lifetime of going up and down in it.'

'But I want to go in it *now*! Uvver children are going in by 'emselves! Why can't I?'

'*Them*selves, Emma. And I never said you couldn't, sweet'eart.'

'Well, can I, then?'

'If you must. If you can't wait for me.'

'Not by meself, though. Billy can take me up and fetch me down.'

'It's a very busy time for everyone and the lift's gonna be in demand . . .' murmured Jessie. She turned to Billy, who was peering at a steam train rushing by on the track above the arches. It had caused a flock of sparrows to flee from their dark nesting-place. He seemed to be in a world of his own.

'Billy, why don't you go up in the lift with Emma and train-spot from the fourth balcony?'

'If you want,' he said, his eyes focused on the railway line, his attention undisturbed.

'Only five minutes, mind. I'm gonna need you to help. Both of you. There's a lot of fetching and carrying to do.'

'I know that,' was his mumbled answer. 'I don't want 'er watching wiv me later on, though. I won't get five minutes' peace . . .'

'I wouldn't want to stop up there with yer!' snarled Emma, her skinny neck stretched and face pushed forward. 'Trains are boring.'

'Good.'

'Go on, then, scarper,' said Jessie, 'and be careful. No climbing down the drainpipe, Billy.'

'Who said I was gonna?' The guilty defensive tone in his voice gave him away: his mother had guessed exactly what he was thinking. Glancing up at the front balconies and catching the eye of Edie who smiled and nodded, Jessie returned the neighbourly gesture.

Stepping out of the way of her neighbours, who

were already carrying things off the lorry, tiredness hit Jessie like a wave. Her legs were aching and she felt as if there were grains of sand behind her eyes. Stifling a yawn and knowing that her belongings would be last off the lorry – they had been picked up first – she went inside the building. The echo of her footsteps on the stone staircase, the gleaming white tiles on the lower half of the walls and the painted green iron hand-rail reminded her of the London Hospital, and she shuddered. Towards the end of the war she, like many local women, had been a voluntary helper, going in to do whatever she could for the victims of the blitz on the East End.

When she arrived at the second floor Jessie instinctively popped her head round the corner to where Edie was leaning on the balcony, waiting for Mr Crow to arrive with her furniture. 'Have you moved in?' said Jessie, above the excited buzz that was coming from all corners and from people of all ages.

'Not yet. I'm waiting for my things to arrive. I bet the dilapidated old truck's broke down.'

'Are you pleased with it, then?' said Jessie, nodding at her neighbour's open front door, all tiredness draining away as her excitement grew.

'I love it,' said Edie. 'I've got a flask of tea inside if you fancy a cup.'

'That was clever. Now, why didn't I think of that? I'll pop back down in a minute, if that's all right. Can't wait to get inside my flat now. I'm up on the fourth floor, right at the top. God help me if that lift ever breaks down. I can't imagine—'

The sudden shrill voice of Sarah James ringing through the block stopped Jessie in her tracks. The woman was scolding Billy. She listened to see if he was going to cheek her. The woman's voice, louder now, continued. 'And you can tell your mother I told you off as well! Bloody nuisance! You break that lift and I'll report you to the caretaker! Then you'll know what being in trouble means! Now, clear off to your own balcony!'

The rapid sound of hurried footsteps on the stairs was a sign that the fear of God had been put into both Billy and Emma-Rose. Eyes on the staircase, Jessie waited until the pair emerged from above, a look of sheer terror on their faces. 'It's all right, kids!' she said, deliberately loudly. 'Slow down, Emma, or you'll fall and break your neck! No one's gonna hurt either of you.'

'I'm not living 'ere!' screeched Billy. 'They've put all the mad people up the top! I'm not living up there!'

'He's right, he's right, he's right!' puffed Emma, grabbing Jessie's arm and shaking it. 'A lady's sitting in the kitchen sink wiv the curtains open and she's singing wiv no clothes on!'

'And that other woman tells *everyone* off!'

Covering a smile, Jessie turned to Edie. 'Sounds like we're in for some fun.'

'Just what I was thinking,' said Edie, looking over the balcony and catching sight of Mr Crow's dilapidated truck being manoeuvred round a lorry and two vans. 'My furniture's arrived at last. If your son wants to run down and fetch up two kitchen chairs . . .' she said, looking down at Billy.

'Course he will. I'd best go upstairs and see what's what.' Jessie tousled her son's hair, 'You'll give the lady a hand, won't you?' The expression on Billy's face and his curled lip said it all: fetching and carrying couldn't have been further from his mind.

'Well . . . if you was prepared to help my daughter Maggie to help Mr Crow bring up our furniture,' said Edie, her voice persuasive, 'I'd give you a silver tanner.'

At the thought of earning sixpence, Billy raised an eyebrow. 'I would 'ave 'elped anyway, but if you fink it's worf a tanner, it must be.'

'Right, then,' said Jessie, amused by his expression, that of a young businessman. 'I'll leave Billy in your hands. Come on, Emma. You stop with me.' She took her daughter's hand. Her nervous daughter, who still had a look of worry in her eyes.

Easier with her hand firmly held by Jessie, Emma-Rose peered up at Edie, the afternoon sun on her snow-white hair. 'Have you got any children like me? I'm ten.'

'Well . . . Maggie's fourteen and she's not got your lovely hair and blue eyes but she's a *bit* like you . . . but more like yer brother.'

'Like Billy?' Emma screwed her nose, aghast at the thought.

'That's right. A bit on the cantankerous side. And right now she's gonna be yanked from the back balcony to help your brother fetch my things up.'

'What back balcony?' said Emma, narrowing her eyes.

'One like this only out the back. She's watching some boys down below racing on their rickety old go-carts.'

'She don't really look like our Billy, does she?'

'Come on, you,' said Jessie. 'Let's go up and see where we're gonna put your bed. The men'll be fetching it up soon.'

Going rigid, Emma-Rose pulled back, her eyes wide. 'Wot about that woman sitting in the kitchen sink? Billy said she probably kidnapped girls and locked 'em in cupboards.'

Jessie looked from Emma-Rose to Edie. 'What on earth have we let ourselves in for?'

'Time will tell,' chuckled Edie, and then, a more serious expression on her face, 'It's gonna be a lot different from living in a quiet turning. A lot different.'

2

From the day that Edie had moved into her new home in late summer and right up until this Christmas Eve she had laboured every waking hour, and every hour she had managed to sleep she had slept well. Out for the count. Using an outdated and clumsy hand sewing-machine, compliments of the factory in which she worked as a machinist, she had made curtains for every window and two bedspreads: one for herself and one for Maggie. She had cut and laid new lino in both bedrooms, the living room, kitchen and bathroom. All of this back-bending and time-consuming work she had tackled by herself after a tiring day's work during the week and again on Sundays. To Edie, though, this was no hardship. She had enjoyed transforming the bare rooms and covering the stone floors to make the flat as homely as her little house had been.

Mr Crow had come up trumps, as promised, on the day he had moved her out of Cotton Street, with the gently faded red velvet settee, which she loved. He had also, during the months she had now been living here, continued to bring furniture to replace other pieces that were old and tatty, and very much out of place in the new flat. He had been and gone so many times that Edie had lost count. She knew that the manner in which he behaved each time he arrived was an act and the stories of how he had picked some of the things up for next to nothing were all white lies, but although it was hard for her, she accepted his kindness and generosity.

The old boy had taken pity on her and even though it hadn't been easy at first for Edie to swallow her pride, she gradually realised, with time, that he *wanted* to help her and soon found it easier to accept his charity. For charity it was. There was no profit for Mr Crow when dealing with war widows, except for the good feeling and warm glow it gave him deep inside. He was, in his own quiet way, doing his bit. Edie now had a lovely furnished, albeit modest, home and clearly he was proud to have helped bring it about and enjoyed bringing his new finds.

Edie's favourite was the four light oak chairs and matching dining table that had been polished lovingly over the decades. She had paid seven shillings and sixpence for this suite, which included the cost of her saviour taking away the old mismatched chairs and rickety table.

Now, as the choir on the wireless sang 'Silent Night' and she sat at her table by the veranda doors, Edie gazed out at the star-spangled navy sky. It was coming up to six fifteen and Maggie had gone to a local youth club Christmas party. Outside, all was quiet and still, except for the echoing sound of a dog barking at sparrows under the railway arch, and Edie was under no illusions as to why. At this time of year families were inside preparing for the next day while young children, clinging to their dreams, were looking forward to a secret visit from Santa. As the night wore on the sounds of song would come from every direction as the festivities began. Here it would be no different from Cotton Street, as far as Edie could tell, except that she would not only hear joyous laughter coming from the houses each side of her but above and below too.

In this lonesome mood, she poured herself a glass of sherry and questioned why her spirits were low. She had the next day to look forward to, when her aunt Naomi, her brother and his wife would be coming to spend the day with her and Maggie. The place would come alive on Christmas morning with everyone buzzing around and the smell of the capon sizzling in the oven, but right now she felt in dire need of someone to talk to. She missed the atmosphere of Cotton Street where she had known everyone and where everyone popped in and out of each other's homes at this time of year for a glass of sherry or ginger wine and a chat.

She switched off the wireless, collected her coat from its hook in the passage and left the flat. Without thinking of where she might walk to, Edie let memories of her husband and herself come to mind instead of blocking them out as she was so conditioned to doing. Before she knew it she had arrived in Cotton Street, her old home ground, and was standing at the end, looking at the two rows of terraced houses opposite each other. With the exception of two homes, and the faint shine from the street lights, the turning was dark.

Tears welling behind her eyes, she walked slowly along the street that was so familiar to her. This had been the only place she had known as home from the day she was born.

When she arrived at the first lighted window from which a warm glow was coming through the thin curtain, she stopped. This was number twenty, the coal man's house. With all nostalgia swept away she was puzzled at seeing the house occupied. Ben, the old Jewish man who had lived alone for as long as she could remember, had moved out on the same day as herself yet the electricity hadn't been cut off. She couldn't imagine that the light inside was coming from candles lit by a tramp who might have set up home there. Tapping her knuckle on the window she waited to see who might appear, if anyone. When the curtain was cautiously drawn back and she saw the worried face peering out into the dark she couldn't help but smile. It was Ben. Dear old Ben. His lovely familiar face brought tears to her eyes.

'I know I'm being silly—' she just managed to say as he opened the door to her, 'but I had to come back and take a look at our street.' She wiped an escaping tear from her cheek with the sleeve of her coat. 'I thought you moved out.'

'I did,' he said, a curious expression on his face.

'Well, then, what are you doing in there, you daft sod?'

'I *was* listening to the wireless, before you blooming well tapped on the window and sent a chill up my spine. Frightened the living daylights out of me. So, what do you want?' he said, a gentle smile spreading across his face, hoping that this really was just a nostalgic visit and no more than that.

'Oh, Ben . . . what have we done? Why did we all leave? Where is everyone?' she asked forlornly.

'How should I know? Moved here, there and every-bloody-where.' Slipping his arms round her he patted her back as if she were the child he once knew and spoke in a low voice. 'There, there . . . Edie. There, there. What's meant to be is meant to be.'

'Is it, though? I don't know any more,' whispered Edie, comforted by his soft shoulder and the faint smell of Lifebuoy soap. Her tears were soaking into his worn thick hand-knit jumper. 'Is whatever 'appens to us meant to be? Was my Harry meant to drown at sea? Was my Maggie meant to grow up never seeing or cuddling her dad?'

Jolted by this remark – for reasons that Edie must never know – Ben cursed the day he had found out the truth about Harry and how he had betrayed her so badly. Since the day he had been listed as missing, presumed dead, he had in fact been lying low in Turkey, with his Turkish mistress, Cicek. 'No, Edie, love. No,' said Ben, guilt rising through his entire being. 'That wasn't meant to be. No. It was a daft thing to say and normally I wouldn't 'ave said it.' He pulled back from her, lips pursed, his own eyes filling with tears, swallowing against the lump in his throat. 'A drop of my Irish whiskey is what we need. That'll warm our tickers.'

'I reckon so. Don't water it down, though.'

'Water down my Irish whiskey?' he said, his face lighting up and more like the face she had always known. 'My only present to myself and you think I'd water it down?'

Closing the street door behind them he pulled a second small armchair close to the coal fire and tapped it with his trembling fingers caused by emotions rather than old age. At seventy, Ben was still wiry and in good health. 'Sit yerself there and I'll fetch another glass. I've got some mince pies that Lilly Cranfield gimme. D'yer fancy—'

'Lilly Cranfield?'

'Sure, Lilly gave them to me. Why wouldn't she? Bloody show-off. Mind you, I've never tasted better pastry than hers. And that's saying something. She's gone to 'er daughter's for Christmas but fetched a few bits and bobs in before she left.'

'But she moved out as well, didn't she? Or am I going mad?'

'Ha. Who said you were sane? None of us are or we'd 'ave jumped off the roof years ago. Bloody world.' The colour was coming back into his face. 'She trundled off and just like me she trundled back agen. We 'ad a fight on our 'ands to get the 'lectric back on but they give in, finally. Well, they would, wouldn't they? They 'ad a queue of people waiting for them one-bedroomed places. I wasn't gone a fortnight and they moved an old couple in.'

'You mean to say you gave up your *new* place?' Edie could hardly believe it.

'Sure. Four of us altogether. Course . . . young Joey's still in 'is place but, then, we expected that, didn't we?' He eyed her cautiously, looking for a trace of confirmation that she possibly knew as much as he did. 'We knew that old sod wouldn't move for no one. Eight grown kids and not one of 'em could persuade 'im to go. 'Now that you have to admire.'

'Young Joey from thirty-eight?' She laughed. 'He must be in 'is seventies.'

'Well, that's younger than his father, old Joey, who's still alive and kicking in his nineties.'

Her response confirmed that she was ignorant to the truth as to why Joey had stopped on.

'And he's not sorry?' asked Edie, sipping her drink.

'Course not. The crafty sod thought he had one up on us by staying put in the end. I think he was a bit taken aback when I wheeled some of my stuff back in on a barrow.' He looked around the room with a look of pride on his face as he sailed a hand through the air. 'I've got everything back in its place as if I never moved out.' He winked at Edie, adding, 'Better to try out the new and change back than never to try at all.'

Can't argue with that, thought Edie. Can't argue with that. Caught up in the moment, she began to wonder what it would be like if they had all done the same: refused to leave or return to bring life back into the old street. Ben had got his place looking as if he'd never left it in the first place.

'I can see what you're thinking,' said Ben, all knowing. 'You stop where you are. You're young enough to start fresh. It's only us old degenerates that can't take change. Christmas can bring out the melancholy side in all of us. Always did. No good clinging to memories.'

'I know. I wonder why that is.'

'It's meant to make us stop and think if you ask me.' Leaning back and gazing up at the ceiling he continued, 'This is the best time of the year. Apart from summer days when the roses are in full bloom. Or springtime when the daffodils and tulips are out.' He surreptitiously raised his eyes to check her expression. 'You're bound to be missing Harry during the festive season, Edie.'

Not wishing to go down that road, Edie smiled at this lone and independent gentleman. 'I'm all right. I've got my Maggie and my brother and you-know-who.'

'Do I ever,' he said raising his eyes. 'How is the old nutcase?'

'Well, funnily enough,' said Edie, 'she's seen as a ray of sunshine by 'er neighbours. Drives the authorities mad, mind you, but she fights for 'er rights – and for the rights of the other pensioners around 'er. She frightens the Welfare to death.'

'I'm sure she does,' he laughed, 'I'm sure she does. Tell 'er I'm back and to drop in when she's passing. Will you do that for me?'

'Course I will.' Edie smiled at the thought of her aunt Naomi swaggering along the turning in her flowing clothes, left over from the twenties. 'She's gonna love it.'

'You think so?'

'You know she'll be impressed, Ben. Miffed at first that some of you are more bonkers than she is – but this baulking against authority and winning, it'll make 'er day.'

Keeping his thoughts to himself, Ben leaned back in his chair, his expression giving him away. To him, this *was* an accomplishment. *This* was what being alive was all about. To stand up and be counted! 'Yes . . . I think you're right, Edie. I think you're right.'

She was, but to agree right then would have taken away his moment of glory. Staring into the flames of the small fire, she felt herself unwind. Coming back to Cotton Street had not been premeditated, but a quiet spur-of-the-moment decision, which she was very pleased she had not shied away from. As she considered whether to stay right where she was with just the two of them uninterrupted, Ben answered for her, saying, 'I fink I'll go an' see if the silly codger wants to come in for a Christmas drink.'

'Joey?'

'Sure Joey. Who else? You never know, the stubborn old sod might be lonely up there.' He wasn't, and Ben was quite aware of the fact.

'I should 'ave brought Naomi. Between us we could've had a little party.'

'I wish you 'ad 'ave done, Edie. She's got a lovely voice, that woman.' He became thoughtful and then added, 'My banjo mandolin's not seen daylight for a while.'

'We could always walk round to see her?'

'We could,' he said, rising from his chair. 'We certainly could. I think that would really make my Christmas Eve.'

'You always did 'ave a soft spot for the fruitcake. My visit not enough for you, then?' she teased.

'Compared to your aunt? Never.'

With his old overcoat on – and now it was at least one size too big for him – Ben pulled on his hat and winked at her. 'See, you can't beat fate. This street wasn't ready to go on the rubbish heap yet.' With that, he left the house, only a *little* unsteady on his feet. The large Irish whiskey he had poured himself before Edie knocked on his door hadn't gone to his head, yet. Ben wasn't a drinking man and on this occasion, it had been medicinal more than anything else. Happy though he had been to get back into his old house *and* having triumphed over the authorities, the reality of having hardly any of his neighbours around him had come as a bit of a knock. If truth had been told, Edie would have heard another story: that he had realised his mistake and had been sitting around his fire regretting his weakness – the lack of ability to accept change. Especially now that Christmas had arrived.

As she sipped her drink, Edie glanced around the small room. The sideboard was heaving with Ben's framed photographs going back to Victorian times. Grandparents, aunts, uncles and cousins and, of course, those of himself as a boy and then a young man. But no wedding pictures. No photographs of him linking arms with a sweetheart. The fact that he had never married had never been an issue. Ben was Ben and lived by himself: he was as happy as anyone else and one of the friendliest people around. He had more friends than anyone, as far as Edie could tell. But where were they this evening? Why was the old man alone on Christmas Eve?

Smiling at the irony of her own thoughts, she sipped her drink. After all, here she was, a young woman with friends and family, and wasn't she in the same boat? Wasn't this why she was here in his house? Hadn't she been drawn to the light in his window like a moth to a lamp? Hadn't the need to talk to someone, and especially an old neighbour, been fierce?

Yes, thought Edie, it had, and somehow in this room it seemed all right to admit it. Not that she would ever confess it to another soul. Never in a month of Sundays would she do that. Her brother's voice floated through her mind. 'You've got nuffing to prove, Sis.' The sound of Ben outside and pushing his key into the street door brought her out of the self-effacing mood which was slowly creeping in.

'He can be a stubborn old mule at times,' said Ben. 'Well, he can sit there and smoke 'is pipe all by himself. Why should I care?'

'Maybe he'd rather be on 'is own—'

'Course he wouldn't. I can read the man like a book. He's a blooming nuisance,' he said, scratching an ear. 'I'd best nip back up there in ten minutes or so with my bottle. Two old soldiers talking about the past round his fire is what he wants. It's not what he needs, mind. He needs a bloody good woman.'

'And you don't?'

'Oh, I do all right. I keep my cards close to my chest, thank you. Love 'em and leave 'em in their own places so they don't go and mess up mine with their knitting and rubbish. So, what about New Year's Eve? Why don't you fetch your aunt Naomi round then? That's if you've nothing else planned, of course.'

'I 'adn't thought that far ahead, Ben.' Edie pushed a hand through her hair. She didn't want to think about New Year's Eve, 'Auld Lang Syne' and her memories. Rising from her chair, she said, 'I'll keep it in mind, though. I daren't mention it too soon or Aunt Naomi'll take it as fixed and I'm not sure what my brother's got planned.'

'Fair enough,' he said. 'At least we haven't lost touch altogether, Edie. That's a good thing. It's how it should be.'

Giving Ben a hug, Edie asked him to pass on her regards to Joey and a message that she was proud of those who had stood their ground. Then, leaving him to fill his hot-water bottle, and to worry secretly over right and wrong before going out again, Edie slipped quietly away from the street where she had once lived and with only a quick glance at her house. She felt better for the visit. Much better. It was as if she had laid a ghost to rest.

As she walked back home, and with more people in the streets now in festive mood on their way to celebrate, Edie was tempted to drop in at her local but thought better of it. She still had the capon to stuff and the mince pies to make. Suddenly she was looking forward to the next day and especially to giving Maggie her Christmas present – a coat she had tried on in Wickham's, the local department store, which Edie had told her she couldn't afford. The next day she had gone back and had it put by with an arrangement to pay it off weekly. The green swagger coat with its jade-green turn-back cuffs and collar had looked as if it were made for Maggie when she had tried it on. Now it was wrapped in holly-patterned paper and sitting under the small tree.

With coloured lights glowing in some of the windows and the sound of laughter and carols coming from wirelesses in the houses she passed on her way home, Edie could feel the joy at long last and it was coming from all corners. Nineteen fifty-two had been shocking one way and another. Earlier in the year there had been the horrifying Harrow rail disaster just outside London, when two trains had crashed and a third travelling at high speed had hit the wreckage – over 300 had been killed or badly injured. King George VI had died in the February from lung cancer and, more locally, there had been gang attacks by Chinese immigrants on American soldiers based in London over accusations that the US had used germ warfare in Korea. In October the first atomic bomb had been tested: this had sent waves of fear through everyone and brought to mind how awful it had been during the war when no one was safe from being blown to smithereens. The thought of what might be in decades to come had been on everyone's mind until it had all died down.

But it had not all been doom and gloom. The modernity of the 1950s meant snack bars, self-service shops, frozen foods and launderettes. Formica kitchen furniture was taking over from drab dark wood. The new pleasure gardens at Battersea were a triumph, as was the Festival of Britain held on the south bank of the Thames, the funfair being the most popular part. Package holidays abroad, affordable to the working classes, had become available, and the more adventurous were beginning to hitchhike to the Continent. Two of the girls in the dress factory where Edie worked had managed to travel to the Riviera on five pounds. Those families who could afford a week's holiday but could not stretch to going abroad could spend a week at a Butlin's holiday camp with Redcoats to entertain them, day and night.

For Edie the most memorable time of the year had been her and Maggie's evening out at the Empire picture palace on the Mile End Road where, to her mind, the film of the year had been Alfred Hitchcock's *Strangers On A Train*.

As her thoughts flew from one thing to another, Edie was entering Barcroft Estate before she knew it. She was thinking about Ben again. Ben and his wonderful droll sense of humour. Edie could only guess at why there seemed to be fewer Yiddish characters around nowadays. During the war the East End had been badly bombed and scarred, and had lost many of its Jewish inhabitants, while the gradual migration to the suburbs was continuing. The friendly old Jewish East End was slowly slipping into the past, leaving its traditions in its wake: markets and communal institutions, boys' clubs, girls' clubs, mixed clubs, synagogues, the cobbled alleys where pawnbrokers and jewellery shops closed on Saturdays and opened on Sundays. The pavement exchange, with tailors milling around looking for work, and noticeboards advertising vacancies for buttonhole makers and Hoffman pressers, the social gatherings in Whitechapel of Yiddish tailors hoping to pick up some business, had been part and parcel of Sunday outings to Petticoat Lane.

The old-style barber shops, where a shave was part and parcel of the service, had all but disappeared over the years, the ladies' hairdressers were going too, the salt-beef bars, the bakeries full of bagels, the delis with the herrings and Hamisher pickle barrels. Not all of these Jewish-run places were gone by any means, but they were diminishing, and creating empty pockets here and there, soulless and silent voids in what had been bustling streets.

To have found her old Jewish friend settled back into Cotton Street was the best Christmas present Edie could have been given. He had lived there since birth, and continued to do so when his old parents had died, and was part of the brickwork now. A glow shining out from a lamp-post that was a landmark. Ben the Jew. That was how he was known and that was how he wanted to be known. Proud as a cockerel, as gentle as a lamb and as reliable as his namesake marking the hour: Big Ben.

Back on her own step and turning the key in her door, Edie saw a light on and berated herself for wasting electricity – but she hadn't been careless. Maggie had returned early from the Christmas dance and was sitting on the settee in half-light and silence. Her eyelids were smudged with Edie's black mascara and her rose red lipstick had been deliberately smeared across her cheeks out of frustration and low self-esteem.

Glancing at her and realising what had happened, Edie put on a pretence of innocence. 'Wasn't it any good, then?'

'It was all right,' Maggie grumbled quietly, keeping her eyes down.

'Did they play records to dance to, or make you play party games and give you jelly and ice-cream?' she teased.

'It wasn't a kids' party, Mum. And I don't wanna talk about it.'

'Fair enough. I won't probe further. At least you gave it a go. I'm pleased you're in, sweet'eart. You can help me with the mince pies. I've got the bird to stuff yet as well. Were there many of your age there?' she continued, pulling off her coat and shaking the cold air out of it.

'I didn't take that much notice. I wasn't bothered.'

'So it was a bit of a waste of time. Never mind. At least you'll know for another day. No use—'

'I'm not crying over it, am I?' snarled Maggie, her face pushed forward defiantly.

'I never said you was.'

'Spilt milk is what you was gonna say. You're too predictable.'

'Ooh, am I now? And what are you? In a right old mood, I'd say.'

'I felt old-fashioned in this dress. Everyone else was wearing full skirts and twin sets and higher heels than these silly fings. And none of 'em 'ad their 'air brushed out like mine. I felt dressed like I was goin' to a tea-party. One of the girls in the ladies' lav said it as well. I nearly squashed her lipstick into her face. Vain cow.'

Edie slipped off her fur-lined ankle boots and sat on the edge of the settee. 'I'm sorry, darling. I tried my best but I must 'ave got it wrong. I thought that frock looked lovely on you and you always *wanted* a red and white and it is Christmas so—'

'That was when I was seven!'

'No, it wasn't. Don't exaggerate. And as for your ginger locks . . . Do you want me to cut it for yer? Is that what this is all about?'

'No. It don't matter anyway. I don't look four-teen – I look seven years old so it's just as well I wore it.'

'Not with that figure you don't. You're nice and slim but you're growing little breasts and soon you'll need a—'

'Don't call 'em breasts! I haven't got breasts! They're tits!'

'Well, all right, then! Call 'em what you want but they're beginning to show. That's all I meant.'

'So why didn't you buy me a brassière?'

Edie leaned back into a cushion. 'Because I didn't think you were ready for it yet. You're only fourteen and – oh, I don't know. But you can 'ave my new one. It's a size thirty-two and plain white cotton. Do whatever makes you happy, Mags. I can't get anything right, that's obvious.'

Closing her eyes, she was at a loss as to what to do to help her child, who meant everything in the world to her. Maggie was about to go through one of the worst phases of her life and Edie was the only one to help her through it. The trouble was, she didn't really know how. She loved Maggie so much it hurt when she was unhappy and so lacking in confidence. She knew that her usual rebellious attitude was an act.

'It don't matter, anyway,' said Maggie, reaching for the glasses she hadn't worn in a while. 'I'd rather stop in by the fire and read a book.'

'Well, there's nothing wrong with that. I s'pose you don't feel like helping me in the kitchen, then?'

'Not yet. I might later. What time they all coming tomorrer?'

'About twelve midday.'

'I s'pose I'll 'ave to wait to open my present for when they get 'ere?'

'You've never 'ad to before, 'ave you?'

'S'pose not. But—' A knock on the front door stopped her short. 'Don't let whoever that is in! I don't wanna be seen looking like this!'

Leaving the room and closing the door behind her, Edie hoped it wasn't her brother, popping in for a Christmas Eve drink. She didn't feel like seeing anyone right then and Maggie certainly wouldn't want it.

It wasn't her brother, it was one of her neighbours: Jessie Smith from the fourth floor. She looked flushed and hurried. 'Edie, I'm sorry to bother you but I'm 'aving a bit of a get-together and I've run out of salt. You'd be amazed how much you miss it when you 'aven't got any. I can't believe I forgot to buy some. I was wondering—'

'Come in,' said Edie, amused. 'It's turning colder.' Her neighbour followed her through to the kitchen and her apologies continued to flow while Edie took her drum of salt from the cupboard and filled a teacup. 'This should be enough to get you through till Boxing Day. Then come back and I'll fill the cup agen.' She smiled as she handed it over.

'You all right, Edie?' said Jessie, who was studying her face.

'Course I am. Lots to do for tomorrow that's all.'

'Honest?'

The expression of sympathy on her new neighbour's face almost broke through Edie's reserve. She lowered her voice, pointed at the closed living-room door, and whispered, 'Maggie's a bit upset.'

'Ah ... Missing her dad at this time of year, I s'pose?'

'No. She never knew 'im. It's her age, between being a kid and a woman. You know what it's like.'

Jessie raised her eyebrows. 'It seems like an age since I was there. Tell you what, why don't the pair of you come up and have a drink with us? A couple of the neighbours on my balcony are coming.'

'Not the woman who sits in the sink and sings?'

'No, Edie, that poor woman never leaves her flat, by all accounts. Someone said her first husband was in a Japanese POW camp.'

'Oh, God, how does anyone ever get over that? There's a bloke who lives in the corner flat on the ground floor who went through it as well. And there was one who lived in our turning. You can almost recognise the poor sods. Skinny as rakes and hunched over – their eyes darting everywhere.'

'Oh, don't,' said Jessie. 'I can't bear to think about it. The woman on the top floor's quite intelligent by all accounts. Or was. Apparently her husband used to talk non-stop about his experiences until he finally took an overdose and died in his sleep, in bed, with her lying there beside him.'

'Oh, my God, that's terrible. No wonder she's flipped. Poor cow.'

'Who wouldn't after something like that? Anyway, back to the party. I've asked the Italian couple in and a woman on 'er own and . . . oh and a few others,' she said, dismissively.

'I'll see if Maggie's up to it,' said Edie, a little hurt that she hadn't been invited before now.

'I bumped into the Italian woman coming back from Whitechapel market. We were both lugging two full shopping-bags. They were practically giving away the fruit, veg and nuts by the time I got there this afternoon.' Jessie seemed embarrassed now not to have thought of asking Edie in a couple of days previous. 'It was meant to be a family gathering but it's growing. I'd love it if you'd come, Edie. You can meet my sisters.'

'I'll give it some thought, Jess. See what Maggie says. If she wants to, we'll both pop in.'

'Try and persuade 'er. There'll be plenty of people so she won't feel out of place. My family alone fill up my flat. And they're all coming, my two sisters and their husbands and both my brothers and their wives. It'll be like Casey's court.'

'At least she'll 'ave your Billy to talk to. He's about the same age, I should think.'

'Thirteen. But you 'ave to drop a couple of years when you're comparing the lads to the girls when it comes to a bit of intellect. What's in their pants grow faster than what's inside their heads.'

'I can well believe that. It would do Maggie good to get out,' murmured Edie, a sad and worried expression on her face. 'It's harder at this time of year with no dad around to help us get in the Christmas mood.'

'Oh, Edie . . .' Jessie instinctively held out her arms and gave Edie a hug. 'I should 'ave realised. I'm sorry.'

'Don't be daft,' smiled Edie, wiping a tear from her eye. 'Maggie's a bit low, that's all. She'll soon cheer up tomorrow when my family arrive.'

'Oh, good. So you won't be by yourselves on Christmas Day. Who's coming?'

'My aunt Naomi, my brother and his wife.' She shrugged. 'There's only the five of us now but we're close.'

Warmed by her neighbour's honesty, Jessie suddenly felt much closer to her. 'Well, come on up as

soon as you feel like it. I want you to come. We're
both new girls in this block of flats, don't forget, and
new girls have to stick together.'

'You make it sound like school. You'll be asking
for my little finger next.'

'What a lovely idea.' Jessie pushed her small finger
forward and Edie fitted hers round it. 'Right then . . .
ready?'

Quietly laughing, Edie then began the chant and
Jessie joined in: 'Make up, make up, promise never
to break up, if you do you'll get the cane!'

The kitchen hatch opened, breaking in to their
laughter. 'What's goin' on?' said Maggie, bemused
at seeing her mother behaving like a schoolgirl.

'We're reliving our youth,' said Jessie, giggling.

'Did you 'ave a row, then?'

'No,' said Jessie, 'we did that in case we ever do
'ave one.' Then having brushed a light kiss across
Edie's cheek, said, 'Come up when you're ready.'

'You're like a couple of kids,' said Maggie, and
closed the hatch.

'That's telling us,' said Edie. 'I'll see you later.'

'Good,' and with that Jessie left the flat.

Her spirits lifted by her neighbour, Edie decided on
the spot that she *would* pop in for a drink, whether
Maggie was up to it or not. Easing herself down into
her kitchen chair, she felt so much lighter for the visit.
Five minutes in another woman's company had done
her the world of good. It was only now that it occurred
to her that in Cotton Street there hadn't been many
women of her age and none she had become friends

with. They had been neighbourly, but looking back it had been the men who were more friendly. Quietly chuckling to herself, it dawned on her as to why. Men, just like the one she had seen on the day she moved in here, couldn't resist sniffing around a woman without a man. Their women, justifiably, were bound to be wary.

Back in the sitting room she poured herself a glass of sherry and was beginning to feel in the Christmas mood again. She glanced at Maggie. The glasses were off and she had wiped her face clean of the smudged lipstick. This, in so far as she could tell, was an ideal moment to begin to treat her daughter as if she were no longer a schoolgirl.

'Fancy a little drink, Mags? We've got sherry, ginger wine, a little drop of brandy to spare . . . and some Babycham.'

Maggie looked taken aback by her mother's new approach, but did her best to seem casual. 'What're you having?'

'Sherry,' said Edie, licking her lips. 'And it's lovely!'

'I'll 'ave a drop of that, then,' sniffed Maggie, nonchalantly.

'We've bin invited in for a drink at Jessie Smith's,' said Edie, pouring her daughter a measure. 'Billy and Emma are staying up late for it. Some of the other neighbours are popping in.'

'Which ones?'

'Laura Jackson and her 'usband, someone elderly who lives alone . . . and I think she said the Italians, but I haven't got a clue who they are.'

Maggie knew exactly who they were: the woman she had helped carry a pram up the stairs on moving day and the dishy son who had winked at her. 'You go, I'll be all right by myself.'

'All right. I think I will. I'm in the mood now.' Edie pushed the glass of sherry into Maggie's hand. 'Get that down you. You'll soon cheer up.'

'I don't need to cheer up. I'm all right as I—' A sudden long ring on the doorbell stopped her midstream. 'If that's another neighbour don't invite 'em into this room!'

'I won't, don't worry. Anyway, you don't look half as bad now you've wiped yer face.'

'Yes, I do! Don't let anyone in!'

'Yes, ma'am, no, ma'am, three bags full, ma'am.' Edie left the room and pulled the door shut hard behind her. 'You're gonna have to be very patient with her, Edie,' she told herself. 'Very patient.'

Standing in the porch Aunt Naomi was a wonderful sight for sore eyes. 'God, your timing's good! Madam's in a right mood,' Edie told her.

'I should think she *would* be,' said Naomi, sweeping past her niece with a dark red bulging carrier-bag in each hand. 'Staying in on Christmas Eve at *her* age!' She spoke in an overly loud voice so Maggie could hear. Throwing open the living-room door she dropped her bags and stood in front of her great-niece with her arms folded. 'What on *earth* are you doing curled up like a pussy cat on a cushion? You should be out there swinging all your bits about and teasing the boys.'

'Hello, Aunt Naomi,' droned Maggie. 'Happy Christmas.'

'Thank you, but *no*, your toneless greeting is *not* welcome. Would you like a bottle of pills to end it all now or later?' Naomi said.

'The brandy's on the sideboard. Save some for the Christmas pudding.'

'I know exactly where to find what I want in this pristine home, thank you.' And then, with her head to one side, she gave Maggie the once-over. 'You look like the fairy who fell off the tree. I thought you were going to have your hair cut and styled, dear?'

'Well, I never did.'

'And that is a *terrible* frock.'

'I know. What's Mum doing? Not leaving me to cope wiv you alone, I 'ope.'

'She is having a pee, my sweetheart. Which is no bad thing. Listen for the flush and you'll know she's on her way back to *fuss* over you.'

'Are my presents in one of them bags, then?'

'Who said you had more than *one*?'

'Are they or not? Cos if it's food for tomorrer, take it all into the kitchen.'

'Oh dear . . . we are in the dumps. Not that I can't see *why*. You went to the dance and ran away – but not exactly the Cinderella, more the *ugly duckling*?'

'Sod off.'

'Oh, *please*, if you must swear at me use something a touch stronger and with a little more venom.'

'Such as?'

Naomi shrugged and splayed her hands dramatically. '*Bugger off?*'

The small hatch into the kitchen flew open. 'Naomi, that's *not* funny!'

'Wasn't meant to be, darling. Give her the carving-knife and let's get it over with. She's *terribly* suicidal, sweetheart.'

'No more swearing!' The hatch was slammed shut.

'*Bollocks*,' murmured Naomi, and then, 'Get that long sexless body off the couch and into your mother's bedroom – *now.*

'Why?'

'*You'll* see. *Up!*'

Downing her sherry in one, Maggie slouched out of the room, secretly thrilled to have her mad aunt in the place. 'You're not touching my hair.'

'Where is your mother's *sewing* box?'

The hatch opened again. 'Leave her alone!'

'Darling, she's *terribly* depressed. If we don't do something about it *now* she may not live to see Christmas Day. That's a *very* sharp carving-knife you keep in the drawer.'

'Don't touch her hair!'

Naomi splayed her hand innocently. 'Did I mention her curly locks, *sweetheart*? I think *not*. I have a little material in my bag and wish to knock up something for her to wear instead of that doll's dress you've deigned to put her in.'

'It's in the bottom of my wardrobe. And I'm warning you—'

'Darling, I know you are. And I am *ever* so petri-fied. You always frightened me and always will. You really ought to have gone on the stage and performed in a chilling Shakespearean play.' Smiling benignly, Naomi left the room before her niece had a second opportunity to slam that hatch door in her face.

Once in the bedroom she closed the door and then pushed a chest-of-drawers against it. 'At last! I have my darling, darling niece to myself.'

'Great-niece.'

'Of *course*, my love. You are terribly great. But, alas, you don't *look* the part exactly in that awful red and white frock.'

'Well, go on then, clever drawers, change me into the Cinderella that gets Prince Charming!'

'Heaven forbid,' said Naomi, rolling her eyes. She then withdrew the sewing box from the wardrobe and opened it to find exactly what she was looking for: the cutting scissors. 'Now, then, you have *beautiful* red hair that Georgia Sitwell would have given up her most favourite lover for. But . . .' she lifted the long strands in one hand, then let them fall '. . . there's no style to it, my love.'

'Who's Georgia Sitwell?'

'Oh dear! Maggie, what am I to do with you? Georgia Sitwell, my love, has been said to be the *rose* of all English roses. A model who catches the mood of youth, no matter what year she is passing through. Sexy, mock-decadent and slinky. She continues in her autumn years to model for Norman Hartnell.'

'Who's he?'

'Never mind,' Naomi said, fanning her face with a hand and sighing. 'It *matters* not. What is *one* wife of one of the three most *eminent* impresarios of the avant-garde in all the arts after all's said and done and the cat's been put out? Is not all the world a stage?'

'Yours is. So you're gonna *cut* my hair, then?'

'Not *cut*, sweetheart,' Naomi said grimacing, then gave her the angelic smile she kept for such times. 'Look at my face, Margaret, and watch my mouth . . . as I speak.' She gracefully brushed her fingertips across her neck and whispered, 'Cut.'

'So? What? I don't know what you're on about!'

'Oh dear! There is a *huge* difference in the way one *speaks* the word. Marginal to most, but to those of us in *theatre* who must assume different tones, it's quite the opposite.'

'To what?'

'To *marginal*, dear, of course. What else?'

'Oh, get on with it,' said Maggie, sitting with her back straight and rigid on the edge of the bed before Naomi could tell her not to slouch like an old feather pillow.

'Now, what I suggest . . . is that we *cut* to chin level. Is that all right?'

'It'll curl up shorter. It's always gone curlier when I've 'ad it cut.'

'And you think that Aunt Naomi hadn't noticed when your mother hacked it to bits? I shall cut the hair according to the texture and the shape of the face. Now, why don't you close your eyes and think of John Gielgud?'

'Who?'

'One of our finest and *most* handsome actors. We are working to please the likes of the very best.'

'I will close me eyes cos I can't look at that orange and red frock you've got on. I'll go blind.'

'My dear Maggie, this *frock* just so happens to have been designed for a part I played in a West End production and by none other than Christian Dior. It will *never* date.'

'Nothing you put on can date. It's not normal. Layers of mismatched, that's what Mum says, anyway.'

'Well, yes, that boring old fart would, wouldn't she? One day she will awake to the woman she really is beneath that sensible front. *Eyes.*'

Secretly thrilled by this daring enterprise, Maggie closed her eyes and relaxed, enjoying the closeness of her aunt and the delicate scent she occasionally wore. Expensive scent bought by a lover some years ago and kept in the dark at exactly the right temperature so it would not go off. The first snip of the scissors sent a chill down her spine but then it all seemed plain sailing. Her aunt seemed to know what she was doing and even hummed as she snipped and cut, sliced and diced. No more than ten minutes later Naomi gave a contented sigh.

'Oh, that has taken me back to the theatre, back-stage, when we all of us trimmed each other's hair.' She ran her delicate pale fingers through Maggie's short locks and tousled them. 'Now, I don't want you to look in the mirror just yet.' She beamed. 'Where does your mother keep her hair lacquer?'

'Shelf at the top of the wardrobe.'

'Well, of course she must. Silly me. Where else?' Humming a jolly tune Naomi retrieved it, then rummaged through her own large, sensible leather handbag. 'Ah, yes. I thought it must be in there but one never knows if one has left it in one's dressing room.'

'You haven't got a dressing room, Aunt Naomi. You're not in the theatre now.'

'Oh, but I have, my dear. A gorgeous crushed velvet curtain now separates my boudoir from my makeup room where one wall has pale pink mirrors with lights above.'

'What are you searching for?'

'Makeup, my sweet, and I search no more for here it is,' she said, smiling radiantly. 'The one thing about working in the theatre is that one is *also* trained as a makeup artist. It is *essential*.' She unscrewed the lid of a large pot of cold cream and smeared some over Maggie's face.

'First we must remove the cheap makeup, and then the work begins.' That done she stepped back to admire her niece's hair. 'Darling, you look absolutely lovely!'

'What? Wiv cream all over me bleedin' face?'

'I'm talking *hair*, darling. Your hair is a work of *art*. Even if I do say it myself. Now we shall let the cream do the work while *you* relax and I look into your mother's wardrobe. There must be *something* we can wear.'

'We?'

'Figure of speech, my love, figure of speech,' crooned Naomi, as she pulled all of Edie's hangers to one side, then slid each garment along, scrutinising it. 'A straight black skirt is always useful. Dull but useful.' She withdrew it and laid it on the bed. 'Now then, something for the top. Ah, a green crêpe blouse, which will go wonderfully well with your red hair. And a wide red belt. Perfect!'

'I'll look like a Christmas cracker.'

'Indeed you will, my sweet. Indeed you will.' Getting down on to her knees, she rummaged through Edie's shoes. 'Oh dear. Red. We need some red shoes. Black and brown, I fear, is all we have to work with.'

'My Christmas shoes are red.'

'What? Your mother allowed you to have *red* shoes?'

'It was her idea. I think she's bought me something to go with them. A bag, probably.'

'Well, she can take back the bag after the season is over. Red is for shopping, and only shopping. Groceries and suchlike. Where are the shoes?'

'In the sitting room. I kicked them off and they're behind the settee.'

And so it continued until Naomi had pushed and fluffed and lacquered Maggie's hair, applied a deep rose-pink lipstick, some powder and mascara and lightly touched up her ginger eyebrows to tone them down and then smudged a little pencil beneath her eyes to make them stand out. Once her *protégée* was dressed, and only once she was dressed, with all the finishing touches, she was allowed to see herself in the mirror.

Stunned by her reflection, Maggie tried desperately to hide a smile. 'I should 'ave put a brassière on. Mum said I could 'ave her new one.'

'No, no, no, Maggie, my dear sweet girl. Soft and natural, soft and natural. Your mother's breasts would no doubt droop down to her belly but yours . . . yours simply sit there with not the least bit of sag. Let a young man brush up against those on the dance floor and he will simply follow you to the end of the world.'

'So you don't think I need to wear one, then?'

'I don't think you *should* wear one, Margaret. There is a difference. But that is entirely up to you,' she said, sailing a hand through the air. 'More to the point, do you like what you see in the mirror, Cinderella?'

'I never said I didn't like it, did I?'

'Well, exactly. I am *so* pleased, darling. My little wallflower has blossomed into a beautiful rose! You look absolutely stunning, Mags.' There were tears in Naomi's eyes – tears of pride for her great-niece.

'I do look different, I must admit,' said Maggie. 'And I feel different. My face and hair feels lovely. And I didn't realise my waist went in like that.'

Pushing her long wiry hair back, Naomi burst into laughter. 'It's called an hour-glass *figure*. Perfectly in proportion at top and bottom and curving in at the waist. The red belt is perfect.'

'Mum's got some red earrings.'

'Good heavens, no. We don't want to gild the lily.

You're perfect as you are. Now . . . let's go and show your mother – and God help me if she hates the hair. I shall be hung, drawn and quartered!'

Leading her great-niece into the living room, Naomi's joy showed in her face and in her eyes. She was proud of her achievement but more than that she was tickled pink with the way that Maggie's self-confidence had multiplied within the hour. Her deeply self-conscious niece whose self worth had always been at ground level was positively blooming. Knowing that Edie was waiting in the living room to see the result and fearing the worse, she threw the door open, stepped aside and allowed the new Maggie to make her entrance.

Edie was overwhelmed. It showed in her face and especially in her eyes. Her daughter looked stunning. The new short hairstyle had almost fallen into place by itself, and her own clothes fitted her daughter as if they had been tailor-made for her, not only enhancing her figure but creating a soft elegant look. A look that would match any of the pictures in a woman's magazine. She could hardly believe it. 'Jesus . . .' was the hushed word that escaped her. 'Where *have* you been hiding, Maggie Birch?'

'Do I look too old for my age?' said Maggie, thrilled with the response.

'No, babe, you just look lovely . . . Well, maybe you could be taken for going on sixteen but that'll change once you take off the makeup. You shouldn't be wearing a straight black skirt, though.'

'Well, had there been a flared skirt in your wardrobe,

Edie, we would have chosen that, but what with you being a touch on the old-fashioned side . . .'

'I can't afford the New Look, Naomi. Flared skirts take more material and more material costs money.' Still, Edie couldn't take her eyes off Maggie.

'Oh. And I thought that with you having been working as a machinist in a factory making ladies' clothes you might have managed to stuff a yard or two of the latest into your shopping-bag . . .'

'That's stealing and I've never—'

'*Bollocks* to that. It's *perks*, darling. *Perks*. Without little treats as such we would *all* be selling hot chestnuts on the pavements. There'll be no dividends in heaven for foolish honesty, Edith. I would have thought you'd have learned that by now.'

'Give me a twirl, Mags,' grinned Edie, ignoring her aunt.

Obliging and very happy to do so, Maggie was suddenly the model on a catwalk, turning first this way, then the other. 'The fing is,' she murmured, 'I don't feel uncomfortable. It *feels* like me. Tomorrow I'll wear my slacks and jumper and still feel the same as I do now. It's the hair, I fink. You've made a good job of it, Aunt Naomi.'

'Of course I have. What else would you have expected? Your hair is your crowning glory, Margaret. Never forget that and you will *always* be picked out in a crowd.'

'So, are we going up to the fourth floor for a drink or not?' said Edie.

'Are we talking party-time, darling, or a cup of tea?'

'Christmas drinks.'

'Well, then, of course we must go, Edith.' Naomi gave her a disparaging look. 'And this was the reason why my great-niece was in the depths of depression? You expected her to go for cocktails looking like a ten-year-old?'

Edie gave her aunt a hard stare. 'If you embarrass me up there I won't talk to you agen. Ever. Is that clear?'

'As clear as a steamed-up crystal ball!'

'Good. I'll go and put a bit of lipstick on.'

'Um . . . you might find your room a *little* untidy, beloved,' said Naomi, waving her fingers. 'The hair and so on . . .'

With her back to Naomi and making her exit, Edie shook her head. 'Why is there always a mess after you've called in? You're a right nuisance at times.'

'I know I am poppet. *Sorry* . . .' purred Naomi, playfully pushing two fingers up after her niece. 'I don't know *why* you put up with me.' Glancing slyly at Maggie to see if she was making her laugh, she called out to Edie, 'I'm just a silly old woman, darling! Forgive me!'

Laughing behind her hands, Maggie said, 'She's gonna catch you doing that one of these days.'

'Well, then, I shall say it is meant purely as a sign of victory. That your mother in my eyes is victorious. Will that do?'

Maggie was giggling too much to answer. She was amused by her great-aunt and she was happy because she knew she looked stunning compared to the old Maggie. Furthermore, she knew that the Italian boy's mother would be at the Christmas drinks party. Whether *he* would be there didn't matter. His mother would be and that would do for the time being. She would befriend her.

'Now, let me see,' purred Naomi cutting into Maggie's thoughts, 'do I need a ten-minute cat-nap?' She stood there pondering for a few seconds, then laid herself flat on the settee, propping a cushion under her head.

'Does this mean we've got to creep about till it's time to go?'

'Of course not, dear. I have worked in a noisy film studio converted from an old horse-tram shed with a cast of a thousand running around me and gone out like the Sleeping Beauty. Lea Bridge Road in Waltham Forest, 1919 was the year, August the month. *The Mystery of the Diamond Belt*, a Sexton Blake thriller starring a dear friend of mine, Percy Moran. Oh, how it *all* flows back,' she said, to the exasperated sigh of her great-niece. 'Another great friend who often worked there was the producer A. E. Coleby, an ex-bookie and actor. The trouble with him was that he always cast himself in his own films.'

'I'm gonna 'ave another drop of sherry, Aunt. D'yer want one?' said Maggie, letting Naomi's ramblings go over her head. She had heard it all before. 'Or brandy? Make up your mind.' Turning to her aunt she saw that she was out for the count, her mouth wide open. Soon she would be snoring loudly. Leaving her to herself, Maggie closed the door gently, so as not to disturb her. She went into her bedroom to admire herself again in front of the long mirror.

Edie, in her bedroom, was sweeping up the last of the red hair and dropped it into a carrier-bag with a touch of regret at the sudden change. Maggie had always insisted on keeping her hair long since she first went to school at the age of five. Lowering herself to the edge of the bed she lifted thick long tufts of golden red from the bag and gazed at it. Her little girl, her Maggie, had crossed the line at which she had been hovering. In no time she would be fifteen, no longer a child but a young lady. Harry's face came to mind and how proud he would have been of his daughter, who looked so much like himself. Same colour hair, and skin with a sprinkling of freckles. Same green eyes.

Clearing her throat and taking a deep breath she berated herself for being sentimental after what seemed like a lifetime of managing to shelve her grief. But things were different now. Both she and Maggie had moved on in their own ways, herself out of the street where she had been born and Maggie from childhood into maturity. Whether she would get used to this new life, and the sense of being trammelled with so many living in the same building, or miss popping outside into her own backyard to hang washing on the line she didn't know. Of course she could hang out her smalls on a line across the back balcony but it was hardly the same thing, and with no copper to boil her washing the bagwash delivery service was her only option until the day when she could afford a washing-machine . . .

It had been painful to give away Harry's clothes, but if she could cope with that she could cope with anything. Giving up her family home was a small thing in comparison. At least she had her war widow's pension from the army, which gave her a sense that he was still alive: he was still keeping her and his daughter. The one thing she was not prepared to give up was the charade she played each week when she placed money in four brown envelopes for bills, electricity, gas, rent and milk, all of which came out of Harry's pension. She still did not, could not think of herself as a widow. Of course, like so many thousands more she might have been hanging on to the shred of possibility that the War Office had made a mistake. When Harry appeared out of the blue in her dreams, smiling at her, she couldn't help but feel as if he were still alive. That he would present himself on her doorstep and everything would go back to the way it was.

The one treat she had allowed herself from the first pension payment was a tiny gold heart on a chain for round her neck, which she had never taken off. She intended to be buried wearing it.

With the carrier-bag in her hand, she went into the kitchen where she could see that Maggie was now settled and sipping a glass of sherry. 'So, what do we do with this then, Mags?'

Maggie peeped into the bag, puzzled as to what the contents might be. The expression on her face showed her disgust. 'Urgh! Chuck it away, Mum! Put it down the chute! I don't want it and you're not gonna put it in a drawer! It's creepy.' She shuddered.

'But you might never grow it this long agen.'

'And then again I might.' She snatched the bag from Edie and stormed out of the flat.

She went along the balcony, opened the lid of the chute and pushed it in, then listened as it tumbled down two storeys and into the huge bin housed within a brick shed. That done, she turned to go back inside. At that moment the sixteen-year-old Italian boy appeared on the stairs.

Returning from the family café where he worked, he seemed a little on the tipsy side. Shy and abashed, because she looked quite different from when he had first seen her – she had been wearing her glasses and her hair was in a ponytail, her Aunt Naomi's words of advice came to mind. 'When in an embarrassing situation, think of yourself dead and you won't go red.' Gazing at the boy, who to her mind was the handsomest specimen she had ever seen, she imagined herself laid out in a coffin all in white, arms crossed. She felt herself go icy cold.

'All right?' said the Italian, with more than a little sparkle in his warm brown eyes.

'Not too bad,' was the cool reply.

'Did I see you before?' he asked, squinting at her as if he were trying to focus. 'You look familiar . . . kind of.'

'I don't think you've seen me before,' she said, blushing slightly. 'Can't remember it and I don't recognise you. Why?'

'Ah!' His face suddenly lit up with a smile. 'That's it.

That's when it was. When we moved in. It must have been your kid sister poking 'er nose in everywhere.'

'Oh, probably. She's a nosy little cow.'

'You really do look alike. Amazing. Except that you're beautiful,' he said, giving her a wink. And then, grimacing, fearing he might have made an embarrassing slip of the tongue. 'I hope she's not eavesdropping?'

'No. No, she . . . she lives with my dad. In Kent. They live in Kent and I live 'ere with Mum. I 'ardly ever see 'er.'

'Oh, that's a shame. Families should be all round each other. Ours is. It's like a railway station at times in our house – I mean, flat.'

'Oh, we visit them quite a lot. We all go down together, aunts and cousins and grandparents.' She knew from a schoolfriend that this was the Italian way and was going all out to impress. 'My stepmother's a bit on the posh side so we don't really get on. Dad won't come into the East End any more. She's put 'im off it. She's American.'

'Can't blame him. Not sure if I'd come back too often if we lived in Kent.'

There was a moment's silence when neither of them could think of anything else to say. Maggie, surprising herself, took the lead. 'You goin' into Jessie Smith's on the top floor for a drink later on?'

'No,' he said, quietly laughing at the idea. 'Mum, Dad and Grandma are, though. Why?'

'Oh, I just wondered. Only I've gotta go whether I like it or not. Give Mum a bit of moral support.

She's not as confident as I am. I just thought there might be one or two of my age there, that's all.'

'I'll try and drop in around eight o'clock, so if you're there we'll have a drink.' With that he turned away.

'Your mum sounds Italian,' she continued quickly, aware that her cheeks were glowing now, 'but you don't. Why's that?'

'Because me and my brothers and cousins were born in this country,' he called back. 'And my mother can speak English when it suits her. "Stay away from bad girls" is her favourite saying, especially when there's one present. And she understands *everything*.' He continued up the stairs, saying, 'Don't be late for that drink. *Ciao*.'

Silenced by this passing exchange Maggie felt as if she were melting. Alone in the cold, her heart beating rapidly and a warm glow spreading through her, she listened to his footsteps echoing as he made his way up to the third floor and along the balcony to where he lived. She waited to hear the closing of his front door, and when it came she leaned against the wall and enjoyed the moment. This experience was new to her. The Italian had aroused something inside her which she had not known was there. She was about to experience the first flush of love and, perhaps, the pain that goes with it.

She could hardly believe that she had fabricated such a silly story about a young sister and blushed at the thought of being found out. But it had worked. He had believed Maggie was a different person from the girl he had seen before.

Inside the flat she could hardly wait to get in front of the mirror to look at herself again, see what he had seen. The new hairstyle, the makeup, the clothes. She was not disappointed and she could not remember feeling so happy before. Now, with a new outlook on life, she went into the sitting room. Naomi was snoring and her mother was listening to carols on the wireless in the kitchen while she prepared the bird for the next day. Leaning over and giving her great-aunt a kiss on the cheek, she realised that she was sound asleep and not pretending, and no doubt living life to the full in her dreams.

With her own small gifts to wrap for her mother and aunt, she went into her bedroom and pushed the tiny brass bolt on the door so that neither of them could come in and spoil her surprises. She also wanted to be alone, in her own private world, and relish the warm glow radiating through her. She was on her bed and brought to mind the face of the Italian boy, the warm brown eyes, the thick black eyebrows, his full lips. Then, more than anything, she thought of his deep, husky voice. She could almost smell his slightly aromatic hair cream. She moved her hand to her breast and imagined that it was his caressing the soft flesh. Then Edie called from the kitchen, bringing her back from those heady heights where she had not gone before.

'Sorry, Mum,' Maggie said, in the kitchen. 'I was just gonna wrap my presents and forgot you'd be needing help. What can I do?'

Turning slowly to face her, Edie could not believe her ears. The new look seemed to have effected more than one change, not only the glow in her cheeks but in her voice and her sentiment. And there was an expression in her daughter's lovely soft green eyes that she recognised but could not put her finger on. 'There's not much to do,' she murmured. 'I was just gonna ask you to make Aunt Naomi a cup of tea for when she wakes up. I want to put a bit of lipstick and powder on and brush my hair.'

'Course you must. And the new frock you bought for Christmas. Wear that as well.'

'Well, it did cross my mind, Mags, but I thought that was going a bit too far. We've only been invited in for a drink.'

'So?' smiled Maggie. 'It's Christmas Eve. Wear it!'

'Well, all right, then, if you really think so I will.'

'Course I fink so,' said Maggie, lighting the gas under the kettle. 'This is our first Christmas on the estate. Might as well make an impression, mightn't we?'

There was a short pause before Edie said, 'And you're not worried Naomi might show us up?'

'She won't. She's too barmy to upset people. She'll crack an awkward atmosphere if there is one in no time. Nobody knows each other that well, do they?'

'That's true. Well, go and give 'er a nudge, then, while I get ready.'

Desperate to tell someone about the Italian boy Maggie was soon in the living room and nudging her great-aunt, who was mumbling in her sleep. 'Come on, you, it's time to wake up.' She poured herself another small glass of sherry and sat by the flickering coal fire imagining mistletoe hanging in the porch of the flat upstairs.

Opening her eyes with no questions as to where she was or why she was lying on Edie's couch, Naomi rambled quietly on as if she hadn't slept at all. Ever amused by her, Maggie let her be and waited. From the faint smile on her aunt's lips she knew she was about to break into another of her orations.

'I can't say for certain whether the Hoe Street studio at Walthamstow was acquired by British and Colonial Films,' Naomi uttered, as if in the middle of a conversation, 'but I do know it was taken on in nineteen thirteen. B & C Films were particularly famous for the *Lieutenant Daring* series. And later, my very good friend Maurice Elvey used the studio to make *It's a Long Way to Tipperary*, with Risdon and Bramble.'

Looking slyly at Maggie's expression to see if she was listening, she continued. 'Lillian Braithwaite, who I personally thought not to be the actress the critics *imagined*, also played in a few films there. Shortly after that there was very little production at Hoe Street, sadly. I had some wonderful parts until then, Margaret, and it was absolutely wonderful.' She went quiet, and observed that her niece was either deeply engrossed in what she was telling her or on another planet.

'I never cried in *public*, you see. That . . . is a

strength that *shows* quality and character. Do try and remember it and you shall *always* be adored.'

'Did you want a drop of sherry, Aunt, or a nice cup of tea?' said Maggie, hoping to stop her before she got into how, when she had been grieving for her husband after the First World War, she had coped remarkably well and taken widowhood in her stride.

'Tea? Goodness, no. A brandy, darling. It *is* Christmas Eve after all. Let's not be mean.' Easing herself into a sitting position, Naomi studied her niece. 'You do look lovely, Margaret. So feminine. A cold-meat sandwich would be very nice, dear.'

'Ham or Spam? But no brandy. It was only a half-quarter bottle, not much more than a nip, and it's for the pudding tomorrer.'

'Is it off the bone? The *ham*?'

'No, it's still on it but Mum'll cut some off if you don't want Spam.'

'Darling, Spam is not a Christmas treat. It's wartime food. Forget the brandy and pour me a sherry. Was I rambling?'

'You always do.'

'I believe I had been dreaming about Will Barker. The professional visionary.'

'I'm not interested, Aunt, and I fink you told me this one before.'

'I'm sure he – no, I *know* he founded the Autoscope Company and built an open-air studio at Stamford Hill, then another at Ealing. The open-air studio con-sisted of not much more than a stage, two scaffolding rods and a backcloth.' She was smiling demurely again, in her old world. 'Humble beginnings from which we artists do rise,' she said and then sighed dramatically for effect.

'Did you want mustard?'

'English, *not* French.'

'It's Colman's English mustard or nuffing,' said Maggie, dragging herself to her feet. 'I know I've got French blood in me but we've never 'ad their mustard.'

'Have you, dear?'

'That's what you told me once, Aunt Naomi. You said your real dad, your mother's lover, was French. I think I was about ten at the time.'

'Goodness me, and now you're fourteen. How time flies when one is getting old. Do you *feel* your age, darling?'

'So he wasn't French, then? Or wasn't there even a lover?'

'Questions, questions, questions. Oh, well, what difference?' she said, flicking a hand in the air. 'Now, Julius Hagen was *quite* a good manager. Of course, he preferred short films. I met Jack Buchanan and José Collins at Hoe Street. And Victor McLaglen. I played opposite him on occasion. I believe I played opposite him in *Heart Strings*.'

'Wouldn't you rather 'ave a cup of tea with your sandwich? You've not stopped talking since you opened your eyes and you might get worse with drink inside yer.'

'Sherry for the aunt,' Naomi carolled. 'Far too late in the day for tea, thank you.' She raised her eyes to meet Maggie's and smiled tormentingly. 'What a pity the studio had to be placed in the hands of the receivers shortly afterwards. Do you not agree?'

'If we go up to Jessie Smith's you'd better not go on, Aunt. They'll label you the Mad Woman without me having to tell them who you are. And we've already got one on the top floor. The difference is, she's got every reason to have cracked whereas you haven't.'

'Oh? How extraordinary. You must introduce me.'

'No, I won't! Try and be *normal* is what I'm saying.'

'But I *am* normal. It's those around me who are half baked. Always trying to stay on a track made by none other than themselves. But if I must live on a council estate then I must and I shall blend in. To please *you*.'

'Good. You're among normal people now.'

'You think so? How interesting. I find that most of the people here are lunatics, if not all. They know nothing of the outside world.'

'Yes, they *do*. They're just *not* interested in smelly old ware'ouses that were once turned into film sets and are back being smelly old ware'ouses agen. It's boring.'

'Well, I suppose that ignorance *is* bliss . . . in a *way*,' said Naomi, enjoying herself. 'Now, Betty Balfour . . . she was an impish Cockney too but with a sense of *humour*. And much loved for it. The star with the huge blue eyes and golden curls. She was rather good in *Blink Eyes* in 1926.'

Wishing to hear no more, Maggie left the room

and closed the door quietly behind her so as not to show that she had risen to her aunt's favourite pastime of teasing and baiting. Even though she loved and admired Naomi, she wasn't always in the mood for her. And this was one of those times. There were far more important things to think about and mull over. Hadn't she just fallen in love for the very first time? And hadn't the Italian dreamboat from above had the look of love in his warm searching brown eyes? Well, she thought so.

With her niece and great-niece stationed safely in the kitchen, Naomi, in this half lit room with only the sound and glow of the crackling fire for company, plumped a cushion and eased it under her neck. Now she could pick up her dream without anyone interrupting her. It had after all been a very long time since she had cavorted on stage in front of a spell-bound audience and only once that the heart-throb Brian Aherne, in the audience, had gazed up at her, mesmerised by her beauty.

'*Brian Aherne*,' she whispered, bringing his handsome ivory face and sexy eyes to mind and imagining herself stroking his blond hair. She could see him so clearly in her mind's eye, as if the photograph in her special album had come to life. He was wearing a white shirt and red silk tie, with matching pocket handkerchief, and an orchid. She could almost smell his scent. Smiling and brushing her fingertips across her neck, she whispered, 'An orchid. Always an orchid.'

The hatch door opening into the kitchen was like a

sharp bee sting on a warm balmy evening. The voice of her niece berating her was worse. Edie's unemotional voice caused Naomi's beloved heart-throb of days gone by to evaporate without a by-your-leave.

'I could have done with a bit of help out here, you know! Laying there as if you're waiting for your slaves to bring you grapes. I've made the tea now so you can bloody well have that instead of sherry!'

'Darling, I *am* in my seventies,' crooned Naomi. 'I simply *must* have my beauty sleep – not that one *may* sleep around here. It is more akin to a railway station than a peaceful home. And if you could possibly make less noise . . . One doesn't want to think that one is resting cheek by jowl to a canteen.'

'This is a kitchen, not a canteen, and tomorrow is Christmas Day!'

'Oh, darling, you don't have to remind your aunt of that. It is the very reason I am resting. Would you have me looking like an old woman on *the* day of all days? I would *hate* to let you down in front of your guests.'

'Well, then, come and pour your own tea once it's brewed to your liking so I can go out for ten minutes and celebrate the season.'

'Of course, dear. I had every intention of doing so. You've jumped the gun again,' Naomi said, smiling serenely.

'I don't think so,' Edie smiled back, 'but my finger's on the trigger!'

The hatch slamming shut sent a shiver down Naomi's spine. 'Would that I was *far* away in romantic Paris or fashionable Rome.' Then, looking around the empty room she realised that without an audience it was all rather dull. 'Trying to entertain within these walls,' she murmured, 'is like pissing in the wind.' Then, much louder, she said, 'Of course, I don't expect anyone to be in the *least* bit interested in my colourful past! Or in the famous with whom I have rubbed *shoulders*, never mind the gods of film who fell *hopelessly* in love with me.'

Coming into the room, Edie bore a smile. Sometimes it was impossible not to. 'I'm just about to freshen up and change. I take it you're coming, but be warned—'

'I shall not open my lips. I bore you and you presume I shall bore your Cockney neighbours. It matters not. But talk to me of the bagwash collection service or the new self-service shops and I shall yawn. If the conversation runs to illicit sex and love affairs I shall *light up* like a fairy on the Christmas tree.'

'Just keep your voice down, that's all I ask.' Peering into the mirror, Edie checked to see if her tired eyes were dark underneath. Surprisingly they weren't. She had been on the go all week, preparing for this festive season, and always after a hard day at the factory. 'A quick brush of the hair, some lipstick and powder, my new frock on, and I'll be ready. Fifteen minutes should do it.'

Remaining in a world of her own making, Naomi stifled a yawn and spoke in a quiet, dreamy voice. 'I have played poker with gangsters, Murder in the Dark with actors, and Charades with backstage people.

Beneath this surface hides *many* secrets. I could tell of scandals to topple the government. Not to mention the *beloved* Royal Family of whom only a handful have the least bit of royal blood running through their veins. Royalty fuck who they fancy and think nothing of the consequences until bellies swell. *Both* sexes. Females are *just* as randy. Birth has been given to many a bastard king. If it were black, of course, and a dead giveaway, it would be sent along the Thames in a Moses basket. Into the Thames and out to sea.'

'You're making it all up, Naomi, and if you start talking like that on this estate you'll be stoned. Say what you want about us Cockneys but we do love our Royal Family. It's all we've bloody well got.'

'Got?' The teasing look was back on her face. 'You think they ride through in their golden coach because they *wish* to see their poor, ragged and filthy subjects? To see, feel and touch them? Darling, they simply don't give a hoot.'

'I'm not listening. I've heard it all before and it's not funny. So drop it now.'

'What on *earth* am I to talk about at the drinks party if not the theatre, film, or the glamorous Royal Family?'

'Stir them into a frenzy over the ninepence they overcharge you on rent and the measly pension you get and whatever else you've gone on about since you moved here. You know, the hours of waiting in the doctor's surgery and the quality of false teeth.'

'I do not wear false *anything*,' said Naomi, and

showed her almost perfect teeth. 'As I have told you many times—'

'Hair, teeth and eyes,' sighed Edie, leaving the room and calling behind her, 'Don't put Maggie in a mood!'

'Is she ever out of one?' murmured Naomi, leaning back and closing her eyes. 'Are either of you? I think not.' Minutes later she was almost asleep again when she remembered she was hungry. 'Where is my ham and mustard sandwich?' she cried. One minute later she was back in the land of dreams. So used to having her cat-naps, they had become more of a habit than a plan. Naomi had always believed in and was practised at snatching ten minutes here and there. In her opinion an hour's sleep during the day was worth at least three hours of night-time slumber.

3

By the time Edie, Maggie and Naomi had arrived at Jessie Smith's flat the place was already bursting with neighbours. Edie was relieved not to be the first of a few and have to make conversation in a quiet room. More importantly, Naomi in her flowing mismatch of colourful period clothes was partly hidden in this crowded room and her crowning glory, the mass of black and silver white wavy hair decorated with her collection of 1920s combs, looked stunning. With an eye on her aunt for the first ten minutes of being there, Edie was somewhat relieved and impressed by the way she swanned from one to another making conversation, asking questions instead of reeling off her glorious past. But Naomi was an experienced socialite and knew exactly how to draw people in and leave them wanting to know more about her.

To remain mysterious was the secret, and until she had captured their interest to the point of their being spellbound, she would, with a delicate brush of the hand, decline any questions she was not prepared to answer or any that she might save and make the very most of once she was in full flow. On arrival into this little soirée, as she liked to think of it, she had promised herself that by the end of the evening, or before then if she was bored, she would, without a shred of doubt, be holding court.

Edie turned her attention to Max Cohen, who was giving a lecture – or sermon, depending on which way it was seen. This immaculately dressed man was expressing his opinion on how the estate might be improved and how important he felt it was to start a tenants' committee with bi-monthly meetings. Max, a businessman, could not keep quiet in a social gathering. He was, after all, an accountant and experience had told him that a new client might come from a grand house, a rented lodging room or, in this case, a council estate.

Satisfied that she could relax for at least half an hour before her aunt might start to misbehave, Edie made her way to Laura Jackson who, with a glass of port and lemon in her hand, was sitting on a faded floral feather-cushioned sofa and gazing into the small fire. As she perched herself on a tall-backed chair, she said, 'You can't beat a coal fire, I don't care what they say.'

'I know. My Jack was going on about us gettin' a gas one to save 'aving to bring coal in and out but I put my foot down on that.' Laura raised her eyes to meet Edie's. 'Settled in properly now?'

'I think so, yeah. Was strange at first, though. Missed the little things you take for granted.'

'I know what you mean.' She turned her head in Max's direction. 'I'm not sure I wanna join a committee. Nor does his wife, Jessie, by the look on her face. She's listening but she's not agreeing, if I'm reading it right.'

Turning discreetly to see for herself, Edie said, 'You're right. I'll try and catch 'er eye. She might be glad of a chance to escape.'

Both women were right. No sooner had Edie smiled at Jessie than she was easing away from the small group and on her way over. 'Hello, girls!' She grinned. 'All right if I join yer?'

Laura moved along the settee, saying, 'More the merrier.'

'Keep your voices down,' said Edie, with an eye on Naomi. 'I'm hiding from my eccentric aunt.'

From that minute on the neighbourly bond that had been struck on the week they moved in changed to one of friendship. At first their conversation was to do with settling into a new way of life and some of the strange people surrounding them, and then, finally, to men, their own in particular. Edie's story of her husband missing, presumed dead, was the first and the saddest but she managed to tell it without depressing the others – it was Christmas Eve and they were here to enjoy themselves. Jessie had read the situation well and offered warm words of encouragement rather than commiseration. Then, it being her turn to tell her story, Edie was all ears.

Jessie told of how Max had been her first boyfriend and how, when the engagement had been broken off, she had been angry. It was easy to understand since marriage between Christians and Jews was still a no-no in this part of London. The fact that Max had denied his family their wish that he should marry a good Jewish girl in the end had proved to Jessie that he loved her very much. His sister Moira, however, still only tolerated their situation.

'The crunch came,' said Jessie, her voice almost a whisper, 'when I found out that Max had been attending Jewish social functions with a girl who was of the same religion. That's when I broke off the engagement. I was so angry.'

'I bet you were,' said Edie. 'I would have been too.'

'I felt as if he'd gone behind my back, really let me down. They weren't sweethearts or anything – at least, I don't think they were – but I felt as if Max's entire family and all his friends were against me marrying him.'

'Do you think you might have married Tom on the rebound, Jess, then realised your mistake?' Edie asked.

'No. It was different with Tom. He bowled me over straight away, whereas me and Max had been friends ages before we started to walk out together. With Tom it was love at first sight – almost.' She smiled. 'Then I learned what a sod he was.'

'But why did Tom storm off in the first place?' said Laura, feeling that some of the blame must surely lie on Jessie's shoulders. Especially since she was back with her first sweetheart.

'I bet it was through jealousy,' said Edie, all knowing.

'It was, as it happens. You've hit the nail right on

the head. He assumed I had been having an affair with Max during the war, which I hadn't. We'd met up again and stayed friends. Max was helping everyone. Say what you will but if it hadn't been for the black-market trade a lot of families would have gone even hungrier than they did if it wasn't for Max. He's too soft but that's not such a bad trait, I s'pose, when you consider some of the bastards out there.'

'And you've not heard from or seen your husband since 1945?' said Edie who knew full well what that was like. 'You must 'ave felt a bit like a widow as well?'

'Oh, yeah. That's just what it felt like. There was no build-up to us breaking up or anything. One minute we were together and happy, the next he was gone. It was Christmas Eve then as well, as it happens. I s'pose you could say this is an anniversary,' she added, a sad smile on her face. 'Although I did cross his path later the next year. Still – least said soonest mended. He *is* the kids' dad, after all.'

'Do they ever ask after 'im?' said Edie, thinking of Maggie, who had not set eyes on her father.

'They did at first, all the time, but not so much now. Billy comes out with something now and then. You know the sort of thing. "I wonder where my dad is now" and "D'yer fink he might be dead?"'

'Poor little sod,' whispered Laura. Then, pushing a hand through her long wavy auburn hair, she said, 'Jack had his faults but abandoning his family wasn't one of them.'

'I try not to think of it like that, Laura.'

Silently berating herself for being thoughtless, Laura

said, 'I'm sorry, Jess. I don't know what made me say that.'

'That's okay. Anyway, he *did* abandon us. All right, it was just after the war but to accuse me of going with other men after all I'd been through – well, it's not worth going over.'

Edie quietly laughed at her. 'But you do and you will. Over and over and over and over again. Once I heard that Harry had drowned in the course of action, I kept on questioning myself. Did I make enough fuss of 'im when we were first married? Were the silly quarrels we had all my fault?'

'You know what I think, Edie?' said Jessie. 'I think we feel the need to blame ourselves so we can cope with it all – so we can sleep at night. The mind's a funny thing.' She then looked into Edie's hazel eyes, and said, 'When did you last go out for an evening?'

'When Harry was alive. Before he was called up.'

'Well, that won't do,' said Jessie. 'Can't 'ave that. Seems like you and me are gonna have to talk to our men, Laura. Tell 'em that from now on there's to be a ladies' night out.'

'Sounds good to me,' said Laura, 'but where would we go?'

Jessie rolled her eyes. 'Forgotten how to queue up at the pictures for a good film or how to dance, have you? It's the fifties, for God's sake. Trad jazz and all that razzmatazz.'

'A bit of be-bop'd do me,' said Edie, her face lighting up. 'Or dancing the fox-trot to one of the bands at the York Hall or Poplar Baths.'

'Give me swing any time. Glenn Miller, Johnnie Ray . . .'

'A little bit of Frank Sinatra . . .' sighed Jessie, melodramatic.

'A big bit of Frank Sinatra,' winked Laura.

'Dancing up close to the big bit and to "Blue Moon".' The three of them shrieked with laughter.

Her eyes fixed on her aunt, Edie could tell she was about to join them. She loved Naomi but there simply was no telling what she might say to embarrass her. 'Here comes trouble,' she warned. 'Dear old Aunt Naomi.'

'Edie, darling, I'm *so* sorry but I'm afraid I must leave earlier than expected. I've suddenly remembered that a *very* dear actor friend might be popping in this evening. I should *hate* to miss her.' Of course, this was simply a way of getting attention, with no truth to it whatsoever.

'An actor?' said Laura, impressed and wholly taken in.

Turning her pained face to Laura and keeping her back to her aunt, Edie said pleadingly, 'Don't. Please don't.'

'Yes, darling, you *may* have heard of her,' said Naomi, tilting her head ever so slightly to one side as she smiled serenely. 'Violet Hopson?'

Laura was beside herself. 'Violet Hopson? She was in an old black-and-white I saw at the Troxy. Let me think, what was it called?'

'*The War Case*?' said Naomi. 'Also starring the London idol of the nineteen twenties, Matheson Lange, the gorgeous Canadian.'

'That's it! *The War Case*! My God! And you know Violet Hopson?'

'Darling, I've worked with her many times. She and Ivy Close were probably my *very* best friends at one time.'

'Ivy Close,' said Jessie. 'Now there's an old name. She was in the same film as Violet Hopson, wasn't she?'

'Of *course* she was. They often worked together, bitching behind each other's back, *naturally*. But I mustn't bore you with all of that. It was *such* a long time ago. Of course, we're all retired now but it was a glittery period, don't you think? The costumes were simply stunning. There was an amazing Turkish foreigner working in Wardrobe. Say what you will about the Turks, but they are terribly clever with the needle.'

'Keep your voice down, Naomi!' snapped Edie, in a whisper. 'There's a Turkish couple in the room!'

'Darling, I meant no *harm*. *Truly*. I was merely paying a compliment. The Turk was simply a *genius* with the needle and thread.' She was sporting her hurt look. 'I do hope I wasn't being rude? It certainly wasn't my *intention*,' she said, a faint smile on her face, enjoying being the centre of attention. 'And the Turks were, after *all* is said and done, neutral during the Second World War, having learned from the First, no doubt, that it's all so futile.'

'It's all right, Edie,' said Jessie, seeing the look of embarrassed unease on Edie's face. 'I don't think they'd mind your aunt saying they were *clever*. Apparently Shereen is brilliant with the needle.'

'It didn't take you long to find that out, then,' Laura grinned. 'I knew 'er before we moved on to the estate. That woman can unpick a really old-fashioned frock and remake it into something you'd 'ave to go up West to buy.'

Edie shook off the icy cold sensation she had experienced at the thought of Turkey where her husband had been killed and focused on what Laura had just said. She had worked in a dress factory as a machinist for so long on piece-work that she had forgotten clothes could be made at home. 'Does she do ordinary dress-making?' she asked, as the luxury of having something made to measure drifted across her mind.

'She can do anything,' said Laura. 'Don't even need a pattern. Tell 'er what you want, she nods and listens and nods agen and tells you 'ow much it'd cost to make it. You take your own material, matching cotton thread, buttons and bows or whatever you fancy. The woman's a genius *and* cheap. She works like lightning and *every* daylight hour. She works with the seasons in the same way farmers 'ave to.'

'I can see why she would,' said Edie. 'Especially if she does hand stitching. It's murder on the eyes when you're relying on electric light to sew by and impossible if you're working on black fabric.'

'Oh, darling,' said Naomi, with a look of commiseration on her face, 'you make it all sound so *tedious*. Costume would knock a garment up for us within hours if the show demanded it.'

'That's different. Costumes for shows are not made to last.'

'Her brother's a bespoke tailor as well,' said Laura, continuing with her own train of thought. 'But that poor sod 'as to work long hours and for peanuts. He'd make a fortune if he could afford to take the risk of working for 'imself.'

'Such a *talented* family! Have they *children*?' mused Naomi, not in the least bit interested whether they had or not.

'Five sons and a daughter, Seriah. The sons are all married, except for Tariq. He's the clever one who passed every exam he took. Went to university and now he works in a solicitor's office in the City,' Laura said proudly, as if he was her own relation. 'Shereen's husband's got a barber shop off Cotton Street and, by all accounts, don't stop bragging about his genius son.'

'Who's the other one?' said Edie, quietly. 'The rude one who keeps staring at me?'

Laughing, Jessie leaned forward and whispered, 'Apparently Turkish men are brilliant lovers by all accounts. And if he was looking at me the way he's looking at you I'd be trembling in my drawers.'

'Mehmet's gorgeous,' mouthed Laura, drawing breath.

'But he's not been looking at me like that. He keeps staring and when I look back he looks away.'

'Well, there you are, then.' Jessie said. 'It works a charm. He's got you wanting to know more.'

Edie raised an eyebrow and left it at that. She had had her fair share of men trying it on one way or another since she'd been widowed but this was different. She had felt his eyes boring into her and the expression on his face had been far from reverential. 'So, who is he, then?'

'A relative. A cousin or nephew . . .' said Laura. 'This must be his third or fourth visit. Got a few bob, I reckon. I'm not sure what he deals in, though. My Jack would know. You should 'ave a word, Edie. Go and say hello. He speaks quite good English.'

'No,' said Edie, blushing and turning her face away from his gaze. 'It's embarrassing.'

'Don't be daft,' said Laura, and then, 'They're really friendly people. The family's got one of the four-bedroom cottages on the estate in Lang Street and they'd put 'im up without batting an eyelid, but I don't think he ever stops with 'em. Can afford an 'otel so I suppose that's why. Who'd sleep on a sofa if they don't 'ave to?'

'How terribly interesting,' purred Naomi, her interest now piqued.

'They are, Naomi, you're right,' said Laura. 'The family came over in the early thirties. Murat owned and ran two dilapidated trucks, which he fixed up, painted and then converted, in his own simple way, into buses. He built up a little business, which he then sold to pay the passage over. As soon as he was settled he found a little place to rent and turned it into a barber shop. His brothers and sisters are still in Turkey and we've been given an open invitation to go and stay with her family whenever we fancy a holiday abroad.'

'Can't be bad,' said Edie. 'A little holiday abroad is something that most of us can only dream of.' The fact that she would also like to pay homage to the place where Harry had been killed in the accident she kept to herself.

'Jack plays cards with Murat and some other blokes once a week,' continued Laura, 'after they've bin to the Turkish baths. They do a little bit of business as well but don't ask me what it is. Jack's got 'is fingers in a few pies.'

'Haven't they all!' smiled Jessie. 'So back to Matheson Lang. What was he like to work with, Naomi? And were you on *intimate* terms?'

'Not *exactly*. We were great chums though. But you don't want to hear about all that old-fashioned and dated theatrical nonsense, do you?'

'You come and sit right down 'ere next to me,' said Jessie. 'We want to know everything. Who slept with who behind the screens would be good for starters.'

'But I interrupt, surely? You were all talking so intimately earlier on. I hadn't meant to burst in.'

Laura patted the sofa again. 'We were making plans for a ladies' night out, that's all. We're going dancing at the York Hall or Poplar Baths one Saturday night. As a treat.'

'*Really?* How simply *marvellous!* Oh, I do miss dancing, you know. I did once play Isadora Duncan . . .'

Oh, no, thought Edie. Please don't . . .

'Oh, well, you'll 'ave to come with us then, won't she, Edie? Edie? You all right?'

'I'm fine, thanks, Jess. Right as ninepence. I'll just go and make sure Maggie's okay.'

'Darling, of *course* she is! More than *okay*, I would say.' Naomi nodded discreetly towards Maggie. 'Need I say more?'

Peering across the room Edie could see her daughter leaning against the wall, a glass of Babycham in her hand, gazing into the eyes of the Italian boy. The young man's parents, Ida and Albino Baroncini, were close by and it was clear from Ida's expression that she, too, was keeping an eye on her fledgling son.

Seeing the look of worry on Edie's face as she watched her daughter enjoying the attention of the lad two years her senior, Jessie gave her a gentle nudge on the arm saying, 'She'll be all right. I wouldn't 'ave minded having a Romeo like that gazing into my face at her age.'

'I suppose so,' said Edie. 'I still see 'er as my little girl, that's the trouble.'

'Well, just cast your mind back to when you was nearly fifteen.'

'I know what you're saying, Jess, but this is a new experience for me. And I don't like it. My stomach's goin' over.'

'Darling, she'll be perfectly all right,' said Naomi. 'You may rest assured that I shall be watching her like a *hawk*. Not to mention the Italian *Casanova*.'

'Well, then, I leave 'er in your good care, Aunt Naomi. I must go. Things to do.' With that she brushed a kiss across her aunt's face and squeezed her arm, whispering, 'Don't let her out of your sight.'

'Thanks for coming, Edie,' said Jessie, 'and have a lovely day tomorrow with your family. Make the most of it.'

'I will, Jess. Thanks for asking us up.'

'And if ever you're by yourself . . .' Jessie added, looking sideways at Maggie and the Italian boy, who could not take his eyes off her, 'knock on the door. Max often works late at the office. We'll have a cup of tea and a chinwag.'

'All right. I'll remember that.' Edie turned to Laura and smiled. 'Have a lovely Christmas. You too, Jessie. I'll see you later, Nao.'

Why Edie had suddenly wanted nothing but her own little safe haven was not hard to fathom. She was so used to her own company and wanted the peace and quiet of her flat and the warmth of her own coal fire. Settled in her armchair with the glow of the burning orange and red coals and the soft radiating table lamp, Edie, in a calmer mood and no longer worrying over Maggie, sipped a refreshing cup of tea. Naomi, her lovable if not bizarre surrogate mother had wheedled her way into a group of younger women who, if appearances were anything to go by, were enchanted by her tales of a glistening star-dusted world they knew nothing about. 'Maybe it's me,' she told herself. 'Maybe I'm too used to Naomi and take her for granted.' It was not new for her to talk to herself: it was a habit she had got into when Harry was called up and she was thrown into a lonely world.

With no regret at leaving Jessie's earlier than planned Edie found another thought coming into her mind.

The leaflet telling of the carol service at St Peter's Church, a ten-minute walk away was drawing her in. She swallowed the remains of her tea and stoked up the fire, then pulled on her fur-lined boots, coat, hat and scarf.

Outside, under the star-studded inky blue sky, which hinted at snow, she was pleasantly surprised that she was not alone. Others, also walking alone or in couples and small family groups, were making their way to relatives or to the local to celebrate their Christmas Eve.

Pushing open the small creaky gate into the dark church grounds, Edie walked slowly behind a frail old man with a walking-stick on his way to the service. At this pace and with the lights from the church and street-lamps, she could not help but see the shapes of the headstones and graves. One in particular took her attention: a spotlessly clean tiny white marble one under which only a small child or baby could be buried. Saddened but not disturbed by it, she touched it with her fingertips as she passed.

Crossing herself, she walked slowly towards the heavy arched doors and went inside to a breathtaking sight: the church was candlelit, and decorated with holly and ivy. It was not the grandest church in England but it felt welcoming. She found a place to sit on the end of a pew and waited for the service to begin; wondering why she hadn't been to church since before the war? Why she hadn't gone to give thanks for being alive and to pay her respects to those who had been killed in battle? More importantly, why had she stopped going to church when her mother had committed suicide? If there was anywhere to find peace of mind, comfort and an understanding, this must surely be it.

Soon Edie was singing her heart out in the almost full church with no thoughts of Maggie, Naomi, her brother or his family who were coming for Christmas dinner. Wrapped in the present, she was carried along with the words of the carols and thoroughly enjoying herself.

The service over, Edie walked quietly out into the churchyard to see that beyond the gates and under the lamplight there was another gathering: the Salvation Army were waiting for the church doors to close before the band opened up and began their song. An almost transparent layer of snow had fallen while she was inside. Just then she saw a familiar figure standing by the tiny headstone – it was Laura Jackson, spending a few special moments alone. Edie guessed that this must be the grave of her baby son.

Waiting in the shadows until she saw Laura walk slowly away, Edie followed in her footsteps. Once they had turned a corner and were almost out of earshot of the Salvation Army band she stepped up her pace until she was at her side. 'He's in the long sleep, Laura, that's all. The long sleep we'll all be in sooner or later.'

Turning to face her, Laura greeted her friend. 'Hello, Edie. I thought that was you back there. I can't help wishing he could be in my arms asleep.' She was pleased that Edie was there giving her company but when she had first seen her in the churchyard she had wanted to run away. 'So this is why you crept off early,' she went on. 'You should 'ave said. There's nothing wrong with choosing to go to church, especially not on Christmas Eve. I only caught the last fifteen minutes but it was enough. I came to 'ave five minutes by myself with baby John but when I heard my favourite carol, well, I couldn't stop myself. It was as if my feet had a will of their own. Maybe one day I'll even stop blaming God for what happened. Who knows?'

'You will. It took me a while,' said Edie, slipping her arm into Laura's and drawing closer as they walked slowly in step. 'And then when you think you're gettin' back to normal bang! In it comes agen. The mighty punch of the fist of God. That's what I used to think. Not now, though. I'm over the anger. It gave me a headache.'

'You mean losing your Harry wasn't the only blow?'

'No. There were two before that. When I was thirteen or so my dad went out one Sunday morning to the corner shop and never came back. I adored and worshipped the ground he walked on.'

'Was it an accident, Ed?' asked Laura quietly.

'No, it wasn't.' Then, 'I can't believe you just called me that. Dad was the only one who ever called me Ed.' She looked searchingly into her friend's eyes. 'Don't you think that's a bit strange?'

'No, I don't. I shorten everyone's name. It's a habit. So what did happen to 'im?'

'He left us. He left me, Mum, and my little brother, who's a lot bigger than me now.'

'Another woman?'

'Yep. Another woman and another child.'

'Phew. I can't imagine what that must have felt like. Someone you love and think you know through and through goes out to the shop and don't come back.'

'Mum never got over it.'

'Not even after all this time?' said Laura. 'Surely the misery turned to anger. I'd 'ave thought she'd 'ave bin bloody furious once she got over the initial shock.'

'Two years. She suffered for two years, and then took her own life. By then she was only a skeleton of her old self. That's what love can do to you,' said Edie, her voice breaking and her eyes filling with tears. 'I missed her so much at first.'

'I know what you mean,' whispered Laura. 'I missed my mum when she passed away and I still long to hold my baby in my arms. I miss hearing him cry for his feed.'

'Oh, Laura . . .' said Edie, stopping in her tracks. 'I am sorry. Come on – give us a hug.'

'Anything to oblige,' said Laura, struggling with her emotions. Wrapped in each other's arms neither woman spoke. They had no idea how moving was the picture they made: two grieving women drawing comfort from each other in this dark thoroughfare with only the light from the moon and cottage windows cast upon them. Other than the distant sound of carol singers it was quiet and the only movement was of a stray cat pattering its way through untouched snow.

Once their weeping had eased off, Edie and Laura walked arm in arm talking quietly about their lives now, their hopes and dreams. As they entered the grounds leading to Scott House, Edie agreed to call in to Laura's flat for a drink. She and her husband were giving an impromptu Christmas Eve party, which Jack had arranged after a few whiskies in the crowded local.

'If you change your mind and really don't want to pop in I won't be offended,' said Laura. 'It'll go on until the wee hours so you can choose your time to suit yerself.'

'That makes it a lot easier. I could get everything done and then see how I feel.'

'Yeah, or you could put the finishing touches to the tree and make brandy butter and peel the Brussels in the morning,' Laura teased. 'No one I know spends hours and hours and hours preparing for one day, Christmas or not.'

'Two days. They're coming back for Boxing Day as well.'

'All right. But we're not talking about a load of visitors, are we? You, Mags, Nao, your brother, his wife. It's Christmas Eve, for Christ's sake!'

'Is it what most people do, then? The night before Christmas Day go out to parties?' said Edie, in a quiet voice.

'Or throw one themselves, yes. Where on earth 'ave you been, Ed?'

'In the kitchen where I could stand the heat. I suppose it's time to see if I can break away from routine. Going out dancing again might help. We definitely must do that, Laura, in the new year. And we'll drag Jessie along – with a rope, if we have to.'

'What makes you say that? Jessie was up for it. Wasn't she?'

'At the time she was, but I'd bet my bottom dollar that once she's out of the Christmas mood she'll change 'er mind.'

'All right. You've got a bet. A dollar it is.'

'You're on.' Offering her hand to Laura, Edie landed a good slap on her friend's palm. She felt the sting as much as her friend and burst out laughing. 'I don't know my own strength. Sorry.'

'Well, that's something anyway. At least you're admitting you're stronger than you think.'

Arriving at the second floor both women were much lighter in heart than when they had set out for the church. But the sight of Maggie and the Italian boy, Tony, sitting on the staircase, his arm round her shoulders, wiped the smile off their faces. The young couple took no notice of them whatsover and simply carried on talking. Collecting herself and without really thinking, Edie said, 'You'll catch your death of cold on them stone steps.'

'Young love stays warm,' teased Laura, giving Edie a wink, then turning towards her flat. 'See you when you're ready, Eddy!'

'In half an hour or so!' returned Edie, not knowing how to react at seeing her girl in the arms of a young man. As she turned to Maggie to tell her the time she would like her indoors, she saw on her face and in her eyes a glow that she had not seen before and had a change of heart, saying instead, 'Why didn't you both go indoors and sit by the fire?'

'Well, that's a nice thought but my mother would beat me with a stick if she thought I would do such a thing,' said Tony, showing perfect white teeth.

'Would she?'

'Well, not quite, but you know what I mean. We're brought up to respect the family, and to go inside someone's home without the parents being there . . .' He drew a line across his neck with his thumb.

'I'm pleased to hear it,' said Edie, relieved. 'Anyway, I'm back now so if you want to come in you're welcome.' She looked from him to Maggie. 'Where's your aunt?'

'Still in Jessie's, entertaining the last few. They can't get enough of 'er.'

'Well practised,' laughed Edie, leaving them to themselves.

Going directly into the kitchen Edie lit a gas ring and put the kettle on to boil. In a strange but calm mood, she went into the living room, which, apart from the glowing coals, was in darkness, and switched on the Christmas-tree lights. She sat on the edge of the settee and gazed into the fire, alone but not lonely. Something was happening to her and although it was scary it didn't feel bad. It was almost as if the Edie of long ago was coming up for air, and that the strong sense of being responsible for Maggie was lifting like mist on a sunny September morning. Her daughter was no longer a child and the time was approaching for

Edie to let go. Be there for her and not be possessive. She, like every woman who had given birth, knew the strong bond between mother and child, but something had happened this evening, and whether it was due to her having gone to church after so many years or that she had seen Laura there at her baby's grave, she couldn't say.

A month ago, had she seen her fourteen-year-old in the arms of a sixteen-year-old handsome Italian she would have been shocked, yet it had been all right. A new feeling of tranquillity seemed to have touched her. She felt as if something was over, although she had no idea what. Soon Maggie would be fifteen and in just a few years' time would be leaving home, but this was not it. Something else was happening and Edie could not put her finger on what it was. Shrugging it off, she tonged a few coals on to the fire, then went back to the kitchen to brew her tea. She had cried in front of Laura Jackson this Christmas Eve instead of alone in the dark night and felt better for it. It was as if she had shed an old skin as a snake might.

The image of her father in the doorway when he had smiled at her for the last time came to mind and she felt for the first time since their parting that now she might see him again. It seemed clearer somehow as to why he had left. He had fallen in love with another woman. It was as simple as that. And that woman had had his son. It was a story that had repeated itself a million times over during the course of history. Her father was a good man and the look on his face before he had turned away from her was of genuine grief. He loved his children, but he had had to go. She knew that now, and as the new thought crept into her mind, she felt she would one day see him again, even if it meant going in search for him to express her love and tell him that neither she, Naomi nor Maggie condemned him for his mistakes.

A few minutes later settled by the fire again with no thoughts of going out, Edie sipped her tea in the half-light and stared into the flames, content to be by herself and talk freely. 'I thought I was strong enough to look after all of us once you'd gone, Dad, but I wasn't. I failed to stop Mum slipping into a dark depression. I did miss you. And I still do. And I miss Mum. I know you wouldn't 'ave gone for no reason. And I did try to make up for your not being there. But I just couldn't do it . . .'

'Darling, of *course* you couldn't,' came the caring voice of her aunt Naomi, who had come quietly into the flat and into the room. 'Flesh and blood, sweetheart. We're all made of flesh and blood. Cut us with a knife and we bleed. Break a heart, and it's scarred for life.'

'Don't knock on the door, will yer?' said Edie, half-heartedly, as she dabbed her tears with her handkerchief, privately pleased to have her company. 'I shouldn't 'ave given you your own key.'

'You didn't actually. I stole your *spare* and had one cut.'

'I know you did. I was trying to forget.'

'I'm sure you *were* . . . as is your wont.' Naomi lowered herself gracefully next to her niece on the settee and stroked wisps of hair off her face. 'Darling, you ought to know by now that those things we wish to forget we *cannot*, yet trifling everyday matters, such as paying the coal bill, slip *completely* from our minds.'

Crying and smiling, Edie looked into her aunt's faded green eyes. 'What would I do without you?'

'Be just as strong and as sensitive as you are now. It's Christmas, my darling, and as I have said so many times before it tends to make us all a touch on the maudlin side. Which is no bad thing. It is a time to clear all the rubbish we hoard and place it where it belongs. In the dustbin.'

'But this feels different. I can't explain it. I never get past this time of the year without thinking of Mum and Dad but I feel as if something's happened or is going to happen and I don't know what it is.'

'And do you not think that I go through something similar? My sister took her own life, and if I had been there for her maybe she wouldn't have – but probably she would because it's what she wanted. To sleep for ever, is what she had said – and more than once.'

'And you really believe that?'

'Yes, I do darling. Truly. Ours is hardly a perfect society. Nature is something else – quite beautiful and one would always be sorry to leave Mother Earth – but we, I am sad to say, are the disease that will in the end destroy the very thing that gives us life. This planet, if a planet it be.'

'So Mum made a wise choice, is that what you're saying?'

'No, of *course* I'm not. She was going to die in

any case – as we all shall do. Nothing is for ever and especially not for us lesser mortals who must rely on trivia and treats to keep us happy.' Stopping for a breather, Naomi pulled back her shoulders and looked her niece in the eye. 'Now, then, Edith, it may not have crossed your mind, but there is something very good and obvious about this little tête-à-tête. You, my darling, for the very first Christmas in a very long time, have not mentioned Harry. Now, what does that tell you?'

Edie gazed into her aunt's ageing but still beautiful face and thought for a few seconds. 'It tells me that at long last, and for no apparent reason, that I've laid the ghost.'

'Exactly.'

'I've been thinking of Mum and Dad while I've sat round this fire, but not of Harry. Even now I can say his name without getting choked. Why is that, do you think?'

'I don't know, poppet, but take it in your arms and embrace it. Embrace the freedom. You've imprisoned yourself for so many years. There's even a different look in your eyes, my darling. A look of resolution. You have it within you to make choices and the world is a very big and beautiful place. And you have many, many years to enjoy.'

'You're right. I will admit I feel different. I'm looking forward to something and I don't know what it is, and that's what gives it the golden glow. I know it sounds daft and I'm not gonna stick holly in my hair and dance all over the place—'

'I'm very pleased to hear it. You must leave that sort of thing to me, if you don't mind my saying so. There is little else for me other than to do whatever I like.'

'And that's got nothing to do with age, Naomi. You've always been the Mad Woman and you always will be the Mad Woman. And we love you for it.'

'Goodness me, Edith, I don't think I have ever seen such light in your eyes! You really are quite content, aren't you?'

'Yes. But don't ask me why – I haven't a clue. Now, then, I'm supposed to be going to another party tonight so I need to put a bit of sliced cucumber on my red puffy eyes.'

'Edie, you are beautiful no matter what and especially now,' said Naomi, cupping her niece's face. 'We are all the more beautiful when we bare our souls. Would that we could remember it when in the depths of despair.' Peering at her 1920s silver wristwatch, she said, 'It is now a quarter to ten and what I *suggest* is that you remain in your place by the fire and sip a glass of brandy, which I shall *fetch* for you.'

'Not brandy, Naomi. There's only a little drop left and that's for flaming the pudding.'

'Oh?' smiled her aunt. 'So you expected me to go through the most special day of the year without my most favoured drink?'

'Oh, right. You've wrapped one up for my Christmas present.'

'Oh, darling, of *course* not.'

'Well, where is it, then?'

'In one of my red shopping-bags, wrapped in a piece of Christmas gift paper from last year, unironed.'

'But you always iron last year's wrapping and use it agen. Don't tell me you've not bothered to press the creases out.'

'I was referring to the bottle of brandy, and only the bottle of brandy, which I have wrapped for your brother's lovely wife.'

Edie burst out with laughter. 'You are such a cow at times.'

'Edie, the best Cognac is *terribly* expensive. I'm sure she'll be very pleased with it.'

'I'm sure she will. But she won't be too happy watching us drain it in two days. You always find a way to wind Helene up like a clock.'

'*Helen*, sweetheart, her name is Helen. Just because she chose to alter it when she moved out into the suburbs doesn't mean we must call her by it.'

'They live in Edmonton and they both like it there and if she wants to be a bit above 'erself for a while then why not? Leave her be.'

'Ed*mon*ton, dear. That is how your brother's wife pronounces it. 'Ed*mon*ton.'

'Whatever,' sighed Edie, 'whatever. Open the brandy.'

'Oh, darling, not before I've given it to her. That would be *awfully* rude.'

'Are you saying you haven't already had a sip from it?'

'Well, yes, of *course* I have. But she won't notice. A little sleight of hand once it's unwrapped . . . as I test to make sure it stands up to its price.'

'Go and get it, Naomi. You can't pull that trick three years running. I've got a box of chocolates from work that one of the blokes gave me – you can give 'er them.'

'Oh. Well, I suppose we *could* do that. They're not too out of the ordinary, are they, darling?'

'No, they're not expensive ones. Just a run-of-the-mill Cadbury's selection.'

'Well, if you think it's not *too* generous,' she said, 'and, of course, your need for the brandy is *far* greater than your brother's wife's at this precise moment. With a little of the delicious liquid inside us we shall *both* be ready for the next party.'

'If you say so,' sighed Edie, easing herself into a comfortable position in the armchair. 'Go on, then. Move yerself. I need a little rest. All this fuss over Christmas time. I sometimes wonder why I bother. What's it all about anyway?'

'It is about everything and *nothing*, darling. This hypocritical society in which we have somehow managed to *land* ourselves is filled with corruption and short-sighted *greed*. The only way through is to accept what we were given in the first place, sun, sea and land. I can see no rhyme *or* reason for us being here at all – but here we most *certainly* are.'

'You forgot rain, snow, ice and the freezing cold,' said Edie, closing her eyes.

'Indeed, I did *not* forget,' said Naomi, as she left the room. 'Nor did I overlook love and *devotion*. Without which we should *all* perish.'

Enjoying the peace and quiet in her place by the fire,

Edie wondered if she might prefer to stay right where
she was until it was time for bed. Two parties in one
day was a touch over the top, to her mind. But then,
remembering what she had heard about the interesting
mix of people who would be at Laura's, she decided to
keep an open mind. After all, if her aunt could keep up
with this social whirl surely she could? With no more
thoughts on chores to be carried out for the next day
she appreciated the stillness and especially this rest.
But this pleasure was short-lived. Maggie, her cheeks
a high colour, came bounding into the room. 'Mum!
I forgot the loft!' she blurted.

'Oh, not now, love. Tell me about it tomorrow. This
is just so lovely, not 'aving to think about anything.'

'But I never went up and got my toy-box down!
It's still there!'

'Well, all right, Uncle Jimmy'll nip in some time
tomorrow and get it. No one will 'ave been up there,
Mags. I passed it today and it's not been disturbed. I
went back to have a look at the old place and—'

'But I need to get it now! The doll's in there!' She
lowered her voice to a whisper. *'Aunt Naomi's doll!'*

'Well, it'll just 'ave to stay there for another night.'

'But I always put it at the foot of the tree! You
know I do! She'll be mortified if it's not there.'

'Mortified?' said Edie. 'Talking in her language
now, are we?'

Ignoring her Maggie said, 'I'm gonna go back and
get it now. Tony said he'll come wiv me and he knows
where the caretaker leaves 'is ladder. We'll take that.
Where's the big torch?'

'In the cupboard under the sink.'

'Right. So that's where I'll be, then. I'll see you in Laura Jackson's later on.'

'I didn't know you were invited, Maggie. She's got a lot of people going . . .'

'She asked me if I wouldn't mind sitting with little Kay in 'er bedroom and reading stories till she falls asleep.'

'Oh. Fair enough. If I'm not there don't worry. I might stay by this fire, all cosy.'

'All right. Don't wait up.' With that, Maggie was gone and Edie was left with a very strange feeling. *Don't wait up?* Had she heard right? Her child was telling *her* not to wait up? What was going on?

The sudden high-pitched voice of her aunt calling out of the kitchen window to Maggie added to her sense of losing control. 'Margaret! Please do *not* forget that your great-aunt has the key to your chastity belt! Which I shall keep for another week, should you stay out too late with the foreigner!'

'Good God,' moaned Edie. 'Oh, spare me that woman!'

Again, the door into her sanctuary crashed open. 'That child,' said Naomi, stretching her arm and pointing a trembling finger at the outside world, 'is behaving as if she were a cow ready for the bull! You should have stopped her going out again! Why on earth didn't you?'

'Because . . .' murmured Edie, enjoying this moment of the tables being turned '. . . I want a grandchild as soon as possible. One with nice dark skin.'

Naomi was all of a tremble now and the finger had been redirected towards her niece. 'You may very well think this is funny, *Edith*, but heed my warning! She is just out of ankle socks and quite naïve. How *dare* you sit there and let her go back to that dreadful house with an Italian? The war is not so many years behind us that you may say you'd forgotten all of *that*!'

'Would it make any difference if it had been an *English*man, Aunt?'

'You know *quite* well it wouldn't! I mention the war *merely* to shock you into action! I told her not even to consider going outside that front door again this evening and she took no notice! None whatsoever!'

'Oh, shut up Naomi and fetch in the brandy.'

'While a foreigner leads *your daughter* through the door of no return! Well, then, *yes* I shall pour the brandy. Two *very* large glasses. We are going to need sedating before this night is through! And please remember when you awake on Christmas morning that it was you who sent your child from here to a desolate house at night with a hot-blooded Spaniard!'

'Italian,' said Edie.

'They are *all* Casanovas!' With that Naomi stormed out of the room and back into the kitchen where she fully intended to sulk for a very long time and drink as much brandy as she wanted! In her present mood, however, she could not settle for two minutes. She was immediately back in the room using a different tactic. 'Edie, darling, please do be sensible! My great-niece is only fourteen and you are letting her loose in the East End of London at night with a foreign young man who, no doubt, is terribly excited, as all men are, at the news of the forthcoming contraceptive pill.'

'It won't be available for years, Naomi.'

'That's as may be but many a cock is standing up at the very thought of it. And apart from this, you have agreed to let her go into a dark, empty house with this fertile young man on one of the most romantic evenings of the year. Are you mad?'

'Well, first, she doesn't look *only fourteen* any more since *you* did the makeover. Second, Tony is not a strange man, he is the son of a neighbour. And third, she is on a mission. They both are. Instead of thinking the worst of the lad you should be pleased he's helping your great-niece. Now, have a drink and sit down.'

'But *why* are they going to that dreadful place? I don't understand. If it's for sentimental reasons, I rest my case. When love is in the air sentiment rushes *immediately* to the penis. I think I have enough experience of men to know that much.'

'I'm sure you have,' said Edie, 'But in this case you're wrong. I know more than you, and that's what's bugging yer.'

'And you are not going to *tell* me what it is I should *know*?'

'That's right.'

'Well, all I can say is that that is terribly cruel. Now, what time exactly are we expected for cocktails?'

Bursting with laughter, Edie said, 'Cocktails? A pint of beer, more like. You'd best not come to this one. Wait here for Maggie to come back and put your mind at rest. That's what I think.'

'Well, I'm awfully sorry to *disappoint* you. I *shall* go. And I shall keep a keen eye open for that young man's *mother*.'

'Whatever,' said Edie. 'Do what you think best.' For all her worldly Bohemian and free-thinking manner, Naomi was, beneath a very thin surface, quite strait-laced and Edie had always been aware of this. It had been a while since this side of her nature had shown itself and it was worth waiting for.

Whether Maggie had gone back to Cotton Lane on this very day that she herself had chosen to stroll down Memory Lane was of no real significance, but Edie couldn't help thinking that her daughter, whether she had realised it or not, had experienced the same need to touch her roots as she had. Though their life had been a struggle, in so far as making ends meet, this time of the year had always been a festive one, and they had decorated the little house together. The memories were still fresh in Edie's mind and most likely in Maggie's too. The one single most important thing that could be attributed to this landmark on the calendar in December was the way everyone managed to switch off from worries.

To explain why Maggie was going back – the tradition of her first doll under the tree being the reason – would be futile in her aunt's present mood. Once she had calmed down and was back in the living room by the fire, Edie would suggest it. With just a few sentimental words she could easily have her aunt weeping with joy and sorrow, and eager to have the young couple return and give her heartfelt apologies for behaving so *terribly* badly!

Having successfully slipped a knife into the lock on the door of her old house, Maggie stood in the front room and shone the torch around to the sound of mice scampering on the floorboards above. Nothing had changed and no one had been in since the day they moved out. Guiding the light towards a small cupboard next to the fireplace, she said, 'That's where we kept our candles and there're still some half-used ones in it.'

'What more could we want?' said Tony, the excitement of this adventure telling in his voice.

'Electricity?'

'No, that's for our new homes. This is more like it. This takes me right back to where we used to live in Rose Lane.'

'Rose Lane eh? Little country cottage, was it?'

'Off Commercial Street? Hardly. That was a slum as well.'

Turning slowly to face him, Maggie said, 'This ain't a slum. I was born in this 'ouse. This is our 'ome.'

'No, it's not,' said Tony, flashing a smile. 'You don't live 'ere any more – and be thankful for it. I wouldn't want to go back in time. Outside toilet. Tin bath hanging on the garden fence. Waiting for the copper to boil. The washboard. The mangle. Old grates that 'ave to be black-leaded. No television—'

'We 'aven't got one in any case,' said Maggie turning back to the cupboard, slighted by his sentiment but not ashamed. She did miss all the things he had mentioned.

'Well, you'll have to come and watch ours then, won't you?'

'Maybe,' she said, wondering just how well-off his family were. Laura Jackson had given her a brief résumé, and at Jessie's she had learned that Tony was from a large close-knit family who ran four Italian cafés in and around Bethnal Green, which served excellent home-made meals. A sudden tap on the front door sent a wave of fear through her. The dark and silent atmosphere was beginning to get to Maggie. With an expression of worry on her face she turned to Tony for reassurance.

'Don't be scared. We're not doing anything wrong.' He strode across the room and opened the door to find Ben the Jew standing there with a torch in hand that was now shining into Tony's face. 'It's all right,' said Tony, shying away from the bright light. 'We've come to collect a box from the loft which the family forgot.'

'Is that right?' said Ben, narrowing his eyes. 'So, you can tell me the name of the family?' His face was dead-pan until he heard a familiar voice call out to him.

'It's okay, Ben, it's me, Maggie. I left a box of my stuff behind.'

With a gentle sweep of the hand Ben eased Tony out of his way and went inside. 'Well, if you're not a sight for sore eyes,' he said, his torch on her but with the light cast down so as not to shine in her face. 'I like the new hairstyle.'

Blushing, Maggie said, 'This is my new neighbour. His name's Tony.'

'Pleased to make your acquaintance,' said Ben, in a fatherly tone but still with a hint of caution. 'She was like a daughter at one time so be a good friend or you might have to answer to me.'

'Of course I will, sir,' said Tony, amused by the old boy in his worn-out overcoat, which was a size too big. And then, offering an affectionate joke, he said, 'I'm sorry I can't offer you a cup of tea.'

'I wouldn't accept in any case,' replied Ben, a touch unsure of this young man's intentions where Maggie was concerned. 'I don't take tea from people I'm not used to.' He then turned to Maggie, pulling back and admiring her new look. 'So what happened all of a sudden?' he said. 'Who did this to you or need I ask?'

'Great-aunt Naomi.' She smiled. Who d'yer think?'

The very name warmed the cockles of his heart. At the tender age of sixteen Ben and Naomi had enjoyed a fleeting romance until she flitted off on her first theatrical tour, in which she impressed all and sundry with her great talent of floating through the air as she danced her solo in a production of *Where Bluebells Grew*.

'For her it's not bad,' he shrugged. 'You could have ended up looking as crazy as she was at your age.' He turned back to Tony and offered him his torch. 'Here. Leave it on the doorstep when you've done.' With that he showed a hand and left, sound in mind that this lad was all right. And if he hadn't returned the torch within ten or fifteen minutes, he could always come back – with the policeman's truncheon he had come by when in a scuffle with the local Blackshirts before the war.

'Well,' said Tony, 'I think I got the gist of that, Maggie. Come on, we'd better get the box and be gone.'

Taking the second torch from him, Maggie led the way up the narrow, dark staircase with Tony following. With enough light for them to see their way, she was happy to be back in her old home. Apart from the chill and the smell of damp nothing had changed. Inside her bedroom she shone the torch to the hatch leading to the loft, saying, 'I really appreciate this. If Aunt Naomi saw no doll at the foot of the tree she'd think I'd put it out with the rubbish.'

'You don't have to apologise, if that's what you're doing.' Tony set the ladder firmly in place and turned to face her. 'I'm enjoying this. It's the last thing I expected to be doing on Christmas Eve, though.'

'At least you've got Laura Jackson's party to go to. I'm not sure if Mum's gonna let me out.'

'Why not?' he said, climbing the ladder. 'Been a bad girl, have you?'

'No. We've got a lot to do tonight. It's all right for you blokes – you don't 'ave to worry about the Christmas dinner being ready on time.'

'Not worry about it, no,' he said, easing the hatch open and pushing it back, 'but we all muck in. Italian men don't think it's cissy to cook. We enjoy it.'

'Men from round this way do – think it's cissy, that is.'

'Brawny labourers might, but not *all* Englishmen. I can't believe that.' With his head and shoulders now in the loft he let out a.low whistle. 'This is great. It's bigger up here than I thought it would be. So long as you stoop it's okay.' He looked down and smiled at her. 'Come on, or are you scared of spiders and mice?'

'Hardly,' said Maggie, climbing up the ladder. 'I've bin living with 'em since I was born.' Shining her torch round the loft she spotted her cardboard toy-box. 'I think we might 'ave to come back in the daylight,' she murmured. 'I want to take my dad's tools, which are in those rusty tins.'

Moved by the sensitive tone in her voice, Tony reached out and squeezed her hand. 'This must be difficult for you. Is it?'

'No. Not really. It feels right being up 'ere.' She pointed at her old pram, which was only good enough for the junk heap. 'Look at that. I wouldn't let Mum throw it away.'

'It's beyond repair by the look of it or I'd take it for my little niece.'

'It was second-hand when Mum bought it for a shilling off the rag-and-bone man, Tony. I scrubbed it till some of the paint come off. Then I stuffed in an old cushion Aunt Naomi give me and put my doll in it. I feel mean now for leaving it up 'ere with this junk.'

'You have to let some things go,' he said, his mind and eyes elsewhere. He was peering into a corner at a First World War army uniform on a hanger hooked on to a nail. 'What's that doing up here? It's a wonder it's not been eaten away.'

'Now you know what the smell is. Aunt Naomi puts mothballs everywhere. That belonged to my Great-uncle Fred. The man she was married to.'

'Well, then, we should take it with us. We can't leave it behind,' he said, crouching and making his way over to it.

Leaving him to enjoy his expedition, Maggie peered into another corner where ancient chemist's bottles were grouped. They had been there when her grandparents had moved into the house. Intrigued now by the dark green shapes she eased her way towards them, stretched her arm as far as she was able and gripped something else: a small brown parcel, thick with dust. Squeezing her arm between two struts of decaying roof timber, she held it under the light of her torch.

'I've never seen this before,' she murmured to herself.

'This uniform is in good condition, all things considered!' Tony's voice came to her from the far end. 'It smells of mould, but after dry-cleaning it should be okay.'

Maggie slipped the parcel into her coat pocket. 'Come on. Let's go. I'm cold.' It had all proved a little too much for her. She felt sad now.

'This uniform,' said Tony, holding it over his arm, 'it shouldn't have been left up here. Wouldn't your aunt be upset if we didn't take it with us?'

'I s'pose so,' said Maggie. 'If you think we can manage that and the box and the ladder . . .'

'Of course we can manage it.'

For no particular reason that she could think of,

Maggie didn't mention the brown-paper parcel. She wasn't even guessing as to what might be in it but her instincts told her it was something to look at alone, in the privacy of her bedroom. She felt sure that, from the fragile and somewhat brittle brown wrapping, it was very old. The string tied around it was a strong twill, thin and oily with grime where dust and dirt had clung to it over the years.

Outside in the street, with the door shut behind them and the torch left on the doorstep for Ben, Maggie sensed someone watching her. She turned slowly and looked across the narrow road to see a man in a dark overcoat with his trilby pulled down over his eyes. He looked like a character in a spy comic, which made her smile. The father she had never set eyes on was the furthest person from her thoughts.

Having been there for a good ten minutes, after ignoring sound advice from Ben and Joey, Harry had come out of hiding to catch a glimpse of his daughter and see if she really did look like him, as Ben had insisted. He had heard so much about her over the past weeks that he felt duty-bound to see her. Once he had lit his cigarette under the street-lamp he glanced at her furtively again, then strolled away, giving Maggie no reason to believe that he was anyone other than a gentleman who had stopped to have a smoke. With his dark grey clothing and trilby he had soon faded into obscurity with only the sound of his diminishing footsteps echoing through the street.

*   *   *

Walking beside Tony as he balanced the ladder on his shoulder with the uniform hooked on to a rung, Maggie felt strange – not miserable, just odd, with a sickly feeling in the pit of her stomach. She wondered if this had been brought on by the box she was holding with her beloved doll inside it and other old toys that had not seen daylight for years.

Respecting her silence, Tony sensed that she was feeling a touch nostalgic for the old times and that painful memories must have been rekindled. To his mind she was far better off living on the Barcroft estate than in a decaying street. 'You okay, Maggie?' he eventually said, giving her the opportunity to talk if she wanted to.

'I think so,' she murmured. 'I'm glad we went anyway.'

'Good. That's good,' was his response. And so they continued on their way, passing others who were out and about, in the Christmas mood. The sound of music coming from a small Dockers' Union club on the corner of Cudworth Street was lovely. Someone was playing the piano and singing, with warmth and passion, Nat King Cole's 'Unforgettable'.

'I love that song,' said Tony glancing at Maggie's profile, the lamplight on her face and copper hair.

'There'll be more than one singing in there later on.' Maggie laughed. 'Especially by midnight. It's always full and lively, never mind at this time of year.'

'Shame we don't know any dockers to get us in.'

'That wouldn't be difficult, Tony. There are plenty on the estate. Laura Jackson's 'usband for a start.

You should see the big blokes going in and out of his flat. Not scruffy ones in work clothes – suits and cufflinks.'

'To do a bit of business. I know. I've seen them,' he said enjoying his private thoughts: the men in suits weren't necessarily dockers but they were certainly bent.

'It takes one to know one,' said Maggie, knowing what he was getting at. 'You Italians can't all be on the straight and narrow.'

'I never said we were. But the gangs don't come into this neck of the woods. They have their own patches in North London.'

'So how come you're so sure about Laura's 'usband?'

'You learn a lot about people working in a café. Men seem to have their own kind of uniforms. You just get to know who's who. And Jack Jackson, I reckon, is the brains of the outfit. Never goes out on a job but plans it all. That's why the suits arrive one at a time with a ten-minute gap between them. I've seen it all before when a job's being planned – when I worked in my uncle's first café in Green Street.'

'So they were customers, then?'

'One or two. Their sort are very good customers. So we look after them. Treat them as if they're royalty.'

'I've seen your dad talking to Laura's husband. Is he involved in all of that as well?'

Tony burst out laughing. 'No, of course not!' Then, amused at the idea, he said, 'But if anything comes up on the cheap that we can use in our cafés he'll have some of it. He was probably putting an order in. I know he's after a small safe for our takings. A second-hand one. One that's had its hinges off. One that's disappeared from a jeweller's shop.'

'You're 'aving me on,' said Maggie. 'I don't believe any of it.'

'No? Try reading this week's East London paper. Spiegalhalter's, the jewellery shop in Mile End, was broken into and the thieves got away with a little safe. It's Christmas. The busiest time of the year.'

Maggie shook her head, disbelievingly. 'I don't believe you. You're wrong. People like that won't be living in our block.'

Turning into the grounds of Barcroft Estate, Tony said, 'Have it your way. And don't repeat anything I've said or my face will be rearranged.'

'Might be an improvement,' returned Maggie, whose attention was now on two very smart men strolling arm in arm with their women, who were dressed up to the nines and heading for the entrance to the block of flats where she lived. 'D'yer reckon they'll be at the party?'

'No question,' he said. 'I'd put a quid on it.'

'Make it a shilling and you're on.'

'Make it a date for the pictures next week instead. You lose, I take you to see *The Day the Earth Stood Still* at the Foresters.'

'And if I win?'

'I'll still take you, but you have to buy the ice creams.'

'I can't really lose, then?'

'No. But we Italians are generous like that,' he said,

placing the ladder back into the caretaker's cupboard beneath the stairs. 'And we've also got a sense of humour.' He looked sideways at Maggie and flashed a beautiful smile. 'Sister indeed – and you thought I'd fall for that?'

'I don't know what you mean,' said Maggie, beginning to blush.

'You don't have a sister. And Ben was right. The new haircut *does* suit you. It makes you look completely different.'

All thoughts of romance now swept away, Maggie became her old defiant self. She pursed her lips. 'Actually it wasn't just the haircut. I was wearing glasses as well.'

'I never noticed that, I must say, just the red hair. But I'm glad you're not wearing glasses any more.' He closed the shed door and looked into her face. 'You've got lovely eyes. Really lovely.'

'Thank you. I didn't need the glasses, actually. I only wore 'em cos they went with the brace I was wearing on my teeth. If you're gonna be an ugly duckling you might as well go the whole way!'

'You were never an ugly duckling, Maggie Birch,' he said, kissing her lightly on the lips. 'You're beautiful.'

Ten minutes later, having parted company, Maggie was back in her bedroom, lying flat on her bed with the door shut and her eyes closed, thinking of Tony. His handsome smiling face. The way he stood. The way he walked. His voice. His gentle manner. It was all so wonderful she couldn't believe it was happening to her. Plain and simple Maggie Birch.

Her aunt Naomi had said more than once that the fifties would be the decade that romance and glamour returned: it would be like the twenties all over again, but without the Charleston. She had also predicted that the feel-good mood in the air would soon capture everyone, and that the glamour of Hollywood films and film stars shown in the press would have an effect on all women: they would yearn for clothes that screamed sophistication and sex appeal.

The domestic scene, however, Naomi refused to praise. She deplored the way housewives were throwing out Bakelite and replacing it with new colourful plastics. She had no wish to see Formica in her kitchen and didn't care for easy-to-keep-clean surfaces. Vacuum-cleaners, however, she held in high esteem. Especially her own. She had nothing good to say about the new family serial on the wireless, *The Archers*, even though she tuned in regularly, but the hilarious *Goon Show* should win an award. The so-called 'teenagers' should get out of the home, hang around milk and coffee bars listening to records blasting out of juke boxes and learn how to smoke a French cigarette with style.

She believed that children were being disgracefully spoiled, which was no bad thing, and adored the euphoria that had come with the interest in outer space. Comic books and American B-movies were awash with horror stories of alien visitations and plots to take over the world that, to Naomi's mind, would shake even the dullest office workers to the core. The rise in the number of UFO sightings to her was the most exciting thing of the century and she adored the new wave of toys: flying saucers, robots and ray guns. Her only regret was that she was too old to add any of these wonderful presents to her own Christmas list.

Recalling the expression of torment on Naomi's face when she had reeled off her predictions and admirations, Maggie smiled to herself. The maddening thing was that her great-aunt was right about most things.

By the time Edie was made up and ready for the party at Laura's, Naomi and Maggie had already been gone for thirty minutes or so, both in the mood to boogie. It was another of Naomi's favourite expressions.

Pleased with her reflection in the mirror, Edie touched up her lipstick and pulled her hair into a French pleat, leaving loose strands to soften the effect. She felt glamorous in her new stilettos. She closed the door behind her, pulled her coat collar up against the freezing cold air and walked along the balcony towards where she could hear laughter, and Rosemary Clooney singing 'Ba-Ba-Baciami Piccina!'.

The door was wide open and Edie made for the kitchen smiling modestly at anyone who caught her eye. She was looking out for Jessie, hoping she would be there too. As expected, she found Laura making sandwiches for the stream of guests. Numberless bottles of brandy, whisky, gin and beer were stacked everywhere. The collection before closing time between the party of family and friends at the Carpenter's Arms had been more than generous for a reason: when drink was left over after an East End do another party was held the following week to finish it.

'You look as if you could do with some help, Laura,' said Edie, looking around for a pinafore.

'Oh, no, you don't. Once I've finished this pile of sandwiches, it's each man for 'imself. With this lot you could end up in the kitchen all night long! Don't worry, Edie, I'm not slaving away, just making it look like that. Find a glass and help yerself to whatever you want. It's too packed to bully my lazy Jack to pour you a drink. Tonics, lime and orange are there by the sink, and the spirits are all over the flat!' Laura was already merry. 'Take your pick!'

'Hello, hello, hello,' grinned one of the guests, who was known within certain circles as Alf the Overcoat. Swaying in the kitchen doorway and gripping a pint glass of beer, he spoke in a very slow voice: 'Oh . . . what movie 'ave you walked out of, sweet'eart?'

'Oh, shut up, Alf and leave 'er alone,' said Laura. 'She's my friend. Edie, say hello to Alf and with a bit of luck he might go away.'

'Hello, Alf.'

'Hello, Edie,' he whispered, gazing into her eyes. 'Fancy a little dance wiv me?' He cavorted about in the small space around him, comically showing his skills, 'I can do this,' he said, 'and I can do that. I can spin and I can sling. Or I can dance like this . . .' He placed his arms round an invisible partner and tried to waltz on the spot.

'What's goin' on in 'ere, then?' said Laura's brother-in-law, Bert, as he squeezed past and pulled a bottle of beer out of a crate. 'Two beautiful ladies all to yerself, Alf? You'll make Jack jealous.'

'Will I? That's good.' He winked at Edie, then backed away. 'Save a dance for me, eh? Cos I'm not only handsome and rugged, look . . .' He rolled up the sleeve of a spanking new shirt and flexed his muscles. 'Feel that, Edie. Go on! Press it as 'ard as you want. Pure bleeding rock-hard muscle that is!'

Laughing, Edie gave his arm a squeeze. 'Rock hard,' she said, 'bleedin' rock 'ard.'

'See? I told yer, didn't I? And just cos of me muscles and me good looks the women run a mile! Frightened I'll love and leave 'em, see?' He suddenly changed and lowered his voice with a little-boy-hurt look on his face. 'I'm very lonely, Edie. I've got no one to cook me dinners or steam me socks by the fireside.'

'Alf, go away,' said Laura, 'and make yerself useful and bring out the empties.'

'See what I mean Edie? Even *she* takes liberties. Now I'm to be the sad old sod who's only 'ere to collect the empties. I bought 'er a lovely big box of chocolates an' all. Cost me over a tenner.'

'Don't tell lies. You nicked 'em out of Cooper's, the sweet shop in Cambridgeheath Road. Liz told me.'

'Oh, what kind of a fing is that to say in front of my new woman? How can you expect the girl to marry me now?'

'Out the way, you ape,' said Bert, ignoring the banter, 'and leave the ladies alone.' He paused for a moment, then turned back to face his mate. 'Tell you what, Alf, there's a beautiful woman in there I reckon you'd like. Lovely singer.'

'Go on,' said Alf, sporting his serious expression. 'Point her out and be discreet, all right? But I'm telling you now, if she's only after my body I'll be offended.'

'Come in and sing a duet wiv 'er.'

'If 'er name's Naomi, I warn you, she'll out-sing anyone,' cautioned Edie.

'Now then, now then,' said Alf, 'don't get jealous. I won't jilt yer. But when the fiddler calls . . .' With that he left them to it, his chin raised as he made his way through the bodies looking for a woman who went by the name of Naomi, his voice almost above the music and noise: 'Where is she? Where's my woman? Naomi, sweet'eart! Show yerself!'

'That's done it,' said Edie. 'She'll really take the limelight now.'

'Leave 'er alone,' smiled Laura. 'She's the life and soul of any do. I'd love her to be my aunt. Free entertainment. What more could you want?'

'A large gin and tonic,' said Edie, helping herself.

Finished with sandwich-making, Laura smiled. 'Your Maggie's a lovely girl, Edie.'

Sipping her drink and leaning against the wall, Edie answered in a quiet voice, 'I know. She could 'ave done with a father around, though. She's missed out there.'

'I know. My Jack's a sod in more ways than one but he's good with Kay. They're really close, which takes a bit of the load off me.'

'Oh, come on, how can your lovely blonde-haired blue-eyed daughter be a load?'

'You know, the baby and everything. I've not 'ad much time for 'er, and to tell the truth I feel guilty. I've been a bit distant.'

'Well, you shouldn't 'ave bin! Shame on you. Poor little thing's got enough to cope with. What d'yer think she must feel like? Baby John was her little brother, don't forget.'

Laura went quiet and then turned to face her friend. 'Thanks, Ed. A bit of honesty don't go amiss. I s'pose you think I've been wallowing in self-pity.'

'Yep. Soaking yourself in it.'

'Do you really mean that?'

'I do. No offence, but I've been there myself, and at the end of the day there's only one person who can help us – and that's ourselves.'

'Laura!' Jack's intervention was well timed. The women had said all that had to be said on the subject. 'Hurry up wiv them sandwiches – I'm starving! Bert ate my plateful, greedy bastard.'

'Jack, please, watch your language,' snapped Laura, giving him a look to kill. 'You're not down the docks now.'

'Sorry, Edie, sweet'eart. I never saw you standing there.'

'Lying toad,' said Edie. 'Anyway, don't mind me, but there are youngsters present, don't forget.'

Jack went quiet, sporting his little boy hurt look. 'I only came in for a sandwich.' Seeing through his act, Laura pushed a small plate of food into his hand

and told him not to flirt with the bubbly blonde from number twenty. Just as he was ready to defend himself, even though he knew she'd seen him giving one or two of the ladies long, lingering kisses under the mistletoe, Naomi's beautiful voice silenced him and the entire flat. It was one of her favourite songs, 'Smile', first heard in 1937 when the Charlie Chaplin film *Modern Times* was revived. Naomi needed no spotlight.

'Do you know what, Laura?' whispered Edie, following her to the doorway of the sitting room where they stood, rapt, 'that woman is full of wisdom. She's singing it for all of us.'

'I've never met anyone like 'er,' said Laura. 'And, let's face it, in this part of the world you meet all sorts.'

Filled with pride, Edie gazed into the living room at this star from a period gone by. Catching the eye of Jessie who was also soaking up the lyrics, she gently smiled at her. No words were necessary. Here, in this small home, in this tiny pocket of the East End of London, were two women who had been thrown together by chance to discover that they had the one most important thing in common: loss. Each had lost men they had loved deeply and the song was poignant. Squeezing her way through the captivated audience towards Edie, Jessie arrived and linked arms with her. 'I sometimes wonder if it's better to have a good cry and be done with it, don't you?'

With held-back tears, Edie glanced at her friend and shrugged. 'It never did me any good, Jess.'

'I'm not so sure. It might 'ave done and you've

not realised. I never did, Edie, that's the trouble. I never cried Tom Smith out of my soul. I was too angry for that – too angry to make any allowances whatsoever.'

'And now?'

'I don't know.' Jessie's gaze shifted from her friend to Max across the room, and she felt her heart melt. Uncomfortable in these surroundings, he was doing his best to blend in. He was with another Jewish neighbour who also looked as if he wasn't used to be among so many East End rough diamonds.

They were chatting quietly in a corner and Naomi's song, for all the attention they were giving it, could have been anything from heart-rending to naughty. It was all going over Max's head.

'I'll tell you what, Edie, if I were to quiz Max on the song your aunt sang he'd look at me all blank. And when I ask 'im if he enjoyed the party, he'll tell me everything about the man he's talking to. He's oblivious to all that's goin' on around 'im. He's so different from Tom. Chalk and cheese.' She nodded towards him. 'He's only just met that man he's talking to but by the time we leave he'll know what he does for a living, where he lives, and where his parents were buried if they happened to be dead. That's Max for you. He has to know everything about someone before he embraces or discards.'

'And what about your ex? What was he like at parties?'

'Tom? Oh, he'd fit in here like a hand in a glove. One of the lads. And he'd have me on that floor dancing to romantic songs while he sang out of tune in my ear.'

'Harry was a bit of a ladies' man as it happened. It wouldn't be me he'd be dancing with but the sexiest-looking woman in the room.'

'And what if you danced with another man?'

'He'd be too busy looking into his partner's pretty eyes to notice. But I knew he'd never stray over the line. He was a sociable man at parties, but there was nothing more to it than that though. I suppose I did get jealous sometimes – no, not jealous, that's the wrong word. Hurt. He'd never ask me to dance yet he'd soon get on the floor with another woman. Especially if he'd never met 'er before.'

Jessie didn't think that was very fair but kept it to herself. 'Max hates dancing. He'd die of embarrassment if I pulled him on to the floor. I think I'd like him to be a little bit more like Laura's Jack.'

'Do yer think so? said Edie. 'I bet you wouldn't. He's a right flirt. Winked at me three times the day I moved in. He's got lovely blue eyes and knows it. Laughing blue eyes. We must go dancing, Jessie. Us three ladies. You, me and Laura. I think it's a smashing idea. The more I thought about it after I came out of your flat, the more I wanted us to go. I haven't let my hair down on a dance floor for years.'

Placing her arm round Edie's waist Jessie gave her a little squeeze. 'We will. It's time you had a little bit of fun, Edie Birch. Perhaps we'll find you a new man who'll take you dancing every week.'

'Wouldn't that be something?'

Jessie looked her friend in the eye. 'It's not exactly the impossible dream, you know. I think you've been cooped up in your own little world for too long. We're gonna 'ave to bring you out of your shell.'

'Maybe you're right,' she said, eager to change the subject now. She turned the attention back to Max Cohen. 'Look at your Max. He's still talking to that man. But they really look engrossed, enjoying it, so you can't blame 'em.'

'Oh, I don't. I just let him get on with it. I'll have a be-bop when the right song comes on. I'll soon be on that floor. That's one thing I do miss about Tom. He did used to love to dance. Once we *were* on the floor we hardly came off other than for a drink.'

'Do you think you might still love him?' said Edie quietly.

Giving her a quizzical look, Jessie said, 'Love him? Course not. I'm with Max now. Whatever made you ask?'

'Oh, nothing. Just a thought, that's all.'

'Max is a good man – and good with the children. At least he wanted to be with me, not like that swine who ran out on me – and more than once. Cos that's what it amounted to in the end – Tom deserted me and his children.'

'You *are* still angry,' smiled Edie. 'You should see your eyes. Still angry and still hurt. And you shouldn't be, not after all this time. I don't think you've buried that man of yours.'

'Oh, yes, I have,' Jessie carolled, 'long ago.' Her tone signalled the end of that line of conversation.

Before anyone could say anything else she turned to face Naomi and joined in with the others as they finished the last line of the song – 'smile.'

If anyone had told Jessie that, at that very moment, in a squalid, silent room just ten minutes' walk away, huddled before a Primus stove, with a grey, moth-eaten blanket draped across his shoulders, was her husband Tom, a lonely, sorry man, she would have laughed in their face. But she would have been wrong to do so. A solitary man now, Tom Smith was weighing his options as he had done on many nights before, with Jessie in the forefront of his mind.

'Well, I can't help thinking he's not out of your heart, Jess,' said Edie, and then, with a different expression on her face, 'I just wish my Harry was here to see this. He thought the world of Naomi and he loved it when she sang.'

'Well, if I'm really honest,' said Jessie, preoccupied, 'even though I don't love Tom any more, I wish he 'adn't gone off like that.'

Edie pulled a face, saying, 'You don't think it could be the time of year by any chance, when the foolish regret their mistakes?'

'No,' said Jessie. 'Not me. I've no regrets nagging at me. Max is a wonderful father to the kids – they think a lot of 'im.'

All the while that Jessie was talking about Tom and believing him still to be leading the life of a rich man, he was filling his empty stomach with a double portion of chips wrapped in newspaper, hoping that boredom would lead to exhaustion, so that by the time his head hit the pillow on his camp bed he would fall asleep and his mind would stop flying back to his wife and children.

Normally, at this time of night, he went on his regular long walk but this evening he had stayed inside, preferring solitude to the constant reminder everywhere of Christmas Eve, a time when families were together. Inside the cheerless room he pretended that this was just another winter's night. Staring into the low flames of the Primus stove, he made a promise. A promise that he would keep. That on New Year's Eve he would go home. Home to his Mum and Dad.

4

New Year's Eve

Arriving in Grant Street in a clapped-out 1930s delivery van Jessie's long-lost husband pulled up to the sound of banging from the exhaust pipe. This was not how Tom had planned his homecoming but, to his way of thinking, life had dealt him a mean hand and it wasn't his fault that he was between the low and good life. Lady Luck waited at the end of the street, was the thought in the forefront of his mind, and this van, which he had picked up for nothing on wasteland because it had lost two wheels had been a present from Lady Luck herself. The few pounds he had earned serving behind a bar in a pub in Wapping had allowed him to buy two second-hand wheels. At last he was on the up, looking forward to getting his life back together again and with no more thoughts of ending it all.

Settled back into his old territory and his new situation, Tom now felt sure the tide was about to turn. This was something he had told himself over and over when he talked to his reflection in the cracked mirror propped against a wall in his dingy room above the breakfast café next door to Trew and Short's, the tripe shop in Bethnal Green.

With a roll-up in the corner of his mouth, he slammed the door of his van and stared at his parents' house, hoping that the door would not be closed in his face. Or, worse, that they had moved on. Nothing about the place seemed familiar. The front door and window-frames had been painted light blue and he didn't recognise the curtains at the windows. His mother, Emmie, had not been one to throw anything away. But, then, as he counted the years since he had stormed away from his family, he chuckled at his stupidity. Even *his* mum wouldn't have kept soft furnishings that long. Tom had walked out on his family on Christmas Eve 1945. Seven years ago.

Unable to look at the house next door, which his late brother Johnny had once owned, and the one further along that he and Jessie had lost. They had purchased it for next to nothing before the war. He stepped forward and gave two hearty knocks on the door of his parents' house and hoped that it would be his mum or dad who answered, not a stranger, and especially not a foreigner fresh from overseas. At the sound of the bolt being drawn back his stomach churned. It was a sound he had not heard in a very long time.

It was Charlie, his dad, who opened the door to him and who stood there in shocked silence, peering at him as if he were looking into the face of a ghost. Charlie, now turned sixty, was wearing his best suit, shirt and tie and seemed quite the elderly gentleman.

From the look of his cheeks, which had always been a high colour, and his clear blue eyes, he had given up the whisky.

'All right, Dad?' said Tom, as if he hadn't been gone a week.

'Stone me!' gasped Charlie, and then, 'I thought you was dead.'

'Thanks. No, it's me, in the flesh and blood. Well? You gonna leave me standing 'ere like a door-to-door salesman for all the neighbours to see?'

'Course not, son. No. Course not.' Charlie stood aside, dazed, and nodded for his son to go through. His son, who had always been proud of the way he presented himself, always smart. Now, although clean-shaven, he had the look of a fallen man. The suit he was wearing had no creases in the trousers and it was a touch on the big side. Underneath the worn jacket he was wearing a thick hand-knitted jumper, which had seen better days. Slowly pushing the door shut, Charlie spotted the old banger parked at the kerb. 'I s'pose that was you making all that bloody racket?' he said, trying his utmost to sound casual and at ease. In truth, seeing his son out of the blue and in this light had truly shocked him.

'It needs a service, that's all. Good as gold, that van is. I wouldn't trade it in for the world. Mum about, is she?'

'She is. But let me go first. I don't want you giving her an 'eart-attack.'

'Pretend I'm just back from fighting for me country,'

said Tom, a touch sarcastic, as he stood aside to let Charlie pass. 'Then you can gimme a hero's welcome agen, can't yer?'

Over his shoulder, Charlie shot his son a black look. 'Still got the gift of the gab, then?' he said, knowing that Emmie would be listening by now to find out who he was letting into their house. He was trying to pave the way. Soften the blow. She had been pining for her son for years but recently the pain she had been harbouring had turned to anger. Many times she had said, 'It wasn't enough that I lost my eldest son during the war and my youngest returned a shadow of himself, oh, no. The one who came through without a scar 'as to walk out on us, 'is wife and 'is kids.'

Charlie was right: Emmie had been listening, and now she was lowering herself into her old feather-cushioned armchair, her mind blank and her heart thumping. So many times she had wished for this moment and now all she wanted was to be in her armchair so that if she passed out she would not crumple to the ground. Bracing herself, she stared at the open doorway, expecting Tom to walk in looking every bit the millionaire. She had believed him to be one since the day her youngest son, Stanley, had returned from a visit to Suffolk, where he had discovered that his brother had been living the life of Riley. Now, seeing him down-at-heel like this swept away all the anger that had turned her heart against him. She held a trembling hand to her gaping mouth and could not speak. Her son, her Tom, had returned a broken man.

'Hello, Mum,' said Tom, forcing a smile while his face showed grief. 'You look all right,' he said, 'younger than ever.'

'Do I?' whispered Emmie, trying to take this in.

'What's it to be, then, son?' said Charlie, clearing his throat.

'Wouldn't mind a cup of Camp coffee with a drop of whisky in it, Dad.'

'We don't keep whisky in the 'ouse no more,' said Charlie. 'I've got some sherry and a bottle of Green's ginger wine.'

'Ginger wine,' echoed Tom, discreetly placing a hand on his open jacket to hide two missing buttons. 'That takes me back. A glass of that and a cup of coffee'd be great.'

'Do you want the coffee made wiv milk?' Without realising it Charlie was treating Tom like a guest instead of one of the family.

'No. Just a drop'll do.' Tom's eyes were on his mother, whom he had missed so badly and who he still loved more than he could express right then. 'What about you, Mum?' he said. 'I s'pect you need a strong drink. You look as if you've seen a ghost.'

'Ginger wine,' said Emmie, giving Charlie a wink. 'A large one.' And then, 'Well, sit down, Tom. You might be a stranger but this is still your home. I turn no son of mine away. No matter how badly he's behaved.'

Sheepish now, Tom lowered himself onto the armchair opposite her and clasped his hands together, his eyes focused on the floor. 'I've not behaved bad,

Mum. Things 'appened, that's all. Things I couldn't stop once they got started.'

'Well, then, you'd best put it all behind yer. And so must we. But I'll say this the once and I'll say no more on the subject. You leave Jessie be. She's settled down wiv Max now and the kids think of 'im as their dad.'

'No, they don't,' said Charlie, coming back into the room with the ginger wine. 'That's where I did put my foot down, son. They call 'im Uncle Max. Not that I approved of that either, but he's gotta be called summink.' He handed them their drinks and then, walking back into the kitchen, said, 'Billy remembers you but Emma-Rose don't. That's the plain truth.'

'Yeah, all right, Dad, I'm not made of stone,' he said, peeling off his jacket to show a shirt that had been slept in beneath his sleeveless jumper. The mention of his family under the wing of another man was too much.

'Well, you're gonna 'ave to convince a few people that you're not made of stone,' said Charlie, his voice fading as he left the room.

'So you've come home at last,' said Emmie, swallowing against the lump in her throat. 'I'm not gonna ask you what you've bin doing, Tom, or where you've been. I don't think my heart could take the sad stories you might have to tell me.'

'What makes you think they'd be sad?' said Tom, only just covering his true feelings. 'I've been all right.'

'Stop telling lies. Spare us that at least.' She raised

her eyes to meet her son's. 'You've a lot of explaining to do, love, but not all at once, eh? Spread it over the next seven years, cos that's how long me and your dad 'ave bin worrying over yer. It's going to take a little while to get over this shock alone. We'd given up on you and that's a fact.'

'I've been moving around, Mum, that's all. I wanted to come back but I thought the door'd be slammed in my face. Then I got to the point where that option was better than never seeing you agen. So . . . here I am.'

Desperate to turn the line of conversation, Emmie pushed a hand through her soft, permed hair and said, 'Stanley'll be in any minute. He's fetching us a bird for tomorrow's dinner. They'll all be 'ere by eleven in the morning. Spending New Year's Day with us, him, Dolly and the kids.'

'Kids,' said Tom. 'How many 'ave they got, then?' He peered into her face as he slipped his braces over his shoulders. 'Mum? You all right?'

'Yes. I heard what you said, Tom, but slow down a bit. Don't rush questions at me. I'm still shaken at seeing you after all this time.'

'All right, all right. I'm sorry. I was just trying to – anyway, it don't matter. Take your time.' Tom could see just how much his mother had aged in seven years.

A few moments passed before Emmie spoke again. She sipped her drink, then said, 'Four children. The youngest are twins. Grace and John. Then there's Hannah who's eight and Annie who's six.' Still Emmie could hardly bear to look at Tom – who, to her mind, was on the edge.

Throwing back his head and laughing somewhat falsely, Tom said, 'Who'd 'ave thought it? Stanley's got his arms full, then. I'm glad he called one of them Hannah. That was nice. I s'pose it was Jessie's idea to call her after her twin?'

'Arm,' said Emmie, dabbing the corner of her mouth with a handkerchief. 'Surely you 'aven't forgotten that? Your brother lost an arm in the war, let's not forget.'

'Course I 'aven't forgot. He's my brother, ain't he? As if I'd forget that. It was a turn of phrase, Mum, that's all. And why wouldn't he name one of his kids after Jessie's twin sister? It stands to reason he would do.' Resting his head back, he stared at the ceiling. 'If you're gonna pick me up on everyfing I'll go, once I've drunk my coffee.'

'No, you won't,' snapped Charlie, returning with the small drinks tray. 'You're going nowhere 'till you've told us where you've bin all this time.' He placed the tray on a small table, dropped down on to the settee and pulled his pipe from his inside pocket. 'We'll be going out for a drink with Stanley once 'e gets 'ere so spit it out now and be done with it.'

'No. I've put all that behind me. I'm back now and I'm gonna settle down. Try and get back into the building and decorating trade. I *need* to put it all behind me.'

'Well, you might be able to, son, but I can't. Just

give me a run-down. Why you walked out on Jessie and the kids'll do for a start.'

'So she could do what she wanted. Move in with Max. And I wasn't far wrong, was I? Then circumstances took over . . . the way they do. Stanley must 'ave told you about High House and the life I was leading in Suffolk – the life of a millionaire. I loved every minute of it. Until Jessie interfered and ruined it all.'

'You might well 'ave been living the life of a millionaire, Tom, but it wasn't your fortune you was spending,' said Emmie. 'No doubt you've served your time for it. And so 'ave we. How d'yer think we felt not knowing if you was in prison or what you might be going through?'

'I got two years' remission, Mum, so I only served two years out of the four I was sentenced for good conduct. And prison was easier than war service. The bloke whose inheritance I was spending never wanted it anyway. He had as much as he needed. And he 'ad no family to pass it on to.' Then, with a smile to cover his shame, he said, 'He used to come and visit me. Had a screw loose but there wasn't any flies on 'im. We got on all right. He sold High House in the end and gave the proceeds to a children's home. He still lives in style in his place in the West End. He's got a girlfriend now as well.' He was smiling but Emmie was no fool: she knew he was bottling his emotions. 'Jessie's sister Dolly could write a book about it,' he said. 'She could make it a bestseller. I s'pose she's still scribbling?'

'She is, and I dare say she could,' said Emmie, 'I dare say she could.'

'What about when you got out?' asked Charlie, more intrigued by the story than he would let on. 'Did the barmy millionaire see you all right?'

'No. Said I could stop wiv 'im whenever I wanted, though, and stay as long as I liked but not one penny would cross palms. Tormenting bastard was loving it. I stopped for a week and lived like a king again but with 'im calling all the shots. I can go and see 'im whenever I want but I don't want. Enough's enough.'

'Maybe he'll will it all to you one day,' said Emmie, with a touch of bitter humour.

'It wouldn't surprise me. It'd be one up on his brother who dumped it on me in the first place before he chucked 'imself in front of a train.'

This was all too much for Emmie. All she really wanted was to hold her Tom close, pat his back and comfort him. For comfort was why he had come home. His need for his family had finally overcome his pride. But she had to contain herself, give him time – and give her and Charlie time to get used to this as well. They had all but given up hope of ever seeing him again.

'What d'yer mean, dumped it on yer?' Charlie again. He was busting to know more. And his wish was soon granted.

Leaning back Tom stared out at nothing as the scene in the train on which he had been travelling on his return from the army seven years ago flooded back. He told of the crackpot who sat opposite him in the carriage and how he had taken pity on him. Charlie was all ears as the sad story unfolded. The story that Tom was only too happy to get off his chest and one that did not interest Emmie in the least. But listen to it she was going to have to. The last thing she wanted was to be reminded of that time.

Leaving the forces for Civvy Street after the war had been a let-down not only for Tom but for thousands of other British troops. The sight of a bombed-out Britain where familiar streets were filled with rubble and debris had been shocking. It was soon apparent that although Britain had won the war she had suffered massive destruction.

Sitting opposite Tom on the train from Northampton, the final part of his journey home to London in 1945, was a stranger who had intrigued him. Sharing a packet of ten Woodbines with the man, who had obviously suffered shell-shock and was not fully recovered, Tom had done his best to reassure him that things could only get better. But the stranger had had a plan when he stepped on to the train. A very tight plan. Everything he had owned was in his kit-bag: deeds to and addresses of grand properties, details of his huge bank account and, more touchingly, his shaving implements and hairbrush.

The kit-bag had been resting on the luggage rack above Tom's head and the stranger had intended to leave it for some lucky and wily character to find. By a stroke of luck, good or bad, Tom had been that man. When the train had stopped at King's Cross station, Tom had hooked the stranger's kit-bag over his shoulder, believing that this would encourage the man to follow him. Instead a spine-chilling scream filled the carriage, bringing silence and a look of horror to the faces of the other passengers. His travelling companion, who had been in one of the worst prisoner-of-war camps, had jumped in front of another train. Too shocked to take in what had happened, Tom had walked away in a daze, with the kit-bag still on his shoulder.

Here, Tom paused for a breather. He looked into his dad's face. 'If I'd known then what I know now I would 'ave tossed that bag over a bridge. That artful sod knew what he was doing. Giving someone a fortune that they couldn't handle.'

'Well, it's a pity you never shared the fortune wiv Jessie and the kids,' said Emmie, seemingly untouched by his tale. 'It would be a different story now if you had've done.'

'Oh . . . and you fink I don't know that?'

'It's all water under the bridge,' said Charlie, warding off a row. 'None of us can think straight all the time.'

'That's true, Dad,' said Tom, and slipped back into the past again, 'I got too hot under the collar when our Stanley told me he saw Jessie having a drink with Max Cohen in the Beggars. Well, I exploded. That's love and jealousy for yer. Worse than having the plague, I reckon. She just couldn't keep away from 'im, though, could she?'

'She met him for one reason only, Tom,' said Emmie, 'which she tried to tell you at the time but, oh, no, you wouldn't listen. Too bleedin' proud! Now look where it's got you. You've lost the woman you loved and your kids!'

'All right, Emmie,' snapped Charlie. 'That's enough. He's back and that's the important thing.' Charlie turned to Tom. 'I'm pleased to see you, son, and so is your mother. She ain't changed, that's the trouble. Still wants to run all of our lives.'

'No,' murmured Tom, hanging his head in shame. 'Mum's right and I was wrong. I was on a short fuse, I s'pose.' He pushed a hand across his face and let out a deep sigh. 'How are the kids?'

'They're all right,' said Emmie, in a tender tone. 'You can sleep in their room. It's—'

'What d'yer mean? Their room?' A look of hope had come into Tom's eyes.

'They stop over for a weekend now and then and a bit longer during school 'olidays.'

Tom took out a comb and drew it through his hair. 'You're still the best.' He smiled joyously. 'That means I can see 'em now and then without Max creeping about in the shadows.'

'Only if Jessie says so you can,' warned Emmie, 'and if she does you're gonna 'ave to take your time. You can't just come barging in and expect them to open their arms to yer. You should know that.'

'Take my time,' he said, 'Jesus Christ, I've got enough of that. More time on my 'ands than I want.' He sucked his bottom lip. 'I never knew what the word lonely meant till I came out of the nick. I can't take it. I can't take the silence any more. No one to talk to.' He drew a deep breath. 'I'll be all right.

Murat the Turk knows someone who needs a van driver.'

'Murat the Turk!' laughed Charlie. 'It's bin a while since I 'eard 'is name mentioned. Don't tell me he's still got that grubby little barber shop?'

'Yeah,' said Tom. 'He's still there. He's slapped a bit of distemper on the walls, though, so it's not as dark as it was.' Leaning back in his chair, Tom stroked his cheek. 'I kept telling you to go in, Dad. You won't get a closer shave anywhere.'

'Leave off. Singes off the last of the bristles, don't he? Nah. Not me. I'll stick wiv me own barber, fanks. A bob for a short back and sides and a cup of tea. Can't moan at that.'

Tom yawned, and flapped a hand at his old dad. 'Stuck in a rut same as ever, eh?'

'I should say so.' Charlie glanced from his son, who looked as if he needed a square meal and a good sleep, to Emmie. 'Shall we put 'im to bed or feed 'im first?'

'I'm all right, Dad. I'll just doze in this chair, if that's all right.'

'Course it's all right . . .' said Emmie, her words trailing away as she realised that Tom was already drifting off. 'He's exhausted, Charlie.' No sooner said than Tom was snoring, out for the count.

'Silly bastard,' said Charlie. 'Look at him. Dead to the world. I'm glad he came home, though.'

'You'd be a sorry father if you weren't,' said Emmie, and then, 'I don't know how Stanley's gonna react when he gets 'ere.'

'We'll just 'ave to leave the pair of 'em to it. It wasn't a good parting, Em, so don't you go defending Tom too much and upset our Stanley.'

Turning in his chair Tom put a small cushion under his head. 'Don't let 'er know I'm back till I've sorted meself,' he mumbled.

'It couldn't 'ave bin easy for 'im . . . walking down this street again,' Charlie whispered.

'No, I dare say it wasn't. And neither must it 'ave bin easy when he made that journey back home all them years ago. Silly sod 'ad bin in the punishment block then as well, and for what? Taking a bit of time off during the war—'

'He deserted on and off, Emmie, and he knew what the consequences would be. But all that aside, yes, it must 'ave bin hard for 'im. Coming back to Civvy Street to find that the place where he grew up 'ad bin given a good blasting.'

Charlie could not have said a truer word. The walk home to Jessie and his family after he had been demobbed *had* been difficult for Tom, as it had for thousands of other men. Once he had arrived in Grant Street on that memorable day he had pushed all that he had seen on his way home from his mind. He had passed through the back-streets where his friends had lived to see house after house bombed out and no more than a heap of rubble and bricks.

When he arrived at the front door of this very house, after his release from detention for desertion in the early part of the war, Tom had been horrified to find that his five-year-old son Billy had not believed

Tom was his dad. The trouble was that Tom had not looked like a hero returning from a battle won. He had lost weight, was pale and drawn and, worst of all as far as his little boy had been concerned, couldn't have been a soldier because he hadn't had a machine-gun slung over his shoulder and wasn't in uniform.

To top it all, his and Jessie's house had suffered severe damage. It wasn't too long, however, before Tom had found them a rented place to live. From then on things had gone well. Jessie and Tom had been together again and very much in love, with their adorable little Emma-Rose and Billy. Then there had been the first Christmas Day after the war and another crashing blow. Tom, his old short temper resurfacing, had ordered Jessie into his mother's sitting room, a thunderous expression on his face. Earlier that month, Tom's brother Stanley had seen Jessie with Max in the Blind Beggars and, with a few drinks down him, had joked about it to Tom. Then, inside this very living room Tom had interrogated his wife, demanding to know if Stanley *had* seen her kissing Max on the corner of the Mile End Gate, then holding his hand in the pub.

Try as she might to explain the innocence of it all, Tom had refused to listen. He had always seen Max as a threat so it was no surprise that a terrible row broke out. He had accused Jessie of sleeping with Max and called her the worst of names.

Later that evening, in a temper and intent on walking out of Jessie's life, he had reached under his bed for his suitcase and dragged out the kit-bag belonging to the man who had jumped off the train. On opening it he had found the files and envelopes, which had been marked *Bank*; *Personal Identity*; *Family History*; *Legal*; *Properties – Grafton Way; High House*. There had also been a bunch of keys and, at the bottom, a sponge-bag.

He had thrown some clothes into a suitcase with the contents of the kit-bag and made his way on foot to the West End and the tall Regency house in Grafton Way off Fitzroy Square, which, as he had suspected, was in darkness and uninhabited. Inside this grand house he had glimpsed a new life, which was his for the taking: ornate crystal chandeliers, Persian rugs on marble inlay floors and ornately framed oil paintings could all be his.

He had gone from one grand room to another, looking in wardrobes and chests until he had found more papers, diaries and vital information that had led him to realise he could take on the dead man's identity and live like a king. From what he was able to tell at that time, the man who had jumped off the train had not one living relative. But Tom had been wrong, as he was to learn not long after he had assumed the life of a millionaire.

He had practised Archibald John Thomas's signature, then paid a visit to the other grand property in the Suffolk village, hoping that High House would be as thick with dust as the London house. It had been, and for a while Tom Smith *had* lived the life of a millionaire with neither guilt nor shame. To his mind, at that time, no-one would have walked away from that fateful opportunity of a lifetime.

'What do we do, then, Charlie?' whispered Emmie, so as not to wake Tom. 'Do we let Jessie know he's back or leave it?'

'It's not for us to do anyfing. Let Tom make up 'is own mind.'

'But we can't keep it a secret. It wouldn't be right. And, besides, his children should know. You can't argue against that.'

'I'm not arguing, Emmie. I'm telling you. Don't interfere.' Charlie settled into an armchair and lifted his head to meet his wife's worried eyes. 'Just leave it be and let fings take their own course. Tom's not ready yet anyway. He's got to get a bit of self-respect back and the way to do that is find proper work. And the way to *that* is through the building trade and our Stanley. He's doing all right and can carry 'is bruvver for a bit until he picks 'imself up. Till he's back on form.'

'Stanley might not want to, Charlie. And you can't blame 'im. Besides, Tom said that Murat the barber's got a job lined up for 'im.'

'He was telling pork pies to save his face. Murat's all he's got, Emmie. He went straight there and I bet it was more to see a familiar face and 'ave a chat than to get 'is 'air cut. Jobs are hard to come by. How's Murat gonna know of one? Talk sense.'

'Wishful thinking on my part, I s'pose. Wishful thinking.'

'Well, we'll just 'ave to wait and see, Em. All I know is that Jessie should be kept in the dark for now. Tom could up and leave, don't forget. He's done it before . . . more than once. Or 'ave you forgot about all that?'

'No. I've not forgotten it, Charlie.'

Tom stirring and shuffling in the chair silenced them. 'How long she bin living there, then?' he mumbled, half asleep.

'Where?' said Emmie.

'High House. The swings 'ave broke.'

'She's not living there, Tom. She's on a council estate.'

'Not council. High House estate,' he murmured, as he changed position and went back to sleep.

'Poor Tom,' whispered Emmie. 'What happened, Charlie? What went wrong with this son of ours? Look at 'im. Curled up like a baby.'

'He's thirty-four years old and all right,' puffed Charlie. 'Now he's back wiv us, he'll be all right.' Turning away from Emmie's watery eyes, he cleared his throat. 'Stanley'll be 'ere soon. He'll know what to do. He's managed to end up running 'is own little building and decorating business and wiv only one arm, so it's 'im who's the intelligent one in this family. Stanley knows wot's wot, all right.'

'Don't forget Dolly. She's been right behind 'im all the way. Doing his books and that. Pity Jessie couldn't 'ave done the same for Tom and changed a few of 'is spots.'

'Stanley didn't 'ave no spots to change. He's a bit

special that one and I'm not the only one to 'ave said it neither. It takes two to tango. Dolly's a good kid but don't go putting our Jessie down now just cos Tom's run down. It's not 'er fault that fings turned out the way they did.'

'I know that, you silly old fool. No need to remind me.' That said, the sad and confused parents of a son who had reached rock bottom, and whom they loved deeply, sat in silence with only the sound of the clock ticking on the mantel shelf. And as Emmie and Charlie sat waiting for one son while they watched the other twitching and moaning in his sleep each of them was thinking their own thoughts. Why had things turned out this way?

Their eldest son Johnny, killed at Dunkirk, was also in Emmie's mind as she recalled her three boys when they were young, playing football together in the streets. Even though she knew that this was not the time to reminisce or wish the clock could be turned back, she couldn't stop herself. 'Onwards and upwards' had always been Charlie's advice, and Emmie could tell that he was now struggling to follow his own words of wisdom. He was suffering just as much heartache as she over this middle son, who had returned out of the blue with nothing to call his own except a dilapidated old van.

'What do we do about Jessie?' she whispered finally.

'Nothing. It's up to Tom. What we've got to do is wait and see what Stanley's reaction's gonna be. He's not got over the way Tom behaved and I've a feeling he's gonna be unforgiving. If that's the case then Tom's gonna 'ave to lie low in his lodging room till he's back on his feet agen and it's bin proven that he's a changed man.'

'So we're to turn 'im out,' said Emmie. 'That's what you're saying.'

'Don't 'ave to say it. He's not daft. He knows he can't stay 'ere where the kids'll see 'im when they stop over and that. We can put 'im up for a few days. Then he's gotta get on with it.'

'Start over agen, you mean?'

'That's right.' Charlie looked Emmie in the eye. 'And it's no one's fault but 'is own that it's turned out the way it 'as. He's got to change his ways, Em, if he hasn't already. He's caused too much upset in the past, one way and another.'

A short ring on the doorbell brought a sigh of relief from both of them. Charlie rose from his chair to answer it while Emmie took the opportunity to brush a kiss across Tom's sleeping face. Then, bracing herself for Stanley's reaction at seeing his brother in her front room, she stood waiting, shoulders back, ready to defend her son. The son she had once been so close to.

Entering the room, Stanley gave his mum a wink and wished her a happy new year. The expression on her face, however, warned him that all was not well. Charlie, biding time, was hanging back in the doorway, leaving things to take their course.

As he turned slowly around to see his brother asleep in the armchair, Stanley was speechless. He looked from Tom to Emmie, then to Charlie, who had slipped quietly back into the room. 'How long's *he* been here, Dad?'

'Not a full hour.'

Again silence filled the room as all three of them gazed at Tom. 'I don't think we need to keep our voices low,' said Emmie. 'He won't wake up that easily.'

'That old banger out there belongs to *him*, I take it?'

'So he said.'

'What, and you think he might be lying again, then?'

'I don't know, son. But look at 'im. Does he look like he can afford to run a bike let alone a van?'

Shaken at seeing Tom in their family home again and looking pitiful, Stanley sat down on the sofa opposite and sat watching and waiting to see if Tom was really asleep or just pretending. 'Does Jessie know?' he said, lifting his eyes to Charlie.

'No. He wants to get back on his feet agen before he makes contact.'

'That's decent of 'im.'

'Don't be like that, son,' said Charlie, tapping his pipe on the edge of the fireplace. 'You wouldn't kick a dog if it was down, so spare some sympathy for yer own bruvver.'

'Like he spared for Jessie and the kids, you mean?' This sarcasm was deep-rooted and both his parents knew not to challenge their son.

Lifting the shopping-bag that contained the bird for the next day's dinner, Emmie went into the kitchen, lighter at heart. She knew her sons better than they knew themselves. Stanley was pleased to see Tom, whether he realised it or not – he hadn't walked out once he had caught a glimpse of him and that to her was a clear sign of good things to come.

'I s'pose he'll be here for New Year's dinner?' said Stanley, the anger in his voice obvious.

'I'd like to think so, son, but his pride's as strong as ever. He said he's found 'imself a lodging room, but I'm not so sure.'

'Well, there's only one way to find out.' Before Charlie could stop him, Stanley was up and standing over his brother, calling his name. 'Come on, you lazy sod! It's not the middle of the night! Wake yourself!'

Slowly opening his eyes, Tom looked at his brother, mumbled something inaudible and then said, 'Go away, Stanley I'm tired.'

But Stanley would not be done. He pulled the cushion from under Tom's neck and hit him across the head with it. 'Wake up, or I'll chuck cold water over yer!'

Suddenly, and without warning, Tom sat bolt upright, his eyes staring as if he was facing the devil. 'Who's that?'

'Who d'yer think it is? Santa come late?'

'Fuck me,' he murmured, rubbing his eyes, not fully awake. 'What're you doin' 'ere?'

'Where?' said Stanley. 'Where d'yer think you are? Back in the glass 'ouse?'

Pushing both hands into his face Tom spoke in a croaky voice: 'I might 'ave known it'd be you. I was in a lovely sleep there. What d'yer want?'

'You owe me ten bob.'

'Take it out of me wallet. It's in my jacket pocket. Happy new year, you skinny little bastard.'

Unable to stop himself grinning, Stanley looked at Charlie. 'Why'd you open the door to 'im, Dad? Bloody nuisance coming back now. He'll want a leg off the bird and—'

'Well, you know the rules, son.' Charlie chuckled. 'The eldest men get the legs.'

'What're you talking about?' Tom peered from one to the other. 'I'm not an old man . . . am I?'

'Well, as far as I'm concerned,' said Stanley, 'only old men sleep during the day! Now get yourself up off that chair and 'ave a sluice. You've got a lot of explaining to do – down the pub!'

'Fair enough,' yawned Tom. 'Your round, though, not mine. Since you woke me from a nice sleep. And since you need a bit of company. You never did 'ave many mates, did yer?' He hauled himself out of the armchair. 'I just 'ope your money's where your good arm can reach it.'

'It is. And my right foot's where someone's arse can be kicked!'

'You and whose army?' said Tom, making for the door, and then, 'All right if I use the bathroom, Mum?'

'Clean towel in the airing cupboard!' called Emmie, from the kitchen.

'Nice 'aircut,' said Stanley, trying to have the last word. 'Short back and sides . . . just like Dad.'

'Yeah, and it wouldn't do you no 'arm to go and

see Murat the Turk. You look like a woman with that quiff.' Tom ran a hand across his chin. 'Left my face like a baby's bum.'

'I suppose he told you he's living a stone's throw from Jessie? On Barcroft Estate?'

This bit of news did jar. Thrown by it, Tom's smile dissolved. 'No, he never mentioned that. But, then, he wouldn't, would he? Got a heart of soft gold that man, not like some I could mention! But fanks for telling me. I'll bear it in mind.' With that Tom went upstairs and Charlie gave his youngest son a black look.

'What's wrong with that?' said Stanley and then, 'Look, Dad, if you fink I'm gonna tiptoe around 'im cos he's hit rock bottom, I'm not. That's *not* the way! All I said, for Christ's sake, was that Jessie was living on Barcroft Estate! What's his problem?'

'Because she's living there with Max! Starting a new life in a new home with Max!'

'Yeah! And she's bin with Max for years!'

'All right, all right,' said Charlie, 'Forget it.'

'Oh, stop it, you two!' snapped Emmie, wiping her hands on her apron. 'Fetch me back a stout and a bag of crisps. And there'll be no rows when you get back in.' With that, Emmie pushed first Charlie and then Stanley out of the room, saying, 'Put your caps and scarves on, as well as your overcoats.'

Dropping down into her armchair, Emmie waited for the street door to slam shut. After a minute or so of shuffling in the passage she had her wish and could relax back in her chair and run the last half-hour through her mind – every expression on Tom's face, every inflection in his voice, and every word he had said. To her mind he had changed, and not for the worse. Tom had come home.

Breaking the news to Jessie that he was back was going to be the difficult bit. Tom had every right to see his children as far as she was concerned and, knowing Jessie the way she did, Emmie had no doubt that she would be fair to the children and to their father. Handled the wrong way, however, Jessie might take umbrage at her world suddenly being disrupted. This sudden intrusion could be the making or breaking of her family.

'You've made a mess of it, Emmie,' she told herself, as she stared into the small coal fire burning in the grate. 'You've got to take some of the blame for all of this. You must 'ave gone wrong somewhere. Three lovely sons given to yer and now look. One's dead and buried, another's disabled and Tom has the look of a man who wished he was dead. Who would 'ave thought it would turn out like this? May God forgive me if I 'ave been a bad mother and got it all wrong. And may God give me guidance because for sure I don't know what to do next.

'One wish,' she murmured, as her eyes glazed over. 'If I could have one wish that was possible to be granted, it would be that our Jessie wasn't so settled with Max.'

Little did Emmie know that sometimes, when Tom came into Jessie's mind, she wished the selfsame thing. But that was Jessie's best-kept secret. She either hated

Tom Smith or she loved him. She wanted him out of her head but not entirely out of her life. She was still angry, fuming at times, especially on certain days of the month when patience is thin on the ground – but she could not bring herself to file for divorce, even though she knew that her refusal to do so really hurt Max's feelings. She also knew that, in the back of his mind, Max worried that one day he might lose her to Tom again. She had tried to reassure him but in her heart she knew that words cost nothing.

If Jessie were ever to air her true feelings to any-one it would be Edie, who had also, under different circumstances, suffered the loss of a husband with whom she had been deeply in love. And in both cases there was no rational reason or sense to it and soon, very soon, one of them was in for a stormy and dangerous ride.

Like Tom, Harry Birch had been lying low, but for different reasons. The serious crime he had commit-ted might see him imprisoned with a long sentence. Desertion alone was grave enough, without the added crime of having obtained false papers and passport. Since his return to England in October, just a month or so after his wife Edie had moved out of Cotton Street, Harry had been in hiding in a house in Bow with others who had also weakened when faced with the opportunity to live a Utopian lifestyle away from the battlefield.

Having made a spur-of-the-moment decision to catch a glimpse of his wife and daughter, Harry had been shocked to see the house in Cotton Street boarded up. During the years he had been living in a faraway world of fantasy in Turkey it had not occurred to him that the street in which he had once lived might have been bombed or pulled down during the government's rebuilding plan. Ben, who had caught a glimpse of him lurking in the shadows, had taken him under his wing. Then Joey had sheltered him as he had others in the past who had mostly been conscientious objectors or men who were too terrified to go to war and had been labelled cowards.

After the tragedy of the boat capsizing close to the rocky shores of Oludeniz, Harry had been nursed back to health by a lovely young Turkish woman and her family. He had worked as a labourer on farmland for the duration of the war and, once Hitler had been defeated in 1945 and peace reigned, he had secured a position as a guide for wealthy tourists who were obsessed with Turkish history, ancient and modern, in particular Gallipoli and the defence of the Dardanelles in 1915.

Having settled into his work as a guide, Harry soon discovered Turkey to be fascinating and far more in tune with modern times than he had imagined. When he had first landed, injured and bleeding, on the shores of what he had thought to be Paradise, he had found that it was not simply the charming ancient world he had thought it to be when back in England, but a modern one too, with education high on the list. Arabic script had been discarded and replaced with the Latin alphabet, and the emancipation of women had not been merely cosmetic:

they had been encouraged to compete professionally with men.

At first, to Harry's way of seeing things, he had been destined to be thrown upon Turkish soil. He had loved the country and the way of life. But as the years went by he had found himself thinking more and more about England and gradually became homesick for his country of birth. It was more recently when Turkey had become involved in the Korean war, with all the talk between Harry's local Turkish friends on the subject, he had felt it was time for him to return to the green fields of home. When he had been called up in 1938 the first flush of patriotism between fellow soldiers had left him stone cold. He hadn't enjoyed the training and he hadn't wanted to go to war and had hated all talk on the subject. His decision to leave Turkey because of the talk of Korea on everyone's lips and to work his passage home had lodged firmly in his mind. He wanted to return to Britain, even though it would mean spending the rest of his life living under an assumed name.

The small harbour, a memorial to the men who had died there after the boat had been smashed into the rocky shore, had brought not only Cicek, a Turkish girl, but her family and neighbours to the rescue. Their compassion and caring ways had saved lives. Since Turkey was neutral during the Second World War the villagers did not have to hide the men from the enemy, they had simply helped the wounded and dying. During Harry's long convalescence, Cicek had fallen for his charms and was soon in love with him.

The handful of other survivors from the wrecked boat had, like Harry, also taken it upon themselves to lie low, close to beautiful Marmaris, where donkeys and horse-drawn carriages travelled along old tracks and roads. There they laid down new roots, in the place where Lord Nelson had moored and prepared his fleet to attack Napoleon's navy at Abukir in 1798. It was a quiet backwater, visited by sailing ships, a perfect natural harbour in a lovely setting, ringed by pine-clad mountains with a soft sandy beach curving around the bays. It was an idyllic place in which to begin a new life with warm-hearted people.

At the time, and during his convalescence as he lay on his sick-bed, Harry had joked that he had died and gone to heaven where an angel had won his heart. He couldn't imagine anyone blaming him for not leaving that paradisical world to return to face the blitz on the already badly war-damaged London, then having to don his uniform and be sent abroad yet again to risk life and limb.

Now, however, back in the East End, he was regretting the live-for-today stance he had taken. Here, in peacetime England and in the thick of winter the reality of what he had done had sunk in and he could not believe that he had been so gullible as to think that he would be able to simply come home and live under an assumed name. Although London was big and London was busy, it had not proved easy to come back and fit into a slot. Furthermore, he had made enemies when he left Turkey, and word of this had spread across the seas to England. Cicek's brothers and cousins had been shocked and very angry at the way in which he had left her without a trace after all she had done for him, and especially since her family had gone against their religion and turned a blind eye to them living together as lovers. They had taken the risk of losing face with their friends, neighbours and extended family when Harry Birch had come into their world, and deep shame when he had left furtively like a thief in the night. Getting away from Turkey had meant that he had had to arrange false papers without Cicek and her family knowing, but this had not deterred him. His work as a guide had given him the opportunity to make the right contacts.

Stealing away from the small village and the people who had adopted him had been thoroughly planned in secret but the consequences of betraying those who had taken him into their hearts had caught up with him. Wheels had been set in motion to find him and take him back to face the family and the people who he had lived among, and who had put their faith and trust in him. In short, Harry Birch was a marked man, with two options open to him: to go back to Turkey and make his peace with Cicek and her family, or remain in Britain and stay in hiding for fear of his life.

5

New Year's Day

The smell of sizzling bacon drifting into Edie's bedroom – and into her waking dreams of being in a strange house, going from room to room where pieces of her old furniture from Cotton Street had been placed – had brought a passing desire to be back in her old home. At that moment, though, Naomi came in and she returned sharply to the real world. Still only half awake and a touch bemused at seeing her aunt dressed in a bizarre mixture of colours, she yawned, saying, 'I thought you always said that blue and green should never be seen?'

'Indeed – unless, of course, one *distracts* with a tasteful clash of colour. Now then, I am *so* sorry to disturb Madam but . . .' said Naomi, '. . . your breakfast awaits and the kitchen maid would rather it did not *spoil*.'

Pulling herself up, Edie rested back. 'I had such a peculiar dream. Or was it a nightmare?'

'I have no idea but let's not worry over it. By the time you are up and dressed you will have forgotten *most* of it, and fragmented bits of dreams when told to others are a *touch* on the dull side.'

'Well, then, I'll bore you for a change, shall I?' Edie yawned again, enjoying a good stretch.

Behaving as if she had not heard the passing remark, Naomi brushed wisps of hair from Edie's forehead. 'Margaret has deemed fit to turn your eggs so I shouldn't let them keep *too* long or the delicate soft yolks will become something to bounce.'

'It must have been all the drink,' murmured Edie, her dream now slipping away. 'God knows how much I got down me last night. You won't mind if I wear my sunglasses at breakfast, will you? I'm not sure if it's because I'm not used to drinking so much or seeing so many strange colours on one frock.'

'Costume, dear. It is a costume.' Naomi trailed a delicate finger across her breast. 'This is a bolero, and beneath is a matching dress. If you like, I could ask the Turkish woman to copy the design.'

'No, that's all right. It looks more in keeping on you.'

'Than? It looks more in keeping on me *than*?'

'Anyone. No one else could get away with it.'

'Thank you, dear. You are terribly sweet to your old aunt. Now, did you have a lovely time? I do so hope you did. It would more than make up for the fact that I had to face New Year's Eve *alone*.'

'Don't tell lies. Ben came round and you got through a bottle of sherry between you. *And* you cut into today's dinner.'

'I said I had to *face* it alone. Luckily my dear friend Ben came to keep me company. And I cut only *four* slices of cold pork. Your *daughter*, however, took a huge chunk. She and the Italian came home famished from their dance. Fortunately, with my clever carving, I have created enough slices to feed all four of us.'

'Four?' Edie peered at her aunt through bleary eyes. 'There's only three of us.'

'Ben is to be the fourth. He *adores* your little flat, so I invited him for New Year's dinner. That was all right, wasn't it, darling? I didn't do the wrong thing again, did I?'

'No, it's fine. Fine.'

'Would you like me to fetch your *breakfast*? So that you may eat in the peace and quiet? You do look as if you might need a little time to *yourself*.'

'No, it's all right.' Edie curled back under her bed-covers. 'A cup of tea would be nice, though. Then I'll get up for breakfast.'

'But the eggs—'

'I don't care if they go hard! Just put a plate over, mind, to keep them warm. I'm hungry so I'll enjoy it whatever it looks like.'

'Very well, Edie,' said Naomi. 'A cup of tea it is. And an aspirin or two *perhaps*?'

'No. And don't go telling Maggie I've got a hangover.'

'Darling, I wouldn't *dream* of doing such a thing. At *her* age one's mother is *already* an embarrassment, whatever she may or may not do. Never mind if she gets herself *defunct* at the local dance hall.' With her final line delivered exactly right for making an exit, Naomi left her niece believing that she would fume just a little. But she was wrong.

Edie was in fact recalling her wonderful night out at the York Hall. Jessie and Laura had finally got their men to agree to let them go dancing instead of to the local pub for a knees-up, providing they were home for the midnight striking of the church clock. They had arrived at the dance thirty minutes or so after the doors had opened and the floor was packed. The music and atmosphere were wonderful, with couples dancing the slow fox-trot. Following the steps of the more practised partners gliding across the polished wooden floor, the younger and less experienced were watching their feet and trying to learn.

Once they had found a table, ordered and sipped the first of several drinks, Laura was on the dance-floor, thoroughly enjoying herself in a quickstep under a revolving light with an older man who guided her majestically around the other couples.

Shy at first to accept any invitation to dance, Edie had resisted one or two requests. She was happy to be by herself at the table and watch others. She did, however, finally give in to a particularly persistent and charming man called Dennis, in his mid-thirties, who on first appearance reminded her of Harry except that Dennis had black and not auburn hair. It was his smile and his silent refusal to take no for an answer that had broken through her barrier. Once they were on the floor with only a few words passing between them she felt as if they had danced before.

With his strong yet tender grip on her waist and his firm hand in hers they did not put a step wrong and when they danced to 'Here In My Heart' Edie had been completely won over. She hadn't been that close to a man since Harry had kissed her goodbye. Moving together, their bodies almost one, they had glided effortlessly to the music with Dennis quietly singing a line here and there, which had sent shivers down her spine and resurrected something inside. Deep inside. Feelings that had been sleeping for too long. The sound of a solo clarinet was almost too spine-tingling, and with her hips fitted into his as they slowly danced around the floor under romantic soft lighting, she had felt as if she could have simply melted away. Now, in this second flush of heavenly bliss in the comfort and privacy of her own bed, she recalled every second of it, and every second had been magical, even though the voice inside told her once or twice that this was dangerous. Without thinking very much about it, the girls had innocently partnered up for the evening and when they stopped for a breather they had gone with their partners to the bar to join their small group of friends. But then with time flying by, Edie realised that the clock was about to strike the midnight hour and she didn't want to leave even though she had promised Laura she would.

All three of them had been so intoxicated by the romance of the evening that they had stayed for as long as the band played, throwing caution to the wind. The evening had ended at one o'clock. Edie's persistent consort, Dennis, however, was not going to let her off the hook so easily. Once outside he hailed a taxi and opened the door for the ladies to get in. Then, in true gentlemanly style, he had paid the cabby and told Edie that he would call at her home the following Saturday at eight o'clock and they would go for a drink in a little nightclub at Tower Bridge.

Jessie and Laura had teased her all the way home about her dishy date, but as much as they tried they couldn't get anything out of her, except his name. Now, on hearing the rattling of china, Edie blew a kiss into the air and whispered his name again: 'Dennis.'

Naomi returned, sat on the edge of the bed and handed her niece a new pretty pink and white flowered cup with matching saucer. 'Here we are, Edith, a little gift for the New Year. Your very *own* bone china. I was going to fetch you a chocolate biscuit but then decided against. We don't want to spoil your breakfast.'

Looking from the cup of tea in her aunt's delicate hand to her face, Edie's face broke into a smile. 'It's lovely. You can be *so* thoughtful at times.'

'And the sun is shining *too*,' said Naomi, as she turned to the window. 'It's such an *odd* thing. It always seems to be sunny on New Year's morning. Have you not noticed?'

'I've never really thought about it,' said Edie, sipping her tea. 'God, I need this.'

'Did you meet anyone nice, poppet?' Naomi asked. 'Someone to dance with?'

'I might 'ave known there was a reason behind you bringing me this tea. Nosy cow. And, yes, as it just so 'appens, I did find someone to waltz with,' she said and then winked at her aunt. 'You would 'ave been proud of me.'

'And was he *handsome*?'

'Very. Like Tony Curtis.'

'Well, I *suppose* that will do. I had someone more like Al Martino in mind. The American crooner and swooner who—'

'I know who he is and I know why you're saying it. His record, "Here In My Heart" got to number one in the charts. We danced to it.'

'Actually, I was thinking more of "Spanish Eyes". A more romantic song one would be hard pushed to find, *these* days, but of course romance isn't everything. Harry had a good head on his shoulders and I suppose you could say he was good-looking.'

'He was very handsome but he's dead, Aunt Naomi, and I've got to get on with my life.'

'My thoughts entirely, Edie darling. I was merely probing a nerve. Testing, as it were. Better late than never is all I have to say. Of course, there is no need whatsoever to keep both legs in one stocking when you next see your lover but please do not go losing your heart to this young man. You are very beautiful and there will be plenty of suitors now that you are ready to come out.'

'I'm only goin' on a date. Take in a show or something,' murmured Edie, a touch of guilt in her voice. 'Is Maggie dressed yet?'

'She is not, and I think I can say I have never seen her glowing *quite* as much as she is this morning. Of course, we *could* put it down to love and the Italian boy—'

'His name's Tony.'

'*Or* to her New Year's Day gift. Once you are up

from your bed you will see *why* I was so bent on sleeping on the couch instead of in Margaret's bed. My good friend Benjamin went home and then fetched it back on his wheelbarrow while your daughter was at her little nightclub—'

'Dance hall, not nightclub.'

'Whatever, dear. But *as* I was saying, she is in raptures over the gift, which really is quite lovely to see since it's more of a *family* presentation. Something we may *all* enjoy.'

The look of relish on Naomi's face was better than any gift. 'Well, go on then, Aunt. Spit it out. What 'ave you bought for her?'

Wishing to make the very most of this, Naomi took a long, slow breath and pushed back her shoulders. 'Had it not been for *Benjamin*, of course—'

'Ben? What's he got to do with it?'

'Darling, he's been *hiding* it for me! He keeps more than one secret actually. We have a great deal to thank him for. Him and *young* Joey, the *elder* of the two. And yet his only reward was a simple night in with an old woman – and a modest bottle of sherry. We owe him so much.'

'Do we?'

'Yes, dear, but please do not quiz me as to why.'

'In other words you want me to?'

'On this occasion, *yes* and *no*. Now, then,' said Naomi, with a glint in her eye as she tipped her head to one side, 'do you not wish to know what the family gift is?'

'Go on, then. What is it this time? A kitten for

Maggie, I s'pose. We're not meant to keep pets, you know.'

'Which is *why* I adopted her rabbit. You have two more guesses.'

'A bird in a cage?'

'*One* more guess.'

'A new Monopoly set?'

'No. There is nothing wrong with a faded board and jaded pieces. So you wish me to *tell* you what it is, do you?'

'You bloody well know I do. Come on. What 'ave you and Ben been up to?'

'Darling . . . that is a *very* personal question. But I will say that I let him go no further than a passionate kiss and a little squeeze.'

'God, get on with it.'

'The gift?'

'Well, go on, then!'

'A twelve-inch—'

'No. Stop right there! It's New Year's Day! Stop being crude!'

'Indeed it is a brand new day. And on this bright fresh start to the year, in your sitting room—'

'*Front* room.'

'Very well, dear, if we must be lower working class – in your *front* room, on your circular coffee table, there now sits a twelve-inch television set.'

Stunned, Edie stared at her aunt as tears welled in her eyes. 'Tell me you're joking,' she said.

'Indeed I am not. *Twelve*-inch, mind, not *nine*. Tell *that* to your neighbours.'

'Naomi, you can't possibly afford to buy a television!'

'Well, it would seem that I *can* . . . and I have.'

'But you said you couldn't afford the rent—'

'Did I say that?'

'Yes, you did.'

'Well, then, I must have been practising on you before I went to the authorities. It obviously worked if you believed me so it is *you* I have to thank for the reduction I managed to *squeeze* out of them.'

'But that still wouldn't pay for a twelve-inch set. Not even one of the small old-fashioned ones. Did you get it on the never-never?'

'Gracious, no. I do have a *little* put by for my old age. I also made friends with a terribly nice young man at Laura Jackson's little *soirée*. I paid at the most half the price I would have been charged in a shop. We couldn't have chosen a better place to move to than this *lovely* estate.'

Chuckling, Edie said, 'I don't know how you get away with it. You weren't in Laura's flat for five minutes before you found out who the fence was.'

'Oh, darling, I wouldn't say he was a fence – a touch wooden, perhaps . . . but what does it matter when one is cutting a good deal?'

Edie put down her cup and saucer. 'If Maggie heard you going on about buying stolen goods . . .' Then, swinging her legs off the bed, she smiled. 'Come on, show me this television set. I still don't believe you.'

Edie found Maggie in the living room in her pyjamas, curled up in Naomi's bedding, transfixed. She was staring at the blank screen and tears were rolling down her cheeks.

'So it's true!' beamed Edie. 'She really did do it.'

'I know – I can't take it in. I keep thinking I'm gonna wake up any minute and it won't be there.'

'Well, then, Mags, she's achieved her usual goal. Two presents in one.'

'Oh, darling, I'm *so* pleased!' said Naomi, from the doorway. 'At *last* you learn! To give an ordinary gift is quite lovely but to give a *surprise* . . .'

'Is the best thing in the world.' Edie spun round, grabbed Naomi and hugged her. 'And you're the best aunt in the world. The very, very best.'

'I know,' said Naomi, thoroughly enjoying the moment, 'but one does *try* not to be.'

'Now I can watch Andy Pandy,' laughed Maggie, her eyes fixed on the dead screen.

'Well, there we are, then. That's made it all worthwhile. Would that I could have purchased a colour set for you, darling, but America will *always* be years ahead of us . . .'

Gazing at the back of the head of her beloved Maggie, Naomi made a wish: that should Harry ever be welcomed back into this family, and she sincerely hoped not, he would not persuade Edie to go with him to some God-forsaken part of Britain so that he could live under an assumed name without fear of being recognised. Snapping herself out of that mode of thought so as not to bring herself down, she said, 'There is one tiny condition with regard to your present.'

'Oh, right . . .' said Edie, 'What's the catch?'

'That you find it in your heart to occasionally invite that poor woman who sings in the sink to come in and watch with you.'

'I'd rather not have the set. You can take it back,' said Maggie, her expression dead-pan.

'Nao, you can't mean that?' said Edie, flabber-gasted.

'Actually, no, it was meant to be a jest. How-ever—'

'No!' said Maggie, desperate to end it. 'She scares me. Or at least all the talk of 'er does. Someone said she's a witch and eats rats if she can catch 'em.'

'Maggie!' snapped Edie, shuddering at the thought.

'Just a suggestion, Margaret, that's all. A little com-passion goes rather a long way.'

'Well, go up and make friends wiv 'er, then. And enjoy a mouse sandwich and a glass of—'

'That's enough, Maggie!' said Edie, the hairs on the back of her neck beginning to stand up.

'What a good idea, Mags!' said Naomi. 'Yes, I shall befriend her. She's probably a very lonely person who needs compassion, not ridicule. And now I shall love and leave you.' She was satisfied now that her present had been a very worthwhile investment *and* that she had sown a seed for the woman who lived on the top floor who was, to her mind, not so many miles from herself. To sit in a sink and sing, thereby jolting the so-called normal people, was brave and wonderful. If, on the other hand, the poor soul *was* completely out of her head, she needed a bit of neighbourly affection.

'I thought you was staying for dinner?' said Maggie.

'I shall return in time, fear not, and no doubt as hungry as a horse. A plate over mine should I be late, would be appreciated. Left on steam, naturally. And it would be especially nice if I may sit and eat it off a tray in front of your television set. It's what they do in America.'

'Going round Ben's, are you?' said Edie, winking at her aunt. 'I hope he's got cataracts with you in that frock.'

'Costume. And, actually, no, on this occasion I am not visiting my friend, Benjamin. I am going to pay a visit to another very old friend of mine. Harriet.'

'God. There's a name from the past. I haven't heard you mention 'er for ages.'

'Which is exactly why I have chosen today to pay her a visit. This is a time when old friends are meant to get together, is it not?'

'Of course it is,' said Edie, slipping her arms round Naomi and giving her another hug. 'And I'm glad you and Ben are getting together again.'

'Darling, we are, and have always been, good friends. No more.'

'Stop fibbing. You might 'ave forgotten the stories you told me when I was Maggie's age, about your first loves. Ben was in there from what I remember.'

'Was he?'

Naomi's wonderful expression of innocence caused Edie to smile. 'Yes, he was, and I think it's lovely that you're . . . mates again. There must be something between the pair of you even if it is only a very close friendship. You did take the trouble to go back to see 'im again . . .'

'Yes,' said Naomi, drawing away from her niece, 'that is perfectly true. On the other hand, I am also about to visit another very old friend whom I have not seen in a while. I do try to keep in touch with all of my chums, actually.' With that she turned away, saying, 'It might do you good to take a leaf out of my book. As a child and later, before you met Harry, you were quite popular from what I remember. Girlfriends were always knocking on your mother's door when you were a child.' Then, giving Edie something else to think about, as she left the flat she added, 'Friends should never be left out to dry, forgotten. You never know when you might need each other.'

Naomi's spur-of-the-moment idea on Boxing Day to call in on Ben to commend him for sticking to his guns and returning to his old home had turned out to be startling in more ways than one. He had confessed that her nephew-in-law was lying low in Joey's house. She had gazed at Ben, speechless. Only when she had been helped on to a chair did she whisper, 'Would you kindly say that again?'

Sorry for Naomi, whom he had always adored, Ben had quietly explained everything, and once she had had a drop of his Irish whiskey and was more herself, he had taken her arm and walked with her to Joey's house along the turning.

The shock of seeing Harry again had been overwhelming and Naomi's immediate reaction had been anger where all three men were concerned. Once she had listened to Joey though, about how several men had taken refuge at his house, her respect for the quiet, brave man had increased. This true gentleman who had brought no attention to himself in all the time she had known him had all the while been one of the silent heroes.

Harry, on the other hand, she saw in a different light entirely. No matter what excuses had been put forward for him by Ben or Joey, she had seen a look in his eyes that had told her the man who had stood before her was in fear of being found out. The expression on his face had lacked feeling and as far as she was concerned Harry was not the man Edie had once worshipped. Either his war-time experiences had changed his personality or his true character had come to the fore in the face of temptation – the temptation having been to cut old family ties and soak up the sun in the arms of a beautiful new woman. Before the war nothing had tested Harry. His life had been on an even keel and day-to-day living pretty much all right. These thoughts had not entirely preoccupied Naomi, but they had been drifting in and out of her mind since that meeting.

Now, on New Year's Day, her feelings with regard to Harry had reached boiling point and the fury she had been harbouring was disturbing her much treasured hours of deep sleep at night. Having had time to get over the shock of finding him alive, fury had

combined with resentment. Questions had been flying
through her mind since Boxing Day and the one that
haunted her was, why had Harry lain low in Turkey in
the first place? He could so easily have made contact
and been returned to a British hospital in England
and then to his family.

That Harry had been involved in a romantic liaison
with the beautiful woman who had nursed him was
not difficult to imagine. But as far as Naomi was
concerned, that was simply a case of love in the eyes
and should have lasted a month or so at most. The
fact that he had stayed away and let Edie believe him
dead was unforgivable and cruel.

Now, with her special present delivered to Edie and
Maggie, she was going to pay someone she could trust
a visit. Someone who would give her advice, for advice
was much needed. Someone of her era to whom she
had been close as a child. Harriet would tell her what
to do in no uncertain terms. Even when they were very
young children Harriet had been far more worldly than
Naomi.

They had met in the winter of 1888 in a Bethnal
Green children's home where Naomi had already
spent six years after her father had fallen ill and
her mother could not afford to feed or clothe her
children. When the high-spirited Harriet came into
her life, Naomi had all but given up hope of ever
escaping from her tormentors, the tall thin woman
in charge of the girls at the home and a grotesque
fat man in charge of the boys, who had abused her as
he had many other children. With her unruly red hair

and defiant blue eyes, Harriet had stirred something in Naomi and the other orphans who had not been so browbeaten as to have given up all hope of escape. Harriet had arrived surly and defiant and had slept just two nights in the home, which was more akin to a workhouse, before she made her escape. Naomi had been lucky enough to have her bedding in the same row as the ragged new girl, and when the gas lights had been down for twenty minutes or so, and with a glow coming in through a small window, she had snaked her way to Harriet's bed and whispered in her ear, 'If you run away let me come wiv yer.'

She could have had no idea of the impact those few words had on Harriet who, with every intention of escaping the place, had believed that none of the other children there had the strength of mind or will-power to do anything other than take what was meted out to them. No time was lost in making a simple plan and that very night, after the exhausted, downtrodden orphans were asleep and their keepers snoring in their beds in a drunken stupor, Naomi had waited with bated breath for her new friend to open the door leading out of the long dark dormitory.

The girl with the ginger hair had not looked back or beckoned. She had told Naomi earlier on that day to follow her: if she wasn't as quick as a fox and as silent as a mouse she would likely be caught and Harriet would go it alone. The tough and surly statement had done the trick. No sooner had Naomi seen movement than she was creeping along towards the door and freedom.

They crept along unlit corridors and quietly unbolted and slipped through the heavy doors, and as soon as they were outside the dour place, the two of them ran as if the devil himself was on their tail, each gripping a thin grey blanket under their arms.

Directly they had arrived in the Old Jago, Bethnal Green, the mumbled greetings from those settling down for the night under ragged coats and covers had been music to their ears. Stopping for a breather, holding their sides and waiting for the cramp-like pain to ease, they had giggled in between sucking in the fresh night air. Where they had escaped to looked no better than where they had come from, but there were no walls fencing them in, no heavy doors and no hostile atmosphere. They had freed themselves from the grip of authority and from worse degradation than would be found in the dark and mysterious streets, which had the reputation of being the filthy bowels of the earth.

Once Harriet had led the petrified Naomi to a decrepit place where market vendors chained and padlocked their stalls and where rats scrounged for decaying vegetables, they had huddled together in a filthy stable where a coalman kept his carthorse. Their blankets over them, they had snuggled into a makeshift bed of hay and fallen into a deep and safe sleep. This was to be their place to rest at night for the following few weeks.

By day the girls had entertained the shoppers in the Bethnal Green and Whitechapel markets, Naomi singing and Harriet dancing in time to the tune. With their bellies fed daily, the girls became stronger and Naomi more used to life on the streets, so that when Harriet upped and left without a by-your-leave, she could fend for herself.

Pleased with the response from her small audiences she had gone further afield to Holborn, Oxford Street and Covent Garden, where she sang and danced outside theatres and music halls until she was finally invited inside to join the chorus in small productions. From then on there was no looking back. Not only had she captivated the audiences, she had captured the hearts of the other performers and musicians. After a few years of living among the avant-garde and bawdy performers when she sang in theatres and music halls, Naomi had blossomed into a self-confident, carefree young singer and actress.

Several years later, while shopping in Whitechapel market, she had come across Harriet and their friendship was rekindled on the spot. They had spent a wonderful hour in a coffee-shop filling each other in on their lives since the Jago. On their departure they made no promises but exchanged addresses and left it at that. There was no need to make a pledge and no desire to live in each other's pockets. But from time to time they got together, telling each other what had happened to them since their last meeting – which had, more often than not, been a few years ago. Today would be no exception. Naomi had not seen her old friend for quite a while.

Passing Riverside Mansions in Wapping she was only a stone's throw from the turning where Harriet now lodged with her daughter and her daughter's family. Shuddering as she passed the forbidding buildings, which had always sent a shiver down her spine, she stepped up her pace. Harriet had loved her two-bedroom flat on the sixth floor, up in the sky, and her husband, Arthur, had decorated every inch of every wall for her. When he passed away, however, heartbroken and lonely, Harriet had moved into her daughter's house for company. And now Naomi could hardly wait to tell her friend that she had also moved and, of all places, on to a council estate, to a one-bedroom apartment especially built for old-aged people.

To turn the tables on her friend and be the one to shock was something that she had always relished and not often been able to do where Harriet was concerned. Striding along the turning, her chin tipped up, she was eager to see her.

'Good God,' said Harriet, as she opened the door. 'What the bleedin 'ell 'ave you done to your face?'

'*Oh?*' said Naomi, tipping her head to one side and brushing the back of her hand across her cheekbone, 'I do hope my fine bone structure has not altered with age? Do you think that *that* is what it might be?'

Standing aside to let her friend in, Harriet rolled her eyes. 'I was talking about the bleedin' makeup. What did yer do? Put it on in the 'alf-light with a trowel?'

'Oh, *darling*,' said Naomi, sweeping along the passage as if she were about to make her entrance on stage, 'it is *so* refreshing to hear a half-truth. I can't tell you how many new friends *and* old insist I have a most enviable natural complexion.'

'A half-truth eh?' sniffed Harriet, in her friend's footsteps. 'You've still got a short memory, then. Wasn't it you who said half-truths are the blackest lies?' Their game of baiting each other was as fresh as it had been on the day they had met.

'Was it?' said Naomi, gracefully slipping down into an armchair by the fire, 'I have always been poetic, dear, I admit, but let's not forget Lord Tennyson. I believe it was *he* who wrote, "That a lie which is *half* a truth is ever the blackest of lies; that a lie which is *all* a lie may be met and fought with *outright*, but a lie which is part a truth is a *harder* matter to fight."'

'Is this a ten-minute fly-in fly-out or are you gonna stop for a cup of tea?'

'Well, I *am* a little peckish.'

'I never said I'd feed yer, but you can 'ave a cheese and pickle sandwich if you want. I'm not gonna cut into our boiled bacon for no one. We're gonna 'ave our New Year's dinner later on in the afternoon – you can stop for that if you want but no falling asleep by the fire.'

'But *why*, Harriet? Why are you not having dinner between one and two? This is New Year's *Day*! Not just *any* old day in the week. And *where* are your daughter and granddaughter? And your *grandson*? Have they walked out on you, darling? They always *said* they would.'

'Course they ain't, silly mare,' said Harriet, going into the scullery. 'Gone to the bloody sales up West!

Went out before light. Right bleedin' mood Iris is gonna be in when she gets 'ome. Can't you stop for dinner?'

'Would that I could.' Naomi peered at the brand new cabinet in the corner of the room, which she presumed housed a radiogram. 'My orders are to be back at Edie's by one thirty sharp. We're having roast pork *cold* for dinner!'

Cackling as she came back into the room, Harriet placed two small glasses on a side table next to the collection of left-over Christmas drink. 'And you wanted it sizzling hot with crunchy crackling.'

'Well, yes, I will admit that I *did*. But there we are. Housewives today take *so* much for granted. Roast pork *cold* when we could have had it *hot*? Would our mothers not turn in their graves at the very thought of it?'

'Do you want sherry or port?' said Harriet, easing herself into the second armchair.

'Oh, sherry, please.' Naomi peeled off her coat and sighed contentedly. 'I do *so* love coming here.'

'And that's why I've not seen 'ide nor 'air of yer for two years or more?'

'Well, you know how it is, Harriet. Time just simply *slips* away. And I *have* moved home after all is said and the dishes done. But, then, you couldn't possibly have known that.'

'Don't you bet on it, smug drawers,' said Harriet, as she poured their drinks to the brim of the glasses. 'Nuffing gets by me. Nuffing.'

'*Really?* And who is the informer? May one ask?'

'Who d'you think?'

'I have absolutely no *idea*.' Naomi sipped her drink and waited, her serene smile back.

'Larry.'

'Larry Simons? Goodness me. I haven't seen Larry for a century.'

'You shouldn't be such a bleedin' snob, then, should yer? If you don't slum you'll stay glum,' she said, with a wink. 'He's living in rooms in that bleedin' old theatre, the Grand Star. Living like a hermit.'

'The one his father purchased in Stratford?'

'That's it. Reckons he'll open it up agen one of these days. Harry stopped there wiv 'im for a week but it never suited 'im. Walked out without a thank-you and went back to Joey as if he was responsible for 'im.'

'But why are they all helping him? Why have they not given him his marching orders – back to his wife and child?'

'It's not that simple.'

'So you have said *many* times. And Larry continues to be the newscaster.'

'Still got a soft spot for 'im, 'ave yer? Well, he's foot-loose and fancy free now so—'

'Don't be absurd, Harriet. This is hardly the time.'

'He's as funny and sharp as ever. So wot's it like, then – your old people's flat?'

'It's absolutely *charming*. I have a brand new kitchen, a *delightful* sitting room, with french windows opening on to the lawn, a fitted bathroom, a bedroom and a dressing room.'

'Well, that's funny,' sniffed Harriet, eyeing her

friend. 'I heard there was only one-bedrooms available.'

'Well, yes, of *course*. Two would be extravagant for someone living alone. But I have converted my *boudoir* to create a dressing room.'

'You've 'ung a bit of curtain up, you mean.'

'A crushed velvet drape . . . and the caretaker's son has fixed pale pink mirrors with lights above.'

'So you can fancy yerself still in the theatre,' said Harriet. 'Well, I take my hat off to yer, Naomi, and I raise my glass. You're as mad as Larry! He lives in the theatre and you live for it. Cheers to the pair of yer!'

'And I raise mine to *you*, my darling. Long may we all live!'

'Too bleedin' right!' grinned Harriet, downing her drink in one.

'So,' said Naomi, resting back in her chair and very much at home now, 'Iris has not remarried, your cherished granddaughter Rosie is to hand, which leaves your wayward grandson – *Tommy*?'

'Who's too bleedin' 'andsome for 'is own good. The ladies still fall at 'is feet. He's never gonna get married while they're prepared to open their legs for 'im. Dirty sod loves it. Still, he treats us well. What d'yer fink of that cabinet, then? Solid Formica, that is. Looks like wood, don't it? Clever wot they can do now. What d'yer fink's inside them sliding doors, then?'

'A radiogram, I *imagine*,' said Naomi. 'Is it?'

'Well, open it and 'ave a look! Brand spanking new,

that is, and only just on the market. Tommy give it to us for a present.'

'You mean he actually went out and *bought* it?'

'I never said that. I said he give it to us. But that's just as good as if he'd paid up front for it. He could 'ave sold it, couldn't he? So it's the same fing in the long run.'

'What a relief. I thought for a *moment* that he might have turned honest and dull. I haven't seen him since I gave him a half-crown for that silver fruit bowl, which I simply *adore*.'

'That's antique, you know. You got a bargain there. Crafty cow. I bet you knew what it was.'

'Of course I *knew* – even though it was almost black with age. He always did have a soft spot for me, did Tommy. Thought I would make a much *nicer* gran than you.'

'So you gonna 'ave a look, then?'

'Well, if I *must*, but I have seen something similar in Gamages of Holborn.' Making the most of the effort of having to rise from her chair, Naomi went to the cabinet and, with grace and charm, slid open the doors to reveal a fourteen-inch television set. Taken back, all she could manage to utter was, 'Oh. What a pity it's so cumbersome.'

'What d'yer mean, "cumbersome"?'

'It does rather *dwarf* the room, don't you think? At least, that's what *I* thought when I chose one for Edith – *her* twelve-inch set was a present to see in the new year.'

'Course it dwarfs the bleedin' room,' said Harriet.

'Ugly great fing. Fank Gawd there are sliding doors to 'ide it!'

'But surely the picture makes up for the *size*?' said Naomi, sorry now that she had been critical.

'No, it don't. On all the bleedin' time it is. At least he nicked me a little wireless set for me bedroom. How am I s'pose to get froo the day wivout me wireless set on? And I'm sure that that fing is wot drew Larry round. Been coming for months, ever since I said we 'ad it. Comes every Saturday now, crafty bugger.'

'Oh, so it wasn't a *Christmas* present?'

'No. Got it in October.'

'How very spoiled you are, my dear. And how *is* Larry?'

'He's all right. Bin 'elping young Joey out wiv them conscientious objector lot,' she said slyly.

'*Still?*' said Naomi, feigning ignorance. 'The war was over seven years since, was it not?'

'That one was, yeah, but they're still sending our boys out to Korea and other God-forsaken places. Besides, not all of the conchies could settle after it was all over. They still get bricks froo their windows even now. And both Larry and Ben know wot that was like from when the Blackshirts were rampant.'

'Larry, Joey and Ben? They have teamed up in order to hide *convicts*? Is *this* what you're saying?'

'Not convicts. You know very well what I'm saying. They've always kept it quiet, though. Well, they would do, wouldn't they? Same as now. There are some fings that not everyone should know.' Once again Harriet looked slyly at Naomi and watched for her reaction.

'And Larry tells you *everything*?'

'Wot are old friends for? If we can't share a secret and that, what hope is there?'

'And you all four shared a secret of which I knew *nothing* until very recently. Boxing Day, in fact. I find that rather hurtful, Harriet. Had I *not*, out of the kindness of my *heart*, gone to visit Ben and Joey on Boxing Day, I should never have known about Harry. You could have spared me this foul play. You could have got word to me *somehow*.'

'Oh, bollocks,' murmured Harriet, 'stop your bloody acting. You're not up West now wiv yer fancy actor friends. I know yer roots, don't forget – where you come from and who got you out of the bleedin' work-house that was under the guise of a children's 'ome.'

'Oh,' murmured Naomi, her feelings still a touch bruised. She avoided her friend's apologetic eyes and stared down at the floor. Then, in a quiet voice, she said, 'That was a *very* long time ago, Harriet.'

'I know it was. I've got stiff joints to remind me.'

'We change because we must, and then it's not easy to go back to what we were.'

'I 'aven't changed.'

'Well, no, but you hadn't the *need*. You were accepted wherever you went and didn't give a toss for those who turned up their noses . . . from what I remember.'

'You could 'ave done the same.'

'No, I don't think I could. I didn't have the *courage* then. But I learned from you and did it my *own* way. We are what we are. But all of that apart, I will say this before I leave you. Beneath the surface *nothing* alters. I am Naomi. I have always been Naomi. If you cannot accept that—'

'Oh, shut up. I wasn't 'aving a go. But fancy saying we was sharing a secret as if we were spies. And 'ow can we tell you everyfing when we never see yer? *We could 'ave spared you?* Wot kind of talk is that? *Rather hurtful?* Do me a favour.'

'Well, you could have come to see me. Ben *knew* where I had moved to. But, no, I had to discover it for *myself* when visiting him on Boxing Day. It was hurtful, *yes*, to find out that Ben and Joey were keeping things from me. And you've confirmed that not *only* did you know about it too but Larry as well. Once upon a time we were all *extremely* close.'

'So you saw Harry, then?'

Raising her eyes to meet her friend's, Naomi pursed her lips. She just managed to get her words out, albeit in a whisper, 'Yes, I saw Harry there. My own dear niece's husband, whom she *believes* to be dead.'

'Well, let 'er go on thinking it, is the advice I would 'ave given once you'd got round to asking. Don't interfere.'

'But Edie has been waiting for *years*! Waiting and hoping that he just might be alive! Saving herself! Hardly *ever* going out! And trying her hardest to make up to Maggie for her not having a father. She's tried to be both mother and father. How *can* I not interfere now that I know?'

'Because wheels are at work. She'll understand if it should all come out into the open and he turns up on her doorstep. You can't rush these things. He'll probably go up north where the rents are cheap and there's work to be had and no one knows his face. Grafters work, true, but beggars can't be choosers.

'And if you really want my opinion I would say let sleeping dogs lie. He's no good to 'er now. It won't just be the law he'll 'ave to hide from. The Turkish family are none too pleased wiv the way he upped and left.'

'Are you saying that Harry committed bigamy out there?'

'No. They knew he was a married man but eventually accepted him into the family for the sake of the young woman. It wasn't easy for 'em and it took a while for their neighbours to accept it. It brought shame on them.'

'You seem to know a lot about it, Harriet,' said Naomi, a tremor in her voice. Gripping her hands together to stop them shaking she managed not to cry. 'As if Edie hasn't been through enough already.'

'Exactly. Which is why the boys are playing their cards close to their chests. Ben asked if I could put Harry up 'ere for a while if the need arose. I'll be honest with yer, Naomi, I said no. That grandson of mine is into crime and we're not talking about boxes of chocolates from Woolworth's. The old Bill would love an opportunity to turn this place over.'

Naomi lifted her head, her chin stuck out. There was a different look in her eyes – of fear. 'Well, then, Harry *must* give himself up.'

'He might 'ave to, if the Turkish family get wind of where he is.'

'Harriet, are you saying that they are *already* in this country *searching* for him? Surely not.'

'Contacts and cousins, Naomi. They're a very close-knit community. They'll want 'im to go back and face the music. If they find 'im and he refuses, he could end up floating down the Thames in bits.'

'Now you go too far. I have worked alongside Turkish people in the theatre and they are the most gentle and warm people you could wish to meet.'

'There are Turks and there are Turks. What if the tables were turned? What if a handsome Turkish soldier did the selfsame thing to a young English country girl? Wouldn't some of the boys we've rubbed shoulders with want to stick the knife in?'

'Point taken,' murmured Naomi, going cold.

'Forget nationalities and religion! We're talking about men and women. Families. Close families. I know what my Tommy'd do if our Rosie was—'

'I did say, "Point taken", Harriet. Let's not bore each other to death over it. Harry must leave London, that is crystal clear. Edie must not have any more trouble on her doorstep. It's hardly fair, after all she's been through.'

'I know,' said Harriet, lowering her eyes. 'And I agree wiv you. He should clear off, one way or another. Edie'll lose 'er widow's pension for a start. Not to mention what the shock of it all will do. I wish Ben 'adn't told you. It's not fair on you.'

'Well, I'm pleased he did. They were all *terribly* embarrassed, I must admit. Harry burst into tears.'

'Crocodile tears, I expect.'

'Actually – I think they probably were. The feeling I picked up was that he was no longer to be trusted.'

'In any case,' said Harriet, topping up their drinks, 'Joey's gonna 'ave to move on. The police 'ave turned a blind eye all these years when he was hiding conscientious objectors and them too terrified to be any use in a war. But not this. They'd be down on 'im like a ton of bricks if it got out.'

'Well, say what you will, but Harry *could* and *should* have come home to his wife and child once the war was ended, never mind after he had been nursed back to health. Edie received the telegram at least a decade ago. It's a disgraceful way to behave, no matter how it's told. And as for Larry and Joey and Ben, I would not give them my *pot* to piss in. They should have turned him away once they had heard his story. It's all bollocks and a disgrace!'

'Atagirl, Nao! That's more like the ragged street urchin of yore that I dragged out of hell and into the gutter!'

'Please don't make fun of me, Harriet. I am *deeply* wounded by all of this. I actually felt sorry for my nephew-in-law when I saw him in Joey's house, but *thankfully* that soon passed.'

Her shoulders pulled back, Naomi drew a deep breath and stilled her slightly trembling voice. Then, smiling serenely, she said, 'He might well have managed to wheedle sympathy from my most treasured friends but I put Edith first. And I shall do anything it takes to keep all of this from her doorstep.'

'So I take it that's a no, then?'

'You take *what* as a no?'

'You won't lend 'im fifty quid to see 'im on 'is way?'

'I would willingly *give* him fifty pounds to get rid of him! I still have my savings from the insurance policy when my husband was killed in battle. And I have my savings and my jewellery. I would give it all up to save Edith and Maggie from the trouble that is brewing. Send Harry out of London, Harriet. You have more than one string to your bow.'

'Meaning?'

'Your son. Get Tommy to arrange his disappearance. Send him to Scotland or Ireland – the Antarctic, for all I care. But he absolutely must *go*! My niece's welfare is at stake! Or I'll see him in prison and be damned! Bollocks to the widow's pension! Edith will manage without it!'

'And what if the Turks get to him first?'

'That, my dear Harriet, is *also* pure cobblers. I have never heard such *tripe*!'

'You think so? Well, heed this, Naomi. The family in question have people living on the estate where you and Edie've moved to. A cousin of the woman Harry lived with as his common-law wife has been over three times already! And now, having seen Edie and recognised her from a photo Harry had left behind with others in Turkey—'

'Harriet, please, do slow down! Which photograph of Edie? And how dare a Turk be carrying a photograph of my niece around with him as if she's to be shot on sight?'

'It was while he was at a little Christmas party in one of the flats—'

'Oh, my *God*,' gasped Naomi, her hand flying to her mouth. 'Oh, *please*, Harriet, *please*, tell me this isn't true. I was *at* the party. I *talked* to the Turkish family. There *was* a cousin there who, according to Edith, looked at her in such a way as to make her go cold.'

'That don't surprise me, and that's why Harry mustn't go anywhere near 'er. I don't think you should go visiting Ben and Joey for a while either. Or come here for that matter.'

'Are you saying I may have been *followed*?'

'I'm not, but it's not that remarkable if you 'ad've bin. Wheels 'ave bin turning for months. But, there, you're bound to be shocked by it all. A week ago you 'ad no idea of any of it.' Harriet patted her friend's knee. 'I think a strong cup of tea is what you need, girl. A strong cup of tea and a five-minute shuteye.'

Naomi dabbed her eyes with her handkerchief. 'Tea, yes, but I hardly think I could sleep with all of this on my mind.'

Smiling to herself, Harriet went into the scullery and lit the gas stove under the kettle. She knew her friend like the back of her hand. Left alone for two minutes and she'd be snoring. Taking one of her notorious cat-naps.

6

By the time Valentine's Day had come round there seemingly had been little to worry about in Scott House, Stepney, the block of flats where Edie had now settled into a comfortable routine. She had been seeing more and more of Jessie for a parley over a cup of tea, which might be about anything to do with their times as children, or their lives when first married and afterwards when each of them had been separated from the men they loved.

Now regularly seeing Dennis, whom she had fallen for on New Year's Eve at the dance, Edie had no idea that her husband was alive and shifting furtively around the East End, going from one hiding-place to another. She continued in her usual routine of going to the dress factory five days a week and did her utmost not to worry over Maggie and the strong developing relationship between her and Tony, the good-looking Italian boy.

Naomi, dropping in whenever she felt like it, had kept a tight lid on the explosive news that Harry Birch had, on the face of it, risen from the dead. She had encouraged her niece to court Dennis, who appeared besotted with her – not just from devotion to her niece's welfare but also because Naomi enjoyed nothing more than house-sitting in front of a coal fire, enjoying fish and chips out of their wrapping paper, while she relished the peace and quiet as she watched the television she had purchased and given to Edie and Maggie. Her presence also prevented the Italian taking advantage of her beloved Maggie. If they chose the one evening when Edie was out to sit cosy round the fire they had Naomi for company. Strangely enough, they had so far avoided it!

Jessie, now Edie's most intimate friend, was enjoying her quiet, pleasant family life, and although she had visited her in-laws with the children each Sunday morning she had no idea that her husband Tom had returned to his roots and was living in the seedy rooms above the tripe shop in Bethnal Green. Jessie's sister Dolly continued to see her, but this blissfully happy mother of three had promised her husband Stanley that she would keep the family secret. She was finding it difficult not to let Jessie know of Tom's return. Her excuse for not paying more frequent visits to Jessie was that the novel she was writing was taking up all of her spare time.

On one of her visits to Jessie, Dolly had met Laura and had found her to be a good listener where her novel set in the hop-fields was concerned. Laura had been going to a hop-farm close to Yalding in Kent since she was first introduced to her husband Jack's family and had taken to it like a duck to water.

This year, because of the move out of her rooms

overlooking the late-Victorian Carlton Square to this estate, Laura had had to give her annual working holiday a miss. She had listened to Dolly's enthusiastic account of the story she was writing, and had encouraged her to go on with it, regardless of what others thought. From then on the two had become friendly and Laura had given her an idea for a sequel to *The Hop Pickers* – she should keep the characters but change the setting to Carlton Square from where she herself had moved.

Laura thought a book about East Enders in the hop-fields of Kent, then another at home around a lovely old tree and shrub-lined square would enlighten those who believed the folk from this part of London were mostly ragged and depressed or villains. Elevated by such encouragement and the idea of a sequel, Dolly, who had been scribbling stories since she was a child, became even more determined not to be put off by rejection letters from publishers. And a new idea had grown in her mind: with the arrival of television, which could only become more popular, she was considering the possibility of writing a dramatised version when she had finished the novel. Then she would have two chances of her work being accepted.

With Laura's support Dolly had been able to shrug off the cynicism of others who believed that no one in their right mind would want to read a book about East End families who chose to live in huts for a month or so, cook over a campfire, and pick hops till their fingers were sore with only one cold-water tap between all forty or fifty families. She knew that Laura looked forward to the ride down to Kent in September and especially the singing with other families as the lorry trundled out of London to the Garden of England when rosy apples, plums and plump green hops would be ripe for the picking.

Content with her work in the offices at Charrington's brewery and enjoying her life in a larger community, Laura still had to cope with her husband Jack's philandering ways while he kept her on a tight rein. On her return from the dance at the York Hall on New Year's Eve, with the faint smell of someone else's cologne on her hair, she had received a good hiding from Jack, and a black eye was the evidence of yet another fight between the volatile couple who both became bitterly jealous when competition drifted into their happy orbit.

The pathetic excuse for her swollen eye had not fooled Naomi, who sometimes enjoyed both Laura and Jessie's company during her special evenings in Edie's flat. Both women, since they had met her at Jessie's Christmas drinks party, had been drawn to Naomi like a moth to the light and an hour spent in her company, either watching *I Love Lucy* or a quiz show, was sometimes a much preferred Saturday-evening treat than trotting off to the local pub with their men. Better than anything was to sit and talk to someone they trusted not to repeat things that ought to be kept private, and Naomi was one such person.

This evening, Naomi had Edie's flat and the television to herself. She was stretched out on the settee, with a bowl of the new Kellogg's sugar-frosted cornflakes watching this week's episode of *I Love Lucy*. It was breaking new ground in television by acknowledging Lucy's pregnancy. Until then they would not show married people sleeping in the same bed! Naomi was in her element, knowing she would not be disturbed. She had told Laura and Jessie to come in after it had finished.

Maggie, wearing the delicate gold earrings Naomi had given her for Christmas looked stunning on this Valentine's evening in her new swagger coat with its fashionable cuffs and collar, and the contrasting red shoes. It had now become natural to her to wear makeup. With her fifteenth birthday between now and Easter she had not long to wait before she would be setting out each morning for work, a young adult. She aspired to be employed as a trainee at a library in Bethnal Green. She had already been for a preliminary interview with a few other hopeful girls from her year at Cephas Street School and had been pleased with the way it had gone, but still she had worried that she might not get through to the next stage. Of the five girls interviewed, two had been selected to complete basic exam papers – Maggie and one other who she thought looked more like a librarian than herself. She talked the worry out of herself by relating the tale of the interview over and over to Edie and Jessie, who she now saw as her mother's friend, not merely a neighbour. It was in a more confident and relaxed mood that she left with Tony for a Valentine's dance at the local Repton Youth Club. Her mother had gone with Dennis to the West End to see a show.

All in all, on this day for lovers, things seemed to be going swimmingly, as far as Naomi could see, and she was blissfully content to have time alone curled on the sofa in front of the television by the fire. Ben, in his own sweet way, had told her he would take her to the local pub if she wanted to go out but she had turned him down with a light kiss on his cheek.

Ben was back in her everyday world and Naomi found that she looked forward to seeing him. Following her instinct, she was keeping things on familiar terms and no more: she did not want to spoil a treasured friendship. She had suppressed the temptation to hold him close when parting – but she had not been able to control the warmth that was growing between them again.

On her last visit to Ben's home he and Joey had promised to persuade Harry not to come into Edie's orbit but to go to the north of England at the very nearest, to begin a new life. Edie having at last found a new man to fill the gap in her life had nothing to do with it and no one mentioned Dennis to Harry. Had they have done so it might well have ignited jealousy and anger whereas at the present time he was still carrying some guilt. In the face of discovering that Dennis was now part of Edie's life, Harry might have rejected out of hand the idea of going away. And this they did not want.

The look on Edie's face when she had left this evening for her night out was something that Naomi had been wishing to see for a very long time. As far as she was concerned, new love was as wonderful as young love and the best of all medicines for someone who had had her heart broken once too often.

Whether Naomi's mood of well-being and contentment had come from the combination of Maggie having arrived at that magical time in life between childhood and maturity, together with Edie's new and developing friendship with Jessie who was always encouraging *her* to have more fun, she neither knew nor cared. This was 1953 and since the British people were being told that they had never had it so good the mood was appropriately fitting the bill, to Naomi's mind. Edie was smiling again, and that she would settle for any day of the week.

Ten minutes after Naomi's favourite programme came to an end there was a timely ring on the doorbell to coincide with the whistling of the kettle. Camp coffee laced with brandy was on the menu for this evening. Opening the door to Jessie and Laura, Naomi graciously waved them in with a warm smile, saying, 'You will be pleased to know that in twenty minutes' time they will be showing *The Merchant of Venice* with Matheson Lang.'

'Sounds lovely,' said Jessie, 'but Max was hoping for a cosy night in together and after the lovely bunch of flowers he gave me for Valentine's Day . . .'

'Well,' said Laura, 'I never got flowers but I did get a big box of chocolates and Jack never mentioned a romantic sit by the fire, but he's made it very clear that if I'm not back in the flat in half an hour he'll be knocking on the door.'

'Ah, well . . .' sighed Naomi, a touch disappointed,

'on a day such as this, love, jealousy and romance must come first.' She looked from Jessie to Laura. 'But you *do* have time for coffee?'

'Oh, yeah,' Jessie spoke for both of them. 'Especially if it's laced with brandy.'

'Oh, it will be,' said Naomi, and told them to make themselves comfortable while she went into the kitchen to see to things. Opening the hatch she said, 'Would you like the wireless on? A little music?'

'No, this is lovely, Nao,' Jessie purred, 'really peaceful.' It was obvious that she loved coming into Edie's home. As for Laura, she welcomed a little escape from Jack to share a tittle-tattle about things of no importance. Marriage was no bad thing, but a little freedom now and then when not granted by husbands was certain to bring problems.

Busying herself in the kitchen with the coffee-making Naomi could hear the girls' laughter and she loved it. It took her back to the days in theatre when the women had got together in one tiny dressing room to secretly smoke Sobranie cigarettes. Then, taking her by surprise, Jessie's voice filled the flat as she sang:

'Bring out your tat and your old felt hat,
Your worn-down boots and your old-fashioned
     suits.
We lost everything in the London blitz
And we'd be much obliged for your rags and your
     glitz and
We promise to keep well away from your very
     own Ritz!'

Carrying the tea-tray in to the sound of laughter, Naomi showed how impressed she was with Jessie's singing voice. 'What a dark horse you are, Jessie . . .'

'Oh, I never made up the little ditty, one of the others did,' she said, bashfully. 'It was during the war when me and Billy, as a baby, was sheltering in a house in Westminster with other women. It seems such a long time ago now.'

'Seven years is no more than seven seconds on life's clock,' said Naomi, setting the tray down on a small side table. Appreciating the lovely mood in the room, she asked Jessie if she had been evacuated during wartime.

'Only for a few weeks to the heart of Norfolk till Tom came on a visit and persuaded me back to London. Billy was in a pushchair at the time. We loved that sleepy little village.'

'Sounds idyllic,' said Naomi. Why on earth didn't you stop longer? Were there other evacuees?'

'A coachload,' chuckled Jessie, as it all came flooding back. 'A mixed bunch, if ever you saw one. But you couldn't 'ave asked for a better welcome. The entire village came out to welcome us and the spread they put on in the village hall was amazing. Home-made cakes of every description. It was like being in another world. As if the war hadn't been heard of.

'We'd been allocated to Alice and Jack Davey – brother and sister who must 'ave been in their fifties.'

'Did you have to sleep in a hay loft?' said Laura, completely drawn in.

'No. It was a lovely little cottage. What a difference to wake up to the sound of birds instead of air-raid sirens. I can still see that little gate into the front garden now. The garden was thick with all kinds of flowers and shrubs and an apple tree. The water we drank came from the well, and they used oil lamps to see by, and the baking was done in an old brick Dutch oven which was set into a chimney breast. The rest of the cooking was done over a little range fuelled with logs. All the vegetables came from the back garden.

'Alice was such a lovely woman and her brother, well, a more comical man you couldn't wish to find. Especially from behind. His baggy trousers, held up by funny old-fashioned braces and safety-pins, were an inch too short and he walked with a limp – but not always, only when he wanted a bit of sympathy.

'Inside the cottage there was always a fire smouldering in the open brick fireplace and above it, hanging on an iron chain, was a black kettle, and on an iron stand next to the grate, a light blue enamel teapot, chipped here and there. And around the inglenook fireplace was a faded flower-patterned three-piece suite.'

'Why on earth didn't you stay for the duration of the war, Jessie? Are you mad?'

'I was mad in those days, Naomi, yeah. I listened to my husband, Tom. He came and fetched me and Billy back to London, and to a worse situation than what I came from when I went to Norfolk.'

Her eyes glazed, Laura said, 'I'd love to live in the country, but Jack's got his heart set on running a pub. He's after one on the square where we used to live.'

'We very nearly did buy a little cottage. There was a pair together and in a right state. Stanley and Dolly were gonna 'ave one and I was gonna live in the one next door. They were so cheap you wouldn't believe it.'

'It's never too late to follow a dream, Jessie. I suppose someone else snapped them up?'

'No. It doesn't work like that in them villages, Nao. I wouldn't be surprised if they're still there and in the same condition. You only get to know about them through word of mouth. Alice, the woman I stayed with, put me on to them.'

'If they're a bargain, maybe you and Edie should think about buying one to share as a holiday home. I could manage Edie's half and if your brother is in the building trade . . . what could be better?'

'Wouldn't that be lovely? Me and Edie getting away from London with the kids. And you and Laura could come and visit us.'

'Well, let's keep it on the back-burner, shall we?' said Naomi, a twinkle in her eye. 'Now, what about Westminster? What was it like boarding there?'

'Good. It was a lovely house and the woman who owned it put us all up for next to nothing.'

'The rich do love to be generous in a crisis,' said Naomi, with only a little hint of sarcasm.

'Westminster?' said Laura, impressed. 'Or was it in the very worst part of it? Because there usually is a worst part of anywhere.'

'No, it was in one of the posh streets. The landlady was lovely. Rich and from the upper classes, but once you scratched the surface she turned out to be just like us. Normal. Poor cow had been left by 'er husband twenty years before we turned up on her doorstep and she was still hoping he'd come back.'

'Well, there's a lesson for *you*, Jess,' smiled Laura, as she sipped her coffee with brandy.

'Tom? No, I don't expect to see him again. I can't ever see him coming back. He's probably still living like a lord . . . or locked away in prison.'

'Prison? Goodness. Let's hope not.'

'I don't think what he did was a crime, Nao, to tell the truth. What bloke in 'is right mind wouldn't have lived the life of Riley when it's dished up on a plate?'

Naomi was intrigued by the flying remarks about things of which she knew little. 'Prison? The life of Riley? Was this man a prince or a pauper?'

'Both, and that story needs more than half an hour to tell. We'll save it for another time.'

'Do you keep in touch with any of the women?' asked Laura, remembering when she had been evacuated to Dagenham.

'No,' said Jessie. 'I s'pose we should 'ave done. I would have written to Joyce, though, had she survived. She was lovely and such an interesting person.'

'Was the house eventually bombed, then, Jess?'

'It was bombed but not eventually – while we were all in it! One minute we were in the big sitting room having a sing-song and the next rushing down to the basement. Joyce had camp beds installed for all of us. Kids as well.

'We were all right down there. Food, blankets, lighting, the lot. But . . . Joyce had forgotten her beloved cats in the panic and went up to fetch them from her snug.' Glancing from Laura to Naomi, she shrugged sadly. 'And that was it. We were hit and it wasn't a Mickey Mouse bomb neither. The sound of that basement door slamming shut behind her still makes me go icy cold. There was an almighty explosion above us and the cellar went black. Everyone was screaming. It was horrible. I honestly thought that me and my little Billy would suffocate with the rest of 'em. Thick dust was seeping in from everywhere. We knew Joyce had had it. Blown to bits with her cats.'

A silence to cut with a knife filled the room until Naomi spoke, her voice soft and quiet. 'But, darling . . . how long were you down there before the rescue team arrived? As arrive they must have or we wouldn't be sitting talking to you now.'

Naomi's question had gone over Jessie's head. The younger woman had been drawn back in time. Staring down at the floor, she said. 'At least it would have been quick. She wouldn't 'ave known much about it. The house was flattened. When we did come up we all looked like ghosts. Our hair, skin and clothes was covered in dust, soot and dirt.

'We weren't the only ones hit that night. We'd copped a thousand-kilogram which 'ad missed its original target, an important building. By the time the fire service got to us we were all in a bad state. We'd been down there for quite a few hours before they got through to us. The lack of fresh air was the worst thing of all. God . . . I've never been so pleased to see the Red Cross and that line of ambulances.'

'Oh, don't,' shuddered Laura. 'I can't bear to think about it.'

'Then we shan't!' said Naomi, spiking their coffee with a little more brandy. 'Here is to a wonderful summer!' She held her coffee cup up. 'And to the whole of nineteen fifty three!'

Later, once the girls had left and Naomi was by herself again she shed a private tear. She, just like Edie's mother, her sister, who had taken her own life, had been brainwashed while in the children's home that one should never cry in public. She wasn't weeping over Jessie's sad story but all that had happened to herself in the past. 'Too much brandy,' she mused, as she discreetly dabbed her tears with the corner of her handkerchief.

Why Naomi's beloved husband's uniform had come into her mind she couldn't say but she had been thinking of Freddy earlier that day and the time when he had first tried it on to show her in 1914, when they were so very much in love and had been married just six years. He was a set designer in the theatre and she an accomplished small-part actress, singer and dancer. They had met and married when she was thirty. Freddy, a younger man, had fallen head over heels in love with her and had blushed madly when he had first built up the courage to ask her out and she had accepted.

Naomi, with a lifestyle of glamour and romance up

until she had met her husband, had had no inclination whatsoever to become a housewife and had surprised all of those with whom she had worked in theatre and film by suddenly turning up for rehearsal one day with a gold band on her finger. Her late husband's army uniform and memories of him flooding back must have come about, she decided, because of the talk of war, which she normally managed to cut short.

Of all conversations war stories were the worse, to her mind, but on this occasion she had to admit that Jessie's account of what she and her small child had been through had somehow made her feel humble. The tragedy of the benevolent woman who had helped the needy had also left its mark. To be blown up by a bomb while trying to save her pets was tragic.

Her offer of the uniform to Maggie's boyfriend, the Italian, had been Naomi's way of making amends with Maggie, who had been very sulky after the little chastity-belt scenario. Half expecting the young Italian to gently refuse the gift, she had been deeply moved to see him walking proudly away with it over his arm with no thoughts of which side of the line his own father would have been fighting on during the latest war.

Now, in this quiet room and on this Valentine's Day, a warm glow was spreading through her. The man she had loved so deeply would, she felt sure, be proud to have a young Italian made so obviously happy with the gift of *his* First World War uniform. Naomi felt she had rung a small bell for peace.

Glancing at the clock she realised that she had missed the beginning of the film and quickly turned it on. Then, back on the settee and reclining, she dipped her hand into a white paper bag and withdrew one of her favourite sweets – coffee-flavoured fudge. When the doorbell rang she believed it to be Laura coming back for her packet of cigarettes and lighter, which she had left on the arm of a chair.

On opening the door she found a tall, broad man in the shadows, his hat pulled down over his face, his overcoat covering most of his body. She was unnerved at first, but then realised who it was. Harry looked like someone out of a 1930s B movie. Standing quite still, his large frame almost fitting the doorway, he said, 'Don't be frightened, Naomi. This is a social call.'

'Frightened? Why on earth should I be? It is you who should be on edge, Harry. Had your widow opened the door to you, she might have had heart failure and fallen in front of your very eyes.'

'I'm sorry, Naomi – I know you told me never to come here but I would like to see my wife before I make up my mind what to do. Just give me ten minutes with her. That's all I need. I want to say I'm sorry and explain the way it was.'

'Luckily,' said Naomi, her voice little more than a whisper, 'she isn't at home. And neither is Maggie.'

'I know that. I thought I'd sit and wait till she gets back.'

'That is a preposterous thing to say and you know it is. Now, please go away and think deeply about what you are doing, Harry. You mustn't turn up like this. Think about Edie and Maggie and not yourself.'

A loud irritated sigh stopped her midstream. 'Would

you stand aside, *please*, Naomi? This is my family's home, not yours.'

'No. I'm most awfully sorry but I can't do that.'

'You've got yourself a nice little old people's place on the estate. And very lovely it is too. Why don't you spend your evening there? You don't want to get burgled. Burglars always choose special evenings of the year to break in, knowing that people are out and about. You wouldn't like it if *your* little place was turned over, would you?'

'How did you know that I, too, live on this estate?'

'Ben and Joey told me. Why shouldn't they? What's all the mystery?'

'Of course they would have told you. I'm sorry, Harry, but the shock of your being alive is still with me. Of course you must come in, but you will only have me for company, I'm afraid. But you mustn't stay long in case either Maggie or Edie returns earlier than expected.'

'Thank you.'

In the living room, Harry peered at her with an expression of apathy in his sloping green eyes. Eyes which, for a man of his age, had too many lines. His years in the sunshine might have given him a natural tan but they had done little for his skin, and his once thick auburn hair was dry and thinning. In the dim light of Joey's house she had not noticed just how much he had aged. Ignoring the touch of compassion that was creeping into her heart she asked if he needed a drink. He said he would like a glass of water and no more.

'This is a nice flat,' he said, dropping into an

armchair. 'Homely. The furniture and fixtures might be different but I can smell Edie's scent.'

'Why have you come, Harry?' said Naomi, handing him his glass of water. 'You surely don't want to shock Edie and Maggie? They believe you are dead. Can you imagine what it would have done to either of them, seeing you standing on that doorstep?'

'You think I should write first, then? Soften the blow?'

Naomi sat down in the armchair opposite him saying 'I don't think you quite grasp what you've done. You have, in a sense, killed yourself off. You should have returned to Britain and gone into hospital until you were well enough to go back into war.'

'Oh, not all that, *please* . . . Ben's already lectured me on that, Nao. I'm bored to death with it.'

'Why *didn't* you come back, Harry? What were you thinking?'

'I *don't* know! All *right*? I was ill for a while, then I was better, and the sun was shining and there was a war on in England. I knew Edie'd be all right. Everyone loves a war widow, don't they? But now I'm back and I want things to be the way they were. That's all. Not too much to ask, is it?'

'I'm afraid it is. Far too much. Would that we could turn back the clock. Life goes on and things change. Surely you can see that?'

'What is it about you, Naomi?' Harry crossed his legs and then his arms, peering at her. 'You're enjoying this. Playing God. I s'pose you miss being up there on the stage with a pathetic audience gazing up at you.'

'Of course I'm not enjoying it! My stomach is churning! I'm terrified that the key will turn in the front door any minute! Now will you please *leave*? I will do what I can to help you but I *will* put my niece first.' A trembling sigh escaped from her mouth as she looked pleadingly into his face. 'Go back to Joey's house and I promise to come and see you tomorrow. In different surroundings we can talk it all through. The best way to go forward and so on.'

Harry gave her an incredulous look. 'There's nothing to talk about, Naomi. I want to see my Edie and explain what happened. I might 'ave to embellish the story a little bit for 'er sake but that's my business. Mine and Edie's.'

'Please, Harry . . . please leave.'

'Ben's not bin giving you one, 'as he?' A goading smile was now on his face. 'Or do they take it in turns, the old men? Ben, Joey and Larry. Cos you've got 'em twisted around your little finger. One word from you and suddenly I've gotta fuck off out the way.'

'Believe what you want, but I will say that those three men have had yours and Edie's interests at heart. They seem old-fashioned but they are worldly, Harry. They've been through two world wars, let's not forget.' There was a quiet pause while they gazed at each other. Naomi was beginning to believe that she was getting through to him. 'They are risking their own freedom by hiding you.'

'From the Turks, you mean?'

'From whatever, and especially from prison. Unless you play this right and feign a lost memory or something similar, you will be imprisoned for a very, very long time. You deserted during a ferocious war when every man was needed. You duped the government into believing you dead. Edie has been receiving a war widow's pension. You have forged papers to take on the identity of another man.

'Surely you can see that you cannot simply walk back into your old world and behave as if nothing has happened?'

'And you think I don't know all that? You've got to stop making speeches, Nao. You're not an actress any more. I had you down for someone with intelligence. There *is* a way . . . and I need to talk to Edie about it. All right? Am I making it clear enough for you?'

'Harry. Of all things that I would love most is to have you back in the fold with your family and to see Edie happy once more. But, apart from anything else, I hear that the Turkish family are looking for you. The woman you lived with as man and wife has a family and they are not best pleased.'

The sudden intrusion of the doorbell stopped her short. Her eyes went immediately to Laura's cigarettes and lighter. 'That could be a neighbour who was in before you called. She left those behind.'

'You can take 'em down later. Tell 'er you was on the lavatory when she rang the bell.'

'Harry, she is no fool. She will realise that something is *wrong*. Will you *please* hide on the balcony just in case it is *not* Laura but one of the Turks? They live on this estate. Did you know that?'

'They don't worry me, Naomi. Bloody foreigners coming over and acting as if this is their country. Fuck 'em. They're not worth worrying over.'

Ignoring him, Naomi was up off the chair and sweeping the cigarettes and lighter off the table. 'Do what you want, Harry. It's your skin, not mine.' Leaving Harry to himself she went to the front door.

It was Laura. 'Sorry, Nao. Left my—'

'Yes, I know. I was just going to bring them along to you,' said Naomi, pushing them into Laura's hands.

Looking into Naomi's face, Laura could tell something was wrong. 'Are you okay?'

'Yes. Of course I am! Why wouldn't I be?'

'Just dozing off by the fire, were you?' she continued, certain that something was amiss.

'Actually, no. Well, yes, I probably was. Thank you so much for calling.'

'Naomi? What is it? Is someone in there?'

'Actually, there is. Please go and come back in ten minutes. Will you do that?'

'You look frightened to death.'

Whispering now, Naomi said, 'It's rather awkward . . . Please come back in ten minutes' time.'

'All right,' nodded Laura, uneasy. 'Ten minutes.'

Smiling graciously at her, Naomi then slowly closed the door and walked, a touch unsteadily, into the sitting room to find that Harry was not there. Thinking that he was hiding on the balcony she sat down and used an old breathing technique to help calm herself before unscrewing her small bottle of brandy and taking a sip. But her time of being by herself was short-lived. The doorbell rang again.

She imagined this to be Laura too concerned to wait ten minutes. Praying that Harry would stay out of the room she went to open the door. But it was not Laura who stared down at her: it was the smart Turkish gentleman who had been looking at Edie so strangely at Jessie's Christmas party.

Speaking gently, he said, 'Please, I am not here to cause a problem.' He then carefully took her hand in his and lightly kissed it before bringing to it to his forehead, showing respect '*Ayse hanim.*'

'What is it you want?' whispered Naomi. 'This isn't my home, you see. I don't live here.'

'This I know.' He smiled. 'I am called Mehmet. My family live here within this beautiful estate.'

Her hand on her neck and worried, Naomi hadn't a clue as to what she should do. 'And I am called Naomi. You are so polite and I would like to invite you in, Mehmet, but—'

'It is difficult for you. I understand.'

'It might be better,' she said, looking over her shoulder for no sensible reason, 'if I were to come to your family's house? Would that suit you?'

'That would be kindly,' he said, placing a hand on his heart. 'Thank you.'

'And I believe that Laura Armstrong is a friend of your family?'

'Yes, she is a friend of my family.'

'May I fetch her?'

'Fetch?'

'Bring her with me to your family's home?'

This brought another warm smile to his face. 'Yes. Yes. Please,' he said, 'Tomorrow? You will come to the house tomorrow?'

'In the evening?'

'Yes, in the evening.'

'Shall we say . . . seven o'clock?'

'Thank you. Yes.' Again the flat of his hand was placed on his heart. 'Seven o'clock.' With that he backed away, gently smiling at her.

Closing the door very quietly, Naomi was dumbfounded. Harry was hiding somewhere in the flat and she had just made arrangements to meet with the man who had probably been sent to bring him to heel. Checking the bedrooms and then the back balcony, she was mystified if not relieved to find that he had gone. She could only assume that he had dropped two flights from the balcony or climbed down the drainpipe.

Lowering herself onto the settee she gazed into the fire and spoke quietly to herself, saying, 'Did I fall asleep? Was it all a dream?' Then, as if in a trance, she lifted her worn leather handbag from the floor, unclipped it and withdrew a packet of French cigarettes kept for emergencies. When the doorbell rang again she felt herself go rigid until she remembered that it would be Laura and was calmed at the thought of her company.

Dragging herself up from her seat once more, she felt a touch light-headed. Steadying herself, she took a slow deep breath and then walked cautiously out of the room feeling as if she might be sick. As she opened the street door she realised that she was still trembling.

'Oh, Laura . . .' she murmured feebly, a hand clasped to her chest. 'Thank goodness it *is* you.'

'Of course it's me, Naomi. Whatever's going on? You look terrible.'

'Do I?'

'Yes,' said Laura, closing the street door behind her and taking Naomi's arm to assist her through to the living room. 'I don't know who's done this to yer but whoever it is will 'ave me to answer for if it's a woman and Jack if it's a man.'

'It's neither, really,' said Naomi, sinking back down on the settee. 'Just life, I suppose. Past life creeping up from behind like the ghastly bogeyman.' She raised her eyes to Laura's face and forced back her tears, saying, 'Could you possibly fetch me a large glass of water, dear?'

'Wouldn't you rather 'ave a weak cup of tea?'

'No. Just water. Thank you. I'll be perfectly fine . . .'

Laura wasn't so sure. Losing no time she went into the kitchen and was soon back again with the drink. 'Here . . . but sip it at first and then slowly drink it.'

'Yes,' whispered Naomi, her usual rosy cheeks now a deathly white.

Standing before her friend, Laura did not take her eyes off Naomi's face and when she rested back and closed her eyes she eased the glass from her shaky hand. 'You don't 'ave to say anything, Naomi. Just rest until you're ready to tell me what's happened. I take it you 'aven't got any pains in your chest or anything like that?'

'No, nothing like that.' Naomi, her eyes still closed, sank her head back into a cushion.

'Don't worry,' said Laura, stroking Naomi's face. 'Just give yourself time to get used to the idea that everything is fine, all back to normal, and no one can hurt you, and that your friend's right here next to you and won't go away till you kick 'er out.'

'Normal. How wonderful that word sounds,' murmured Naomi. 'You are kind, Laura. I think I might cry but please don't worry if I do. It's not that I'm unhappy or frightened. I do so hate to see old people cry myself so I'm quite used to stopping should—'

'Naomi,' said Laura, softly, as she placed a hand on her arm, 'shut up for five minutes and wipe your tears away. Here.' She offered her handkerchief. 'It's clean.'

'Tears?' said Naomi suddenly, her face coming alive again. 'Gracious me, yes,' she said, stroking them away with the tips of her fingers. 'How *silly.*'

'No, it's not,' smiled Laura. 'It's what the tear ducts are for. Ask any Italian family. We're supposed to shed a tear every day apparently to release tension. Little worries build up if we don't let it all flow.'

'Well, yes, that does make sense. I can see the logic.' Naomi smiled and the colour slowly came back into her face.

'That's better. More like your old self. *Now* would you like a cup of tea?'

'No, I'll stay with the water, thank you.'

'Good. And when you're ready, if you want, you can get it *all* off your chest. Whatever it was that upset you like this.'

'I *would* like to get if off my chest but . . . it is rather *shocking*, I'm afraid. And I shall have to ask you not to say a word of it to anyone. Not even your husband. Do you think you could agree to that?'

Unable not to laugh at this lovely genteel woman, Laura said 'You really are a one-off, you know. Course I won't say a word. I'm your friend.'

'Well, yes, but I think you had better sit back in your seat. I'm certain this is going to give you quite a jolt.'

'I'll cope. I've not *quite* 'ad enough jolts to last me a lifetime yet. Go on, then.'

Drawing breath, Naomi said, 'Edie's husband is not dead.'

Silenced by this statement, Laura felt an icy-cold tingle in her spine. Raising her eyebrows, a look of disbelief in her eyes, she murmured, '*Not* . . . dead?'

'No. And I assure you I am *not* about to tell you I have experienced a spiritual happening here in this room while alone. Harry was here – in the flesh.'

Laura straightened, her face expressionless, and then sank back into the armchair. 'Does she know? Edie?'

'No. So you can see why I was a little on edge when I opened the door to you the first time. He was here in this very room. And I'm afraid there is *worse* to come.' She then slowly unfolded the whole story from beginning to end realising just how much good it was doing her to have a spellbound audience – albeit of just one person. All through her incredible speech Laura did not utter one word.

'So,' Naomi said, relaxed now her story was told, 'what on earth *am* I to do? I have committed myself to going into the Turkish family's home and having all sorts of questions, if not accusations and insults, thrown at me.'

'No, they're not like that,' said Laura, her voice quiet. 'They won't accuse you and they definitely won't insult you. They have inborn respect for their elders. But I think I should come with you. Unless you don't want—'

'Oh, Laura . . . *would* you?' said Naomi, her face showing her sense of relief and appreciation.

'Course I will. Or, rather, I'll meet you there. I'll tell Jack that we're both gonna be measured for a frock for summer and if your Edie or Mags 'appens to spot you going in or coming out, that story'll suit them as well.'

'Oh, how clever you are. You've made me feel so much better about things already.'

'That's all right,' said Laura, and then, 'So you think that this flat was being watched? I mean, it's a bit of a coincidence that he turns up soon after Edie's husband.'

'Well, either that or they know exactly where he is, and every movement of Harry's *is* being watched. I imagine that is the way they would do things. Watch and wait to see what his next move will be.'

'That does sound like the Turkish way of doing things. The good and decent Turks, that is. I don't know about the others who hang around in Cable Street. But just thank your stars that he did run. You don't want all of that on your doorstep. If you ask me, they probably 'ad a man watching out the back as well who saw 'im scarper. I think that Mehmet came up to see *you*, Naomi. If Harry had been followed here and he was informed of it, then he came to give a silent message to him through you. That's what I reckon anyway. He knew you wouldn't ask him in. Not with Harry in here. The Turkish are so bloody clever the way they go about things.'

'Slow and mindful, you mean?'

'I think so. Weigh it all up rationally so they know the outcome before they get started. I wish I could be more like that.'

'Don't we all, Laura, don't we all? So, then . . . I shall be perfectly safe going to the Turk's cottage and not quite the lamb to slaughter?'

Touched by her innocence Laura said, 'Don't be silly. I'll be there with you. They're friends.'

'And you won't mention this to anyone? We've got to keep it from Edie and Maggie as it is. All we can *hope* is that Harry will go as far away as possible, and without your nice Turkish family ever finding him. We don't want blood on our hands. We none of us need that.'

'Well . . . I'm sure you'll be a good peacemaker and once you've got your side of the story over, Shereen's family'll end up the ones feeling sorry.'

'Oh? Do you really think so?'

'I'm sure of it. You'll 'ave 'em in floods of tears by the time you've finished.'

'I see what you're getting at,' said Naomi, as the light dawned. 'I must not be defensive but calmly attack and with the best weapons of all – love, tears and devotion to my beloved niece and great-niece.' She pushed her face forward with an expression of query in her eyes. '*This* is what you think I should do?'

'Well, it's the truth, Naomi. You won't 'ave to be theatrical. Just tell it in your own honest way. Edie *did* suffer badly, Maggie's never seen 'er dad, and you've fostered them both in a way. Tell 'em about Edie's dad as well and how he ran off. And what it did to Edie's mum. She committed suicide over it, for Christ's sake. Surely all that's 'appened is enough grief to go round a dozen families let alone one!'

Pausing for thought, Naomi glanced at Laura's face, and the look of passion in her eyes confirmed that every word she had uttered had been heartfelt. 'Well, when it's all wrapped up in a small parcel like that – yes, enough is enough.'

'That's right, and I'll be by your side when we go to Shereen's. I'll be there but I won't be centre stage, just in the wings ready to give you a congratulatory hug when you take your bow.'

'Well, put like that, Laura, how can I possibly do anything other than to follow your intelligent advice? And how can I *possibly* thank you?'

'There is something, as a matter of fact. Talk to Jessie's sister, Dolly, for me.'

'Dolly? What an unfortunate name,' said Naomi, her head tilted to one side. 'And what would you like me to talk to her about?'

'Your world. You've bin around so you must know the way things work. In 'er spare time, and by the sounds of it sometimes working into the wee hours on 'er old-fashioned typewriter, she writes novels. She told me about the one she's working on and I reckon it'd make a good film or be great on the television screen.'

'Really?' Naomi's face lit up. 'How fascinating. Do fill me in.'

'No. Let her tell you. That way you'd get a better picture. Anyway, I might be wrong in my judgement but I don't think so. You know a lot more about these fings than I do. And I know she'd love it if you showed interest.'

'Yes, I can see that. But it is extremely difficult for new writers and *especially* one who has not had the education. Those coming out of our universities stand a far better chance of getting attention.'

'But look at what you've achieved.'

'Well, yes . . . but I danced barefoot through all weathers and for pennies and farthings in the last century. Things are very different now. And it was by sheer persistence that I eventually got through the back door. The managers in the theatre in those days would rather have had me inside entertaining instead of outside drawing my own crowd, which is exactly what I had hoped for.'

Taking a breather, Naomi leaned back with a look

on her face that showed she had more to say. Laura knew this, and although Jack was hovering in the back of her mind she was prepared to throw caution to the wind and let this mellow lady of a certain era talk about her past. Jack would be angry with her for staying out too long but this being Valentine's evening she would easily be able to woo him out of his mood with a little hint of an early night and romantic pillow talk.

'But I'm afraid there isn't anything *I* can do for Jessie's sister, even though I still have some very good contacts. But I will tell her all I have learned from other writers, that whether published or produced or not, she will be unable to stop the words *flowing* on to the page. It is either a blessing or an encumbrance that she has been given. The gift, depending whether or not she is in the right place at the right time when offering up her work, can sometimes be a cross to bear.'

'And you're gonna tell 'er all of that, are you,' said Jessie, ever amused by her honesty.

'Into the bargain,' said Naomi, carried away, 'she will be the butt of mockery until she is published or produced. Then it will be a different matter entirely. But none of it matters when all is put on the table to be counted. Should she have success much later in life her writing will be all the better for it.

'We have each to experience for ourselves to find the truth. The thick and prickly bramble bush must be gone through in order for us to see that the field on the other side is not necessarily greener and possibly much worse than what we are running from.'

Having said all she wished to say on the matter

and exhilarated by her own voicing of what she truly believed, Naomi plumped the cushion behind her and then lifted her feet to lie full stretch on the settee. 'Does that make any sense at all, Laura, or have I simply been rambling?'

'You did go on a bit but it makes sense, Nao.' Laura checked her wristwatch. 'Now I'm gonna 'ave to love and leave yer or I'll get a clip round the ear from that possessive man of mine.'

'There is nothing so good as jealousy to keep the pot boiling. Jack obviously knows this?'

'I'm sure he does but he won't give me an inch—'

Breaking in, Naomi rushed her words, 'Are we talking about a wife beater? Because if so I really don't think that—'

'No, we're not,' said Laura. Naomi obviously remembered the black eye Laura had appeared with after New Year's Eve.

'Good. Well, then, you and I must have another little tête-à-tête some other time. You should have a lover, that is the nub of it. Unless, of course, you are a prude?'

'No, actually, I'm not. I just don't get the chance for a little bit of romance on the side. He'd smell another man on me a mile off.'

'But you *have* told me that when you go to this dreadful place in the country to pick hops and so on, your husband, like other dockers, must stay in London and only visit at *weekends*.'

'But that means that none of the men are there during the week except those who've managed to cry wolf at the doctor's – and they're under the eyes of their women all the time we're there.'

'Ah,' smiled Naomi, satisfied, 'you *have* been in search of a lover.'

'Actually, I think I might 'ave found one who I could run with, Nao. One of the sons of the wealthy owner of the hop-farm we go to.'

Slowly drawing herself up from her makeshift bed, Naomi leaned to one side and studied Laura's face. 'Is this true?'

'I said *might*, Nao.'

'Has he touched you in secret?'

'No. We just met in a small lane which runs alongside the hop-fields one Sunday and walked side by side talking, that's all. He was taking his dogs for a run and I was out for a stroll.'

'And?' Naomi waited, with bated breath. 'Laura, *please*, do not leave me in mid-air like this. What *happened*?'

'Nothing. We just enjoyed each other's company and from then on if ever he saw me on the hop-fields or in the lanes he stopped for a chat, or if he was in his car or jeep he'd offer to gimme a lift. That's all.'

Floating back down into her most favourite lateral position, Naomi sighed deeply, saying, 'How terribly *romantic*. It would almost be a sin to spoil it all by letting him take you. But that's really asking for too much. Next September it will *all* happen, I assure you. You will be loved by that man as no other woman has been loved before!'

'Yeah, well, if you think so,' said Laura, 'all I know

is that if I don't get back to Jack pronto I'll be interrogated as no woman's been interrogated before. For all we can tell, he might have caught a glimpse of Mehmet coming to your door.'

'Oh, *surely* not!' said Naomi, the fear back in her eyes.

'I'm only kidding. If he had of done I would never 'ave bin allowed to come back. Believe me, that's how possessive he is.'

'Thank goodness for *it*. To have a jealous man at your heel is no bad thing. You will see yourself out for me, Laura? I feel a little cat-nap coming on.'

'Of course I will. I'll see you tomorrow at Shereen's,' she called back over her shoulder, leaving Naomi to drift off by the fire.

Once she had heard the front door shut, Naomi spoke with a contented sigh. 'Everything has a way of turning out in the end, Naomi, you know that. And would not the park be dull without broken swings, roundabouts, and seesaws to add a touch of danger?'

Twenty minutes later, after a heavenly cat-nap, Naomi awoke with mixed-up visions swimming through her mind as she tried to cling on to the remnants of her nightmare. Her dream of sitting in Edie's kitchen sink, her drawers round her ankles with legs dangling and all of this to the sound of her dear friend Ben coming into the room. Amused by the vision now, she mopped the beads of sweat which were trickling down the side of her face with her lace-edged handkerchief. 'Heavens above,' she murmured, 'what can such a dream mean? That I, too, will end up like the wretched soul on the fourth floor? The poor woman who has deigned to come into my most precious sleeping hours and whom I have yet to meet?'

Taking in her surroundings so as to get things into perspective, she was pleased that she was not in her apartment for once but in Edie's front room. 'Is it Christmas? If so then where are the tree and fairy-lights?' She saw the two Valentine cards on the mantelshelf. 'Ah . . . of course. Silly me. It is that time of year when the heart will rule the head.'

A little more alert she swung her legs off the couch, leaned back and yawned a lovely long stretchy yawn. 'Bring me a cup of tea, slave!' she called out, and then, 'If *only* one had a servant just for those few waking moments when tea is more important than anything else in the world.'

Glancing at the small side table she saw that there in her glass was the remains of her sherry, and Harry's face clouded her mind. She lifted it to her lips and sipped the delicious sweet liquid. Comfortable again she sank back into her cushions and gazed into the dying embers of the fire, with the clock softly ticking the seconds by. She had been asleep a full hour, which meant that several of her cat-naps had been taken up. She recalled a tiny section of her dream – herself in the kitchen sink and singing. Whether this had been brought on by the fact that, in a tiny part of her mind, she felt a touch guilty for not paying a brief neighbourly visit to the wretched woman who lived in the same building as Edie, she couldn't be sure.

Questions were flying through her mind. Was the

little cameo a warning from the guiding spirits? Were they showing her the path she was on and should get off? Was it possible that she, too, might end up bathing and singing in a sink? She had, after all, bathed in deep puddles and public ponds when young and living on the streets.

'There but for fortune . . .' she whispered. 'There but for fortune.' Had other more immediate and dangerous matters not pervaded her mind, she might just have gone upstairs and introduced herself to the woman right then. The woman who, to Naomi's mind, was in need of someone to talk to or, since she would have little to talk about, someone to listen to. And Naomi knew that she could draw people out.

Back in the immediate time with the immediate problem working its way through to the front of her mind, she told herself that Harry turning up out of the blue to find her alone had been a blessing in disguise. Had Edie or Maggie been at home it would have been a disaster, a horrendous shock, which could only lead to worse things.

Stoking up the fire with coke, a fuel she disliked intensely but which Edie had changed over to, Naomi wondered if her niece was having a romantic evening with the new man in her life. To her, Dennis seemed to be a lovely ordinary man with good looks and fair ambitions to attract women who could be content with a middle-of-the-road way of life. And after all that Edie had been through, he seemed to be ideal for her – so far. Time would tell, and if there were any skeletons in *his* cupboard that would one day be aired, she could only hope that it would be sooner rather than later. Naomi's first impression of Dennis had actually been correct. He was steady, reliable and with no past to worry any of them.

His having worked all hours as an apprentice to an electrician since the day he had left school had paid dividends. He now ran his own little business of which he was not only the employer but the sole employee, except for a fourteen-year-old lad, his apprentice.

As far as Naomi was concerned life had shown her that there would always be room for the experienced and reliable electrician, plumber, decorator, not to mention builder. Especially now with the widespread desire for central heating, which was becoming more popular.

With these thoughts sweeping through her mind she could not help recalling the great Wall Street crash in America during the thirties when investors took to throwing themselves off skyscrapers. She had felt at that time, and still did, that the tragedy was clear evidence of the fragility of the world of commerce where the rich and prosperous could be made poor overnight. Much better to have a pile of pound notes in the bank, where one might look at it whenever one chose, was her opinion.

The sound of the front door opening and closing brought an end to her rambling thoughts and a stop to her rising temper, which had, in earlier years, erupted when conversation had come round to dishonest politicians and mercenary businessmen. Checking her worn silver wristwatch, she saw that it was only ten thirty and she hadn't expected Maggie until gone eleven. Never mind the ground rule of *ten thirty*, which had not come from herself but from Edie. If Naomi's second mention of chastity-belt had embarrassed her into coming in earlier than she might have, then she could expect either a sulky mood or a dressing-down from her great-niece, who had grown rather confident since her new look. But it was not Maggie returning early, it was Edie, her Edie.

Showing the flat of her hand as she dropped into an armchair, Edie was making it clear that she wanted no questions as to why she was home earlier than expected and that she would explain when she was ready, and this more than suited Naomi. With the earlier drama returning to her mind, she welcomed the silent request for no interrogation as to how the evening had gone.

From the expression on Edie's face, it was obvious to Naomi that she was not so much upset as worried. She spoke quietly with no hint of commiseration in her voice. 'How strange,' she said, offering a faint smile, 'I was just going to make myself a cup of tea and you came into my mind. Not that I was feeling lonely, but just thinking how cosy this room is and how nice it would be if you were here to share it with me.'

'And here I am,' said Edie, her eyes cast down. 'Not too much milk.'

'I don't suppose you're hungry? I was considering making myself a Welsh rarebit . . .'

'Tea'll be fine.'

Leaving the room and Edie to have her few quiet

minutes alone, Naomi went into the kitchen telling herself that it couldn't be possible for Harry to have crossed her path and that something else had upset her. Whatever it was, she was not going to probe but simply wait for her to unload her anxiety for that was what she had seen in her eyes. Naomi had been acting the surrogate mother for so long that she knew Edie inside out as a birth-mother would. Engaged in her tea-making and wrapped in her thoughts she didn't hear her niece come into the kitchen.

'I'm gonna ask you a question, Naomi, and I need a straight answer, no theatricals, no rambling on about your past loves, nothing.'

'Very well, Edith – you have my word,' said Naomi, keeping her back to Edie.

'Do you think there's any chance whatsoever that Harry might one day be found alive?'

Stunned by this, she spoke instinctively: 'No, actually – I don't.'

'But how can you be sure? What if he's in a hospital miles away, paralysed and lost his memory?'

Turning to face her, Naomi did not on this occasion cover her true feelings. 'I can be more than sure because it has been almost ten *years*! Had Harry been in the condition you *mention* he would by now be six foot under. And if he *hadn't* suffered head injuries or paralysis then he would have found his way back long before now, wouldn't you say?'

'I don't know. That's why I'm asking you.'

'Well . . . he must have been killed during the war or deliberately keeping away from you. And if the latter *should* be the case he will only be keeping away from you because he has nestled down with another woman. You of *all* people should know that this kind of thing *does happen*. Let's not forget what your own father did to my sister. Left without a word and has never been heard of or seen since.'

'So you think I'm free to marry, then?'

Taken aback yet again by this stark question, Naomi stretched to her full height. 'I think you are free but not ready.'

'Why not?'

'Because you have known Dennis for only three months! You are not a teenager, Edith, you are a grown woman! One who has given birth to a baby who is herself now a young woman! How can you speak of such things?'

'So . . . what you're really trying to say . . . is that Den's not the man for me? That you don't like him?'

Drawing her shoulders back and tilting her head ever so slightly, Naomi said, 'Goodness, this Valentine's Day really has had an effect on you, as it has no doubt had on your new friend. Has he proposed by any chance?'

'As a matter of fact he did . . . sort of.'

'So you ran home early? From fear, one wonders, or plain common sense?'

'He fetched me back in a taxi,' sniffed Edie, 'like he always does.'

'And your answer to his premature hint of a proposal?'

'I said I would need time to think about something so serious if someone were to offer me a diamond ring.'

'Well, that's a relief. At your age you need to think very carefully—'

'You never answered my question! Do you think I'm free to marry?'

'I said free but not ready. Ask me again in a year's time and I should have a clearer picture of Dennis. As it is, just like you, I know little about him and he has not in my opinion had time to be tried and tested. Have you been out on a romantic evening with him while having a period?'

'Oh, for Christ's sake! Why do you always have to bring things down to lavatory level?'

'Because at the end of the day that is what makes for a civilised society. Without the lavatory pan where would we be?' Naomi then sported her favourite smile. 'And I know that you know perfectly well *what* I meant. When you have a period you are in a foul mood, come rain or shine, and if he has survived that he will survive anything. Now, if you really do want my advice then suggest to Dennis that you will give him an answer in a year's time but not, under any circumstance, on Valentine's Day. Even in your present mood you need not have me explain why.'

'What if he won't wait a year?'

'You see? Talking things through *is* the best remedy when doubt clouds the mind. You have answered your own *question*, have you not?'

'No.'

'I think you *have* and you *know* that you have. You were confused by your own scepticism and ran straight home to your aunt Naomi. And I have, whether you wish to accept it or not, taken on the responsibility of making the right decision for you.

'Confirmation is what you were seeking and confirmation is what I have given. A man who proposes having known the woman only twelve weeks or so, and on Valentine's Day, is not to be entirely depended upon. What might he do on the following *Guy Fawkes*? – one cannot help wondering. Light the blue touchpaper and perhaps *blow up* the said marriage? Historical romance is no bad thing to read about, Edith, but not something to mould one's life around.'

'The kettle's boiling,' said Edie stiffly, and went back into the living room.

'Indeed it is,' murmured Naomi. 'Indeed it is.' Pouring boiling water into the brown teapot, she thought that perhaps she had said too much too soon. 'All will come out in the wash,' she told herself 'all will come out in the wash.'

The hatch door suddenly opening startled her, even though it was something that Naomi had come to get used to since visiting this new flat of Edie's – but she was more comfortable on the other side of it, in the living room. Placing the kettle back on the stove, she said, 'Do try and behave in keeping with your age, dear. I am far too old to be continually shocked by you.'

'So what's wrong with him, then?'

'There is nothing *wrong* with him, and if we are to continue this conversation I would rather come into *that* room or you come into *this*. I feel as if I am talking to a presenter on the *television* set.'

'So you think I should turn 'im down?'

'That is not what I said. I said wait a year . . . or so.'

'Just checking,' said Edie, going quiet and causing Naomi to feel a touch confused. 'He's coming round tomorrow for dinner and to spend some time trying to get to know Maggie. Do you want to be in on it or not?'

'Well, it's very nice of you to ask, Edie,' said Naomi, setting the tea-tray, 'but I do have somewhere else to go tomorrow, which, I fear, will leave me quite drained. I'll sit and have a chat with him some other time. Will that do?'

'Perfect,' said Edie. 'I just didn't want you to feel left out of it.'

'Oh, I shouldn't worry too much about that. Whether it pleases me or not it would seem that I am never to be left out of it when it comes to your affairs.'

'What's that s'posed to mean?'

'Oh, nothing to write home about. Just the ramblings of an *old* woman who really at this time of her life *ought* to be sitting in a corner armchair with a shawl wrapped around her, while knitting *cardigans*.'

'When you're eighty we'll let you do that.' The hatch door closed again.

'And now let us hope that is the end of it for this

evening,' Naomi told herself. So much had already happened that all she wanted was peace, quiet, and to be adored and perhaps even comforted.

7

True to her word, when Naomi arrived at the Turkish woman's house, Laura was there to welcome her. Unable to cancel a previously made appointment Shereen, in the sitting room, was fitting a coat she had altered for an ageing Jewish woman, her next-door neighbour. Sitting on a small couch in the corner was the Jewish woman's husband, Nathan, who came into this home at the least opportunity. He was drinking Turkish tea from a small glass cup.

In an armchair next to him was Shereen's husband, Murat the barber, his shirt collar off and the buttons undone. His trousers were rolled up to his knees showing his skinny legs, and his feet were in a bowl of warm soapy water. On another armchair sat Shereen's brother Ismet, the bespoke tailor, who was taking his turn in having a draw on the family Turkish pipe.

All of those in the house, with the exception of the old Jewish couple, knew exactly why Edie and Naomi were there but they gave nothing away. Each of them shook Naomi's hand and welcomed her, and in answer to their customary greetings of '*Hosgeldiniz,*' she gave a short courteous nod, saying, '*Iyi aksamlar.*' This she had learned from the Turkish seamstress backstage some years since.

The warm room was cluttered with furniture as well as people, and a fire was burning in the grate and was reflecting its glow in a mirror hanging from a chain on the opposite wall. On another wall hung an attractive, albeit faded Turkish rug, which blended with the turquoise and rust throw that almost covered the settee. In another corner, on a large ragged cushion, sat a contented cat.

'You sit on the long-bench, please,' smiled Shereen. 'I finish soon and then you sit on the comfortable couch.'

'Oh, I see,' teased Nathan, the old Jewish man, 'we're gonna be slung out early tonight on account of royalty!'

'Take no notice, Shereen,' said his wife Becky, rolling her eyes. Then, turning to Laura, she said, 'A few minutes and we'll be gone.'

'It's all right, Becky,' said Laura, as she and Naomi sat down on the bench, which was covered with an old hand-woven donkey cushion. 'I've bin given some time off. Jack's listening to the boxing on the wireless. Pity Nathan's not doing the same.'

'I would if the set wasn't crackling like bloody fireworks. It's not bin the same since we moved. You did all right, Laura, you know that? You did the right thing,' said Nathan. 'Taking a flat, I mean, instead of one of these bloody things. At our age we should 'ave gone for a place with a lift. But no, *she* wouldn't hear of it.'

'Who's *she*? The cat's mother?' droned his wife. 'We get a lovely two-bedroom house with a room in the attic and he complains.'

'And if your mother wasn't so bloody fussy and slept in the attic we could have had a one-bedroom place. Why pay for two bedrooms when one will do? All you can see is walls and metal bloody windows. They put you in army barracks and then say you're lucky. Lucky to get a modern house. Ha!'

'You sleep *down*stairs, still, Nathan?' asked Shereen, as she pinned the hem of Becky's coat.

'Course I do. I never go up there. I stop down and pretend I've got the little flat I always wanted. The kitchen's downstairs, the bathroom's downstairs, and that's where I listen to the wireless plugged in. When it's working. I've got a self-contained flat with my own front door and back garden. It's freezing bloody cold up there anyway.'

'It's not freezing cold. Cold, yes, but freezing, no. Don't exaggerate. Anyway, it's lovely now I've got a one-bar electric fire. I move it from one room to the other and then leave it in the passage in between. It's beautiful and warm up there. What with that and my thick blanket, I sweat like a pig. You wanna be alone downstairs, be alone. You'll be sorry when you look back. A man should sleep in his wife's bed. It's not right. Still . . . if he wants to be a double meshugener, let him. I should care. If he doesn't want me in his bed, fine.'

'The put-u-up's too small for two. Silly cow. And you can't get two of 'em in that front room now. She brought every bloody bit of furniture with her. I said I'd take it to Club Row and flog it for good money, but no. No, she has to bring all the old shit with her.'

'If I get rid of it, would you sleep upstairs?'

'What are you talking about, woman? What has that got to do with anything? I'm telling you, Shereen, she's losing her mind.'

Used to the banter between this couple, Laura was as usual thoroughly enjoying it; no matter where she came across them, in the shops, the markets, or especially now that she had her favourite orange-flavoured Turkish tea to sip, courtesy of Ismet, the brother of Shereen. She could tell that Naomi was in her element in the room with this mix of colourful people. Even Naomi knew that, should she try and get a word in edgeways, she would be upstaged. Besides which, this was a light interlude, as far as she was concerned, for what was to follow.

'If I'm losing my mind,' mumbled the Jewish woman, 'it's not as bad as having lost it as you did, years ago. Premature senile dementia is what they call it now. Did you know that, Nathan?'

'So now *I'm* the crazy one? Well, then, how come you don't see me pulling myself up by the banister groaning a dozen times a day? Up and down, up and down. Up and bloody down. Just because the stairs are there, she must use them. It doesn't make sense. Not to me anyway.'

'So what do you think we should do with the stairs? Get rid of them?'

'That would be one way to keep your mother up

there and out of my hair. Bloody daft question to ask. Put plants on the bloody things – what do you think you should do with them? Plants and some of your sodding ornaments. No wonder you flop into your bed exhausted. Waste of energy. You should sleep downstairs like me, by the fire.'

'There's not enough room for another put-u-up. You said so yourself.'

'There would be if you let me sell the furniture we don't need,' he said, sucking on his teeth and grinning slyly at Shereen's husband.

Shaking her head slowly and looking at Laura, Becky rolled her eyes. 'You can see what I have to put up with. But will he go to see a doctor?'

'I don't need no doctor to tell me what's wrong,' said Nathan. 'I know what's wrong. And I know when it went wrong. When I married you.'

'I think it's all the Friar's Balsam. Always got his head stuck under a tent of a towel and cooking himself. I think he might be addicted,' she murmured gravely. 'My sister had the right idea. She never married. Had a few good-looking boyfriends, mind. Did I tell you she bought her own house, Laura? She never paid a penny more than a hundred and eighty pounds for it! That was two years ago. And she's doubled her money . . . if not more.' Again Becky shook her head, saying, 'I should 'ave listened to her.'

'She never doubled her money, woman. And it's a shoe box.'

'She doubled it!'

'I'm telling you she never doubled it!'

'So maybe she trebled it, Nathan? I don't know! I don't care! She made money, and without a bloody man to nag her day and night!'

Sniffing, he sipped his tea. 'She never doubled it.'

'If God should have come down just once and give me one request,' said Becky, 'I would have asked that the man I marry should have the brains of my sister.' This was Becky's best weapon: Nathan and her sister were the world's worst enemies even though they loved each other.

'Do you know what, Laura? That woman opened her downstairs window and sold bric-à-brac and cut sandwiches out of it. The sandwiches she made out of floppy white bread and cheap Spam with a bit of French mustard and the bric-à-brac she collected from rubbish dumps. She cleaned it, she polished it and she sold it. How else do you think she could save to buy her own house? She could sell anything . . . and *always* doubled her money.'

'How can she *double* it if she never paid a penny in the first place?' said Nathan. 'And she might have a house but she's walking around on cracked lino, which is on top of three decaying layers that's been there since the First World War.

'Can't blame her for it, I s'pose.' Nathan raised his eyes to heaven to contemplate. 'When you've come from the gutter anything is gonna look like a luxury. Take my wife, Naomi,' he said, hoping to get her under his belt, 'she couldn't see a thing once upon a time. So I treated her to a pair of

National Health glasses. *And* she turned stone deaf as well. So I took her to see the doctor and left her there. Doctor Brynberg couldn't *believe* what he saw. Enough wax to make candles to last one family a lifetime. I don't want to brag – but I've been good to my wife. Very good.'

'Haven't I been good to you?'

'You've been bloody marvellous,' was the droll reply. 'A bloody saint!'

Leaning forward and pushing his mouth closer to Naomi's ear, Nathan said, 'She's a bit touched. You can't take too much notice of what she says.' He then nodded towards his neighbour, Shereen. 'She knows. She knows she's a bit wrong in the head. Not altogether bonkers but a bit touched. Am I right, Shereen, or am I wrong?'

'You're a wicked man,' smiled Shereen. 'A very wicked man,' she chuckled.

Keeping a droll face while her tormenting husband was trying to make her laugh, Becky spread both hands and hunching her shoulders said, 'They drag other poor sods off to the lunatic asylum when there's no need . . . but will they take *him*? Of course not.'

'One day, Becky,' laughed Shereen, 'one day they take him.'

'I tell her what to do most days – guide her along, so to speak.' Nathan was now addressing Naomi and only her. She had become his victim and, for once in her life, Naomi was quite speechless. In all of her years mixing with oddballs she had never met a couple like this. 'I give her advice on what to say, that kind of thing.'

'That's right,' said Becky. 'Do this, do that, skin the cat.'

'She thinks the bloody world of me, that's the trouble. Don't you, Beck? Think the world of me?'

'That's right, Nathan. I think the world of you. Especially when you had a tanned body instead of a crooked white one.'

'See what I mean, Naomi?' said Nathan, looking for sympathy. 'But she's harmless enough. She likes cooking and baking and keeps the place all shipshape. Loves running round after me. But that stands to reason. I've been bloody good to her. Lovely spanking new house. What more could she want? All right,' he said, swirling a finger at his temple, 'she's not all there but that's not her fault.'

'Okay. It will do. You take off your coat, Becky. Eight o'clock tomorrow evening it will be finished for you.'

'Good. My feet are killing me,' puffed Becky, carefully pulling her arms out of the coat that once fitted her. 'I'll try not to lose more weight but with him nagging all the time, what can I expect?'

'You shouldn't keep going up and down the bloody stairs,' groaned Nathan, pulling himself up. 'Perhaps now I'll get some supper, woman? Just because you're as skinny as a rake doesn't mean to say that I want to look as if I've just come out of the camp.'

Becky gave her husband a black look and held her stare. 'That's not funny.'

'No . . . but if we keep on not mentioning it we're as bad as the bloody Germans.' With that he offered Murat, the head of the house, his hand.

'Goodnight, my friend,' said Murat, 'Good night.'

'Sleep well,' returned Nathan, and then went to Ismet, the quiet gentleman, and repeated the gesture. Turning to Shereen he simply put a hand on his heart.

Once they had left the house, the room where they all sat went very quiet until Laura said, 'Is your cousin coming soon, Murat?'

'Mehmet is here,' he said, 'upstairs. Now he'll come down.'

True to his word, Mehmet came quietly into the room and went immediately to Naomi, gently lifting her hand to his forehead and then kissing it. To Laura he nodded politely and then sat in the chair, which had been pulled forward by Ismet to whom he whispered a question, '*Ozur . . . nasil denir Ingilizce?*'

'I apologise,' said Ismet, 'the word is a-polo-gise.'

Mehmet looked at Naomi and placed a hand on his heart. 'I apologise for coming to your house. I did not wish to offend you.'

'Actually it isn't my house,' said Naomi, her expression one of a relaxed person in a stranger's home. 'But thank you for the apology. I accept it graciously.' She smiled.

'Thank you, Madam.' The atmosphere in the room immediately changed, especially since Shereen had arrived carrying a tray of fresh Turkish tea.

'I expected to find the husband of your sister's daughter in the house,' continued Mehmet.

'Yes, I did wonder. Please don't be abashed. It is *quite* forgotten.' Looking from him to Shereen, who was offering her a glass of tea, Naomi thanked her and carefully lifted a small cup and saucer from the tray. Not certain as to the Turkish etiquette she waited until the last glass had been accepted, and watched. Rising from their seats the family touched glasses with each other and then with Naomi and Laura, saying, '*Serefe, sihhate.*' To our honour and health.

Settled back in their seats, a warm mood in the room, Naomi, anxious to know what this gentle family had in mind with regard to Harry, began, 'First and foremost, I would like very much to apologise for any *upset* that my niece's husband, who we all believed to be *dead*, has caused your family *here* and in Turkey.'

Clearly, by the warm gestures as the family looked from one to the other, she had said exactly the right thing. Realising this, she continued while ahead: 'Also, I would like to *add* that the news of Harry being alive and back in England came as a great shock to *me*. And this shock I have had to absorb. My beloved niece and great-niece know *nothing* of this and do in fact believe him to have been killed, at sea, by accident. Their hope is to *one day* visit the coastal shore of Oludeniz, where they *believe* the boat capsized and brought an end to his life.'

Lifting their eyebrows the family voiced in Turkish their sympathies for mother and child. 'Do you think that Harry will journey with us to our country?' said Mehmet.

'Back to Turkey? I really cannot say,' said Naomi. 'I wish he would. It would be good for all of us if he returned to the woman who is now considered to be his wife. Your cousin. But, alas, I think *he* might prefer to remain in his own country. He is an Englishman after all is said—'

'Yes,' said Mehmet, 'I understand. But,' he swept a graceful hand across him, 'here in this room my family would sometimes prefer to be in Turkey. They made a—' Concentrating, he tried to think of the word.

Laura helped him out. 'Decision?'

'Yes. They made a decision to come to England to make a life. And they will stay, Naomi, even when the winters are very, very cold and ice is on the windows. The elders in my family miss the wailing of the muezzin calling the faithful to prayer five times a day, and the smells of spices and sights of the bazaar, the lined Asiatic faces of the Anatolian peasants, the camels slow-stepping through our village streets, Turkish carpets airing on balconies.' He paused for a few moments, the silence in the room a touch emotional, then said, 'Why did Harry come to the family home?'

'I believe he had hoped to find Edith, my niece, and Margaret, my great-niece – his daughter – inside. Presumably he wanted to worm his way back into the family. But he found only myself. We had words and I wanted to hit him with a frying pan.'

Turning to Shereen, who suddenly burst out laughing, Mehmet looked puzzled. 'Why do you laugh, my cousin?' Shereen then conveyed all that Naomi had said in her native tongue, and when she explained the frying-pan, quiet amusement from the others gradually built up to soft laughter. Even Laura was having trouble in keeping a straight face.

'I am sorry to say that I would love to have thrown him over the balcony.'

Shereen related this to the family.

'Then you came to the door, Mehmet, and out went Harry to hide on the balcony. When I returned to tell him what had happened he had gone. I can only imagine that he climbed down the drainpipe like an ape to escape you.'

The vision of this clearly amused Shereen: she could hardly translate it for laughing. Joining in with the jest, Naomi actually felt heavy at heart. To her mind, whether she was breaking the ice or not, this family was not going to let Harry off the hook. The atmosphere in this house was good but elsewhere there might have been plans afoot to cut Harry's throat for all she knew. To cover her true feelings she drew on her acting ability. Looking from one to the other, she waited graciously for their expression to change as the room quietened.

It was the cousin who changed the mood back to one of slight tension. 'But you know where he is living, Naomi? He told you this?'

'He told me nothing. He said he would wait until my niece, his wife, came home and talk to her. I said he would do no such thing and that the shock of seeing him would be devastating.' Again Shereen translated this into Turkish – herself serious now.

'He became angry, we had words, and that's when I lost my temper.'

His face serious, Mehmet said, 'If he returns you would let my cousin Murat know?'

'No. I'm awfully sorry but that is *not* the way we do things. Family must *never* give away family.' This was tripe but Naomi thought that it might go down well. 'We are from a very ancient old English line and tradition is of the *utmost* importance! *Never* betray the family!'

As the family talked among themselves in Turkish, Naomi glanced at Laura who raised an eyebrow, herself looking a touch edgy. This scene, for whatever reason, gave rise to Naomi's indignation. How dare they sit as judge and jury? Stilling her temper, she clasped her hands together and waited. Depending on what might be conveyed next, she would respond accordingly.

'We feel,' said Mehmet, 'that this family and your family must have a meeting. We believe that your niece, Edith, must be told that Harry has a woman in Turkey.'

'Well, I'm most awfully sorry to be disparaging,' said Naomi, 'but that is not the way we do things over here. I'm sure you must have been deeply shocked and wounded to learn that your cousin, Cicek, had taken a *married* man as her lover. A *British* married man . . . and so I can understand why you would want Harry to face her and perhaps take some of the blame and to apologise. No doubt your family must have been *terribly* angry with Cicek. She did *after all* live with a man knowing that he had a wife at home. Which must have brought great shame to your family name.'

Since Naomi was speaking without pauses, Mehmet looked to Shereen to interpret and by the grave expression on Shereen's face, she knew that this was going to squash any hopes of a peaceful ending to this meeting. Slowly, with gesticulations that she was not finding easy to convey, Shereen quickly ended her translation.

'I understand,' said Mehmet, 'but my cousin Cicek could not know that Harry was married. This she heard from someone else, much later on.'

'Then why did they not marry in the first place instead of living as lovers, which is against our Christian religion and surely against your faith too?' said Naomi, a sanctimonious smile on her face, trying anything she could to win this battle of wits. She was hardly a church-abiding woman!

'It is far too complicated to explain,' said Mehmet.

'Yes, I can see that now, my courteous friend, and I also see shame and regret in your eyes. You, like myself, are deeply embarrassed by what has happened. My niece, who has had to struggle to bring up a child alone, has not once up until this very year, in fact, gone anywhere near another man. She has been waiting for ten years, hoping that her beloved husband, the father of her only child, might return. That he might have been lying in a hospital somewhere having lost his memory.

'Can you imagine what that must have been like? Ten long years of waiting and hoping and all the while with a broken heart. With your hand on your heart, can you look at me and say that my niece should be punished *further*? She must *not* be told that Harry is alive, especially since she has recently found someone who cares deeply about her. It is far too late to mend bridges and she must never learn that he has been living in sin all the while with another woman in Turkey and for so many years.

'Now I don't care what you do or how far you must travel to find Harry. But I do mind very much if you upset my niece! And I, Mehmet, you must understand, come from a long line of proud East London people! The men in our family would close ranks around me, should I deem fit to make just one telephone call. So please do not tell me what my niece or my great-niece must suffer. It simply will not do. I may have risen from a childhood of poverty but, like others from the East End of London, my roots are in the East End and such roots are *never* forgotten!'

'I don't think that Mehmet was threatening you, Nao,' said Laura, sensing that this was the time for her to step in as the peacemaker. 'He was just trying to see if it could be sorted out by sitting round the table and talking.'

Pleased that Laura was on the mark and her timing perfect, Naomi responded as if she believed that her wise friend was right. 'Well, if I misunderstood and spoke out of turn, I apologise profusely.'

'It's all a misunderstanding,' said Shereen, hunching her shoulders and waving her arms. 'A terrible misunderstanding on both sides.'

'Perhaps,' murmered Mehmet.

'Perhaps?' said Naomi, her eyes narrowing, determined not to let the fish off the hook now that she was this far ahead.

'It *is* a misunderstanding,' he said, 'and all because of my cousin Cicek and your nephew Harry.'

'He is no nephew of mine, Mehmet! I have washed my hands of him. Where Harry is concerned you are most welcome to him. But if you want my advice you will leave well alone. That man is clearly heading for the depths of degradation. If I were you I would turn the other cheek, and when you return to Turkey, help your cousin Cicek to forget Harry.'

'Yes. But Cicek is carrying his child.'

At this point, with the stony silence that had pervaded the room, the sound of a key in the street door was like the rattling of chains. Tariq, the genius son of the proud parents, Shereen and Murat, came into the room and bade them all a good evening in true Turkish style and then, with a lovely smile on his face, said, 'It's so peaceful in here after a day at the office.'

'Sit, Tariq.' His mother, squeezing his arm had eyes only for him now. 'I bring you some tea and soon you will have supper.'

'Tea'll be great, Mum,' said Tariq, 'but nothing to eat. I had something in town – it's why I'm late.

A client wanted to go over a few things and it took longer than I thought it would.'

'Okay. No food *again*.' Shereen, went into the kitchen reeling off a stream of words in her native tongue, which her family had all heard before with regard to mealtimes.

'I don't think we've met,' said Tariq, addressing Naomi while taking her hand and showing the usual respect to an elder.

'No, we haven't,' smiled Naomi, with a certain tingling in her spine that she had not experienced in a very long time. This twenty-five-year-old was not only charming and natural but very good-looking. The pity of it was that he looked too young for Edie and too old for Maggie.

'Do you live on the estate?' said Tariq, pulling a round faded leather pouffe to her side and sitting down.

'Yes, I do . . . and so do my *niece* and *great-niece*. Have you an inkling as to why I am here this evening?'

'Yes.' Tariq was smiling. 'I think I know why you're here. It has something to do with one of my cousins in Turkey?'

'Cicek?'

He looked around the room and settled his attention on his father, Murat. 'I thought you might have sorted things out by now.'

Murat spoke and became the philosopher, saying, 'It takes longer to mend a pair of trousers than it takes to make them.'

'Well, you know my view on it. It's none of our

business and Cicek's probably better off without him.' said Tariq.

'My sentiments entirely,' said Naomi.

'But she is with his child,' said Mehmet to his cousin.

'I realise that, Mehmet. But nothing can be gained by your dragging Harry back to Turkey. The damage is done. They'll stone him,' he joked, to ease the tension building in the room again.

'And what if Cicek wants to come to England – to make a home with Harry?'

'Well, then, let her, Dad,' said Tariq. 'That would solve everything. Uncle Turgut can afford the passage and she can stay here until they find rooms.' He then cautiously turned to his mother as she came back into the room with his tea. 'I might be moving out soon in any case,' he said, sidetracking to bring the attention on to himself and his personal life. He knew he could rely on his mother to want to know more. He was, after all, more important to her than all of her relations in Turkey.

'Moving out?' said his mother, true to form. 'You *found* somewhere already?'

Taking the tea from her he said, 'Yes. Somewhere in London and only two stops on the Underground to the West End.' He knew this would impress. 'I've finally found exactly the right thing for a very good price.'

'The West End,' she said, impressed. 'Near to Harrods?'

'No,' he said, catching the eye of Naomi, who was

loving this, 'it's just off Tottenham Court Road.' He refrained from telling her that the studio flat he was about to purchase was in Greek Street.

'It's a real bargain. The old woman who lived there used to be in the theatre. She passed away a month ago aged ninety-six. The flat needs a lot of work but it's a very big room with a small bathroom and kitchen off it.'

'There is space for two beds?'

'Yes. A bed and a studio couch that pulls down into bed. So you can stay overnight. If that's what you're hinting at.'

'How else will it be cleaned if I don't come? And who will do your washing? Iron your shirts?'

'You, of course. And in return I'll take you out to lunch, to Harrods.'

'My son the billionaire,' said Murat, secretly thrilled with his youngest offspring. 'How much is the rent?'

'I won't pay rent, Dad. I'm buying it. I'll borrow the money and pay it back monthly. It's called a mortgage.'

'I know what a mortgage is, Tariq. When I first came to England I could have a house twice as big as this with a hundred pound notes as deposit. But then . . . poor Turks, as we were seen, were a risk. No mortgage. But things are different now. Luck be with you, my son, luck be with you. *Inshallah*!'

'Do you know the name of the thespian who lived in this studio flat, Tariq? I had many friends from the theatre living in and around Soho. Which street did you say it was in?'

'I didn't,' said Tariq, 'I, er . . . I can't quite remember. And, no, I don't know the woman's name. It's all come about so quickly.' He then turned back to his mother, who was gazing at him with tears in her eyes. 'It won't be for a while, Mum. It takes a long time for everything to go through and then even longer to get the place into a fit state to live in.'

'So you won't be leaving soon?'

'No. Not for a few months, I shouldn't think.'

'Well,' said Shereen, 'you must know about it.' She looked at Naomi and smiled with modesty. 'Tariq is a solicitor. He went to university. Won a scholarship.'

'Anyway,' said Tariq, 'enough about me.'

'Not at all,' said Naomi, 'you've left us all wanting to know more. But . . . as you know we must resolve this business of Harry and Cicek. I personally would like to wash my hands of the whole thing. But I do have *one* request, which comes from the heart.' She glanced around at the others. '*Should* you deem fit to bring the lover of my niece's husband to this country, would you *please* be so kind, for the sake of Harry's wife and child, who have been in mourning for him for ten years, as to make absolutely certain that the couple live at the furthest end of the map, be it south or north of Britain.'

Turning to Tariq, Naomi continued. 'Edith believes her husband to be dead and has at *last* come to accept it. His *daughter*, Margaret, has been brought up without a father to guide her. Now, at almost *fifteen*, it would be devastating if she were to learn that her father has been alive all of this time and living in sin and in secret . . . and that the woman he has taken is with child.'

'I can understand that,' said Tariq. 'It was really good of you to take the time to come here and explain your side of things. I'm sure my family will be discussing this for many more hours . . .'

'Yes, of course they would want to,' said Naomi. 'And this ageing lady is *very* tired and quite weary of it all.'

'Come on, then,' said Laura, standing up and ready to leave now that Tariq the peacemaker had usurped his cousin, whether he had meant to or not. 'Thank you for your hospitality, Shereen and Murat.'

'Ah,' smiled Shereen, 'it's a pleasure. Next week you bring Edith and I will fit you both at the same time. She knows to bring her own—'

'Yes,' said Laura, 'her own material, cotton, buttons and bows.'

'Edith's coming here?' said Tariq. 'The wife of Harry is coming to this house? After all that has happened?'

'It was arranged before we knew that Harry was back,' said Laura, 'and that you were related to . . . well, you know . . .' She wished now that she hadn't got into this particular arena. 'If you want me to lie to Edie and make an excuse I will, but I'd rather not. The webs we weave and all that.'

'No Laura!' said Shereen. 'You come with her and we forget all this! I have met Edie and like her.' She then turned to the men in the room and spoke in rapid Turkish. Sheepishly they backed down and went quiet. In this house, as in many East End people's homes, the woman ruled the roost when push came to shove.

'I'll see the ladies out, Mum,' said Tariq, rising to the occasion, and for reasons the rest of the family could not know.

At the door, and safe in the knowledge that they could not be heard, he said, 'Don't worry. It's all been arranged. Cicek is coming over by boat and she and Harry have been found a small rented house in Glasgow.'

'Goodness Tariq,' murmured Naomi, taken back by this. 'How can so much have happened in such little time?'

'It's been going on for a few weeks but I tried to keep my family out of it. Sometimes a drama can be turned into a crisis and I didn't want that to happen. It would have been bad for all of us.'

'You're incredible, Tariq, do you know that?' said Laura, her face lighting up under the glow of the small light above the front door. 'That was a brilliant performance in there.'

'Well, it's not over yet,' he said, 'this will go on for days. Debating and discussing something that's already settled. But I wouldn't want their feelings to be hurt . . .'

'We won't say a word,' said Laura. 'Not a word.'

'Thank you so much, Tariq.' Naomi smiled. 'You have made a silly old worrying woman very happy. I take it that Harry will be warned not to show his face in these parts?'

'Oh, I think he's got the message now. Two Turkish friends have been talking to him.'

'Really? And when was this?'

'Last night. After he left Edie's flat via the back way. It's the way this lot do things I'm afraid. It's all a bit amateurish but it works. He's been watched for weeks and they followed him last night to your relatives' flat. I'm sure they'll make a good life for themselves in Scotland. Work in a leather-goods factory has been laid on for Harry and for Cicek, until she has the baby.'

'A Turkish firm, I presume,' said Naomi, finding this so incredible.

'Don't worry. It'll all work out.' That said, they bade each other farewell and Tariq went quietly into his family home.

'Well,' said Laura, linking her arm with Naomi's. 'What a turn-up! All problems solved.'

'Yes,' said Naomi, suddenly feeling very sad by it all. 'Poor Edie.'

'I know . . . but sometimes things do happen for the best. That's cold comfort, but she really does like Den, you know. And he's smitten with her. You should 'ave seen him the first time they met at the York Hall—'

'On New Year's Eve.'

'Yep, on New Year's Eve. He couldn't keep his eyes off her lovely face.'

'I must admit that his name is on her lips quite a lot. And from my first impressions he seems very nice. Almost too good to be true.'

'No. You're only thinking like that because so many bad things have happened to Edie. All that's really happened is that she's come out of the shell she's bin hiding away in. She might not stay with him . . . she might even go mad and date a few men, make up for lost time. I shouldn't worry over it. She knows what she's doing – and she's hardly a kid, is she?'

Naomi had to agree with her younger friend, who was more in tune with the times. 'So . . . what do I do *now*, Laura? Go through life *keeping* this dreadful secret from both mother and daughter?'

'I don't think you've got any choice, Nao. In fact, I know you 'aven't. They won't find out. Once he's in Scotland that'll be that. The only reason he came back, I reckon, was because he thought she might be pregnant and he scarpered before she showed. You can't tell me that he thinks much of Edie, not after what he's done.'

'No. No, I don't think he feels anything for any of us.'

'Well, he's on the run and not only from the authorities, don't forget. He's bound to be on edge and scared.'

'No. The way he stretched himself out in Edie's armchair, the expression of contempt on his face – for me, that is, because I've grown old. There was a look in his eyes that spoke of detestation.'

'Well, you can stop thinking about it now. He's out of your life. Gone.'

'That's as may be, but it will take some time before the memory of him in that room, grinning at me, fades away. He tormented me in that oppressive way, which will haunt me for a while.'

'No, it won't. You'll forget all about it when something nice happens. Come and 'ave a drink indoors with me and Jack, we—'

'No, I don't think I will, if you don't mind, Laura. I really *am* ready for my bed. It's *all* been a bit too much for me. And that is something that one can only admit to a *friend*.'

'Daft thing. Go on. Home you go. Or do you want me to walk back with you?'

'No, no, I'll be perfectly all right. It's not even a ten-minute walk and it's *very* well lit *en route*. But thank you, thank you for *everything*. And really I do mean that, Laura.'

'I know you do. Night, night.' She kissed Naomi lightly on the cheek and watched her walk away. Then going into the entrance to her block of flats, she herself felt quite drained. She had not lived a life without her own problems to solve but this was something else. Still, she could hardly take it in. She wondered how she would feel if Jack made another woman pregnant. She shuddered at the thought of it and felt very sorry for Edie.

Making her way home, Naomi, for the first time that she could remember, felt quite alone. A lonely soul on her way home to her ground-level flat for one. It was a miserable evening too, dark and cloudy with the kind of rain you could feel on your skin but not see. And it was quiet. A quiet February night with not even a hint of snow to brighten things. Other than the sound of footsteps echoing in the distance it was silent on the estate.

Arriving at the small green square with the single-storey units surrounding it, Naomi was uplifted by the warm glow coming from the windows and the familiar low sound of a wireless coming from her neighbour's sitting room. Her next-door neighbour, who was in her nineties and doing very nicely for her age. Turning her key in the front door she pushed it open and felt for the light switch. Inside the small hall she disrobed and felt a little more cheerful at being back in her own home where she could sit quietly with a glass of brandy and run the evening's events through her mind.

In her tiny kitchen she lifted the kettle off the gas stove to fill it ready for a cup of tea after her brandy. As she reached for the tap she suddenly replaced the kettle on the draining-board with a bang. Feeling as if her blood had turned cold she stared at it as the horror that all was not as it should be gripped her like a vice. The kettle was not cold. Nor was it lukewarm. The water inside had recently been boiled and she suddenly felt as if someone was there.

Turning slowly around, she gasped and her hand flew to her mouth. Harry was in the kitchen doorway, leaning against the door surround, a grin on his face. 'You've gotta be more careful, Naomi. If I was a cat burglar I would 'ave cleaned you out of treasures by now. Your jewellery, your money stashed in the air vent, your album wiv all them signed photos of famous actors . . .'

'How long have you been here?' she said tightly, hardly able to get the words out. She felt as if every single joint in her body had locked.

'About . . . half an hour to an hour. Dunno. Made meself a cup of tea and found your biscuit tin. Nice shortbread.'

'How did you get in?'

'My penknife, which admittedly is bigger than normal, slipped between a window-frame and Bob's yer uncle – up wiv the catch. You've got little locks on yer windows, Naomi. I know they're crap but if you'd 'ave used 'em, I might not 'ave bin *able* to get in.' The patronising tone was back.

Pressing his lips together he slowly shook his head. 'I never 'ad you down for turning into a silly old woman. Now go and sit by the gas fire, which I've lit so as to make the place warm for yer, and I'll pour you a cup of tea.'

An icy tingling in her spine caused Naomi to feel sick and rather faint. Anyone in a normal state of mind would not behave in the way that Harry was presenting himself. Speaking as if he had every right to be in her house. As if it were his home too. 'Please leave this house now,' said Naomi, a telltale tremor in her voice as she stuck out her chin defiantly.

'Don't be silly. Come on. You're as white as a sheet. Take my arm and I'll help you through. We don't want you ending up flat on your back, now, do we?'

'I *shall* go into my sitting room, thank you. But I do not need an arm to support me. I don't know what has happened to you, Harry, but you are not the young man I knew. You would never have broken into my home—'

'Stop *talking* for five minutes. I'm trying to *help*, Naomi. You're the one who's changed. You've aged. Face facts. It's not me who's changed but you.' He was treating her as if she were an imbecile.

'Please leave the doorway and let me pass, Harry. I don't need assistance.' Trembling now, Naomi knew that she had to sit down. The tea could wait.

Standing aside with the air of a true gentleman, Harry gave a gallant bow, saying, 'Have it your way . . .'

Dropping into her armchair she raised her eyes. 'Would you be so good as to pour me a brandy? The bottle is in the—'

'Sideboard,' grinned Harry, cutting in. 'As are the glasses.'

Her eyes following his every movement, Naomi could hardly believe this was happening. He had been through her cupboards, touching her things, and now he was behaving as if he lived here. This was akin to a horror film in slow motion directed by none other than Alfred Hitchcock himself. The perspiration on her brow had turned cold but with her head rested back into a cushion she gradually began to feel better. She turned the palms of her hands upwards and began to take long slow breaths of air as she and other actors used to do before going on stage to perform.

'The thing is, Nao,' said Harry, shortening her name for the first time ever, 'we're in a bit of a predicament, you and me.' He handed her a small brandy while looking directly into her face, unblink-ing.

'Thank you,' murmured Naomi, taking the drink from him. 'Tell, me what it is you want of me, Harry, and all I can promise is to listen. I'm too old to play psychological games with you.'

'*Games?* I'm not one of your queer actor friends, Naomi. You've got to stop clinging on to the *past*. You're in the *real* world now.'

'What do you want from me, Harry? Why are you here?'

Closing one eye and concentrating, he said, 'Well . . . even though I don't think that this country's worth a light, I do believe that my Edie would want me to stay put if she knew I was back. That I was still in the land of the living. So I need time to think things through. Should I go abroad or stay put? That is the question, Nao. That is the question.'

'And the Turkish family. They are out for your blood. Or are you thinking of returning to Turkey? To Cicek. Is that it?'

'Who gives a fuck about Turkey? I can't stand the Turks. They're still living in the Dark Ages, Naomi. Travelling around on the back of stinking camels!'

'Then you will go to Glasgow – with Cicek?'

'Fucking Glasgow. Leave off. Glaswegians? One was on our boat that capsized. Turned 'imself in as a survivor. Yellow belly. If anyone'd blab, he would. I wouldn't wipe my arse on his toilet paper. Not that he'd use toilet paper. Old newsprint more like. Lowest of the low,' he said, shuddering. 'Horrible people.'

'Well, then, why *are* you here? What is it you want from me? Money? Are you here because you need money? Is that it?' Naomi could not fathom the way his mind was working. She felt as if he was leading her around in circles.

'This *is* a nice little place you're got,' he said, sprawling on the settee where he had placed himself. 'Very nice. And this sofa's comfortable. But for ever? No. It's one step from the grave, if you think about it.'

'You can't stay here, Harry, if that's what you're after.'

'Course I can. Your neighbours are too senile to catch on. It'll only be for a week . . . before I sail away.'

'No. I'm awfully sorry but I don't want you here.' She was staring into his face now. 'Harry, I will not be manipulated. I would rather be dead. So, if you must, then murder me. Strangle me tonight. I would rather that than have you living under my roof.'

'Once the actor always the actor. You kill me, you know.' Kicking off his shoes, he swung his legs up on to the sofa and pulled a cushion into the crook of his neck. 'Oooh, that's better. I'll sleep like a baby on this.'

Lost as to what next to say, Naomi tried another tactic: 'Am I to be a prisoner then – in my own home?'

'Prisoner?' He relaxed into a smile. 'You've bin in too many dramas, Nao.'

'So I am to be let out?'

'I don't see a warden with a key anywhere.'

'And you're not the least bit worried that I might go to the police? Or the Turkish family of whom I have become fond? Or Ben and his friends?'

'What good will that do? What would be the point of it?'

'I would have you out of my home.'

'Please yourself. If you don't think enough of Edie to put up with me for a week you're more of an actor than we all caught on. This is the fifties, Nao, not the twenties. Mobsters can't go around knifing or shooting people the way they did then.' He made himself more comfortable. 'If you go to the authorities, however, that would be a different kettle of fish. Then I *would* be worried. But if *I* go down – Edie comes down with me. I'll say she knew I was alive and kicking all the time and still took the pension. Never mind the shock she'd 'ave when she sees me in the flesh and not as a ghost.'

'You should have thought of that when you turned up at the flat. You're a very selfish man, Harry.'

His eyes closed, arms folded, Harry said, 'I knew she wasn't in. I'm like the Scarlet Pimpernel. Do we see him here? Do we see him there? You never see Harry anywhere.'

'So why did you turn up?'

'I wanted to see you. I guessed that Edie'd go out on Valentine's with that drip she's been seeing. And that daughter of mine'd be off with the Italian. Fourteen and going out with a man! I don't know what Edie thinks she's up to.'

'Maggie is almost fifteen and Tony, her boyfriend,

is just sixteen. But how could you know all of this? Of their movements? Were you spying?'

'You see him here, you see him there, that Harry Birch gets everywhere.' Enjoying himself now, he continued. 'How do I know? Because I watch, look and listen – and I love it. It's a lovely feeling to know what everyone's doing and especially since they don't 'ave a clue that I'm there, watching.'

Obviously Harry had thought everything out in detail, Naomi realised. Questions slowly crossed her mind and one in particular: did she have a choice other than to let him stay? 'How long do you think you will need to hide in my flat, Harry?'

'A week. Gimme a week without nagging or threatening to go to the police and I'll be gone from your and Edie's life for good.' The tone of Harry's voice had changed yet again, but this time it was more like the old Harry's. Naomi could not guess that deep down inside this man was grieving for the life he once had. The life he had lost because of staying in Turkey. He had sold himself down the river. He knew that he could never live under his real name again unless he was prepared for a very long prison sentence.

'I don't know what made me go to Edie's flat,' he said at last. 'It was stupid, really. But I just wanted to see the inside of where she lived. Smell it. Be there. I knew she'd gone out for the night and so had Maggie. I thought you of all people would 'ave let me in without a fuss. But I was wrong. I had to leave by the back door and scale a drainpipe, like an intruder. An unwanted person.'

'Harry, please . . .' whispered Naomi. 'I am not made of stone. Please don't test me any more. You change from one mood to another and confuse me.'

'What you see right now is all there is. I've blown it, Naomi, chucked it all away, and for what? Sun, sea, freedom and another woman. A beautiful woman at that. But I never loved 'er like I loved my Edie.' He paused to swallow against the lump in his throat. 'I'll be gone soon. Out of everyone's way.'

'Gone? What do you *mean*? Is this another of your *stories* to upset me? Do you intend to kill yourself as Edie's mother did? Will you let it be made *public* to get the very most out of it? Write to a newspaper before you slit your throat? Thereby having my niece suffer yet again. Is this what you have in mind? You have a *plan*?'

'*Yes*, Naomi,' he groaned, 'I *do* have a plan. I came back to England because I thought I missed it. Now I know different. Fucking black men everywhere you look. Freezing and miserable in the winter. And overcrowded with these bloody new estates they're shoving up. No. It's not for me. I'm done with this miserable little island. In a week's time I'll be off to a sunnier place. Not fucking Turkey, though.'

'A week,' said Naomi. 'Your ticket is booked, then, is it?'

'*Yes*, my passage *is* booked. At last the penny drops.'

'And you would like to lie low here until then?'

'It would help. A week that's all.'

'And once you've gone to this sunnier place you won't return to England?'

He turned his head slightly to look into her face. 'No, I bloody won't. If you knew where I was going you wouldn't even ask that question.' He returned her sceptical look with a smile. 'Don't you wanna know, then?'

'Does it matter?' Very tired by all of this, all that Naomi actually needed was her cat-nap.

'Spain. South of fucking Spain. Beautiful—'

'Harry! You never used to swear.'

'You should see the picture of the place, Nao. A three-storey house in a terrace of white-painted Spanish 'ouses with little balconies and beautiful flowers growing up the walls. And in a lovely little cobblestone turning.'

To Naomi this sounded very much like a fantasy he had created for himself. 'Well, I'm sure you'll fit in very well.'

'Course I will. They're more relaxed, the Spanish.'

'So someone is giving you a very generous handout?'

Predictably, Naomi had touched a raw nerve. 'Call it what you want. Who cares? So long as I'm away from this miserable country. Sod the past. I can't say I fancy Edie any more, if truth be told. I prefer dark women. Not niggers but . . . Spanish. Yeah. A nice plump Spanish wife should do me a treat. Anyway, Edie's second-hand goods now. Another bloke's had her. And as for my passage and some-where to live in Spain, I'm being paid in kind for work carried out so far and work to be carried out in the future.

'I rub people out, Naomi. People who mess with

professional business dealers and have to be . . .' He pointed a finger at his temple and shouted, 'Bang!'

'That's not funny, Harry, and please try to remember that while I'm not accustomed to being an *audience* I know exactly how the mind of the performer works. What you have to try and remember is when to switch off.'

'Oh. Right. I can see what you're gettin' at. Wot a wise woman you are underneath all that garbage.' Staring at her, a studied expression on his face, Harry went quiet, and Naomi saw through his act. He was back in his intimidating mode.

Leaving him to it, glad that at least he had shut up, she took off her shoes, pulled her rug from the floor next to her chair where it had fallen and covered her legs. Her head sunk into her feather cushion. She hoped that he at least would allow her to sleep. Fifteen minutes later he was gently nudging her.

'The question is, Naomi, shall we 'ave fish and chips or saveloys and pease pudding? It's a ten-minute walk to the chip shop and fifteen to the café at the top of Globe Road. I don't mind either way. What would you prefer?'

His voice drifting across her head, Naomi spoke in a whisper: 'Fish and chips would be very nice, Harry.'

'Fish and chips it is, then. I'll pick up a bottle of cider from the pub as well.'

Semi-awake, Naomi murmured. 'Not the pub, Harry, someone might recognise you . . .'

'All right. It'll 'ave to be milk. From the machine.'

Rubbing her eyes and yawning, she said, 'I think that's sensible.'

'Stop worrying about me. The Turks have got sawdust for brains. Bloody Cicek's family 'ave at any rate. Certain others would knife you while you're saying your prayers.'

Almost fully awake now, Naomi peered at him. 'You can't be serious, Harry?'

'Course I'm not. You take things too earnestly. Do you want a wally and a pickled onion?'

'Both, please.'

Once he had gone out, Naomi went into the kitchen to percolate some strong coffee. Having listened to Harry's ramblings earlier and seen the way his mood and expression changed within seconds, she did not cherish the thought of being in a deep sleep with him in the house. She was relieved to have a little time by herself so that she could think things through.

Back in her comfortable armchair and sipping her lovely fresh cup of coffee, Naomi felt easier about him breaking into her quiet, calm home. 'You are going to have to go out during the day,' she quietly told herself, 'but not to Edie's, or to see Laura or Jessie. And you dare not go anywhere near Ben for fear of him drawing it out of you. You have one option, Naomi . . . and that is to lay all of your trust in your most trusted friend. Harriet.' She drew strength from the fact that in a week's time Harry would be gone.

8

On this early April evening, and five weeks after Harry had furtively packed his bag and gone in the night without saying goodbye, Naomi was looking forward to the party that Edie was giving in honour of Maggie's fifteenth birthday. During his stay with Naomi Harry had made it his business to see as little of her as possible. Out for most of the day, when he would go to work as a casual labourer on a site close by where another modern estate was in the early stages of being built, Harry had been trying to carve himself a niche back in the East End.

Working on the foundations of the new Ocean Estate on the Mile End Road, he had enjoyed the company of other men, as he always had, and especially those like himself who were a touch on the clandestine side, existing in a way to ensure confidentiality for fear of being exposed. Harry, to his relish, had discovered that he was not, by any means, one of a few to have changed his name. There were hundreds in the same boat working in London and especially in the East End.

Reasons for taking on new identities the men kept to themselves, with no questions asked. A wink and a nod on pay-day was all that was necessary for a man to show he was in the same club. Those men without cards would go into a shed on the site to receive their cash in hand while others employed legitimately went into the site office.

But Harry had not been able to keep himself to himself quite as much as he should have, and his habit of goading and baiting others had not gone down too well among the workers. The consequence of which was that other men gradually began to keep their distance from him until, as the case had been when he left Naomi's flat, hostility had crept in.

However, with the local government's massive rebuilding scheme in the East End, Harry had not found it necessary to move on. There was plenty of employment. He had now secured himself work on the newly built Rogers Estate in Bethnal Green as a casual caretaker's assistant while going from one place to another to lay down his head – namely the homes of Ben and Joey.

With Harry out of her life and her thoughts, Naomi was thoroughly enjoying herself and was, as one might expect, proving to be a wonderful hostess at Maggie's fifteenth birthday party, with Edie's friend, Jessie, as her best supporting helper. The Italian family had been invited as well as other neighbours, together with friends from Cotton Street and a girl from Maggie's class at school who was becoming her best friend. This was Rita, the other contender for the post at the library. The final decision made had pleased each of them. They had *both* been offered a position, Maggie as junior librarian and her friend Rita as assistant to the chief historian.

The celebration party having got off the ground, Edie's new man, Dennis, had brought a hush to the room when he had stood up and called for attention in order to make his speech. Shy at first, he soon warmed to the friendly faces and gentle asides to help him relax.

Not wishing to milk the attention, he told his captive audience that the one thing he had always wanted in life was to be part of a family, a happy, contented family. With his gaze on Maggie, whom he had drawn to his side, he stroked her hair and then withdrew a small velvet box from his jacket pocket. Giving her a fatherly wink he flicked open the lid and then, taking her by surprise, lowered himself down on to one knee, asking if she would do him the greatest honour of becoming his beloved daughter.

Overwhelmed, Maggie's hand flew to her mouth to stop herself crying. Offering her hand to him he slipped the ring on to the third finger of her right hand to the sound of clapping and cheering. Then, still on one knee, he turned to face Edie, who had tears rolling down her cheeks. 'I know I've taken a big risk by asking Mags to be my daughter when I don't even know if her mother will take me for her husband but, well, I wanted to show that I'm ready not just for marriage but to settle down to a family life. We've only known each other since New Year's Eve, but I feel as if I've known Edie all of my life. I know that Naomi's been a bit sceptical at this lightning romance but I aim to prove her wrong.'

To the sound of polite chuckling, Naomi was touched by his honesty. 'I shall buy myself a rolling-pin for the cause, Dennis. So do be careful.'

'I don't doubt that for one minute, Naomi,' he said, quietly laughing. Then, reaching into his other pocket, he produced a matching velvet box and held it in the flat of his hand. The room fell silent as he looked across to Edie and waited for her to come over to him. She walked slowly across the room and stood before him.

Taking her hand in his and looking into her eyes, he said, 'Edie . . . marry me,' his prepared speech having flown from his mind.

'Is that an order?' She said, 'Or a request?'

'A request. Please will you marry me?'

'Yes, you daft sod, I'll marry you.' Holding out her hand she looked into his face and mouthed the words, 'I love you,' and then, as he slipped the ring on her finger, she burst into tears.

To the sound of laughing and joyous cheers, one by one the guests hugged and congratulated the happy couple and Naomi, who was standing separate from the crowd, looked silently on as the warmth of love for her niece charged through her. She hadn't had time to really get to know the handsome young man that Edie was clearly in love with but that had been partly her own fault. When asked, on Valentine's Day, if she thought Edie should accept a proposal from Dennis, Naomi had been scared that her niece would get hurt again.

Catching Edie's eye, Naomi blew her a kiss as Edie eased her way through the small, happy crowd and wrapped her arms around her mother-figure and hugged her, 'I know I said I would wait a year but I really love him, Nao. Be happy for me.'

'I am, my darling,' said Naomi, 'I am so terribly happy for you. I love you very much, Edie.'

'And I love you,' she said, stroking Naomi's back. 'You've been more than a mother to me. Much more.'

So, with the evening of Maggie's birthday now on a high note, Edie could not have been happier. Tony's parents, Ida and Albino Baroncini, were clearly enjoying themselves and Ida was getting on very well with Naomi who was probably, and without trying, the star of the evening. Among other things she was a natural-born hostess, who couldn't help making sure that she spoke to each and every guest. Eventually, as with such people as herself who pushed themselves to the limit, she felt the need to break away and lie down on Edie's bed for a quick nap.

Slipping discreetly out of the room she heard a short ring on the bell as she passed the front door. Believing this to be another guest, she opened the door to find Laura and Jack's friend Alf standing there. 'Goodness me, I didn't know you were coming. How wonderful.' Her natural smile gave away her feelings. She really had been taken by this funny man when at Laura's party.

'Hello, sweetheart,' said Alf, in a quiet voice. 'You're just the person I was gonna ask to talk to. In private.'

'Am I?' A hand on her chest, Naomi was puzzled.

'Yes, you are,' he said. 'Come outside a minute and put the door on the latch.' He then removed his much treasured overcoat and placed it round her shoulders. 'There we are. You're the only one that's ever had that put on by me.'

'Well, how very sweet,' said Naomi, nonplussed. 'And to what do I owe this pleasure?'

Placing a finger on his lips, he ushered her away from the street door, along the balcony and down one flight of stairs to where Ben and Joey were waiting. 'I can see you've had a couple of brandies over the top,' grinned Ben. 'How's the party going?'

'Very well, thank you.' Naomi looked from one to another. 'What on earth is going on?'

'Come on down to Alf's motor-car. We've someone in there who's got something to say to you.'

'To me?'

Allowing herself to be guided down the stairs and to the car, her mind was a complete blank. Then, with their captive in the dark and in the front seat of the locked car, Alf pushed the key into the back door and held it open. 'In you get, my darling.'

Slipping in beside her and closing the door, while Ben and Joey waited in the entrance of the block of flats, Alf said, 'Here we are, then, all nice and cosy. So,' he said, addressing Harry, 'what 'ave you got to say for yerself?'

Turning slowly to face Naomi, Harry sighed as if with frustration. 'I'm very sorry that I broke into your little flat, Na-o-mi.'

'But I thought you were in Spain. What *is* going on?'

'Now say it as if you mean it, Harry,' said Alf.

'Oh, what is this, for fuck's sake? I said what you told me to say, and I'm not gonna say it agen.'

'Yes, you are.' The tone in Alf's voice had completely changed. It was authoritative. Holding up his hands as if in submission, Harry repeated his line in a dead-pan voice, which just about appeased Alf.

'But I thought you had gone abroad five weeks ago? To the south of Spain,' said Naomi, puzzled by all of this. 'Were you lying, Harry?'

'He made the biggest mistake of 'is life, Nao,' said Alf. 'He went from you to Joey's with no idea that we knew exactly where he'd been holed up. With enough whisky inside 'im and wivout needing much encouragement he started up with his silly talk. We let him ramble on till we knew the score.'

'Now tell Naomi your little story of Spain, Harry.'

Harry spoke deliberately slowly. 'It was *all* hopeful wishing. And I'm sorry I told a *big* lie. All right, Overcoat? Will *that* do?'

'It's Alf to you. And you're pushing your luck, son. You really are.' Alf then gave Naomi's arm a little squeeze, saying, 'He won't be troubling you agen.'

'Oh . . . but you're not going to hurt him?' said Naomi, a tremble in her voice. This was all proving too much for her.

'Not one finger will be laid on Maggie's father, don't you fret. And only *because* he's her father. The main point, Nao, was for 'im to apologise and for you to know for definite that he *is* catching a plane and I'm gonna make sure he gets on it. He'll be met at the other end, and once he's out of the airport, his passport'll be taken away and kept in a safe place. He won't be able to come back here of his own free will. We wanted you to know that, Naomi, and we want Harry to say goodbye so you know that he's gone for good. From what I gather, he never even left a note when he left your place.'

'No, but that was all right.' She leaned forward towards Harry and said, 'But *where* are you going?'

'To an island in the sun,' Alf answered for him. 'A contact of mine'll be waiting for 'im. He's gonna work in a kitchen of an 'otel. A very busy kitchen. Washing up, fetching and carrying.'

'I see.' She went quiet and then, addressing Harry, said, 'Why did you say you were going to Spain, Harry? That seems rather odd.'

'It put your mind at rest, didn't it?'

'Well, yes . . . but, then, a lie often does. Where have you been staying?'

'I've bin drifting. Leave it at that.'

'He's a bit of a Roger the Dodger so we're gettin' 'im on that plane first thing tomorrer. He slipped Ben's net and come round 'ere earlier, on account of it being Maggie's birthday, he said, but then let it slip about Edie's new feller . . .'

'I wanted to make sure he looked all right,' said Harry, talking as if he were bored to death with all of this.

'I'm sure,' murmured Alf. 'Call it a premonition,

if you like, Nao, but I 'ad a feeling this is what our trouble-maker had in mind. He picked up the fact that there was a party tonight from Ben and Joey since they'd bin invited. I knew we'd find 'im skulking around down 'ere. Wondering how he could break up the party and the engagement that I happened to know was gonna come about. Dennis, your future nephew-in-law, is no stranger to me.'

'Can we go now, Alf, *please*?' said Harry. 'This is gettin' on my nerves.'

'I didn't even realise you knew Ben and Joey, Alf, never mind Harry.'

'Oh, we all roll around each other, Naomi. Off you go, then, sweetheart. You enjoy yerself up there. It sounded like it was goin' well.'

'Yes, it is.' She reached out and touched Harry on the shoulder. 'Try and make a new life for yourself, Harry. Especially now that Edie is to be married.'

'Oh, get out the car, Naomi. And Edie can't get married – not while I'm alive. That's bigamy.'

'Take no notice,' said Alf pushing open the door for her. 'He's not coming back.'

'Go away, Naomi, will yer? So we can get off this bloody estate. It gives me the creeps.'

'Well, then, why come here?'

'To remind me of what I'm going *to* and getting away *from*. Sun, sea and sand for stinking old bomb sites and pee-smelling bricks everywhere. Can't be a bad swap, can it?'

Having spent a week in Harry's company, seeing his moods swing from all levels, she had realised that underneath it all he was the same person she had always known, except angrier and resentful. 'It's time to move on and begin again, Harry. Cut the ties.'

'I already did that in Turkey. Can't wait to get away agen.'

'And why shouldn't you? You're a free man once abroad. You may marry again and have children. Don't look back. Never look back, Harry.'

'Tell that to the Turks,' said Alf. 'He's left a young woman carrying his child. Give my overcoat to the boys once they've seen you to the front door, sweetheart.'

'I will,' said Naomi. 'Goodbye, Harry.'

'Ta ta, Naomi. And don't forget to bolt yer windows. You never know who might break in,' he said, laughing none too convincingly.

Once Naomi was out of the car, Alf turned to Harry, saying, 'You're a tormenting bastard, you are. Got no respect for women whatsoever.'

'They're all *whores*, Alf. You should *know* that by now. No common sense, *nuffing*. And when they get old like that, they smell,' he said, shuddering. 'Cheap talcum powder, mothballs and pee. *Yuk!*'

'But you'd give up your right arm if you could live with someone like her. She's a one-off. Gawd knows how she put up with you for a week. She did it for Edie, I know, but all the same—'

'I wasn't in that much, Alf. She bored the shit out of me.'

Knowing that that could never have been the case and that Harry was still covering his true feelings of failure, he said, 'You know we 'aven't got no choice, don't yer? You've been a silly boy and dug yerself into this hole.'

'Alf, I don't give a *fuck*. I'll be *back*.' He grinned. 'Stop worrying. If you wanna pay for me to go to a desert island, well, *do* it. Sorted me out some work as well, *lovely*!' He was grinning again. 'You wanna be a charity – *all right*. Nuffing wrong wiv it. Fucking stupid but that's your problem, not mine. Stop *worrying* over it. You should try an' relax a bit more. Keep your nose out of other people's business. Shouldn't *interfere*.'

'Yeah, all right, Harry. That's enough. Wind me up a fraction more and I'll shove my fucking fist in that face of yours.'

Back in Edie's flat all that Naomi wanted was her much cherished lie-down in as quiet a room as possible. But this was not to be. Maggie, concerned that she hadn't been able to find her aunt, was in the passage looking for her to show off the lovely delicate gold and topaz ring that Dennis had given to her. When she saw how drawn Naomi looked, she went to her and placed a hand on her shoulder, asking if she was unwell.

Not wishing to get into conversation Naomi gently curled a hand and said, 'Darling, I'm going into your mother's bedroom for a rest. Wake me in twenty minutes' time, would you?'

'Course I will,' said Maggie, peering into her pale face. 'Are you just tired or not well?'

'Tired. We must remember my age, sweetheart.

Once upon a time when love was in the air, as it is this evening, I would have lasted to the very end. Dancing in moody nightclubs converted from cellars or sitting and holding hands with my lover while listening to the music of Fats Waller and Duke Ellington. Alas, youth and I parted company long since.'

'Well, you've bin a brick in there going round talking to everyone. You've worn yerself out, that's what it is. I wanted you to have a proper look at this.' She spread the fingers of her right hand.

Taking Maggie's hand Naomi admired the ring. 'Mags, sweetheart, it is quite beautiful. And *such* a clever choice. Topaz is the perfect stone for your hair and complexion. Dennis has put a lot of thought into it.'

'I know,' said Maggie, and then, 'Did you hear what he said to me?'

'Of course I did. I heard and I saw and it was very touching.'

'It would be nice to have a dad – even if he's not really my dad. Do you like 'im more now you've got to know him?'

'I like him in the same way as I have always liked him. I was being cautious, sweetheart, that was all. Your mother is deliciously happy and that lifts my heart. Now, I really must lie down.'

'And you do like Tony, don't you?'

'Yes, I do. Just don't get *too* carried away. You've *years* ahead of you to experiment with sex.'

'Aunt! What if someone heard you say that? Mrs Baroncini's in there and she's very strait-laced!'

'She couldn't possibly have heard, as you well know. Now, go back into the sitting room and help your mother by being a wonderful hostess.' With that Naomi turned away and went into Edie's bedroom.

'You all right, baby?' whispered Tony, kissing the back of Maggie's pale, soft neck. 'Your aunt been teasing you again, has she?'

'No. She's just tired, that's all.' Flashing him a radiant smile she stretched her arm out and wiggled the finger adorned with her prized piece of jewellery. 'I love this ring,' she said. 'Wasn't it nice of my stepdad to buy it for me?'

'Mmm,' he said, gazing into her lovely soft green eyes. 'Mags . . . can't we . . .' He nodded towards her bedroom door.

'No way. I'd get skinned alive if we got caught.'

'Just for five minutes, that's all. I want to kiss those lovely lips and stroke . . . your beautiful hair.'

'That's not what you was gonna say, you tease,' Glancing around herself, with the celebratory drink having taken effect, she said, 'Five minutes, and only five minutes. And no wandering hands.'

'I promise,' he said, kissing the tip of her nose. Then, looking furtively about him, Tony took her hand and led her into her bedroom, quietly closing the door behind them.

'God, Tony,' whispered Maggie, 'what if someone comes in?'

'We're not doing anything wrong,' he said, pulling

her close to him. 'I'll open the curtains a bit more so I can see you better from the street-lights.'

'Open them properly,' she said, keeping her eye on the door. She could hear people in the kitchen and living room and, although nervous that they might get caught, was thrilled by this daring adventure. Returning to her, Tony lost no time. His hands gently laid on her shoulders, he kissed her lightly on the lips and then slowly drew her closer until they were like one body, swaying as they kissed with no more thoughts of anyone outside that room. His breath hot on her neck. 'Maggie . . . I think I'm in love with you.'

'And I think I love you Tony,' she murmured, responding to the wonderful sensation as he slowly massaged her small soft breasts and pushed himself hard against her. She could feel the heat of his erection pressing between her legs. Kissing as they had never kissed before, she slowly parted her legs a little. Every inch of her was throbbing and she felt as if she might explode if it didn't stop soon, but neither did she want it to end.

Slowly inching her skirt up with one hand while the other squeezed her breast and his mouth sucked at her neck, Tony quietly moaned in ecstasy. 'Oh, God, Maggie . . .'

Pushing his hand inside her knickers he slowly massaged until she urgently whispered, '*Inside. I want you inside of me.*' Slowly he slid a finger into her moist hot vagina until he could stand it no more and tugged at her silky knickers until they slipped to the floor. To the sounds of her heavy breathing he slowly and carefully eased himself inside her. Maggie was in heaven and would not have cared if the roof caved in.

'Ah, Mrs Birch! At last I find you in the crowd!' cried Tony's mother, Mrs Baroncini. 'It is a lovely party! And you are engaged to be married! I am very pleased for you! We are both pleased for you!'

'She's a romantic, no?' said Albino, her husband, hunching his shoulders and splaying his hands. 'She always cries when somebody fall in love! She cry if somebody get engaged to be married! She cry when baby comes. Thank you for your very kind hospitality. To be with your family at such a time is magnificent!'

'It's a pleasure for us that you're here,' said Edie, 'and we must have a meal together with the young ones. Maybe they went for a walk.'

'Or maybe they are on the stairs again, talking. Talking when they should be canoodling.'

'Albino!' Tony's mother looked horrified at this. 'Too much *wine*. Too much *talk*!'

'I drank only beer! Is this wine? I don't think so.'

'It's all right, Ida, I didn't take him seriously. Maggie's probably boring your son to death about the library. She starts work in three weeks' time.'

'Ah!' cried Ida, delighted. 'Mama's baby is no longer a child! She is a working girl! I congratulate you. She is a good girl! I always say Maggie is a good girl! Did I say that, Albino?'

'She said it! Now we go home! She tell me I drink too much so – I go to bed!' They wove through the bodies and Edie watched with a smile as Tony's mother gripped Albino's arm, scolding him in Italian.

'If they're gonna become family,' said Jessie, coming up behind Edie, 'you'll have some wonderful evenings in their place. The Italians celebrate at every opportunity.'

Turning to face her friend, Edie said. 'I think you're right, but let's not forget that Tony *is* Maggie's first boyfriend and she's only just out of ankle socks.'

'It happens. I've known Max since I was fourteen. We never courted till later on, though, it's true. Anyway, you can't go far wrong if it is a long courtship and ends in marriage. Ida loves your Maggie.'

'You know . . . you *always* manage to make me feel more at ease about things. And you seem to have got to know our neighbours already. I wish I—'

'That's because I'm inquisitive!' said Jessie. 'Got to know who's living below and beside me. Now, then, where's Nao? My sister is dying to meet her. I'm gonna arrange something. She wants to know if she can visit Nao in her flat.'

'Oh,' said Edie, puzzled. 'Why?'

'Dolly's the one writing a play about hop-picking and wants a bit of advice on how to go about sending it in once it's finished. Nao said she'd 'ave a word apparently.'

'Sending it in to where, Laura?'

'The BBC.'

'Television?' Edie frowned. 'I don't think Naomi's got any contacts there.'

'No, but she might know someone who knows

someone. A producer or editor. She told Laura and she's really excited about it. East Londoners on the hop-fields and the follow-up set round the square where Laura and Jack used to live, here in Stepney.'

'I'll remind 'er, then,' said Edie, looking around the room for her aunt. 'She must be having a little lie-down on my bed or Maggie's.'

'Anyway, I'd better get back. Max 'as had to work on a Saturday agen and late. I'm gonna do 'im a corned-beef salad. I've 'ad a lovely time, Ed. And congratulations again.' She gave her a hug, saying, 'Den's a good man. Caring. I wish you well to wear 'is ring.'

'Thanks,' whispered Edie, the joy showing in her eyes. 'It's all a bit fast but—'

'No, it's not. We none of us are getting younger. Grab a bit of happiness if you can. You made the right decision and the right choice.' Giving her friend a wink, Jessie slipped away.

A few minutes later, squeezing past some guests in Edie's passage, Laura almost bumped into Maggie as she crept out of her bedroom with Tony following. She gave her a tormenting grin and said, 'Been looking at your stamp collection, 'as he?'

Blushing madly, Maggie mumbled inaudibly, giving a humble reason for them being in there. She then eased her way through to the living room while Tony slipped out the front door in Laura's footsteps.

All he wanted was to be in his room, on his bed, to think about Maggie. Things had changed now. Both of them had crossed a certain line and with it came the realisation that he was hopelessly in love. His girlfriends so far, pretty though they had been, were nothing compared to Maggie, and the flirting and petting had come nowhere close to what he had just experienced for the first time in his life. He couldn't wait to be on his own to absorb all that had happened in the privacy of his own room.

Taking the stairs two at a time he had no idea that Laura had followed him out and knowing exactly where he had been could only imagine what he and Maggie had been up to.

As she walked along the balcony towards her flat, she was reminded of when she was young and Jack was hot and passionate.

Smiling to herself, Laura pushed the key into the lock of her door, still reminiscing. 'Love's young dream,' she giggled, going inside and closing the door behind her.

'What? Found yerself a nice little boy to dance with, did you, Laura?'

'God, Jack! What d'yer think you're doing? Creeping about in the passage like that,' she said, going into their living room. 'Frightened the life out of me.'

'I wasn't creeping. I was on my way to see what you was up to. Kay's bin asking for yer. You know . . . your *daughter* Kay!'

'Don't tell lies. I've only bin gone an hour—' she said, brushing past him.

'Hour and twenty minutes!'

'She shouldn't still be awake at this hour in any case.'

'She's not now. Your dad read 'er a bedtime story.'

'Dad? I didn't know he was coming round.'

'He fancied a walk. And he's left some bingo tickets for Bert and Liz. So, who was there, then? Some of dozy Den's mates?'

'One or two. He popped the question with a beautiful diamond ring,' said Laura, taking off her coat. 'I wish you'd 'ave been in there. It was really lovely the way he did it. Got down on one knee—'

'Fuck me,' groaned Jack. 'Well, there you are then. Dozy Den. The glove fits.'

'Ah, but he never got down on his knee for Edie. Not at first, anyway.'

'If you're gonna tell me he proposed to you for a lark I'll go and smack 'im in the face right now. Showing me up.'

'He got down on his knee and, with a lovely topaz ring in a little velvet box, he asked *Mags* if she'd do 'im the honour of becoming 'is daughter! It was lovely.'

'Jesus, he's worse than I thought.'

'Then he proposed to Edie and gave her a lovely diamond ring.'

'Well, at least he's got a few bob. I s'pose that's somefing.'

'Ah, but,' said Laura, moving in close to him, 'he 'asn't got your laughing blue eyes and broad shoulders.'

'Stop trying to get round me,' said Jack, loving it. 'You said you'd be half an hour.'

'I wanted you to miss me,' she purred. 'I thought we'd have a nice romantic cuddle by the fire.'

'Did you, now? Well, you'll 'ave to wait, won't yer? I'm bloody starving. Go and get us some fish and chips. Then I'll fink about giving you a cuddle.'

'You go and get 'em while I change into something more comfortable,' she teased.

'You want *me* to go out and buy fish and chips?' He was aghast at the thought of it. 'What am I now – a woman?'

'I just thought—'

'Yeah, well, don't. And get me skate, not rock nor cod. And tell the fryer that if the fish is not white I'll go in and ram it down 'is throat. And don't go flirting with any of the men in the queue. Not that it'll do you much good. Men who go shopping for their women're all a bit on the limp-hand side.'

'I know they are, darlin'. Now, give us some money and—'

'Take it out your purse,' sniffed Jack, as he dropped down into his armchair by the fire. 'And get out of the way of the wireless! The boxing's about to start.'

Leaving the room. Laura could hardly believe that Jack honestly thought that if anyone blocked his view of the wireless it messed up the picture of the boxing ring in his head. If asked he would insist he could see it all by looking at the set – even the bell and the rowdy audience!

Checking on her eight-year-old daughter, who had

her thumb in her mouth and was sound asleep, Laura whispered before quietly closing the door behind her, 'Night night, Kay, love.' To Laura, Kay was everything. She had her dad's blonde hair and blue eyes but, in so far as she could tell, she was a replica of her mother in every other way. Since becoming friends with Edie, Laura had taken strides in coming to terms with the death of her baby son and to appreciating what she had – her lovely gentle Kay.

With her coat back on, she went out of the flat on her way to buy her and Jack's supper and, for no reason in particular, Naomi's words floated through her mind: 'Next September it will all happen I assure you. You will be loved by that man as no other woman has been loved before!'

Shuddering at the thought of what Jack would do if he had heard her, she dug her hands deep inside her pockets and braced herself for going alone in the dark to the local fish-and-chip shop. Whether Naomi's prediction came true or not, she would enjoy the thought of it and look forward to late August when she would be returning to the lover of her dreams' hop-farm.

'Going out on the razzle, Laura?' joked Jessie, as they met on the staircase.

'I should be so lucky. No, fish-and-chip shop, I'm afraid.'

'That sounds like a good idea,' beamed Max, as he turned to face Jessie. 'What do you think? We could get some chips for Billy and Emma. I'd rather that than sit in a Chinese restaurant.'

'All right. I s'pose anything is better than a cold salad after a day's work.'

'I should say so.'

'Is that what was on offer, Max?'

'Mmm,' he said, cautiously. 'It's not my most favourite meal, I must say.'

'I should 'ave known, really,' said Jessie, embarrassed.

'Ne' mind. I'll get some for yous while I'm going. What fish d'yer want?'

'Wouldn't dream of it.' Max showed the flat of his hand. 'I'll go and get them for all of us. It'll be my treat. And I'm not taking no for an answer.'

'Well, put like that, how can I refuse?'

Relieved that she wasn't going out at this time in the evening by herself, Laura placed her order and then went with Jessie to her flat. 'He's like a knight in shining armour, that man. Especially when you compare him to Jack.'

'Oh, right,' said Jessie, 'so he made you go out as a punishment for stopping too long at Edie's, then?'

'No. It just wouldn't cross 'is mind to go. I even asked him to this time. He's so bloody old-fashioned, when it suits 'im. As far as he's concerned, fish and chips is a meal and it's the women who get the meals. It's his sister Liz's fault. She practically brought 'im up and spoiled 'im rotten.'

'But you wouldn't change 'im for the world,' said Jessie, watching her face. She hadn't quite worked out their relationship – it was fiery, that much she did know.

'Probably not, if push came to shove. But who knows? If someone like Den came along and wanted to sweep me off my feet . . . What about you?'

'No,' said Jessie firmly, as she pushed her key into her street door. 'Max *is* a knight in shining armour, as you so rightly said. He'll see me out.'

'And if Tom ever came back?' she asked, knowing full well that Tom was on the scene.

'He won't, Laura. That's all in the past.' She suddenly stopped and cocked an ear. 'It's a bit quiet in there. I can't believe they've put themselves to bed.'

Inching the door open, Jessie popped her head round the door to find that Billy and Emma were still playing Snakes and Ladders with farthings. 'You look nice and cosy,' she said, not really wishing to break the silence. 'The fire kept in, then?'

'I 'ad to put some more coal on,' said Billy, throwing the dice.

'Did you now? Who's winning?' The response was silence as the pair of them fixed their eyes on the rolling dice until they finally stopped.

'Yes!' yelled Billy. 'Five and home!'

'You're a cheat,' snarled Emma. 'You cheated when I went to the lavatory.'

'I never.'

'Did.'

'Never,' said Billy, and then, 'You can go first this time.'

'Winners go first.'

'Suit yerself.'

'Cheat.'

'Liar.'

Having heard enough, Jessie closed the door and joined Laura, who was already in the kitchen and filling the kettle. 'Little sods.' Jessie chuckled. 'They know they're meant to be in bed.' She opened the hatch into the living room. 'Max is gonna fetch you some chips. Or 'ave you stuffed yerself full with biscuits after you ate your tea?'

'No. I'm starving 'ungry,' said Billy.

'So am I,' said Emma, watching Billy slide his farthing up a ladder. 'I 'ope he gets some wallies as well.'

'And some onions.'

Jessie closed the hatch. 'They're a peculiar pair at times. Either yelling at each other or so close you couldn't slip a knife between 'em.'

'*That's* close?' chuckled Laura. 'I'd hate to hear when they're having a row.'

Happy that Laura was taking control of her kitchen, Jessie sank into a chair and kicked off her ankle boots, yawning. 'God, I'm tired. I think I might drop one day off my working week. Go in four days instead of five.'

'Don't blame you. What did you do for a living before you was married?'

'Same as now. Book-keeping and typing. God, when I think back to then, Laura, it seems a lifetime away. So much has happened,' she said gazing out, deep in thought. 'It doesn't seem possible that all of that could 'ave been fitted into . . .' She counted the years under her breath. 'Blimey . . . it's thirteen years ago. That's when I left the company where I'd worked since I left school.'

'Billy's age. You should 'ave remembered that straight away.' With the kettle on the stove and the cups ready, Laura sat down opposite Jessie at the small Formica table. 'So you stopped before you dropped,' she grinned. 'Was Tom around then?'

'On and off.'

'Oh, right,' said Laura.

'Oh, right, what?'

'Nothing. Just . . . oh, right. That's all. Don't be so touchy.'

'Why must you always try and get me to talk about Tom? You're such a nosy cow.'

'Ah, but not a gossip,' said Laura, wagging her finger. 'You can tell me anything you like, knowing it will never be repeated. And I mean that and I hope you believe it.'

'Of course I do.' Pausing, Jessie leaned back in her chair and looked into Laura's face. 'You are right, but then again you're wrong.'

'About what?'

'You know full well. I probably do still love Tom but not in the way I did.'

'Do you love Max in the way you *did* love Tom?'

'Oh . . . so this is cat-and-mouse is it?'

'No,' said Laura, and then, 'yes.'

'I've never loved anyone the way I loved Tom. And I never could love anyone now in that way. But . . . I'm not still in love with 'im. It's over, Laura, and I would rather think of it like that than have the image of him with another woman living in the lap of luxury while his kids have to get their own tea when they come in from school, because I don't quite get back from work in time.'

Lowering her eyes, Laura fiddled with a small blue china cruet set on the table, and after a short silence said, 'Jessie . . . I'm really sticking my neck out here but . . .'

Jessie waited, and then said, 'But what?'

Lifting her chin, a heedful look in her eyes as her stomach churned, Laura spoke in a quiet and worried voice: 'Tom's back, Jessie.'

Recoiling, Jessie simply stared at her friend. After a few moments, she opened her mouth to say something, closed it again, then whispered, 'What did you say?'

'It didn't seem right for you not to know. Tom is back in the East End.' Pushing both hands through her long auburn hair, Laura turned away from her friend's searching eyes. 'I'm sorry but I couldn't stay silent any longer. It just doesn't seem right. I could really get into a lot of trouble for this.'

'How do you know?' said Jessie, going cold. 'Who told you?'

Looking into Jessie's light blue eyes Laura shrugged. 'He's really down at heel, Jess. Jacket with no buttons, trousers with no creases. Last time I spoke to Murat about it, which was just after Christmas, he said he'd put him on to someone who needs a van driver.'

'Murat? The same Murat who came into my house for a Christmas drink? Murat, whose wife made my new frock?'

'I know it sounds too much but this is a small community and, well, Tom goes to him to get his hair cut and—'

'Jesus . . .' murmured Jessie. '*Murat*'s the Turkish barber that Tom used to—' She stopped mid-sentence, flabbergasted. 'I can't believe I'm hearing this. Why didn't he say something? I invited him and Shereen to my party—'

'Apparently that's the first place Tom headed for once he was back in the area, according to Murat anyway. And that was *after* Murat'd been in your flat. It didn't click who you was then.'

'So why didn't he tell me once he did know? And why 'ave *you* kept quiet over it?' she asked, wiping away a tear.

'Tom told Murat that he wanted to get back on his feet before he asked if he could see the kids. But Murat never ever told him that you'd moved on to the estate. I don't think he knew what to do about it. He took me aside and asked if I thought we should tell you the state your Tom's in. I said no, I didn't think we should interfere, but I've not stopped thinking about it on and off ever since.'

'He's not *my* Tom. Not any more! What about Emmie and Charlie?'

'Who are they?'

'Tom's mum and dad. You've got chummy with my sister, Dolly. Has she never mentioned them? They're like a mum and dad to her. She's married to Stanley, their other son. Tom's brother!'

'Oh,' said Laura, as the penny dropped. 'Well, Dolly did say that Stanley's mum and dad didn't think they should go against his brother's wishes. I didn't know they were called Emmie and Charlie.'

'So *they*'ve been two-faced as well,' said Jessie, and drew a breath. 'I can't believe this.' Then, blinking against tears, said, 'And my own *sister*? What have I *done*? Don't they like me any more? Have they *all* been pretending? Putting on a front? Surely they've not been lying all these years? And not Dolly as well? Not my own sister?'

'Of course they've not been lying for years, and of course they like you. They love you! And it's been really hard for Dolly. She asked what I thought she should do. Apparently Tom's mum and dad agreed that he should stay away from you because you were nice and settled with Max. They didn't think it would be good for the kids. Neither did Stanley. Dolly's the only one who argued the case. Tom's only recently turned up on the doorstep.'

'When exactly?'

'New Year's Eve.'

'And you really think that Emmie and Charlie stopped him coming to see us so as not to rock the boat?'

'Not think, Jess, *know*. They thought it would disturb Billy and Emma, not to mention you and Max.'

'And what did you tell 'er? When Dolly asked your opinion?'

'That I didn't know – which is true. But it's been playing on my mind. I couldn't *not* tell you. And I'm *not* sorry. I think you *should* know. And that's it in a nutshell. I think you should know that Tom's back and broke.'

'Is he living with his mum and dad?'

'No. He's told them that he's renting a little flat, but Murat . . . Murat told me he's staying in a dingy room above a tripe-and-onion shop in Bethnal Green. Once he's got a bit of self-respect back and a job he's gonna take up the offer from 'is brother, Stanley, to go in the building trade with 'im.'

'Good for Stanley,' said Jessie, deep in thought, 'good for him.'

'I hope we can still be friends—'

'Of course we're still friends,' said Jessie, cutting in. 'And of course a good friend sees more than other people do.'

'Like what?'

'I do still love Tom. And you picked that up, didn't you?'

'I think so, Jess. I can't advise you what to do . . . The ball's in your court.'

'So it would seem,' she said, staring out.

'As if one's not enough . . .' said Laura, her thoughts moving elsewhere.

Her back immediately up, Jessie stiffened. 'What's that s'posed to mean? I wouldn't deceive Max by seeing Tom in secret! How could you think that?'

'I wasn't thinking about you, Jess. You're too on edge. I was thinking of poor Edie.' She raised her eyes to meet Jessie's and drew a breath. 'You're not gonna believe this. Not in a million years. Her late husband Harry, missing, presumed dead, is *back* from the dead.'

Numbed, her mouth gaping, all that Jessie could say was, 'Come agen?'

'No . . . you heard me right the first time. I won't go into the details now but, honest to God, Jess, it's been scary. And as for poor old Naomi, I can't tell you what she's bin through.'

'And Edie?'

'She doesn't know.'

'But she's *got* to be told! You can't keep something like this in the dark! She's just accepted an engagement ring, for Christ's sake!'

'It's more complicated than that. But Harry Birch is not the man she'd remember. He's not right in the head. And I do mean not right. He broke into Naomi's little place and stayed for a week, tormenting 'er. Hiding out until his ticket came through for Spain – or at least that's what he told her. The bastard was living with a woman in Turkey all that time. Now she's pregnant he's done a runner.'

'Turkey?' said Jessie, as the penny dropped. 'Of course . . . Murat again?'

'Yes,' said Laura, 'Murat again.'

The sound of the doorbell stopped them in their tracks. It was Max back with the fish and chips. The two women looked at each other in silence each conveying their thoughts. From Jessie: *Please don't ever say anything about Tom in front of Max.* And from Laura: *Don't do anything rash*. 'Here he is,' said Laura, passively, 'Good old reliable, lovable Max.'

There was no need for either of them to open the street door to him. Billy and Emma were already in the passage trying to get there first. 'Does Naomi know about Edie's husband?'

'I told you, Jess. He broke into her place and stayed – against her wishes.'

'So you did, Jessie.' She was still unable to take this in. 'So you did.'

9

One week later with spring in the air and only a month before Maggie would be walking away from her school for the last time, she was looking forward to stepping out into a brand new world and earning a wage. In love with Tony, she was strolling around with stars in her eyes and this was seen by Edie as sweet and innocent. Dennis was reserving his judgement. He didn't think that someone so young should be in a relationship.

His private thoughts were that a broken heart was on the cards. Now that he and Edie had decided to be married the following Christmas, and if possible on Christmas Eve, he was beginning to take his role as stepfather seriously. The wedding was planned to take place at the Stepney Register Office, which was the very place where Edie's parents had been married.

The pledge that she and Dennis had made to each other was that, until that day, under no circumstances would Dennis sleep overnight in Edie's bed. This was not only for the benefit of Maggie and the embarrassment it would cause but for their own self-respect too.

Oblivious to the fact that she was not a war widow, Edie was looking forward to her wedding day and to sharing a new and fuller life with Dennis. For this reason alone, Jessie and Laura knew that they had to keep the secret. The explosive secret that Harry was alive. Should it come out, they knew that it would not only bring terrible grief to Edie and Maggie but would certainly delay the wedding.

Naomi, as far as Jessie was concerned, was best left out of any discussions on Harry and whether he might one day turn up on the doorstep again. She had been through enough already and, just as if she had read their minds, Naomi was tacit where Harry was concerned. The least said about him the better!

For Jessie, the strain of having to keep up a front, and not mention to anyone that she had been told that her husband Tom was now back on the scene, was beginning to show. She had been snappy with Billy and Emma and distant towards Max until he had pointed it out to her. She loved him no less than before but with this news of Tom having hit rock bottom, she was finding it hard to simply carry on as usual. Visions of him living in a squalid room and reflections of the past when he had been fun-loving, the light of her life, continued to pervade her thoughts.

Now, in the quiet of her kitchen, with Billy and Emma-Rose in the front room playing board games while she peeled root vegetables for the evening meal, Jessie allowed herself to wander back through time to when she had first met Tom and to the day when he had pulled up in front of her mother's house in his first old clapped-out banger.

Having turned up on the off-chance of seeing her,

and with a mutual friend in tow, Tom had sent the girl to knock on Jessie's door with a message that he would like to have a few words with her. The friend had made herself scarce while they had shared private words.

Remembering the way he had looked at her through the open window of his car when she had peered in at him, Jessie felt a nostalgic rush as that old black magic returned while she slowly peeled parsnips. Her stomach churning, she remembered his words and the scene that had followed as if it were yesterday.

'I was told you wanted to have a word with me,' Tom had said, between blowing smoke-rings. 'Well, here I am. You gonna get in the car then or what?'

'I'm not sure now,' she had said, having had second thoughts even then.

Leaning back and stretching one arm, Tom had smiled that irresistible smile when she had finally opened the door and slipped into the passenger seat.

'I remember the first time I saw you . . .' was how he had begun his apology for standing her up previously. 'You was outside Stepney Green station, looking sad. Then there was the dockers' march when you were smiling and lovely. I'm sorry I never turned up for the date but I couldn't get there. I'll say this once and then it's up to you. I've not been able to get you out of my mind. I knew you was getting engaged to Max Cohen so I kept away. Then I learned that it was all off.'

Jessie had warmed to his boyish devil-may-care front and had admitted to him then that she had been thinking about him, too, since the day they had first met on a dockers' march where she had been waving the banner for her dad, then a stevedore. Tom's face had lit up once he had heard what he had considered to be her declaration of love and had opened up even more. Pushing a hand through his hair, he had said, 'I'm crazy about you, Jessie, but I thought you didn't care.'

Wasting no more time he had pulled her close to him and kissed her and confessed his love. Something that Tom, the cocky lovable chap, had never done in his life. Gazing into her face, his voice deep and husky, he had spoken openly, saying, 'I'm putting my trust in you, Jessie. Please don't leave me a broken man. I couldn't bear it. I'll never be unfaithful and I'll never hurt yer. I'm yours for as long as you want me. I don't know how long that'll be, maybe for ever or maybe for a while. You might go off with someone else, or go back to your boyfriend and leave me for dead – but I'm willing to take that risk.'

'I won't hurt you, Tom,' had been Jessie's response. 'I'm not a heart-breaker.'

Rinsing her hands under the tap and then drying them, Jessie forced those memories from her mind. She dared not take the risk that, should one of her children come into the kitchen to look into her eyes and ask if anything was wrong, she might just break down. She was already on the verge of tears.

As she sank into her kitchen chair, she covered her face with her hands, asking herself why it had all gone so wrong. Tom had been true to his word and loyal right up until he had taken a new identity as one of the landed gentry – almost seven years after his pledge of devotion and only because he believed she had been sleeping with Max, while he had been away fighting in the war.

Sorry that something beautiful had turned sour, Jessie decided that it was time for her to pay a visit to her in-laws, Emmie and Charlie. Tell them that she knew Tom was back and that he was welcome to see his children whenever he wanted, providing he always wrote first to say when he was coming or that they made fixed regular times for him to pick the children up. Her mind settled, and sure that this was the right thing to do, she realised that she was going to have to tell Max that Tom was back, confident that he would be considerate and as gentle as a lamb about the whole thing.

Among those she did not wish to know that he had returned was her own mother, Rose, who had never really taken to Tom, and had always believed that Jessie had married down from her own middle-lower-class background. Stephen, her youngest brother, now living with his partner Josh, in Holborn, adored Max and was still angry with Tom for walking out on her, his niece and nephew, and would most likely do everything he could to stop Tom crashing into her life again.

Her other brother, Alfie, would, she felt sure, take the news as the best thing he had heard so far. Inspired by Tom when young and impressionable, Alfie had done his best to mould himself on his hero. Now, having moved up in the world of crime, Alfie was living in a terraced Victorian house in Hackney, which had been renovated and restored – and all from his dodgy wheeling and dealing.

Tom was no saint but neither was he a hardened fraudster. Jessie was surer by the minute that the sooner his presence back in Stepney was brought out into the open the better – and that his children had every right to see him.

'Worse things happen at sea,' she told herself, as she rinsed her root vegetables under the tap, and thought about Edie and how she would not wish to be in her shoes. If her husband Harry had really gone from her life for good, then of course there would be nothing to worry over, but from what Laura had told Jessie, she did not believe for one minute that Harry would not turn up again one day. 'Poor Edie,' she murmured, 'As if she hasn't had enough grief already.'

In her cosy sitting room, her legs curled under her, the armchair pulled close to the fire, Edie was flicking through a fashion magazine looking for something special that Shereen could copy for her wedding day. Lying on the settee, her head sunk into a feather cushion, Maggie was trying to read small handwriting written in black ink. The only sound was of the crackling fire and the rustling of pages from Edie's magazine.

'Wasn't Aunt Naomi s'posed to be coming round?' said Maggie, as she looked up from her reading.

'She'll be here, don't worry,' said Edie, her eyes on a lovely picture of a cream-coloured costume, which looked stunning on the model. 'Why do you ask?'

'No reason.'

Raising her eyes, Edie glanced at her daughter's troubled face as she stared up at the ceiling. 'What's the matter?'

'Nothing's the matter. It's just that this diary is really old. Eighteen eighty-eight.'

'What diary?'

'This one,' she said, holding up the small black book. 'I found it in the loft when I went back for my doll and stuff. It was wrapped in this old brown paper and string.'

'Does it say whose diary it is?'

'No.'

'Maybe it's something to do with Uncle Freddy. It might have fallen out of his uniform pocket as Tony was carrying it out.'

'No. I found it in a different place. Next to them old green medicine bottles and other bits of rubbish. The brown paper was filthy. I 'ad to give it a wipe over before I could bear to handle it. There's some writing on it in pencil but I've nearly wiped that off. Can't make out what it says.'

'Well, I don't remember putting it up there.' She held up her magazine for Maggie to see. 'What do you think of this costume?'

'Not bad. Keep looking, though. You've got months to find a pattern, don't forget. I think you could do better than that. Cream's a bit—' The sound of the doorbell stopped her mid-sentence. Maggie was off the couch in a flash and out the door with Edie staring after her, puzzled. She thought that her daughter was a bit too eager to see her aunt and wondered what was going on. She glanced at the black journal and old brown wrapping paper. 'Must 'ave caught her interest,' she told herself.

'Hello, my darling Edith. Guess what I have brought for you,' said Naomi, swanning into the room, positively glowing as she waved the local paper in the air.

'I've no idea,' said Edie, bemused.

'I have,' grinned Maggie. 'It was our secret.'

'Shall I read aloud? Or would each of *you* rather read your own pieces?'

'Give us it,' said Maggie, 'I'll read it aloud so Mum can get the proper gist of it. You'll only dramatise it as if you're on stage.'

'Very well, sweetheart. I do so hope you'll be pleased too. Page *twelve*, column *three* and then . . .'

Flicking through the pages Maggie was clearly amused once she she saw the column marked Announcements. 'Oh, God, Mother, she *has* put you and Dennis in.' She quickly scanned the page until the smile drained from her face. 'This is *not* funny, Aunt Naomi.' She held the open page for them both to see.

'Oh . . . but it wasn't meant as a joke, Margaret,' said Naomi, hurt by her sharp tone. 'I thought it would be a nice touch to have both mother and daughter in there. And look who you share the page with! That is a charming, albeit small, picture of our new Queen.'

'Look at it,' wailed Maggie. 'Why did you have to give 'em that horrible picture of me in my glasses, with the brace on my teeth and my hair in a ponytail!

I hated looking like that, you know I did!' Furious and genuinely embarrassed by it, Maggie, red-faced and with tears in her eyes, stormed out of the room.

'Oh dear. I seem to have put my foot in it *again*, Edie.'

'Take no notice. It's her age. Here. Show it to me.'

Taking another copy from her red shopping-bag, Naomi handed it over, saying, 'I've bought six copies to hand out but it looks as if that was money down the drain.'

'Don't be daft,' said Edie, reading the announcement of her engagement to Dennis. 'That's really lovely. I'm pleased! I would never 'ave thought to do that.' She then saw the announcement under Maggie's photograph. 'Mmm . . . you did take a bit of a risk there. She read the piece aloud: '"Daughter of Edith Birch, Margaret, also received a proposal from the husband-to-be who, when down on one knee, asked if she would become his beloved stepdaughter."'

'But whatever's *wrong* with it? It's just a bit of *fun*, Edith.'

'There's nothing wrong with it, but like I said, she's at that age. You might have got away with the announcement, but the photo?'

'A bit of fun, that's all. She doesn't look like that *now* so Tony will imagine it was taken when she was ten years old.' Pausing for a moment to think, Naomi said. 'No actually. I'm sorry, but I think she is being *completely* childish. Something *else* must be troubling her!'

Disappointed, she slumped down on the settee and on the diary. Pulling it from under her, she slammed it down. 'These childish tantrums of Margaret's have got to *stop*, Edith. She will soon be employed in a *library*. It's time she behaved like a young *adult*.' Clearing her throat, she folded her arms and cast her eyes down so as to avoid Edie's face, should she hit back.

'I know,' murmured Edie, 'I'll have a word with 'er. She shouldn't be so rude to you either. It's time she showed respect.'

'Well, let's not go *too* far, dear. I'm not *that* old.' Naomi glanced at the black diary and then her eyes fell upon the wrapping paper. 'Oh, my *God*, Edith, where on *earth* did she find that?'

'Find what?' said Edie, reading the announcement of her engagement again.

'The loft! Christmas *Eve*!' exclaimed Naomi. 'She went back for some of her *things*! Oh, my God . . . Edie.'

Looking up from the newspaper, Edie frowned. 'It's not your private diary, is it?'

'No. Much worse, I am sorry to have to tell you. I was asked by a very close friend to keep this *safe* and let no one see it, with strict instructions to pass it on to you should I be on the brink of death. I had *completely* forgotten about it.'

'Well, whose is it?'

'Harriet's. Margaret should *not* have unwrapped it. It says *quite* clearly "Not to be opened until the death of Harriet Smith" on the cover!'

'Maggie said there was some pencil writing on it

but it's faded away. She couldn't make out what it said so she opened it. I don't think we can blame 'er for that, Nao.'

'No, of *course* not. Of course not.' Naomi's eyes were fixed on the black diary. Then, shuddering, she spoke in a quiet voice: 'There's something quite *evil* in it. My only regret is that Maggie has touched it. Read it, even.'

'She said the handwriting was small . . . and it was scary.'

'Well, never mind . . . what is done is done. I shall take it away and find a hiding-place for it. But *should* I pass away before Harriet then I must ask you to keep it until she joins me in the great blue sky. Then, and *only* then, may you read it and do with it what you will. But *never*, never on any account, must you *destroy* it.'

'Why not? What's so special about it?'

'It is no *ordinary* diary, Edith. It is the diary of a murderess. And it is dated eighteen eighty-eight. Does that tell you *anything*?'

'No. Just that it's a bit macabre and some nutcase's fantasy.'

'Does eighteen eighty-eight not mean *anything* to you?'

'No!'

'Jack the Ripper?'

The room fell silent as the two women looked into each other's eyes. Then, breaking the silence, Naomi said, 'I have been told of its contents but have not fully read it . . . In fact, I don't believe I got through the first three pages of those which are separated from the rest with tiny bookmarks. I *can* tell you, however, that this diary is of significant historic importance and should not be taken lightly.'

'If all you say and think is true, Naomi, hand it over to the police. You can't keep something like that a secret. You said it was the diary of a murderess and it's written by a midwife. Are you telling me that she was the so-called Jack the Ripper?'

'Jacqueline the Ripper, my sweet, Jacqueline.'

'I don't believe you. You're making this up. You must be. You wouldn't have just . . . *ignored* it. No one would. And especially not you.'

'Does it really matter, when all is said and done? It was a very long time ago.'

'Of course it matters!'

'Besides, Harriet and I go back a long way. We know more about each other than most people know about themselves. If a trusted friend asked you to keep a secret, would you?'

'Not if it was something as serious as this I wouldn't. No.'

'Well, then, we must beg to differ on this occasion. Wipe it from your mind. Forget you have ever seen it or risk becoming an interfering busybody who could cause grief to someone who once saved me from a fate worse than death.'

'Such as?'

'Such as when I was in a dreadful children's home in eighteen eighty-eight. Would you like to hear the sordid details?'

'You were in a children's home? This is news. Stop making things up.'

'I did not tell you before now, Edith, because I had no wish to pass on misery when it was unnecessary. I have managed to bury it, thankfully. Why would I want to burden you with the knowledge that there had been a dark time in my life when I was at an age when all that one wanted was one's mother?'

The room fell silent as Edie and Naomi's eyes met and held. Drawing breath, Edie spoke quietly. 'You are being serious, aren't you?'

'Yes, my darling, I am. And, really, I would much prefer to forget all about it. I promise you, no good will come of dragging it all up. You must trust me on this.'

'Okay. No need to upset yourself over it, Nao, is there?'

'No . . . you're right, darling. It doesn't matter. It's all done with, and talking about it only serves to bring back memories best left in the dark. It is now and the future that counts. If you walk through a filthy puddle and dirty the hem of your skirts which then dry from the sunshine by the time you reach home, you do not think of the puddle, only the stain left by it and how best to clean it away.'

That said, Naomi left the room to have a few moments by herself in the kitchen, only to hear the slow opening of the hatch and Edie's broken voice: 'I'm sorry, Naomi. I wouldn't want to upset or hurt you for the world.'

Shuddering, Naomi went quiet, and then said, 'Edie,

darling, *will* you keep it safe and when the time comes – when both Harriet and myself have passed away – pass it on? Will you?'

Seeing the look of anguish on Edie's face, she changed her tone to one more light-hearted. 'Harriet is a similar age to myself even though she looks *much* older. I doubt we will live beyond another fifteen years or so. That will take us into our *eighties*, by which time I shall have had quite enough of dodging between *motor-cars*. I shall smile down from heaven while you must *all* get on with it.'

'Tell me where you'll hide it then, because that would be a help . . . if I'm to pass it on.'

'Will you, Edith? That would so put my mind at rest. You see . . . Harriet was in a strange way involved in it all. In fact, the hand that killed two of the Whitechapel prostitutes almost murdered her and she was no more than ten years old. It mustn't come out while she's alive – it could affect her so badly and we don't want my friend to end her days in a straight-jacket in a padded cell.'

'God, Naomi, you certainly know how to deliver your lines. Put it in your handbag and forget it. And no more talk about once you've pegged it. It's too bloody morbid for any time of day.'

'I will admit that it is all much darker than the worst horror film of all time in which I had a rather menacing part—'

'Stop it! Drop the subject! Left to you we'd all be 'aving nightmares.'

'Very well. But you will pass it on to someone you

trust?' said Naomi, a hand on her heart, her head tipped to one side, a gentle expression in her eyes. 'It is important.'

'I said I would and I will. You're scaring me. Just let me know where I'm to find it.'

'With my other treasures. In a space behind the cupboard under the sink in my bathroom.'

'Well, that's that sorted out,' said Edie, lifting herself out of her chair and not wishing to think about the time when Naomi would be gone. 'I'd better go and see if Mags is all right.'

'Yes, *do*, darling, while I pour myself a little drink.' She went back into the living room and pulled a half-bottle of brandy from her shopping-bag. 'And tell her I *am* sorry about the photograph but I happen to think she looks lovely in it. I miss seeing her looking like that, as a matter of fact.'

'Well, who's to blame for it?' said Edie, leaving the room.

'I know, I know,' murmured Naomi to herself. 'And I *also* know that it is time to change the way I approach my great-niece who, I *suspect*, is no longer an innocent child. If I know anything at all about the Italians it is that they are the most ardent of lovers.' She warmed at the memory of one such love in the 1920s when playing opposite the very handsome tenor, Luigi Valentino in *Passion for Paris*.

Glancing again at the diary lying on the couch she felt herself go cold. Then, with a cautious hand, she picked it up and let it fall open to a page at random. Shrinking back from it, at first she had no wish to read anything that was written inside. Then glancing down at the page with a sense of foreboding she read:

1 September

There will be more drowned rats in the sewer. The rain is easing off but the gutter beneath my window is like a fast-running stream. Such peculiar weather. Today the scorching September sunshine heated the paving stones to such a degree that it felt as if I were walking on hot ashes. Just a few hours and it will be dusk and later, after dark, the streets will be devoid of any decent folk. The air is heavy with fear and the quickening sound of footsteps is mixed with the slamming and bolting of doors. Inside the houses, there will be conjecture, vague suspicion and rough guesses as to what might be in tomorrow's newspapers. And I, too, wonder. Will there be another murder tonight?

The sound of Edie's footsteps in the passage caused her to close the diary, and when her niece came into the room said, 'You are quite right, my darling. This must be hidden away and forgotten about. It has nothing to do with us, after all. Forgotten, that is, until—'

'Yes. I know. Now put it in your handbag and trust that I'll do as you've asked. It was written by a midwife and not your friend. It's probably just wild fantasies of a lonely spinster.'

'But you won't throw it away once—'

'Naomi, please! That's enough! I know what Mags would do with it if it became her inheritance. Chuck it in the bin. Why don't you give it to Jessie's sister

Dolly? She's the one who wants to write novels and plays. She might find it more interesting than any of us would.'

'Actually, that is a very good idea. I shall think very carefully about it. It is a possibility. I may well consider entrusting it to her.' Naomi carefully lifted the diary and the brown paper and twine and dropped it into her bag.

'Whatever,' said Edie, back in her chair and with her magazine. 'I'm looking for ideas on what to 'ave made for my wedding day.'

'Something *white*?' Naomi said, hopeful, her soul having just been filled with something very dark.

'I don't think so. I like this, though,' she said holding up the picture of the model in cream.

'A little on the bland side, I think,' said Naomi. 'If not white, then something quite different altogether, is my humble opinion. Your natural colours, hair and so on, are warm. Brown hair, hazel eyes. Apricot and powder blue would look lovely, but since it will be a winter wedding, why not go for burnt orange and navy or a mix of autumn colours with a dash of Christmas red?'

'So, not cream, then?'

'Lovely in the summer, darling, but not in the depths of winter.'

'But I like the suit. What if Shereen was to make it up in a warmer fabric and in rust?'

'Wonderful. And you could always have a cream hat and gloves with a dash of red?'

'Mmm . . . I'm not sure about the red—'

'And another thing!' said Maggie, bursting into the room. 'You never told 'em how old I was when that picture was taken!'

Eyeing Edie and containing a smile, Naomi said, 'People will realise that you were very young there, Margaret. It won't even enter their minds that this could have been you a year ago. Romance will always win over sense.'

'Anyway,' said Maggie, a half-apologetic tone in her voice, 'I thought it was nice of you to put me in as well as Mum. But in future check wiv me first.' On that note she turned away, making for her bedroom.

Waiting for the sound of Maggie's bedroom door to close behind her, Naomi raised an eyebrow. 'Our little girl is growing up at last. An apology? Now that *does* show signs of a mature young lady.'

'Don't speak too soon,' mused Edie, 'she'll be back agen, I guarantee.'

'Better she stands up to us than sulks in her room. It's only a *small* step but a great one. Thank goodness I did *not* send pictures in to the Sunday paper.'

Raising her eyes from her magazine, Edie spoke with caution: 'Sunday paper?'

'Yes, darling. I want the world to know that you have found happiness at last. The world and all—'

'I know why you did it, Naomi. I'm not daft. And don't think I've not had the same thought. I have. I just couldn't think how to word it without putting on pressure.'

'Please don't speak in riddles, Edith. I have no idea what you are talking about.'

'No? Well, in a word . . . Dad?'

Her hand floating to her bosom, Naomi's face was a picture. As if a momentary shock had silenced her. 'Goodness, whatever gave you such an idea?'

'Because, as I just said, it's crossed my mind too. But not on this occasion and yet it's so obvious. You're unbelievable. What do you do – lie awake at night thinking these things through?'

'I don't know what you mean, Edith,' she said, her face all innocence.

'It's a brilliant idea, Naomi, and I'm really, really pleased you thought of it. But how will he get in touch – if he wants to?'

'Via the newspaper, dear.'

'But will they give him an address? Surely not.'

'I have already been down that road. Your address is carefully tucked into the piece.'

'Edith Birch of Scott House, you mean? That kind of a thing?'

'Yes. That kind of a thing, with a little more detail. Stepney, E1.' Not wishing to disturb the silent pause, Naomi waited before saying, 'Will you be terribly upset if he doesn't get in touch, darling?'

'No. Not now. Water under the bridge and all of that. But . . . I think he will. If he reads it, he will. Did you put your name at the bottom of it?'

'Well, yes, I did but, darling, he may not read *The Times* and he may not have returned to this country after his emigration—'

'I know. But it's worth a try. You know that the pair of you were close. He liked you and he'll know why you've put it there. Which is why you put your name in the ad. He'll know that you're calling him.' With that Edie burst into tears.

A while later, with no word from Edie's father, Naomi was thinking about him as she knocked on the door of Harriet's home. This time, however, Harriet had known she was coming. Her grandson Tommy had had a telephone installed in the house and a postcard giving the number had been sent to close friends to either impress or inform, depending who the recipient happened to be. For Naomi it was meant simply as information since Harriet wanted to be at home when her old and trusted friends came to visit.

'See?' said Harriet, as she opened the door. 'Modern machines. Can't beat 'em. Normally I wouldn't 'ave bin in this morning—'

'Normally,' said Naomi, following her friend along the passage, 'I would not be visiting today. It was arranged on the telephone at my expense, let's not forget. The charge is fourpence a call which is not expensive but the business of press button A or press button B to get through is something I cannot be bothered with.'

'That's as may be,' returned Harriet, speaking over her shoulder, 'but you've got to admit it's a bloody good invention.'

'And quite an old one. Now, *fortunately*, it is available to the likes of *ourselves*. Although I for *one* would not have one installed in *my* home.'

'Oh, shut up and sit down, Naomi. I know you're

jealous. You don't 'ave to admit it, though. I've made us some Cheddar cheese sandwiches and I've got some chocolate ice-cream in the freezer bit of the new fridge. Wot do yer want? Cup of tea or coffee?'

'Tea, please. Three sugars.'

Dropping into a chair, her handbag on the square wooden dining-table, Naomi looked about herself. 'It's a pity Tommy doesn't spend a little of his ill-gotten gains on decorating. It's a touch dreary in here, Harriet. Dark green paintwork is terribly out of date.'

'Well, then, I'm in front of the times, ain't I?' called Harriet from the kitchen. 'In a year's time it could be all the rage. Back to Victorian colours!'

'You could be right, Harriet, of *course* you could. But I don't think that the *Victorians* had Formica, which looks exactly like wood with a television set housed *within*.'

Placing the plate of sandwiches on the table and setting out two small ones, Harriet was quiet until she said, 'So Harry's bin shipped off, then?'

'So I am to believe.'

'He shouldn't 'ave frightened you like that,' said Harriet, to the sound of her kettle whistling in the kitchen. 'Breaking in as if he was a burglar. He's lucky they let him off so lightly.'

'Well, all's well that ends well, as they say,' mused Naomi, helping herself to a sandwich.

Once the women were settled and enjoying their lunch, Naomi got round to the real reason for her coming today. 'Your diary has surfaced, Harriet. What do you want me to do with it?'

'What diary?'

'You know very well. The black one.'

'I thought we'd already settled that. You said you'd keep it and pass it on to your Edie on your death-bed.'

'Well, yes . . . but that was then and this is now. Maggie, I am sorry to say, found it whilst rummaging around in the loft of the old house. The scribbling of yours in pencil had completely faded and so . . . she opened it and read some of the contents.'

Harriet sipped her tea, imagining the look on Maggie's face. 'What bit did she read?'

'I have no idea. She has not mentioned it since and neither have I. But Edie was in the room when she discarded it so I told her where I would hide it until the long sleep.'

'Well, that's all right, then. Nuffing's changed.'

'Well, no . . . but I was wondering if you might not want to put it out into the world now? I'm sure a journalist would pay quite a bit for it.'

'I'm sure a journalist would and that's no different now to any time. The point is, I don't want it coming out while I'm alive and kicking, thank you very much. It's too bloody macabre!' She looked slyly at her friend saying, 'You're the only one I'd 'ave trusted with it. If I thought you would 'ave let me down I'd 'ave chucked it in the Cut.'

'You *can* trust me, Harriet. I was merely making a suggestion.'

'Well, don't. Keep your airy-fairy thoughts to yerself. I've gone freezing bloody cold at the thought of it.

What did yer wanna bring that up for? There was no need.'

'No. And I'm sorry now that I did. I can see that it's upset you and I apologise. I hadn't meant to bring back bad memories. I may be getting old but I'm not getting nasty, Harriet.' She placed a hand on her friend's. 'You're still my dearest close friend, whose company I cherish.'

'If I didn't know you better,' sniffed Harriet, leaning back in her chair, 'I would say that that was all bollocks. But I do know you. Better than anyone.' Casting her eyes upwards, Harriet gazed at her ceiling. 'I will admit, though, I do find I can think about that time a little more as I get older. As the distance stretches between me and then. Especially knowing that that poor cow is dead.'

'The midwife?'

'The midwife. She gassed herself in the end.'

'Yes, I know. You've told me before.'

'It wasn't 'er fault. It was no one's fault, not really. Daft Thomas wasn't evil, just not all there. Some are born without sight or sound and he was born with a few screws missing. Bloody world.'

'Try not to think about it. Edie is to be married, you know. At Christmas.'

'Course I know. You already told me. Your memory's worse than mine. So what's your opinion of this Dennis bloke, then? You never did say.'

'Oh, I don't know, Harriet. One minute I think he's just what she needs and then I wonder if he's too good to be true.'

'You don't trust 'im, then?'

'I wouldn't say that exactly. It has all been a whirl-wind romance with no time to test the waters. Do you know, they haven't had one cross word?'

'How do you know?'

'Edie would have told me! We tell each other every-thing, Harriet. Everything.'

Harriet told her friend not to be such a fool. 'You were the closest adult to her when she had no one to love or be loved by. But now she 'as got someone and I'm afraid, Naomi old girl, you've gotta accept the fact that you're in the back seat. Iris was the same. Once she met Bill I stopped being Mum and became Mother.'

'Well, yes, I can see what you're saying, but Edie and I are very, very close. We kept nothing from each other.'

'That was then and this is now. It's a story that repeats itself over and over again. Ask any mother. If they're truthful they'll tell you the same. Daughters, or sons, come to that, let you down once they're in love. You'll take second place now, gal. In fact, by the sound of it, third place. Cos the girl Maggie's now a young woman, from what you tell me, and her and Edie'll be talking to each other from the heart. Just like you and Edie did. Shifting sands is what I call it.'

'So you think that Edie and Dennis may have argued and so on and she hasn't told me?'

'Exactly. And don't bother to ask because she'll tell you not to interfere. To mind your own business.'

'Never. No. Not Edie. We're too—'

'She will, I tell yer! But if you must, see for yerself and ask personal questions about her and this bloke, wotsisname. You'll fall out – trust me.'

'Well, thank you so much for that, Harriet. You've lifted my spirits no end. I was going to talk to you about Harry but I don't think I'll bother now.'

'What about 'im?'

'Ask me again, Harriet, as if you really are interested.'

'Very well, Naomi. *What do you think about Harry, pray?*'

Amused by her friend, but not letting on, Naomi kept a straight face. 'Actually, I think that you and the boys have got it all wrong. He's rather nice, if you take the trouble to sit and talk to him.'

'Well, he would be, wouldn't he? When he's being given a roof above 'is head and fed and watered. Did he pay for 'is keep?'

'I would have refused, as well he knew. He was *my* nephew-in-law, let's not forget.'

'But that was a while ago. People change. Men in particular. Especially after they've served in a bloody war . . . bedded a beautiful woman who then lived wiv 'im as a wife—'

'But he came back for Edie – and let's not forget he suffered a head injury.'

'Oh, don't give me all that bollocks about lost memory. Hundreds 'ave tried that one on, for one reason or another. The trouble with you, Naomi, is that you lived so long in the theatre that you've lost touch wiv reality. Harry's a self-centred bastard.

Bloody good job he's bin shipped off to that island in the Canaries. Good riddance, I say. Now, can we talk about my family for a change? Iris, for instance. Or that bleeding granddaughter of mine. Or Tommy.'

'Of course we may. I am all ears. But first, one more question. Would you like to come to Edie's wedding?'

'What about Iris, Rosie and Tommy? They invited?'

'I don't see why not, but I doubt they'll come. They're hardly on intimate terms. It is you and I who are best friends.'

'Is that right?' Harriet said, looking her friend in the eye. 'I lost my first baby, you know. Me and Arthur was really cut up over that.'

'Oh, I didn't know that. I'm so sorry it must—'

'Just after we'd bin banished from Bow in nineteen five. The worst time of my life. Worse, even, than when we was kids living on the streets.'

'Really? I am sorry. I didn't realise.'

'Obviously not. No sight nor sound from you at the time.'

'Well, I must have been touring in a show, Harriet. Otherwise—'

'Must 'ave bin at least five years between us seeing each other agen. And do you know why that was? You. You was so involved wiv your fancy actor friends that you forgot about me. Which is understandable and I don't bear a grudge. But don't start telling me now that we're best friends. We were best friends once upon a time. But a lot of time 'as gone in between then and now.'

'But all good friends lose touch for a while . . . branch out on their own. I always believed that the best friendships are those that can be picked up with no resentment or apologies. I suppose that having worked in a world of make-believe for so long it could have coloured my emotions.'

'Or common sense.'

'Yes, that too, Harriet. That too.' The room went quiet and turned from an everyday family space into something else – a sanctuary away from the outside world where two women who had lived through seven decades were each counting the cost.

'If we hadn't 'ave bin proper friends I don't s'pose we'd be sitting in this room now, would we?' said Harriet, her voice soft and quiet.

'No,' murmured Naomi, 'we wouldn't.'

'I should think we've both been friendly with hundreds of people over the years and yet I could count on the fingers of one hand to come up with the figure of them I still see. Them I count as friends. And you're one of 'em.'

'Thank you. And you're one of mine. In actual fact, I believe we share the same few people. Ben, Joey, and now Larry, who I once adored. He made me laugh until my sides hurt . . .'

'Two Jews and a Catholic . . . better than the Scotsman, Irishman and Englishman,' grinned Harriet. 'Ben was always the funniest, though.'

'Do you think so? I would have said that Larry was. Droll and dry and very clever.'

'And poor old Joey was the stunt man.' After a few

moments both women burst out laughing, remembering different incidents and happenings from the past.

Caught up in their own recollections, the room went quiet again until Harriet said, 'You know what I think? I think that Jacqueline Turner, the midwife, came back from America with one purpose in mind. To find me and get back that diary.'

'Who, darling?'

'The midwife.'

'Oh. Of course. But whatever made you think of her when we were talking of friends?'

'Because the shadows of people who mattered are always there. Friends and enemies.'

'Well, yes, I suppose that's true. Does she still frighten you?'

'Course not. She's dead, ain't she? But that don't mean to say she's gone. One day I'll lay the ghost, though. I swear it. The poor cow gassed herself in front of a stove in a lonely bed-sit above a tobacconist. The last thing I should be is frightened of someone so dispirited, but there we are.'

'Memories are always more disturbing than present life. But let's change the subject and talk of happier things.'

'Can you imagine what that must be like? To want to end your own life?'

'Oh, please, *do* change the subject, Harriet.'

'You brought it up in the first bloody place. It's bin out of my mind for years and now you've dragged it all back telling me about that sodding diary.' Harriet sipped her tea, leaned back in her chair and smiled mischievously at her friend. 'So, what's it like living on a camp site, then?'

'If you mean the lovely estate, actually it's very nice. And so much going on. People coming and going all of the time and so many skeletons in the cupboard. So many are living in sin and yet you would never believe it. On their second round of marriage without the certificate. Or third or fourth in some cases. It all reminds me so much of the world of theatre. Dramas and comedies all around us. Walton-on-Thames studio comes to mind. Opened in nineteen five by Hepworth, the producer. During the First World War we were stationed there for at least a month while *Dream Painting* was being filmed. It was a small part but so, so wonderful. When I wasn't rehearsing I was making tea and so on. The gossip was absolutely thrilling – just like the snippets I pick up on my estate. I absolutely adore it there. I never thought I would but I do.'

'Rather you than me, is all I can say.'

'Yes, but you are a touch on the old-fashioned side,' she said, 'All of these dark colours . . .'

'I love 'em,' sniffed Harriet. 'Iris goes on now and then about light blue and cream walls. Bollocks to that. I'd fancy I was living in a children's bleedin' nursery.'

'And does she not insist on change?'

'Wouldn't do 'er no good. This is my 'ome and she's gotta get on with it.'

'Yours? But surely you moved in with your daughter and grandchildren when Arthur died?'

'That's right, an' I do all the cleaning, washing and cooking while they're out there 'aving a lovely time at work. So it's *my* home. I scrub this place top to bottom every six months. If Iris 'ad her way it'd be scrubbed every soddin' week. God help me when she packs up work next month. House-proud cow.' Then, looking her friend directly in the eye, she said, 'Don't bring up this business of the diary agen, will you? I don't wanna start 'aving nightmares.'

'Of course not,' said Naomi. 'I just wanted to check that I was doing the right thing by continuing to hide it. You might have wanted me to burn it.'

'No. No, don't do that. The truth must be told one day. Too many were blamed wrongly and lives ruined. And too much was going on at Scotland Yard for it not to come out.'

'Very well, then, I shall do as you ask and I shall not mention it again.'

'Good. Now, what's all this wiv you and Ben? From the glow in your face you look as if you're getting some of the other, you lucky cow. Still good, is he?' The laughter coming from Naomi was contagious, and within seconds both women were enjoying a good belly chuckle and being as filthy as filthy can be, when the door is closed and there is no one there to tell tales.

10

A few months after Jessie had discovered that Tom was back in the area she – with the June sunshine on her face and a little trepidation inside, having seen the children into school – walked slowly along Barcroft Road on her way to Grant Street. This visit she was about to make she had not mentioned to Max and now she was asking herself why not. He of all people would understand why she had to see her mother-in-law, Emmie, to find out what was going on with regard to her wayward husband, Tom.

Since the day that she had discovered Tom was back Jessie had not referred to it once, not to her friends, her sisters or brothers or her mother. And neither had she told Max. Not one word. But now guilt was waking her at night. She had risked turning something that could so easily have been aired into a secret. Worse still, since Laura had enlightened her as to the whereabouts of her husband she had found Tom to be forever drifting in and out of her thoughts.

That he might be there at his mother's house when she arrived had not crossed her mind. When Tom answered her knock on the street door of Emmie and Charlie's house she could do no more than stand there, looking at him as if he had risen from the dead. He was, however, not as she had imagined him to be – gaunt, pale and shabby. He looked nothing like the picture that Laura had painted.

But time had not stood still for Tom Smith. With the help of Stanley, his brother, he had found his old confidence and he was working again. Working alongside Stanley, the way they had planned it many years ago.

'So you found out at last,' said Tom, quietly gazing at Jessie as the love he had hidden away came flooding back. 'You'd best come in.'

Once inside the sitting room, which was so familiar to her, Jessie gave her mother-in-law a kiss on the cheek saying, 'Sorry if I've come at the wrong time.'

'It's not the wrong time, Jessie. No. There is no wrong time for you to come into this house, you should know that by now.'

'I'll put the kettle on,' said Tom, choked at seeing his lovely Jessie again.

'No, you won't, Tom. You and Jessie sit in the armchairs and get used to seeing each other before we have a chat.' With that Emmie went into the kitchen and closed the door behind her, something which was rarely done in this household. The kitchen and sitting room had, over the years, become like one room.

'You look well, Jess,' said Tom, as he tried his best to be at ease in her company. 'You've lost weight. You look more like you used to.'

'When did I look any different?'

'In the early days when we was first married. I

s'pose you'll tell me that it's peace of mind and contentment. That Max is looking after you the way I should 'ave.'

'Could be. It didn't do my health much good your walking out on me, but I picked up.' She wanted to remind him who was to blame for their break-up.

'Point taken. So, what about the kids? Are they doing all right?'

'You know they are. Your mum would 'ave soon said if not and you would 'ave been round like a shot.'

Chuckling, Tom said, 'You always was too quick for me. Course I know they're okay, but it don't stop me missing 'em.' He raised his eyes to meet hers. 'It's not fair, Jess. I was robbed of being with 'em as babies cos of that bloody war and now I'm missing out on their growing up.'

'And whose fault's that, Tom? Mine?'

'I never said it was your fault. I was just telling you 'ow I feel. I might not get a chance to see you on your own again so I'm clearing the air. That's all.'

'Good. It's what I want. And we need to do it. You're the kids' father and they should have contact. Now that you're on your feet agen—'

'I've never bin off me feet. Who's bin talking to yer, running me down?'

Checking herself Jessie quickly changed tack so as not to let him know that she had heard from others how low to the ground he had been. 'You look like your old self is what I meant. And I haven't been talking to anyone about you. Don't forget that the last time I saw you, you was dressed up like a boring old squire . . . and you'd put on weight as well, from what I can remember. You 'ad a beer gut when I last saw you in that mansion in Suffolk.'

'It wasn't a mansion and I never 'ad a beer gut. I've never 'ad a beer gut in my life.'

'Well, whatever. Anyway, I came to ask your mum if she'd give you a message. I didn't expect to find you in.'

'And what was the message?' Tom was leaning back in his chair now, his fingers locked.

'That we should arrange to see each other here. To talk things through . . . how and when would be the best time for me to tell the kids you're back, for instance.'

'So how did you find out that I was back?'

'Mind your own business. What difference does it make, anyway? I heard, that's all. Let's leave it at that.'

'How's Max?' said Tom. 'Made 'is first million yet?'

'He's all right,' she said. 'He doesn't work for 'imself any more but he's got a desk job as accountant and that suits him.'

'And the kids?'

'You've already asked me that. They're fine. Fine and funny. Especially Billy.'

'So Mum and Dad said. Apparently they reckon me and him are like two peas in a pod.'

'You could say that.'

'And Emma's still got that lovely blonde hair and them blue eyes.'

'Yeah. She's not changed much.'

He turned away and gazed up at the ceiling, his emotions in check. 'So she still looks like her mum.'

'A bit pudgier, that's all.'

He turned back to face her and smiled. 'I like your hair like that, Jess. Free and casual. Don't fink much of the lipstick, though. Too bright. How's Max?'

'I told you, he's all right. Fine.'

'I meant to *look* at. I can imagine he's put on weight?'

'No. Looks much the same as when you last saw 'im.'

'Oh, right. Good. So, what *did* you want, then?'

'I told you that as well. I think it's time to bury the hatchet. Time for you and the kids to see each other.'

'And what about you? Do you love Max? Or do you still love me?'

Amused by him, she couldn't stop herself laughing. 'You've got a nerve.'

'You already told me that,' he said, parroting her for the fun of it. 'Years ago and more than once. Well?'

'Well, what?'

'You know what.'

'Tom . . . I'm not here to play silly games. Stop—'

'All right,' he said, putting a hand up as in defeat. 'Just one answer and then I'll stop. Do you love Max?'

'That's not something I'm prepared to talk to you about. It's none of your business. Max 'as been really good to us. Totally unselfish. Great with Billy and

Emma. Loyal to me. I'll never leave 'im. If that's what you're getting at?'

'That's all I wanted to know. So I'm free to fall in love with someone else. That's all I need to know.'

'Ah. So you've met someone, feel guilty, and want me to make everything all right. Same old Tom. Same old predictable Tom.'

'No, I 'aven't met anyone and I don't intend to go out looking – but I do intend to go out. Now I know you couldn't care less about me I feel freer – if someone 'appens to come along. Who's gonna start the divorce proceedings, you or me?'

Shaken by the finality of the word 'divorce', Jessie went quiet. 'Ask me in six months' time. There's no rush. It's only a bit of paper, after all's said and done.'

'Thanks. Is that 'ow you always saw our marriage certificate, then?'

'Shut up, Tom, you're getting on my nerves. If you want to set the wheels in motion, fine. You do it. I've got enough to think about. Do what you want.'

'What about Max? Surely he'd rather be married to you, Jess. His family must be cringing wiv shame. Them Jews don't forget,' he said, loving the tease. 'Especially that sister of 'is. She turned orthodox, didn't she? Wasn't that what you told me all them years ago?'

At that moment Emmie came in with the tea-tray and Jessie was thankful for the intrusion. Tom had a way of cutting things to the bone or, as he would put it, speaking the truth. But he was doing no more than playing cat-and-mouse as far as she was concerned.

Setting the tray on the table, Emmie held her tongue. She had no intention of filling an empty silence or playing the game of peace- or match-maker. Her considered opinion was that these two were going to have to sort themselves out by themselves. She had intervened in the past when it had been necessary, and although it had helped, one way or another she no longer had the strength or desire to absorb her loved ones' sorrow. And Tom was a tormented man when it came to Jessie. She knew he still loved her and there was nothing she could do to help him. Advice, yes, this she would give if asked and only if asked.

'I've got some nice fresh crusty rolls, Jessie, if you're peckish,' she said, behaving as normal as possible under the circumstances. 'Help yerself to sugar – I hope it's not too milky for you. Charlie still insists I put too much milk in tea.'

'I had some toast with the kids this morning, thanks, Em,' said Jessie, spooning sugar into her tea. 'And this looks perfect to me, but we've gotta let Charlie 'ave something to air, haven't we?'

'That's very true, Jess,' said Emmie, taking her seat on the sofa. 'So . . . have you worked out the best way forward, then?'

'As to what?' said Tom.

'The kids. I take it that's why you've come, Jess?'

'Yeah. That's why I'm here.' She turned to Tom again, saying, 'Would you rather I fetched them round here for visits?'

'Visits?' chuckled Tom forlornly. 'You make it sound as if I'm in prison.'

'No, I don't. That's *your* interpretation. Nothing changes!' snapped Jessie.

'Fetch 'em round Mum's. I don't particularly wanna see the marvellous Max in a home which he considers to be his and should be mine.'

'I wouldn't even think of going down that road, if I were you, Tom,' said Jessie, peering at him. 'It's not clever and you know it. You're worthy of better than that.'

'All right, all right. Point taken.' He turned to Emmie to ask her opinion. 'What d'yer think, Mum? Sundays? After they've bin to synagogue?'

Jessie looked from Tom to his mother. 'He's not ever gonna change, is he?'

'I doubt it,' said Emmie, keeping a straight face. 'I doubt it very much. Still . . . he's working alongside Stanley now. He won't stand for his nonsense.'

'What?' Tom sported a look of innocence. 'Why wouldn't Jess 'ave converted? She likes the Jews . . . and so do I. It wouldn't bother me if our Billy wore a skull-cap of a Sunday.'

'Saturday, actually,' whispered Jessie, straight-faced.

'I know. I was just testing. So you'll fetch the kids this coming Sunday, then?'

Jessie and Emmie looked at each other and the room went quiet as each of them were thinking their own thoughts. 'And you'll be happy about that, will you, Em? Them coming here? Every other Sunday.'

'Course I will. And I must admit that *every other* does

suit me better. They wear me out, Jess, you know they do, and I'm not gettin' any younger. What with your two and Dolly's little gang . . .'

'Why don't we say every three weeks, then? Every third Sunday?' said Jessie cautiously, eyeing Tom for his reaction. 'What do you think?'

'It's up to you two, Jessie. I'm just the granny.' Emmie glanced at Tom, saying, 'That'd suit you, wouldn't it? Every three weeks to start off wiv and then see how it goes. They might end up coming round every bloody day straight from school, if we're not careful. Well, Billy would do, anyway. He loves it round 'ere and messing about in the backyard with 'is granddad and them bleeding chickens and rabbits.'

'So you'll fetch 'em round next Sunday, then? We'll play it by ear from there.'

'Suits me, Tom.'

'Good. Cos that's what it's all about. What it's always bin about. Suiting you.'

'All right, Tom,' snapped Emmie. 'Don't start!'

'Don't make no difference to me now, Em. He can goad as much as he wants. It'll all go above my head. I've been there before many times.' Jessie turned and smiled broadly at Tom. 'You're a tormenting sod but this little fish won't rise to the bait any more.' With that she stood up and ruffled his hair. 'You're still a boy inside, Tom, no matter what you've been through. A spoilt little boy who won't grow up.'

'Man enough to make two lovely kids, though, wasn't I, Jess? Cos you never had any by Max, did you?'

'That was out of choice. Two's plenty.'

'Mind you, pacing the floor at night trying to quieten a screaming baby wouldn't be that easy for 'im, would it?'

'Because of 'is two left feet, you mean?'

'Well . . .'

'Well, Tom, how about this for a laugh? Max never did have anything wrong with his feet. He got away with not going to battle though. You should 'ave tried something as clever, instead of playing truant and getting my army pension stopped over it.'

'Oh, here we go,' groaned Tom, 'always back to money. Don't open your purse or the moth'll fly out.'

Leaning over Emmie, Jessie kissed the top of her head. 'I'll see myself out. Don't let him get to you.'

'Chance'd be a fine thing,' said Emmie, 'chance'd be a fine thing.'

Strolling back home, Jessie was not so much confused as bemused by her situation. Now that she no longer considered herself Tom's wife she found him amusing. His good looks had been the thing that had first attracted her to him but it was his personality that had captured her. Instead of feeling low at this point, which she had expected, she was light-headed and happy. This she put down to having finally sorted out whether to tell the children he was back yet or not. Now she could see it was the obvious thing to do. Be very casual about the whole thing. And, yes, Jessie was pleased to see that Tom was getting back to his old self. She no longer loved him in the same way as she once had but he was still her Tom and more like an irritating brother than anything else.

This was, in fact, a reversal of the way she felt when she had first met him. The hot passion between them had been unparalleled but his reckless live-for-the-day stance used to irritate her. Now the former emotion had gone cold and the latter was attractive. She surprised herself as she turned the key in the front door of her flat with a warm glow in her chest as the words, *Only a few days, Jessie and you'll see the sod again,* floated across her mind.

Unbuttoning her coat she was surprised to hear a remote sound of talking coming from the wireless in the living room. Pushing the door open with one finger she cautiously stepped inside to see Max in an armchair, staring into the unlit fireplace and miles away. The wireless was on but clearly he was not listening to it. 'Max? What are you doing home from work? Are you all right?' said Jessie, worried.

Turning to look at her he pinched his lips. 'I think I might be going down with a cold. I had such a headache that Goldstein told me to take the rest of the day off.'

Kneeling in front of him she laid a hand on his and looked into his face, but could see no sign of sickness. 'Have you taken some aspirin? For the headache?'

'Before I left. I'm fine now,' he said, stroking her hand. 'A bit tired, that's all.'

Her worry growing, she looked into his eyes and she saw an expression she recognised – sorrow. 'Max, has something happened? I can see you're upset. You haven't got a headache, have you? Did Goldstein give you the sack?'

'No, of course not. I'm not a complete failure, Jessie. I'm a good accountant . . . even if I don't work for myself any more. But that will change.'

'Of course it will. You'll build a client list—'

'But you're right. I haven't got a headache. I came home because I wanted to. I had a feeling this morning before I left that you would go and see Tom and I couldn't stop myself thinking I was about to lose you back to him.'

Stunned by his admission, and by the fact that he had known all along that Tom was back, she lifted herself from the floor and dropped into the other armchair, speechless. Knowing him like she knew the back of her hand, she said nothing, just waited. Max had more to say and if she didn't give him centre stage now he would withdraw into his polite, sensitive world of silence and tell her that everything was all right when it wasn't.

'Max . . . how could you think that, after all we've been through together?'

Avoiding her eyes, he focused on the floor, on the patterned rug. 'I won't hold you to any promises made, Jessie. I love you and I love the children, but they are Tom's children so you might want to do the best for them.'

Touched as ever by his sincerity and lack of self-ishness, she almost wept. 'Daft thing,' she murmured, 'And how did you know he was back, may I ask?' Even though Jessie had lived in the East End of London all of her life, the broadcasting service that went on between friends and neighbours still mystified her. 'Who told you?'

'You did, without realising. Then I did my own checking and didn't even have to knock on Emmie's door. I saw him coming out. He didn't see me so you needn't worry about that. I reduced myself to a cheap detective – unpaid, of course.'

'*I* told you?' said Jessie, wondering if it was her going mad or Max. 'I don't think I did, sweetheart.'

'You talk in your sleep sometimes, Jess. I love it when it happens. It's usually amusing. You said it a couple of nights ago, as clear as if you were wide awake and wanted me to know. "Tom's back." I jokingly asked you where he was living and you said, "In rooms. Bethnal Green." Then I asked how he was and you said, "Down at heel. He needs me."'

'God, I don't remember that. I talk in my sleep? I can't believe it. Why didn't you tell me, you rotter? I dread to think what else I might 'ave said.'

'Well, that's for me to know and you to find out. Might tell you in the future and I might not. It all depends.'

'On what?'

'Whether you'll be absolutely honest with me.'

'Max, I've never lied to you before so why would I start now? I know I never told you that Tom was back but that was withholding information and only because I thought it would worry you. Besides, I didn't know how to deal with it in any case.'

'And now you do?'

'I've just done it. I've been round there. I went to see Emmie to tell her I was gonna bring it all out into the open but Tom opened the door to me.'

'I knew you were going round there, Jess. Don't ask me how I knew, I just did. Right in the pit of my stomach I knew. And that's why I'm not at work and why I've been sitting here trying not to bite my nails. This morning you were different. I can't put my finger on it but you were preoccupied and looking forward to something. I went to work but couldn't concentrate on any of the tax returns. All I could see in my mind's eye was you sitting in Emmie's talking to Tom.' Then, lowering his head into his hands, he forced himself not to shed a single tear. 'I can't live without you now, Jessie. Or Billy and Emma. You're my life. Everything I do or think or feel is to do with you, Emma and Billy. I feel as if you're already my wife and they're my children.' He pulled his sparkling white handkerchief from his pocket and blew his nose. 'I'm terrified, and I do mean terrified, that I'll lose all three of you.' He leaned back in his chair and sighed deeply. 'Well, at least that's got *that* rubbish off my chest.'

'It's not rubbish, Max. It's genuine fear. But, sweetheart, you've got nothing to fear. Nothing. I'm not leaving you and I'm certainly not giving the children up to Tom. I went today to Emmie's to arrange things. They'll go to their grandparents every third Sunday when Tom will be there. How long that will last, God only knows. Tom could take off agen and leave without saying goodbye, even.'

'Do you really mean that, Jessie?' said Max, clearing his throat. 'Do you really mean that, given the choice, you'd rather be with me?'

'Yes, Max. I do mean that. And if there were any doubts in my mind Tom certainly cast them out. That rotten bastard brought your sister Moira up and how she was the cause of our engagement plans going awry. On the way home I ran everything we'd said through my mind and when I came to that bit my heart leapt. The thought of losing you again is not one I even want drifting across my mind. I love you and always will.'

'Then you won't leave me?'

'Sweetheart, I will never, never leave you. I love you. The children love you. I'll get a divorce, if that's what it takes to make you feel all right about everything. We'll get married. Anything. Just say what you want.'

'You don't have to go that far,' he said, pushing both hands through his hair. 'Although I would prefer it if you were free to marry me.' Turning to look into her face he managed a smile, saying, 'That's better. I feel much better for that. I wouldn't mind a strong cup of tea.'

'Is that it, then?' said Jessie.

'Is what it, then?'

'Your worry over me and Tom – gone?'

'I think so. No . . . I know so. I believe you and I trust you.'

'Good. I might just lace that tea with a little drop of your whisky.'

'No. Mustn't do that, Jess.' He glanced at his wrist-watch. 'I have to get back to the office. I've a family to think of, don't forget.' He caught her eye and said. 'I will do it, Jessie. I will rise and make enough money to move us out of the East End. We'll live in a house you'll be proud of, and the children will have a good education. I'll work every hour I have to, if that's what it takes.'

'But, Max, you don't understand. I'm happy here. These are my roots and the kids are not suffering. You don't have to work so hard.'

'I do, Jessie. I don't want this. I don't want to live on a council estate for the rest of my life. I want a house in the town and a cottage for weekends in the country. I want a nice family car and I want us to be able to take holidays on the Continent. I've been poor and I've been well off and now I'm broke again—'

'We're not broke! Far from it.'

'And,' he continued, determined to finish, 'I want to be wealthy.'

Unnerved by this, Jessie could think of nothing to say other than, 'Well, if it's what you want and you're prepared to work for it, I suppose that's it. But for my part I'm very happy as we are. If that's any consolation.'

'No, you're not, Jessie. You're thought yourself into that frame of mind because you think that this is all there is. It isn't. There's more. Much more.' He stood up and stretched, a smile on his face. 'I feel much better. I'll be able to focus on my work now. Now that I know we're okay and nothing's troubling you.'

'Troubling *me*? Haven't you got that the wrong way round?'

'Talking in your sleep like that,' he said, as if he hadn't heard her, 'it shows a deep-rooted worry. I'm glad we spoke about it. It's much better than bottling these things up. Don't you agree?'

'I s'pose so.'

'You know it is.' He then kissed her on the cheek and told her not to worry about the tea. 'Best get back to the office. Time waits for no man.'

'No, I don't s'pose it does,' she said, as she watched him take his leave.

Later that day, as evening fell, with Max in the sitting room reading a paperback and the children playing Lotto to the quiet background music from the wireless, Jessie could hardly believe that she had got out of bed that morning. It all seemed like a weird dream. She had been to see Tom and he had behaved as if they had been parted for just a short while and Max had – for the very first time since she had known him – broken down and cried and then gone off to work as if all the world and its troubles had been lifted from his shoulders.

In need of some female company, and one who had her feet firmly on the ground, Jessie pulled a white cardigan over her shoulders and slipped out to knock on Edie's door. Her hopes that she would be alone were not dashed and, furthermore, her friend, happy enough to have a quiet evening by the television, was pleased to see her. Earlier on Edie had collected Jessie's finished summer frock from Shereen, which had been made to measure and was simply beautiful:

it was mid-blue with navy spots and a heart-shaped neckline.

'Well,' said Edie, as she opened the door to Jessie, 'I think I know what you've come for.'

'Do you?' said Jessie, as she followed her friend through. 'And what might that be?'

'Close your eyes before you come into the living room, Jess,' said Edie, lifting a hand as if barring her way.

'What 'ave you been up to? You haven't got a tall dark handsome man in there, 'ave you?'

'No,' said Edie, leading her in by the arm, 'but there will be plenty of them following you like puppy dogs when you put this on. Open your eyes!'

'Oh, my dress!' squealed Jessie. 'It's finished! Oh, my God, I love it! I love it, Edie! Shereen is a bloody genius!'

'I know, I know! And mine'll be finished in two days' time. I can't wait. You should see the white collar she's made for it.' Taking a breather, Edie, her eyes shining, said, 'Go on, then. Try it on in my bedroom.'

'No. No, I won't do that. I'm gonna leave it on that hanger until the day I wear it. I know it'll fit me.'

'Shereen said you shouldn't wear a belt with it but she knows you will.'

'Sometimes I will and sometimes I won't,' said Jessie, a smile spreading across her face. 'Tom would say that was drop-dead gorgeous on me.'

'Tom?'

'I mean Max. I was thinking about Tom earlier and I

s'pose he's still hanging around in my mind. Oh, Edie, it *is* lovely. I love it. I really love it.'

'Good. Don't forget to go and pay 'er tomorrow. I never had enough on me . . .' she said, a touch embarrassed '. . . or I would 'ave.'

'Don't be daft. Shereen won't mind. She trusts me. I'm gonna feel a million dollars in that.'

'There's booze in the cupboard left over from Christmas. Some sherry and some vodka. Shall we—'

'Definitely. We'll have a cigarette and a brandy on the veranda,' she swanked. 'Just like in the movies.'

'Speaking of which, Jessie, guess what's showing at the Popular next week? Gary Cooper in *High Noon!*'

'Right. That's when I'll wear my new frock and you'll wear yours. Get the Wednesday afternoon off work, Edie. Go sick. And we'll go to the matinée performance!'

'You're on! I've not been to the pictures in ages.'

'So where's old Nao's brandy, then?'

'There's only a drop of that left but we've got a full bottle of sherry, and vodka.'

'Any orange juice?'

'Yep.'

'Good. Mine's a vodka and orange.'

'Coming right up.' Leaving the room Edie felt really happy. 'I'll start with the sherry and then finish Naomi's brandy.' Then, opening her beloved hatch to ask if Jessie wanted a small cup of coffee as well, she caught her friend gazing at the new creation and wiping a tear from the corner of her eye. Her discretion to the fore, she quietly closed the hatch again and poured out their drinks.

Almost an hour later the women were curled in armchairs, having chosen privacy and comfort to the romantic notion of sitting outside, and slowly getting drunk. 'I was really nervous about moving on to an estate, Jess,' said Edie wistfully, sipping her second large drink. 'I thought I might not like it.'

'Me too. But I do. I love it. I feel as if my life has *turned around*! At last. It's been a long time coming, though. Maggie loves it as well. And she was worse than *me* when it was first offered to us. Did her pieces. Said she'd rather run away . . . than live in a flat.'

'Well, she got lucky, didn't she? Fancy having a *gorgeous* Italian all over you at *her* age. She's in the pink all right. Yep. She's in the pink!'

'What about your Max? Has he settled to it?'

'He has, Edie, yes. But will he admit it? No. He still goes on and on . . . and on . . . about the house he's gonna buy for us *all* to live in . . . one day. Still, everyone has to have a pipe-dream, don't they?' There was a quiet pause while each of them absorbed their own thoughts. 'I saw my husband today. *Tom*.'

'Oh? So, he's back in the area, then?'

'Living with his mum and dad – until he finds a couple of decent rooms to rent. He's working with his brother now, Stanley.'

'Got bored with living the life of Riley, then, did he?'

'I really don't know what happened, to tell the

truth, Edie,' said Jessie, and then, 'Can I tell you something . . . in confidence?'

'Course you can! What are friends *for*?'

'It's very personal – and I feel rotten talking behind Max's back but . . .'

'You saw Tom and realised that you still love 'im,' said Edie. 'I won't be surprised if that's what you were going to say. I guessed that right from the first time you told us about him . . . at Christmas.'

'It wasn't that obvious, was it?'

'Only to us women. The two of us, I mean. Me and Laura. I could see from the expression in her eyes at the time, she thought the same as me. So . . . what will you do *now*?'

'Nuffing. I wouldn't hurt Max . . . not for the world.' Then, 'I love him as well, but in a different sort of a way. He's solid. And reliable. And a lovely bloke.'

'Whereas Tom is anything *but*?'

'No, I wouldn't say that. He *is* unreliable, *yes*. And I wouldn't call him a *lovely* bloke, no.'

'But?'

'But . . . he's a bastard that you can't help loving! Simple as that.'

'Sounds to me like you're in between the devil and the dark blue sea. Have an affair with Tom. Sod what the neighbours fink!'

'No! God, Edie, I can't believe you said that!'

'Nor can I! So what, then?'

'Stay with Max, of course. Stop with him, and hope to God that when Tom finds someone else he'll move far, far away. I couldn't bear seeing him with another woman. Arm in arm and in love. I think that would be too much to bear. Stupid, I know. Very stupid.'

'No, it's not. You can't help what you feel, Jess. None of us can.'

Throwing caution to the wind, after a brief spell of silence, Jessie said, 'What if your Harry were to turn up out of the blue? Would you tell Den to go?'

'Oh, Jesus, what a thing to ask.' Edie reached out, picked up the sherry bottle and refilled her glass. 'Help yourself to the vodka and orange cocktail while I think about it.'

As the next hour slipped by easily, the two friends talked and drank non-stop. They spoke of their worst and best schoolteachers and remembered classmates long forgotten. They recalled their childhood fears and dangerous ground where they had trodden. Their favourite famous heart-throbs made the longest stretch of conversation.

Having refilled the white china jug with more vodka and orange juice, Jessie filled her glass to the rim again. 'The thing is,' she said, her speech more than a little slurred, 'both my kids love Max but I know that if Tom were to move back in, which is definitely not gonna happen, after a while when everything settled down, they'd love 'im. He can be funny at times. And he'd do things with them. Take Billy fishing and that. And down Brick Lane on a Sunday morning. And I know that 'is mum and dad'd be as chuffed as anything.'

'You don't have to make excuses to me, Jess,' said Edie, giggling and certainly feeling the effect of the sherry. 'If you want him back, do it. You've only got *one* life . . . and, by Christ, that's hard enough. If you can get yourself a bit more joy, what's wrong with that? Eh?'

'It can hurt other people,' said Jessie, downing her drink in one go. 'That's the trouble. One gets loved and the other gets hurt. I wish I'd have been born a cat. Cats can 'ave as many toms as they like, can't they, and no conscience whatsoever? What if your Harry's bin going from one beautiful woman to another? Would that make you jealous?'

'Harry?' Edie topped up her glass. 'What are you talking about, Jess? Harry's dead.'

'Well, yeah . . . but what if he wasn't? What if he was only playing dead? Would you be pleased to see 'im back in Stepney – or bloody furious for hoodwinking yer?'

'Well, there's not really an answer to that, is there? It's not a proper question . . . is it? If he's dead. He is dead. So he can't come back like your Tom has. Can he?'

'But what if he did?'

'Well, he won't, will he?'

'But he could do.'

'Course he couldn't.'

'Well, he has. So there! I know more'n you do.'

'That . . . Jessie Smith . . . is a very wicked if not funny sort of a thing to say. And I can't remember the question which made you say it.'

'If he came back would you still marry Den?'

'I don't remember you saying that.'

'Well, I did or I might not have done but that is what I was going to say. Harry or Den? Who are you gonna choose?'

'Den, cos he's alive, thank you very much.'

'Ah, but so is Harry. Been living in sin with a Turkish woman.' Jessie tapped her nose. 'I know things. A little bird came to my window-sill and sang.'

'Jess . . .' said Edie, resting her head back on the armchair. 'Is the ceiling going round?'

'No. No, that's the room. The walls. It's like the spinning wall of death at Southend. Except we're not pinned up against the wall of the drum . . . are we? Edie? Did you hear what I said? "We haven't got our bum against the drum!"' Roaring with laughter, Jessie very carefully, while swaying, placed her empty glass on the small coffee table. 'Bum on the drum!'

Pushing her head forward and stretching her neck, she peered into Edie's face. 'Have you got your eyes closed? You have! Some host you are. Falling asleep while I'm still talking.' With that Jessie flopped back in her chair, closed her eyes and immediately began to snore.

'Who's drilling a hole in my walls?' murmured Edie. 'Someone's drilling . . .' Pulling herself into a sitting position she pushed her foot forward and nudged Jessie. 'You're snoring!'

'I'm not,' said Jessie, her eyes suddenly open. 'When I think . . .'

'Yeah. When you think? What?'

'What we were like at thirteen, Ed, twelve, even,

when we had a crush on a boy, it makes my hair curl. My Emma-Rose is ten but she's still a baby.'

'To you she is, Jess, but she won't be to a ten-year-old boy, will she?' said Edie, all knowing as she pointed a finger and then wiggled, saying, 'No.' And then, 'Shall we have some coffee now, do you think? The drink might have gone straight . . . to my head. You can bet your life she's played kiss-chase in the school playground.'

'It's hard to imagine,' said Jessie, pulling herself up from the chair. 'Tell me where the kettle is and I'll make us some coffee.'

'Look at my Maggie. One week my baby and the next . . . she's a young woman overnight. Now she's going steady. That's Naomi's fault. She did it. Making 'er look too old. It's her fault.'

'I was fifteen when I met Max . . . I think,' said Jessie, in the doorway. 'He was my very, very . . . first boyfriend.'

'Well, there we are, then, Jess. What goes round . . . comes round. I've got so used to seeing Maggie with Tony now that I can't imagine them apart. God help us when it does break up.'

'Maybe it won't all fall apart, Edie? You never know . . . Do you want this coffee or not?'

'Not. I'm having another little drop more of this sherry. It's lovely.'

'Oh, well . . .' said Jessie, stumbling back to her armchair. 'In that case – I'll 'ave a drop more vodka and orange juice. Sod it.'

'She was fourteen when she met Tony and now she's

fifteen. You can't stay with the same person from the age of fourteen, Jess, surely?'

'Some do and they're very happy. Don't forget, she grew up without a father. They reckon that girls who go through that . . . do marry early and often . . . the first boyfriend.'

'Well, maybe having a stepdad will make a difference . . . He's all right, is my Dennis. Never thought I would fall in love agen, Jessie. No. But I have. And it's very, very nice.'

'You best go easy on that sherry. You sound drunk.'

'So do you.'

'Tell you what, Edie, let's make this the last one. Let's 'ave a toast. To us. And to the men in our life. I've got Max and Tom, and you've got Dennis and Harry. Lucky cows, ain't we?'

'You are. I've only got Dennis.'

'No, you haven't. You've got Harry an' all.'

'Harry's dead. I keep telling you but you won't listen to me.'

'And I keep telling you, Edie, and you're not listening. But who gives a shit? Cheers, mate!'

'Cheers bloody cheers, Jess!'

Happy in their blissful intoxicated world, Edie and Jessie rambled on about nothing of much importance but with one clear thought, which they continued to return to – that they had the lovely future to look forward to, even though they agreed that neither of them could possibly know what might be in store. Each of them had had so much grief that they agreed that nothing bad could happen to them now. They believed that it was all plain sailing from now on.

But each of their lives, by the time this very day came round the following year, were going to be very different from now. So drunk had Edie been when Jessie told her that Harry was alive that she would not even remember it being said and likewise Jessie would not remember having said it.

Harry *had* been sent packing, and had sailed off to a remote island, but had every intention of sailing home again when the opportunity arose. England was his place of birth and no one was going to exile him from it for ever. Fuerteventura, the quietest of the Canary Islands to which Harry had now been delivered, would certainly not be to his liking. It would afford him only one vocation: to work in the kitchen as a skivvy in one of the first hotels to be built for the promised tourist trade. Also, in this faraway paradise, there was no crime, no night-life and plenty of men to watch over their women. An ideal place for Harry, in so far as Alf and the boys were concerned – especially since the very good English contact who ran a little bit of business out there had promised to keep an eye on him.

But Edie, if asked in the future what had been the worst shock of all during her lifetime, would have to say nothing could come close to what she is about to find out. Her treasured fifteen-year-old daughter, Maggie, is pregnant . . .